Where Dinosaurs Roam

MINTARI II
Where Dinosaurs Roam

DANIEL ARENSON

CHAPTER ONE
God of the Deep

There was a terror underwater. There was a monster in the depths. And Figaro was rowing closer, closer toward its waiting jaws.

Her hands tightened around the oars. Even in the cold night, sweat trickled down her spine. Her teeth chattered. The rowboat creaked as if shivering with her. It was too quiet out here on the open sea. Eerily quiet. Fig's pulse pounded in her ears, and her heart beat against her ribs like a wild bird in a cage.

We should turn back. We should never have come. We're going to die.

"Aww, look. She's shaking!"

Wrenly pointed at her. The girl sat in the boat, wrapped in a plaid blanket, cradling a mug of hot chocolate. Ribbons adorned her blond pigtails. She was sixteen, same age as Fig, but a head taller.

That wasn't saying much. Everyone at school was taller than Figaro Triplehorn, *la petite enfant sauvage.* Fig had grown up in the wilderness. Raised by dinosaurs. She had been living among humans for five months now. But what was five months? Her years in the outback, scrounging to survive, had left Fig scrawny, smaller than her classmates, and full of demons. When she closed her eyes, she still saw them. The fangs. The claws. The beasts that prowled Mintari. She had left the wild, but the wild still howled inside her.

And now we're rowing toward another beast, she thought. *A monster that rules the sea.*

Another shudder ran through her.

"Aww, she's terrified, guys." Wrenly pouted. "Look at her!"

The boys turned to look. Two of them sat in the boat. And they could not be more different.

Grayson was broad-shouldered, square-jawed, and tall (and not just compared to Fig). He sported auburn locks, an easy smile, and a gleaming dinoball medal that he always wore around his neck. Whenever he was around, Fig found her eyes straying toward him, seemingly of their own will. And whenever he met her gaze, she blushed. Yes, Grayson was a handsome young man. Even Fig, who had just crawled out of the wilderness, could see that. Some instincts were inherent. Appreciation of beauty was one.

Al, the second boy, could not be called handsome. He was short, overweight, and pimply. Scraggly black hair covered his head and upper lip. Despite his prominent gut, he boasted muscular arms. He spent every day at the gym, he often bragged. That seemed ridiculous to Fig. Calories were precious. Every calorie was a trophy from a battle won. You had to fight for your energy. Why waste it lifting weights?

I'm still thinking like a dinosaur, she realized. *It's different here in human society. You don't have to hunt or gather for food. It's right there in the fridge.* A fact Al, no doubt, knew all too well.

"Hey!" Grayson said, the wind in his auburn hair. "Hey, cavegirl! You cold or something?"

Fig tried to stop shivering. She could not. It was a cold night, and she was only wearing her school uniform. Tan trousers. A button-down shirt. A green neckerchief, denoting her a freshman. But she had survived colder nights with fewer clothes.

She wasn't shivering because she lacked a coat. No. She wasn't cold. She was terrified.

Talking was difficult for Fig. She could understand language perfectly. Despite what people believed (usually because she told them so), she had not spent her *entire* life among dinosaurs. Until Fig was four, a shaman raised her. They lived in the forest, far from civilization, but Fig heard human speech in those years, and her memory of language remained. Speaking was a different matter. Between ages four and fifteen, she had communed with dinosaurs. In those years, Fig had not uttered a single word, instead growling, yipping, and snorting with the pack. Her tongue had gone clumsy with disuse. Her mouth had forgotten how to shape syllables. Since joining civilization last spring, she had been practicing, and she was making progress, though speaking still made her so nervous. She opened her trembling lips and gave it a try.

"M-m-ma-ssss-sir! Innnn . . . in . . . da wada!"

Mosasaur! In the water!

The other youths stared at her, then burst out laughing.

Grayson struggled to catch his breath. "What the tar pit did she say?"

Al guffawed. "She said she's got the hots for you." He elbowed the taller boy. "Careful or she'll bonk you on the head with a club, then drag you back to her cave."

Grayson flushed and clenched his fists. "Shut up."

Wrenly pouted. "You boys are horrible."

The pigtailed girl wriggled closer to Fig. She smelled of vanilla and apple blossoms. Fig still thought it strange how humans masked their natural scents with perfumes. Wrenly's blue eyes softened, and she placed a hand on Fig's knee.

"Try it again, cavegirl."

Fig paused from rowing and opened her mouth.

"I didn't say stop rowing." Wrenly frowned. "You can row and talk at the same time, can't you?"

Fig blushed. She had done something wrong. She had embarrassed herself. Human society was so complex! She resumed rowing the boat, and she tried speaking again.

"We . . . we . . . tun ba. M-m-mossasir in wada!"

We must turn back. Mosasaur in the water!

But the others didn't understand. They simply stared at her. Wrenly wrinkled her forehead and tilted her head. Tar it! Why was talking so hard?

"Dude, she's a stegobrain," said Grayson. "Dumber than a stegosaurus, and those dinos have brains the size of walnuts. She just talks gibberish. Probably a dinosaur stepped on her head." The tall, handsome boy contorted his face, making himself ugly. He curled up his hands as if forming T-rex arms, and he spoke in a slurred voice. "I'm . . . I'm . . . Imma a stupid cavegirl duhhhh I can't talk good."

The others burst out laughing. Al laughed so uproariously he nearly fell overboard. Fig smiled hesitantly. She let out a shaky laugh, trying to join the merriment. Normal humans laughed at jokes, didn't they? And Fig had to be normal now. No longer a wild child running with dinosaurs. Human society confused her. But she had to learn. How to laugh at jokes. How to make friends.

The past five months had been hard. The hardest in her life. For a while, after finding her way back to civilization, Fig had lived with her family. Her grandmother taught her how to wear clothes, cook her food, clean her body. Her father taught her to be strong, brave, proud of her humanity. They both taught her how to feel safe. Feel loved.

But they wanted her to learn more. To read and write. To do her numbers. To socialize with her peers. So they placed her in school.

And that was where all the trouble began. School was crueler and more dangerous than the wilderness of Mintari. Different sorts of predators prowled those halls. Fig had learned that at school she was no longer a hunter. She was prey.

There was the teacher who rapped her knuckles with his ruler until she cried. The students who shoved her into lockers. Who dunked her head into toilets. Who called her "cavegirl" and "stegobrain." She tried to learn her numbers. She tried to read and write. She failed. And again the ruler struck her knuckles, and again she cried, until one day she lashed out, grabbed the ruler, and struck the teacher back. They had dragged her to the headmaster that day. Beaten her. Then shoved her into the remedial class where she remained. Exiled and forgotten.

In some ways, the remedial class was easier. The students were known by many terms. Special needs. Mentally challenged. Autistic. In the schoolyard, some called them crueler words. But Fig found shelter there. There was one big boy who liked to grab her hair, to pull it, to shove her, but not too often. No teachers hit her, and nobody mocked her. She learned a few letters. A few numbers. She still cried every night.

"Weirdo!" the normal kids called to her in the hallways.

"Cavegirl."

"Freak!"

"Stegobrain."

They shoved her. Spat on her. Spilled her lunch across her chest. They laughed and she laughed with them. A funny joke. She had to laugh too, didn't she? It was what normal people did, wasn't it? So she laughed, spaghetti in her hair, chili on her clothes. And when her father asked her how school was, she forced a smile and said she loved it. She only cried at nights after he was asleep.

Then earlier tonight—a breakthrough.

Three normal kids approached her. Not only normals—but popular kids. The alphas of the human herd. Grayson, blond and handsome. Al, burly and tough. Wrenly, beautiful and adored. They surrounded Fig outside school, taller, stronger, paragons of human excellence. They were actually talking to the runt!

Fig had recoiled at first, expecting a blow. But they smiled.

"Join us tonight, Fig," Grayson said. "We're taking a boat out. Just some friends, some drinks. We'll have fun."

She had smiled, shaken her head, tried to mumble apologies with her clumsy tongue.

"C'mon, cavegirl!" Al had told her. "We'll just row a little offshore. Have a few drinks. That's what normal humans do. You wanna be normal, don't ya?"

Yes. She did. More than anything. Back in the pack of achillobators, Red Scar had accepted her—the powerful alpha male of the pack. He had protected her. Kept her alive in the wilderness. Fig had learned to imitate him and other achillobators, and thus she had survived. This was a different kind of wilderness, and these were different kinds of predators. She needed their protection.

So she had accepted. And now here she was, rowing so far into open water they could not see the shore. The ocean was deep here. Fig knew what people called this ocean. Hell's Aquarium. A realm of sea monsters. And most monstrous among them—the mosasaur.

Fig had never seen a mosasaur. Few had and lived to tell the tale. Fig had heard those tales. The dreaded reptiles lived out here in the open sea, larger than whales and meaner than sharks, prowling the depths.

A wave rocked the boat, pulling Fig back to the present. Just one wave and there was no wind. Something was stirring in the depths. Fig peered over the boat's gunwale, but she couldn't see a thing. The water was so dark it might as well be tar. Clouds hid the stars and moons, trapping the boat in endless blackness.

"P-pees," Fig whispered. "P-pees go . . . go baka!"

The other girl stared at her.

"What?" said Al. The burly boy guffawed. "You gotta pee?"

"Not on my father's boat, you're not," said Grayson.

Wrenly crossed her arms. "She said *please*. You boys are horrible. She's terrified! Can't you see it? Look at her. Trembling like a leaf on the wind." The pigtailed girl leaned closer to Fig, and a strange light filled her eyes. She smiled crookedly and bit her lip. "You're scared of the mosasaur, aren't you? They call him Ryujin, Lord of the Depths. They say he's a god. That he eats misbehaving children." She pinched Fig's arm. Painfully. "But you got nothing to worry about. No meat on you."

Fig pulled her arm back. Her skin throbbed. It was true. Fig was still so skinny. Her life in the wilderness had left her malnourished. She was eating better these days, albeit not at school. If she was lucky, the bigger kids stole her lunch. If she was unlucky, they dumped that lunch on her head. For dinner though—ah, at dinnertime she feasted. Most evenings, dear old Barnum—the rotund owner of the Fossil and Firkin saloon— served her his famous shepherd's pie. Fig was gaining weight. Not a lot. She was still scrawny compared to Wrenly and the others. But slowly and steadily, she was putting some meat on her bones. Maybe she would even grow a little taller. Barnum said it was not too late for a growth spurt.

To the mosasaur, it wouldn't matter. Skinny or plump, short or tall—he would eat anyone who entered his domain. Fig didn't know much about human society. But she knew something about predators. They were not picky eaters.

"D-d-dis no game!" Fig blurted out. "D-dis deen-ger-is! M-m-mosasir is . . . is . . . leel!"

Yes, the mosasaur was real. No, Fig had never seen one, but the shamans of the wilderness spoke of him, and theirs was an ancient wisdom.

Another wave rolled across the water. The boat rocked. Fig leaned overboard, and while she saw nothing in the darkness, she imagined the terror coiling below. A carnivore larger than a T-rex. Large enough to devour a T-rex. A god of the ocean. A god of hunger.

"W-we g-gon back!" she said.

Fig resumed rowing. But this time she turned the boat around and began oaring back to shore. At least where she thought the shore was. In this darkness, she felt lost. The abyss seemed eternal.

"Hey, what are you doing?" said Grayson. "I didn't tell you to row back."

"Yeah, we're not done drinking yet." Al cracked open another beer.

Fig ignored them and kept rowing. She peered into the distance, seeking the lights of the shore. Nothing. She could not navigate by sight; even the stars were hidden. But a cold wind blew, and wind this time of year blew from the west. She rowed with the wind. It would lead her home.

"Hey, stop that!" Grayson said, lunging toward her. The boat rocked.

Fig tried to keep rowing. But Grayson grabbed one of her oars. He stared at her, his blue eyes so cold. The lanterns swung on the boat, painting his face with demonic firelight.

"You row when I tell you to row, cavegirl. You stop when I tell you to stop. Do you want to go back to your losers in the remedial class?"

Fig glared at him. "D-dey my frens!"

Everyone laughed. Other than Fig. She was done laughing. Done appeasing them. These predators were not welcoming her into their pack. She was their prey. And they were toying with her.

I was a fool. Tears stung her eyes. *A tarry fool.*

"Awww!" Wrenly pouted. "Look! The cavegirl is crying."

Fig wiped her eyes. She would not give them the satisfaction. "I emmmm nao criiin!"

Her clumsy words only made them laugh harder.

"Awww, she misses her dinosaurs," said Wrenly.

Grayson snorted. "Probably misses her fellow stegobrains in the remedial class."

Al cracked open yet another beer. "Drink it." He shoved the can at Fig. "Let's see what happens when cavegirls get drunk."

The burly boy grabbed Fig's jaw, forced her mouth open, and poured the beer down. Fig spat it at his face. That made Grayson and Wrenly laugh even harder. Soon the pair were rolling around on the deck, almost crying with laughter. Al flushed, wiped his face, and clenched his fists.

"I'll show the stegobrain for this." He snarled. "Spitting on me! Disgusting. I'll teach you a—"

A rumble sounded from the depths.

A loud rumble. Deep. Rolling like thunder.

Fig shuddered.

"M-m-mo-sa'sir," she whispered.

Everyone in the boat fell silent. For long moments, nobody dared speak, not even breathe. The rumble faded and the sea calmed. Not a gust of wind blew nor a wave rose.

It was Al who finally broke the silence.

"What was that?" the beefy boy whispered.

Wrenly smiled wickedly. "Ryujin. Here to eat kids." She poked Al in the gut. "And you're the juiciest meal."

He shoved her hand away. "Shut up."

"Shut up, both of you," Grayson said. The dinoball player was still gripping Fig's oar. "I've had enough of this mosasaur talk. Some fish burped, and you're all pissing yourselves. There's no such thing as ocean monsters. The monsters on Mintari live on land. The sea is safe. We came out here to have fun, drink some beers, and—"

"Immm . . . gon back!" Fig said. She wrenched her oar free and began rowing with all her strength. She was small but strong. She had built that lean strength during her years in the wilderness.

"I said stop rowing!" Grayson said.

Fig ignored him. She had hunted parasaurs. She had battled raptors. She had faced King Ivan, the greatest T-rex on Mintari, and lived to tell the tale. She was not going to fear Grayson Hardback no matter how broad his shoulders were or how many dinoball trophies he boasted of.

"I said"—the tall boy grabbed the oar again—"stop rowing! We're staying right here."

"No!" Fig wrestled with the oar. But strong as she was, Grayson was stronger. He tugged the oar free.

Fig made a grab for it. Grayson pulled the oar out of her reach.

And suddenly Fig was back in the wilderness. She was a predator again, a huntress on the plains, racing with the pack toward her prey.

She pounced toward Grayson and lashed her hand like claws. Her fingernails slashed his cheek. Blood spilled.

Grayson let out a screech. It was almost comically high-pitched. If Fig weren't so terrified, she might have laughed.

"What the hell?" Grayson cried. "That stegobrain scratched me!"

"I do ee agen!" Fig cried, lunging forward for more. Grayson cowered, but Fig was beyond showing mercy. She pressed the attack.

Before she could draw more blood, beefy arms wrapped around her waist, holding Fig back.

"Not so fast, cavegirl."

Al! He had grabbed her from behind! The burly boy lifted her off the deck. Fig kicked in midair, struggling against him. But Al was twice her size. She could not free herself. His arms tightened. Tightened. Crushing her. She couldn't breathe.

"Al, put her down!" Wrenly leaped to her feet. Fear filled the girl's eyes.

"Should I put her down?" the brute said. A strange note of mockery tinged his voice. "Grayson, what do you think? Should I put the cavegirl down?"

Grayson was clutching his wounded cheek. He stared at Fig through narrowed eyes. The flame of pure hatred burned in his gaze.

"Yes," the square-jawed boy said. "Yes. Put her down."

Al lifted Fig higher. "Thought so."

Fig squirmed in his grip, suddenly understanding. With a grunt, Al hurled her off the boat.

For a terrifying second or two, Fig tumbled through the air, limbs kicking. Then—

A crash.

Icy water flowing over her.

Salt stinging her nostrils.

She sank into the depths, kicking wildly, heart pounding. She was blind. The darkness wrapped around her like a living thing. No matter how much she floundered, she wasn't rising, and she heard muffled screams far above. Her lungs ached. She kicked again, but she kept sinking.

A voice spoke inside her.

You are a huntress of the pack. You are an achillobator. You are a survivor. Live!

She kicked again and again, propelling herself upward. Her head burst over the surface, and she gulped down air.

The world spun. For a moment she didn't know up from down, left from right. Salt water stung in her eyes. Lights dazzled her, and she blinked away the salt, trying to orient herself, to focus on the lights. They were the lanterns on the boat. Al must have tossed her far. The boat was several meters away now. The boys were laughing uproariously, pointing at her. Wrenly had her hands on her hips.

"You've gone too far, you jerks," Wrenly said. "What if she drowns?"

"Let her drown," said Grayson. "The freak cut me."

Wrenly lifted a life jacket and prepared to throw it overboard.

"Stop that." Grayson grabbed her wrist.

"Let go of me." Wrenly wrenched herself free, leaned over the gunwale, and tossed the life jacket. "Grab it, Figaro!"

The jacket splashed down near Fig. She swam toward it, gripped it, but struggled to pull it on. So many tarry buckles and straps! The buckles were magnetic, and she kept getting the poles resisting each other. It didn't help that her fingers were shaking with cold.

"We're outta here," said Grayson. He began rowing deeper into the ocean. "See ya later, freak."

Al laughed and pointed at Fig. "Swim back to shore, loser!" He tossed an empty beer can off the boat. It hit Fig on the head.

"Perfect shot!" Grayson high-fived the shorter boy. "Nice work, buddy."

"Yeah, I should be the one on the dinoball team."

"Shut up and grab an oar."

"Sorry, Grayson. Rowing!"

Another rumble sounded below.

Just a murmur this time. Barely audible. But the sound chilled Fig more than the icy water.

The kids on the boat didn't hear. The boys were laughing, chugging beers, and rowing away, leaving Fig behind. She floundered, still struggling with the life jacket buckles.

"Stop this!" Wrenly said. "It's not funny. Turn this boat around right now! Go get her."

"She'll be fine," Grayson said. "Sit down, Wren. Stop feeling bad for freaks. I thought you were cool."

Wrenly looked over the gunwale at Fig. The pigtailed girl's eyes were soft with concern. She sat down and crossed her arms.

"You guys are jerks," she said.

The boys rowed vigorously. The boat moved farther and farther away from Fig. She tried swimming after them, but she was too slow. She looked around, seeking the shore. It was too distant to see. Nothing but blackness above, below, all around her, and the lights of the boat were shrinking.

This must be what death is like, Fig thought. *Nothing but cold blackness all around.*

Then—the rumble again. Louder this time.

The black water roiled.

Currents tugged on Fig. She managed to buckle the last magnetic strap, securing the life jacket around her torso. But the current strengthened, pulling her legs like ropes of water. Even

17

with the life jacket, Fig could barely keep her head above water. She paddled madly, trying to swim away from the undertow.

The boat rocked. The lights bobbed in the distance like fallen stars on the water.

Wrenly's voice carried over the darkness. "Hey, quit rocking the boat."

"We're not!" answered both boys.

"I'm not kidding, stop it!" said Wrenly. "I—"

The creature bellowed again. Louder. Much louder now. The boat jolted. Swimming in the cold water, Fig rose and fell on a wave. Ripples spread through the ocean. A grumble bubbled up from below, and a stench like tar filled the air.

On the distant boat, Wrenly screamed.

"What the hell is that?" Al shouted.

"What's that sound?" cried Grayson.

Watching from a distance, Fig knew.

"He's here," she whispered.

Funny. With nobody near enough to hear, she spoke perfectly.

Then, as fast as the disturbance began, the sea stilled. The rumbling ceased. The wind died. All was silent and nothing troubled the night.

For long moments, nobody dared move. Fig just floated there.

"Is he gone?" Wrenly said, voice trembling. She was a good distance away, but in the silence, Fig heard her clearly. "Is he—?"

A rumble tore the ocean. Deafening. Booming. The sound of a world splitting in two. Great waves soared. Water sprayed through the air, forming archways like a liquid temple. And from the ocean he rose. Gargantuan. Larger than any predator on land. Larger than anything Fig had thought could exist. His skin was the color of the ocean, charcoal gray and bruised purple and mottled indigo, covered with lumps and barnacles and remoras. His mouth was a volcano, widening, growing and growing, lined with teeth longer than Fig's arms. It was a mouth that could devour the world.

He rose higher from the water, a craggy pillar looming from the ocean, a force of nature, a landmass, a formation of magma and scales and hunger. A scar shaped like a *Z* blazed on his head. His cry shook the air, rippled the water, and slammed into Fig with a physical force.

There he rose. The mosasaur. The god of the ocean. The terror of the depths.

Ryujin.

The boat tried to flee, to ride a wave, to glide to safety. It never stood a chance. Those monstrous jaws opened around the boat. Not just *below* or *beside* the boat but *around* it. The teeth scraped across the hull, digging grooves into the wood. The kids inside screamed. They fell to the deck. They reached for the gunwale, trying to pull themselves out, maybe just to hold on to something.

"Figaro, hel—!" Grayson began.

Then, like a bear trap the size of a car, the mighty jaws of the mosasaur snapped shut.

The boat shattered into a million splinters.

Blood splashed with the waves.

The boat's lanterns fell into the water. One fizzed out and sank. Another. A third. Only a single lamp floated on the water like a burning buoy.

The mosasaur sank back underwater. Chunks of wood floated toward Fig, rising and falling on the waves.

Fig stared through the darkness, bobbing on the water like another piece of flotsam. Her heart pounded. Were the others gone?

Then she heard the screams.

"Oh God, oh God, oh God, help us!" It was Grayson, splashing near the ruins of the boat.

"It's him! It's him, I told you!" It was Wrenly—her voice panicked, high-pitched. She cackled like a madwoman. "He's come for us!"

"Oh God, where is Al?" Grayson splashed in the water. "Oh God, there's so much blood. Where is Al? I want to go home. Oh God, I—"

The rumble rose again, washing over his words.

Water splashed skyward—geysers of salt and fury and tar and strands of sticky kelp.

"Ryujin!" Wrenly cried, and the lamplight caught her eyes. They shone, two blue orbs of awe and terror. "Ryujin rises!"

The jaws rose from the water. Algae dangled from the hellish mouth, marinated with blood. A body lay impaled upon the jagged teeth. A burly body with a big gut and muscular arms. Torrents of water rushed into the open maw, pulling Wrenly and Grayson into the churning pit. One eye of the beast emerged from underwater—a pale white eye like a silver moon. Inside the terrible open mouth, Wrenly began to pray. The monstrous mouth snapped shut.

Her prayers died.

The mosasaur withdrew into the depths, leaving ripples in the water.

Wrenly was gone. They were all gone. They—

"Figaro!"

She gasped. Grayson was still alive! He was floundering in the bloody water, barely staying afloat.

Fig began swimming toward him. She knew the mosasaur could return. Knew the blood would intoxicate him. But she kept swimming closer. Grayson was drowning. She could share her life jacket, maybe save his life.

The rumbling of the mosasaur rippled through the deep. The undertow tugged Fig. He was coming back for more, she knew. He had eaten only two humans so far. That would not sate his appetite.

She swam faster and reached out to Grayson. His hand clasped hers.

"Cam on!" she cried, pulling him through the water.

Fig swam with all her strength, dragging the boy behind her. He was bigger, heavier than her. He was sinking, losing blood, losing the will to fight. The undertow grabbed him, was pulling him under. Fig bared her teeth, tightened her grip on his hand, and swam even harder.

I'm getting you out of here! We're going to live. We. Are. Going. To. Live!

Chunks of wood floated around them. A shoe bobbed on a wave. Wrenly's shoe. The lantern rose and fell on the water, still burning like a fallen star, but the light was fading fast. Blood filled the water. Fig swam onward. Even Grayson managed to paddle with his feet, gasping for air.

But the currents strengthened. The vortex was sucking them under. Grayson sank down to his nostrils. The depths caught Fig's legs like liquid fingers, pulling her deeper, deeper. The murk beckoned. Ryujin was swimming underwater, churning the ocean, pulling them under. He was a god of barnacles, an emperor of flooded palaces and sunken cities, and he was calling. He wanted them in his watery realm. Fig sank down to her ears, swallowed water, and coughed. The rumbling vibrated the sea around her. Fig could almost hear words in the rippling bass.

Come to me. Sink with me. Come home . . .

It would be so easy to let go. To sink into that realm of forgetfulness. To never more feel pain. To never more feel like an outsider, a freak, a weirdo. She could sink now. She could dance with the watery god in his flooded palace.

No. No!

She rose and spat out salt water. Her mind was hazy. Her body was weak. She squinted, trying to clear her mind, to breathe, and—

There! On the horizon! Lights! The shore!

Fig laughed.

"Land!" she cried. "Grays'n! Look! Land!"

She swam with more vigor. She took deep breaths, coughed out more water, swam harder. She pulled Grayson along. She was going to make it. She—

Once more the mosasaur breached the water.

He rose like a jutting mountain of scales and teeth, riding a tidal wave. The jaws widened, sucking up water, sucking up air. The hellmouth was like a black hole, pulling in gravity itself, devouring light and ripping apart the particles of the universe. Fig screamed and kicked and swam away from the toothy abyss. The wave caught her. The jaws snapped shut behind her with a shower of water and a spray of kelp. Fig tumbled along a foamy crest. Her head went under. She spun underwater, rolling, rising, hurtling along with the storm. But she kept her grip on Grayson's hand. She did not let go.

She was alive and she kicked and swam. Grayson was no longer pulling her down. The weight of him seemed much lighter now. Perhaps he was finally swimming too. She tightened her grip around his hand.

We're going to make it, Grayson! she thought, too weary to attempt to speak. *I've got you!*

She glanced over her shoulder at him. But Grayson was gone. She was still holding his hand. But the rest of him was gone.

With a startled cry, Fig released the severed hand. It floated away and vanished into the darkness.

A maelstrom churned behind her. Slats of wood rose and fell, and the vortex sucked them under. Ryujin was spinning in rings below, drawing down the water and the last bite of his meal. A little morsel named Figaro Triplehorn. She tried to swim away, but the whirlpool was too strong. It caught her, spinning her round and round the pit. The last lamp from the boat plunged downward into the funnel, casting light upon walls of water, kelp, and there below—the insatiable mouth of the beast, ringed with teeth. A portal to hell.

Fig kicked desperately, but the current was too strong. The magnetic buckles of her life jacket ripped apart. The inflated jacket slid up her arms, and—

The mosasaur mouth snapped shut below.

The beast rumbled.

Waves tossed Fig upward. She tumbled out of the whirlpool, and a current carried her along the surface. The surging water ripped her life jacket off. She grabbed the inflated jacket before it could float away, clinging on for dear life, and stared around, seeking the mosasaur.

The last light was gone. She saw nothing. Only darkness. For a terrifying moment, Fig thought she might have drowned, that she was underwater, dead and doomed to forever haunt the abyss. But then he rose again. Only the top of his head emerged from the water, and his mouth remained closed. The head was enormous. Larger than the boat had been. The clouds parted, and moonlight caught his eye. He stared right at her. It almost seemed like sentience filled that silver eye.

Fig stared back. She could see her reflection in his orb. A girl lost at sea, clinging to an orange floating jacket. A girl broken. A girl grieving. A girl who was as lost on land as she was here at sea.

Then Ryujin turned away.

His massive body flowed beneath Fig, roiling the water. His scaly back grazed her, knocking her aside. His tail churned the ocean. He sank, drawing down water, and vanished into the depths.

Clouds hid the moon once more. All light faded. Hell's Aquarium settled into silence. He was gone.

Why did you spare me? Fig thought. Her eyes stung. *Why did you kill my friends but let me live?*

A last ripple snaked across the water, the only hint that the monster had ever been there. No sign of the boat remained. No sign of those lost.

Fig turned in the water. And she finally saw them. The lights of the coast twinkled in the distance. Tears in her eyes and guilt in her heart, she swam toward the shore.

CHAPTER TWO
Scars

"Come on, you useless clumps of tar, move it!" Joe shouted.

The useless clumps of tar groaned. They kept running, drenched in sweat, wheezing. Their cheeks were red. One boy was clutching his side, moaning that he was going to rip open. Joe checked his stopwatch. He had been running the recruits for only four minutes now. They already looked half-dead.

"Come on, move it!" Joe said. "Give me another lap."

The recruits took a few more wobbly steps. One of them, a stocky lad with a wispy beard, collapsed with gasps. Another recruit, a skinny girl with thick round glasses, slumped down and puffed on her inhaler. One recruit almost made it to the finish line. Almost. He fell a step or two away, reached out a twitching hand, but the finish line remained just out of reach.

Joe switched off his stopwatch. He shook his head in disgust. "Pathetic. Look at you. A turtle could have outraced you. An old one. With arthritis. Who was run over by a jippi." He spat onto the dust. "Get up and dust off. I want you at least half-alive before you hit the firing range."

The recruits pushed themselves up, wobbling and panting. Only seven of them. That was it. Seven recruits, too fat or too scrawny, too young or too old. One man, a scrawny fellow, was pushing sixty. The youngest was only sixteen.

It's not enough, Joe thought, looking at them. *We need more recruits. We need strong, determined killers with fire in their bellies.*

Like the recruits, Joe wore a khaki uniform. But unlike them, he wore a ceratop hat on his head. Modeled after park ranger hats from ancient Earth, the ceratop was a symbol of Mintari. Rangers wore them with pride. On his chest, Joe displayed a badge shaped like a stegosaurus dorsal plate. The words MINTARI RANGER were etched into the brass.

He tapped the badge. "You want a badge like this?"

The recruits all nodded their sweaty heads. "Yes, sir!"

"You'll have to earn it," Joe said. "You'll have to be faster. Stronger. Fiercer. This is a war, tar it all. I'm going to turn you into soldiers."

One of the recruits, a pudgy lad with pink cheeks, raised his hand. "Um, Mr. Triplehorn, sir?" He glanced around nervously, then looked back at Joe. "With all due respect, sir, aren't we just training to become Rangers? You know, to pull baby dinosaurs from quicksand, give directions to tourists, prevent forest fires, that kinda stuff? Not um . . ." He blanched. "Fight a war."

Joe stepped toward the kid. He was young, only eighteen, but big and heavy. Bigger even than Joe, who was not a small man. Mason Proudfoot was his name. Clan of the diplodocus.

"You're a big guy, Mason," Joe said. "We're going to need big tough guys like you."

Mason gulped and wiped sweat off his forehead. "Um, so we don't just save wounded dinosaurs and stuff?"

"Do you know why most dinosaurs are wounded?" Joe said calmly.

The kid shook his head. His pink cheeks wobbled.

"Because poachers shoot them!" Joe barked. His voice was so loud the kid jumped. "Because poachers have been shooting millions of dinosaurs on my beloved planet. Hundreds of poachers are on Mintari now. Maybe thousands. They all have guns. And they don't hesitate to shoot Rangers. This is war, boys and girls. A real war. Mintari doesn't have a military. It has us. The Rangers. And we will fight this war as soldiers. Is that understood?"

They all stared at him, pale. Heather Hardback was crying, her thick round glasses fogging up. She only paused from weeping to puff on her inhaler.

"Is that understood?" Joe repeated louder.

"Yes, sir!" they all answered. But he saw the fear in their eyes. Good. They needed to be afraid. Because Joe himself was afraid. Only five months ago, he had fought in the Battle for Dinovia. He had seen comrades die. He himself had nearly died. His leg still hurt from the wounds he had suffered that night. Worse were the scars inside him.

Amissa is still out there, Joe thought. *My murderous sister. She will strike again. We must be ready.*

Pain stabbed Joe. He closed his eyes, and he saw it again. Amissa, his younger sister, here on Mintari. Firing her gun. The bullet plowing through his leg. Her eyes—God, her eyes. The madness in them. The inhumanity.

She was running wild across this world, leading an army of poachers she called Hell's Hunters. The devastation spread across Mintari, and the Rangers were in ruin. So many heroes had fallen. So many warriors lay deep underground. The survivors must fight on. These recruits were green now, but by God, Joe would make them warriors. When Amissa struck this city again, she would face an army.

"Hey, Heather, no fair! I was going to buy that last Chocosaurus bar."

"Nya nya, it's mine."

"Are there any banana chips left?"

Joe opened his eyes. The recruits crowded round the vending machine at the back of the yard. Raymond Greatwing was fishing for coins in his pocket. Heather Hardback was gobbling up her Chocosaurus bar while Mason Proudfoot stared in envy, salivating.

"Get back here!" Joe roared. "Did I say you were dismissed? You've just earned yourselves another lap. Now run!"

They all moaned. But they ran.

Joe heaved a sigh. He didn't want to be here. He missed the Last Home Hollow, his cave outside the city. He missed Simone, the woman he loved. He missed Fig, his long-lost daughter, finally found and back in his life. For two weeks after the Battle for Dinovia, precious two weeks, Joe had remained in his cave. To recover. To learn to walk again. To be with Simone and Fig, two souls he loved. For two weeks, he had laughed with them. Swapped stories. Shared meals. Those were two weeks of pain. His leg was a mess. A T-rex tooth had slashed it, then Amissa's bullet had bored through it. Talk about adding insult to injury. But with Simone and Fig, he endured the pain. He found joy every moment. For so many years, Joe had been alone. For fifteen years, he had lived as a hermit, a grieving widower, nursing his pain. Simone and Fig came into his life as angels, bringing bliss.

But it was not to last. He had a duty here in Dinovia City. Arban Clubber had called him personally. And when Arban Clubber gave you an order, you followed it. He commanded the entire Mintari Rangers. He was the boss of bosses. The big kahuna himself. And he was also family.

Arban had a little sister. Mina Clubber. Joe's late wife. They both still mourned her loss.

The two men didn't always see eye to eye. They were not close. They were not friends. They had barely spoken since Mina's death. But they were still family. And to Joe, *family* meant more than just *boss*.

So Joe had left the Last Home Hollow. He had come here to the city to serve in Fort George, headquarters of the Rangers.

While he no longer needed crutches, he was still limping. He could not fight in the field. But he could train new fighters. He could do that. As much as Joe wanted to remain in his cave, to spend every waking hour with Simone and Fig, he answered the call of duty. So here he was. Trapped in Dinovia City, far from the comforts of his cave. A drill sergeant.

This wasn't his dream. He hated yelling at recruits. He hated being stuck here in the barracks when the battle raged in the wilderness. He should be out there. Facing Amissa and her poachers on the field. A bolt of pain reminded him why he was here. Joe grimaced. It had been five months. Would his leg ever stop hurting? He supposed he should be thankful. He had kept the limb. But with his limp and pain, he felt like a wounded old dinosaur, too weak to fight.

He fingered the silver crest on his lapel. A triceratops head. Symbol of Clan Triplehorn. The most hated clan on Mintari. A clan that had betrayed this world, that migrated to Cloventia, that came back with guns to hunt and destroy. But not Joe. Not this Triplehorn. He stayed true to his clan values. The triceratops symbolized strength, courage, and honor. Perhaps honor most of all. Many had told Joe to remove his crest, that the triceratops head, while once noble, had become a symbol of poaching. Joe refused. Someday he would restore his clan's honor. Every day that he fought was another step toward that goal.

The little pin was tarnished. So tarnished it was nearly black. Joe had vowed not to polish the symbol until his clan was redeemed. Someday this crest would shine.

"Sir!" A young Ranger came running toward him. His ceratop hat wobbled on his head, and his uniform was creased. A fabric rectangle was loosely sewn onto his sleeve, peeling off in one corner. His rank was *tenderfoot*—the lowest rank in the force. The kid had just been sworn in last week. He stopped before Joe, panting, and saluted. "Sir, the chief wants to see you in the yard."

Salutes. That was new. The Mintari Rangers had never saluted one another. But this was wartime. The Rangers were quickly becoming more militarized. Mintari only had a population of three hundred thousand people. Half a million if you included tourists. A tiny population for an entire planet. The Rangers were Mintari's only uniformed service. Their prime directive was to protect the delicate ecosystem of Mintari, this planet-sized nature reserve for dinosaurs. But they were also a police force. A rescue service. And now—a military.

Joe was a forester. A higher rank, a more experienced Ranger. He had never thought much about ranks, but he supposed they mattered now. Things were changing. He returned the kid's salute. "I'll be right there." He looked back at his recruits. "You get a break. Go hit the showers. You stink."

Joe walked through Fort George, headquarters of the Mintari Rangers. Named after George Cuvier, the father of paleontology, the barracks rose in the center of Dinovia City. Other important buildings shared the neighborhood. The Dinovia Library was a short walk away. Pangaea Hall, center of the Mintarian government, had collapsed in the battle, but it was being rebuilt down the block. *Darwin's Ark*, the starship that had delivered the first pilgrims to Mintari five hundred years ago, stood on Buckland Hill nearby. All the important achievements of humanity on Mintari were here within walking distance. But to Joe, it didn't matter. His heart still yearned for the wilderness. He did not live on Mintari for humans. He was only here for the dinosaurs.

But that's not entirely true, Joe thought as he walked down a corridor, passing by Ranger bunks. *Not anymore. I have Figaro now. And I have Simone. I have people I love. People who love me.*

At that thought, his heart swelled. He rarely saw them these days. He was here in HQ six days and nights a week. But he thought about Simone and Fig constantly, and when Sundays came, and he could pull the loves of his life into his arms, it was all worth it.

He looked around him at the barracks, and sadness mingled with his joy. These halls had once bustled. They were now nearly empty. Photos hung on the walls, depicting smiling men and women. Photos of the dead. So many had fallen in this war. Most had fallen right here in Dinovia City, resisting Amissa's invasion. Two hundred Rangers. Two hundred heroes. Gone too soon.

By all rights, I should be rotting underground with them, Joe thought. *I got lucky. It was just luck. That was all.*

His fists clenched. His eyes stung. He was no better, no braver, no stronger than all those who had fallen. The bullet had hit his leg instead of his torso or head. Just luck, that was all. And that luck came drenched with sticky guilt like tar.

Joe stepped through a doorway into the dinosaur yard. He squinted in the sunlight. For now, he pushed his feelings down. He was on duty.

Not many dinosaurs lived inside Dinovia City. Dinosaurs belonged in the wild, not among humans. But the Rangers did work with a small number of specially trained herbivores. Most of the rangersaurs (as the Rangers unofficially called their trained dinos) were out in the bush now, helping Rangers track and battle poachers. But three rangersaurs remained here at Fort George, resting in the yard, kept safe behind high walls. Safe for them. Safe for the city. Not that a rangersaur would ever deliberately harm a human, but they could accidentally step on a child without even noticing. Or on an adult. Or on a building.

Dozer was one of them. Joe's beloved triceratops normally lived in the wild, guarding the foothills below the Last Home Hollow. But dear Dozer had refused to leave Joe's side, so here he was in the city. He contentedly stood in the yard, munching leaves from a trough. When he saw Joe, he raised his beak from his meal and wagged his tail. Dozer was twice as massive as an elephant, battle-scarred and burly, with horns that had slain tyrannosaurs. But when he saw Joe, his face lit up like a puppy. Joe nodded at his beloved companion. He couldn't wait for tonight, when he could spend some time with the old trike.

An edmontosaurus stood farther back. He was an enormous hadrosaur, also known as a duckbill dinosaur. He was even taller and longer than Dozer. Joe only stood as tall as his knees. A howdah was mounted onto the dinosaur's back, large enough to hold five Rangers. They called him Eddie. Mostly Eddie stayed here in the yard, playing with Dozer and munching on uprooted trees the Rangers brought him. But in emergencies, Eddie could be used for riot control. Even for war. The sight of a multiton scaly dinosaur lumbering forth could disperse any enemy formation.

The third dinosaur in the yard was an ankylosaurus, a bull named Bumpy. Some people called triceratops a living tank, but perhaps the moniker fit ankylosaurs even better. Armored plates covered the dinosaur head to toe. Even his eyelids were armored. Spikes rose across Bumpy's back and thrust from his sides like scythes on an ancient chariot. Everything about this dinosaur was optimized for war. His greatest weapon was his tail. A bony club like a wrecking ball swung on the end. That club could knock down a T-rex. Knowing this, even the mighty tyrannosaurs gave ankylosaurs a wide berth.

Arban Clubber stood beside the ankylosaurus, polishing the dinosaur's armor with an oiled rag. He was a burly Ranger of fifty years. The Clubbers traced their ancestry back to ancient Mongolia, and indeed, Arban resembled old paintings of Genghis Khan. Certainly he was just as fierce. A pin shaped like an ankylosaurus club shone on his lapel. Clan Clubber had chosen the ankylosaurus for their sigil, and like their house dinosaur, the Clubbers were big, stubborn, and aggressive. Arban Clubber led both his clan and the Mintari Rangers.

Joe approached and saluted. "Chief, you wanted to see me?" He winced. "I hope it's not to break my nose again."

It was an old joke. Twenty years ago, Joe had asked Mina Clubber to marry him. She had said yes at once. But her older brother, Arban Clubber, had been less enthusiastic. More accurately, he had gone ballistic. The Triplehorns were traitors! They sold guns to poachers! How dared this impudent Triplehorn boy marry Mina, a proud Clubber? Well, he had eventually accepted the marriage. But not before punching Joe in the nose. Once Joe got out of the hospital, his nose held together with splints, the two headed together to the Fossil and Firkin, shared an ungodly amount of beer, and made amends. Since then, Joe never missed the chance of reminding Clubber of the incident.

Normally the joke could make Clubber smile. But now the big man remained somber. He lowered his rag. Bumpy snorted in displeasure and shook his head; he had been enjoying his spa day. His rows of spikes gleamed with oil.

"Joe." Clubber's broad, scarred face seemed as hard as ankylosaurus armor. "There's been an incident. It involves Figaro. She's fine, Joe! She's fine. But we need to talk about it."

Joe stood silently, listening as Clubber spoke. At first, rage bloomed in Joe. His daughter, sneaking out of the city and traveling cross-country to the port? Stealing a boat and rowing out to sea with alcohol? He would ground her! He would punish her so hard her head would spin! But as Clubber kept talking, horror replaced his rage.

"A mosasaur?" Joe whispered. "The other kids?"

Clubber put a hand on Joe's shoulder. "The others are gone. Three dead children. Fig was the sole survivor."

Joe's breath shook. His very bones tingled. He no longer wanted to punish Fig. He wanted to hug her and never let go.

"Where is she?" Joe said.

"I sent a Ranger to pick her up from the port. She's on her way here to Fort George." Clubber patted Joe's shoulder. "I'll get someone to cover for you, to train the recruits. Take the rest of today off. I've got to return to the field. Stay strong, brother."

"Chief, don't you want to finally meet Figaro?" Joe said softly.

The big man nodded. "Aye. Someday I do. Not today. She's hurt now. She needs her father."

The chief wandered off, moving a little too fast.

Joe sighed. For months now, Clubber had known about Fig, a girl they had all thought dead. Finally, after growing up in the wilderness, Fig was back with her family. But Clubber refused to meet his niece, always making excuses.

Joe thought he understood why. The pain of Mina's death still hurt them both. So did the pain of Clan Triplehorn's betrayal. And Fig, whom everyone said looked just like Mina, bore the Triplehorn surname. Maybe Clubber just needed time.

Best he waits until he's ready, Joe thought. *I don't want him punching Fig in the nose.*

With the chief gone, Joe waited anxiously in the yard. He couldn't even pace. Not with his tarry leg.

The sea was a two-hour drive from here. Fig must have hitched a ride with her friends. She had actually traveled across dino country without armed guards. And stealing the boat too! What had gotten into her? His mind reeled. Thankfully, Dozer was here in the yard with him. Joe found comfort with his triceratops, stroking the dinosaur's beak, placing his head against the lumpy hide to hear the steady heartbeat. Dozer had a heart the size of a beer barrel, and he had always been there for Joe.

This feeling, the anxiety of parenthood, was new. For fifteen years, a hermit in a cave, Joe had worried only about himself. Now he had Fig in his life. A long-lost daughter finally come home. She filled his life with love but also endless anxiety. He worried about her integrating into human society after fifteen years in the wild. He worried about her life at school. Could she catch up? Could she learn at sixteen what other children learned at six—to read, write, count? Fig could barely even speak. Was she too old to learn those skills, doomed to forever remain behind?

Well, if Fig remained the way she was—so be it. Joe would accept her. He would love her just the same. The worst part was not seeing her for six days a week. Joe was stuck here at Fort George from Monday to Saturday, day and night. He worked around the clock, barely even finding time to spend with Dozer, let alone stumble into his bunk and sleep. He had left Fig to fend for herself. True, Simone was with her. The two were renting a room at the Fossil and Firkin, a cozy saloon. It was hardly the wilderness. But tar it, Fig needed a full-time father. With the war on, with Joe desperately training new recruits to fight Hell's Hunters, he simply couldn't be there for his daughter. He had chosen his planet over his child, and it tore him up.

This is my fault, he realized. *All of it. I neglected Figaro. Because of me, she almost died last night.*

Dozer seemed to sense Joe's despair. The big triceratops moaned and licked Joe's arm, slobbering all over him. Disgusting. But the trike meant well.

"Dad?"

The voice came from behind him, soft and shaky.

Joe turned around.

Figaro entered the yard. She took a few steps toward Joe, then stopped, daring not walk closer. She looked so much like her mother. Fig could have been Mina reborn. She had the same olive-toned skin, the same delicate features, the same almond-shaped eyes. But while Mina had worn her black hair long, proud of the lustrous locks, Fig kept hers cut short. It was as if Fig tried to appear smaller, to draw less attention, to hide from the world. Joe knew something about that. She had inherited her mother's looks and her father's personality. Like Joe, she was introverted. Like him, she was stubborn and defiant.

Like me, she's a pain in the butt, Joe thought, and a wry smile twisted his lips.

Then he noticed the tear rolling down Fig's cheek. She looked up at him, eyes damp. "Dad. I sorre. I sao sorre."

She began trembling. Joe rushed across the yard toward her. He pulled the girl into his arms and held her close, rocking her gently.

"I'm here for you, Fig. I'm here for you. You have nothing to be sorry for. I'm here for you always, and I love you."

Father and daughter rode Dozer down the streets of Dinovia, heading home. Five months after the devastating Battle for Dinovia, the city was still recovering. Scaffolds surrounded the new Pangaea Hall, and bricklayers bustled across the wooden slats, rebuilding the grand rotunda. A diplodocus plodded toward the building and craned his neck high. A sack of bricks dangled from his neck like a lumpy bolo tie. Several stories up, workers collected the bricks, rewarded the dinosaur with some cantaloupes, and began slapping on mortar. Riding by, Joe nodded at the workers and waved. They waved back. Fig blushed and waved shyly.

They kept riding down the block. Dozer was a big dinosaur, even for a triceratops, tipping the scales at over ten tons. At least that's what Joe estimated; there were no scales on Mintari big enough for Dozer to actually step on. Despite his size, Dozer was surprisingly gentle, treading carefully without knocking down buildings or leaving potholes. He caused no damage to cobblestones or bricks. Gardens were a different matter. Whenever he passed by a pot of petunias, Dozer couldn't help but munch.

The trike lumbered by the old clock tower, a historic building. It was too badly damaged to restore. The tower had fallen. The clock had broken. The foundations rose from the ground like the shattered teeth of a giant. Two ankylosaurs were there, swinging their clubbed tails, knocking down the remains. In time, the clock tower would rise again with new bricks. The historic clock would be repaired and tick once more.

Joe looked at the diplodocus crane, the ankylosaur wrecking balls, and the living bulldozer he rode. Humans using dinosaurs for their needs. Rangersaurs, they called them. A cute name. But there was nothing cute about this, if you asked Joe. This all went against the ethos of Mintari. When Joe had become a Ranger, he had vowed to protect the vision of Mintari's founders. Mintari was a nature reserve. The planet belonged to dinosaurs. Humans were here as caretakers, not masters. Yet now he saw dinosaurs serving humans. Perhaps that was the reality of war; they must bend their morals for the greater good. He still didn't like seeing it. These dinosaurs should be in the wild, not here in the city. But for a while, dinosaurs and humans must work together to protect Mintari.

Then again, maybe I'm a hypocrite, Joe thought. *I've been riding Dozer for years. Even before the war.* He sighed and patted his dinosaur.

Everyone in the city was working to rebuild. Joe saw them carry bricks, pave roads, plant gardens (much to Dozer's delight), and raise barricades. Many buildings had fallen during the battle last spring, but the city was healing.

"You gotta give it to Mintarians," Joe said. "We're a tough lot. No matter what disaster strikes, we rebuild."

Fig rode ahead of him, holding on to Dozer's frill. She gazed into the distance. "But dinosirs can . . . nit re-bid. Dinosirs . . . jis . . . die."

She struggled with every word, but she was getting better at speaking. Joe understood her perfectly.

"You're right, Fig. Dinosaurs can't rebuild. When poachers kill them, they simply die. But that's why we're here. The Mintari Rangers."

Fig swiveled around and looked at him. Her eyes shone. "Kin . . . I . . . be a R-r-rin-ga?"

Joe's chest swelled with pride. Figaro, his daughter—a Ranger! Now there was a thought! But he hid the smile that threatened to bloom across his face.

"First graduate high school," Joe said. "Then you can apply to become a Ranger."

Fig rolled her eyes. "Dad! B-b-but school sucks!"

Joe laughed. "I know, Fig. I know. You're like me. You don't play well with others. You don't respect authority. You're wild at heart. I'm too old to change, but you're young. You can be all the things I never was."

She looked at him with soft eyes. "But I wan be like you."

Joe's eyes dampened. "I love you, Figaro."

"Liv you, Dad."

She leaned against him. Her talking was getting so much better. Yes, she was smart, she was learning, and she was improving every day. Figaro would not be held back.

This girl survived fifteen years in the wilderness, Joe reminded himself. *She can survive anything.*

Dozer turned onto a side road. They moved along the narrow, cobbled street. Homes rose alongside, almost close enough to graze Dozer's lumpy flanks. Balconies rose above them, blooming with the last flowers of autumn. Clotheslines stretched over the street, adorned with a thousand Mintarian flags. The flags were crimson with a golden, three-toed footprint in the middle. The footprint represented a megalosaurus, the first dinosaur species discovered on Earth and the first one cloned on Mintari. Joe looked at the flags fluttering overhead. He had been born on Cloventia, but Mintari had become his home. He would forever fight for this flag.

"What happened last night?" Joe said softly.

For a long moment, Fig said nothing. She sat stiffly on Dozer, and Joe sat behind her, while the triceratops lumbered down the road under the sky of flags.

"I . . .," Fig said. "I try-tried to h-h-halp but . . ." Her voice cracked. "M-m-mosasaur. He got dem. He . . . he . . . bit dem. I try to pall dem. To safe dem." She sobbed. "Dey die. Why? Why Fi-ga-ro live?"

He wrapped his arms around her. "You did nothing wrong, Fig. You were brave. You were so brave. And I'm so sorry you had to see what you saw."

They rode the rest of the way in silence, Joe holding his daughter in his arms. It would be a long few days. Fig would need to give a formal report to the Rangers. To recreate the terror. To live with the guilt. Right now they just felt dazed. Right now Joe just needed to get his daughter home.

Dozer rounded a corner, and there it rose. The Fossil and Firkin. The best saloon in the city, if you asked Joe. No tourists allowed. Just the kind of place Joe liked. He had spent his youth there, playing piano, eating Barnum's famous shepherd's pie, and drinking the home-brewed beer. He had met Mina in this saloon. After she died, Joe had fled the city, had lived in exile for years, hiding in his cave. But the Fossil and Firkin was still home. Joe didn't own the place. But he knew he and his family were always welcome there.

This is a good place for Fig, he thought. *A safe place. A place of love and camaraderie.*

They parked Dozer outside. The trike headed straight toward the petunia garden and went to town. Barnum always left out bales of hay for the dinosaur, but Dozer knew what he liked. While Dozer's head was lowered toward the flowers, Joe grabbed a horn, slid down Dozer's flank, and landed with both feet on the ground, wounded leg and all. He held out his arms for Fig. She didn't need help. As quick as a velociraptor, she scampered off the dinosaur.

Fig hesitated outside the saloon's batwing doors. She glanced at Joe. "Dad. Am scaret."

He knew what she meant. They rented a private room on the second floor. To get there, they had to pass through the busy common room. The regulars were always there, day and night, socializing, eating, drinking. They would notice something was wrong. Would ask questions. Joe understood his daughter perfectly. He had never felt comfortable in crowds, especially not since Mina had died. Fig was the same.

He wrapped an arm around her. "Come on, Figgy. I'm with you."

She tilted her head. "Figgy?"

Joe grinned. "I just made that up."

She smiled softly. "Figgy. I like."

Armed with smiles, they stepped through the batwing doors into the common room.

As always, the locals were there. Merl sat at his usual table, splatters of paint covering his overalls. He was picking his ear while eating beans from a can. Edna was chewing tobacco, sometimes leaning over to spit into a spittoon. Her curly white hair spilled out from under her ceratop hat. Abernathy sat by the fireplace, warming his old bones and whittling a sauropod. Vinnie, Joe's pet velociraptor, lay atop the piano. The turkey-sized dinosaur was curled up into a ball of feathers. Young Billi, the proprietor's granddaughter, stood on a ladder, dusting the dinosaur fossil that stood propped against the wall, still trapped in a slab of stone. It was a real dinosaur fossil, seventy million years old, dug out of the ground of Earth. The only real fossil on Mintari, Barnum claimed. Every other dinosaur on the planet was genetically engineered, and Barnum prided himself on owning the real deal.

Barnum—owner, manager, and chef—stood behind the bar. It was his favorite place in the saloon, and who could blame him? A wonderful bar it was, carved from live-edge wood, lovingly polished and oiled countless times. Casks of ale rose farther back, and clay mugs hung from above on hooks. Barnum was an old man now. He boasted bushy white muttonchops, a big belly, and a bigger heart. As soon as he saw Fig enter the saloon, the rotund barkeep raced around the bar, his speed belying his size and age.

"Oh, darling." He pulled Fig into an embrace. "I heard the news. Oh, sweetheart, we're so glad you're safe."

Joe glanced above the bar. The holographic television floated near the ceiling, broadcasting the news. It showed a chaotic scene on the shore. The victims' families stood on the sand. Tricopters flew over the water, seeking the three lost children. A caption orbited the holographic tableau, each letter a little satellite. THREE YOUTHS LOST AT SEA. ONE GIRL RESCUED.

But Joe remembered what Fig had told him. Those youths would not be found alive.

The image on the holographic television changed. Now it showed an image of Figaro. A voice sounded over the image.

"The girl rescued this morning was Figaro Triplehorn, granddaughter of the infamous Tobias Triplehorn. Our loyal viewers will remember that Tobias Triplehorn was charged with treason in Mintari's high court and has been living in exile. Our viewers might also remember the extraordinary story of Figaro, who was abandoned by her father, left to fend for herself in the wilderness until only last spring. The girl's aunt, Amissa Triplehorn, is the same poacher who led the attack on Dinovia. Viewers, one can't help wonder why Clan Triplehorn seems connected to every tragedy that befalls—"

Barnum tapped the remote, switching to the Dino Derby. Fig's image vanished. Holographic dinosaurs raced around a track while the crowd cheered.

Nobody in the common room was watching the derby, though. They all stared at Joe and Fig, silent. Edna's eyes were soft. Merl's were damp.

"Tarry news," Barnum muttered. "Buncha rubbish." He looked at Fig and his expression softened. "Sweetheart, can I fix you a plate? Hot shepherd's pie? Cold ice cream?"

Fig couldn't meet his eyes. She stared at her toes, cheeks flushed.

"I think we'll head up to our room," Joe said. He took Fig's hand, prepared to lead her to the staircase.

"Dad. I . . . wan stay. Here." She raised her eyes, hesitant, and looked at the people all around. "Wif . . . wif frens."

That surprised Joe. In her shoes, he would want to isolate himself, to hide from society. He would have locked himself in the darkness with his ghosts. Fig preferred the company of the living. Smart girl. And like Mina in more than just looks, it seemed.

They headed toward their usual table. It was close enough to the fireplace for warmth in winter, close enough to the window for a breeze in summer. The piano was just the right distance to appreciate good playing and tune out bad playing. Sitting there, one could see the full common room, the batwing doors, the bar, and the fossil. A perfect view of this cozy oasis on a planet of savage danger. That table was their happy place.

Before Joe and Fig could sit down, a cry tore across the saloon.

"Figaro!"

A woman came flouncing down the staircase. She had a Cloventian accent, but she wore Mintarian clothes. As she descended the stairs (moving with all the grace of an avalanche), she revealed hiking boots, a safari outfit, and a neckerchief. Another step, and her head came into view. Her face was the color of porcelain and strewn with a thousand freckles. Her eyes shone a startling blue. But what most people noticed first about Simone LaRue was her flaming red hair. It was her only vanity. The fiery mane spilled out from her ceratop hat, cascading down to her waist.

"Figaro!" Simone repeated, rushing across the common room toward the girl. On the way, she managed to bump into a table, spill Merl's can of beans, bang an accidental chord on the piano, and step on (a very terrified) Vinnie. Joe stifled a smile. Simone's heart was courageous, her mind was sharp, but her dexterity left something to be desired.

When she reached Fig, she pulled the girl into a crushing embrace. "Oh sweetheart! You poor little thing."

Fig gasped. "S'mone! Air!"

"Oh. Sorry." Simone loosened her grip. "I'm just so happy to see you. The news is dreadful. Dreadful! The journalism on this planet!" She placed her hands on her hips. "As a journalist emeritus, I'm appalled by the state of Mintari's media. Details not fact-checked. Reporters stumbling over their cue cards. Shaky camera angles, bad lighting, and don't get me started about the fashion choices—"

"Simone, let's focus on what matters now," Joe said. "Figaro."

"Right. Right." Simone nodded, her red hair bouncing. She held the girl's hand. "We're here for you."

"Eveeone say dat!" Fig blurted out. "Everyone say . . . we here fo yoo. I . . . just wan . . . food."

The girl knuckled her eyes, sat down at the table, and crossed her arms.

Joe glanced at Simone. She met his gaze, concern in her eyes. They both understood. Fig was in denial. The horror had not yet sunk in. It had not yet hit Joe either.

He looked at his daughter. Fig was perusing a menu even though she could barely read, and she always ordered the shepherd's pie anyway. She stubbornly avoided his gaze.

I've seen friends die in battle, he thought. *But I was already an adult, a hardened Ranger. You're just a child, my sweet Figaro. You're new to death. You suffered a terrible trauma. The waves of grief will wash over you—as surely as the waves at sea tossed you off that doomed boat. And I'll be here to catch you, my beloved.*

It was a funny thing. He had only known Fig for a few months. But he had fallen in love with her that first day, and his love had only grown since.

Barnum brought over three plates of steaming shepherd's pie. The aroma of beef, onions, gravy, and creamy potatoes filled their nostrils. The barkeep poured two cups of strong coffee for Joe and Simone, a cup of milk for Fig.

"Shepherd's pie for breakfast?" Joe asked.

"Don't look a gift horse in the mouth," Simone said, speaking through a mouthful of potatoes.

The portly barkeep nodded. "Shepherd's pie is comfort food." He looked at Fig, his eyes soft. "And this morning, we all need some comfort."

Barnum smiled sadly, patted Joe on the shoulder, and shuffled back to his bar.

The common room was quiet. Too quiet. Normally the sound of conversation filled the Fossil and Firkin. All Joe could hear now was the crackling fireplace, the muted sounds of the Dino Derby, and the scrape of Fig's cutlery on her plate. The girl was feasting with gusto.

"Mmm. Good." Fig stuffed in another spoonful, then reached across the table for the bread basket. "Pess roll?"

Simone nudged the basket closer to Fig. The girl grabbed a roll and took a huge bite. Then a bite of shepherd's pie. Then another mouthful of bread. She was barely chewing, and she kept her eyes on the Dino Derby.

"Mmm . . . good race." She gulped and wiped her lips. "Galmimi G'all fast toe-di."

Indeed, Gallimimus Gil, a favorite of Fig's, was running a good race today. He was only second from last, which was good for the lanky dinosaur. But Joe only spared the derby a glance. He kept his eyes on Fig. The girl was chattering away, stuffing her cheeks like a hamster, and savoring the moment.

Joe glanced at Simone. She looked back, eyes sad.

"Fig?" Joe said, shifting his chair closer to his daughter. "Are you all right?"

She nodded and reached for the bread basket. "More . . . roll? Pees?"

"Figaro."

A tear rolled down her cheek. "I fine. Bread! More bread."

Nobody moved to pass her the basket. Fig glared at them, swallowed her mouthful of shepherd's pie, and wiped her mouth.

"I fine! I fine. I . . ." Another tear flowed. Fig lowered her head. "I em alive. I em alive . . ."

And she was sobbing. Big, ugly sobs, her body shaking, her face hidden in her hands. Joe and Simone were at her sides at once, embracing her. Barnum rushed forward with a handkerchief, then joined the embrace. Even Merl joined the hug, nearly crushing them all in his wide arms.

"Hey, what are we hugging for?" the big man said. "Aw, who cares! Merl loves hugs!"

Fig managed to smile. But Joe knew that nothing he, Merl, or anyone might say could fix this. He had felt the same after Mina had died. After Rangers had died. Survivor's guilt. Grief. Terrible, crushing emptiness. All he could do was hold his daughter, be there for her, a pillar of stability in her crumbling world.

CHAPTER THREE
Through Dangers Untold

There was a dinosaur in the center of the labyrinth, and Two Crows knew he was going to die.

He stumbled through the maze. He had no yarn like Theseus. No breadcrumbs like Hansel and Gretel. They had given him a rifle, that was all. Against the terror in the heart of this labyrinth, it might as well be a peashooter. Two Crows ran, took a right turn, then a left. His head spun. He was lost. Hopelessly lost. And in the distance rose the hungry grumbles.

Long ago on planet Dagon, his father had carved him wooden dinosaurs. Young Two Crows had delighted in the toys. They were poor farmers. Far too poor to ever visit Mintari and see real dinosaurs. Two Crows would spend hours on the farmhouse porch, playing with his toys, making them fight, making them roar.

Now his childhood dream had come true. He was on Mintari. And he learned that dinosaurs did not roar. They rumbled. A sound like thunder rolling over the fields. A sound like nightmares. A sound so deep it vibrated across the ground, pounded his chest, and clanged his ribs like hammers. It was the sound of oncoming death.

He missed his home.

He had always found Dagon boring. An entire planet covered with farmlands. Nothing but crops to the horizon and beyond. Most days the only wild animals were the crows that covered the fields, pecking at seeds. Two of the birds had landed on the porch the day he was born. It was a difficult birth. A premature birth. A struggle against death while the crows cawed.

"A curse!" his mother had cried. "Crows are the messengers of the god of death."

His father, according to the stories, had only laughed. "Call him Two Crows. He conquered death. Let him carry his victory in his name."

Now, running through the labyrinth, Two Crows knew his parents had been wrong.

Crows were not messengers of the gods. Crows, like all birds, were dinosaurs.

And today a much larger dinosaur would finish the job.

It sounded again. That terrible rumble. That thunder that shook the bones. It sounded almost like laughter. Two Crows had not seen the beast. But he had seen the footprints. Huge footprints with three toes, with claws the length of his forearms. The stench of the beast filled the labyrinth. The grumbles echoed, flowing through the halls. It was impossible to tell where the sound was coming from.

Two Crows ran onward. Why was he running? There must still be hope in him. Hope he could find his way out. Could survive this terrible place. Hope filled his chest. He was strong. He was young. He could do this. He could still escape, still solve the labyrinth, win the prize.

The prize. Yes . . . the reason he was here. The desire of his heart, the object of his dreams. He could already imagine it. He could almost touch it. A hundred thousand Mintarian mints. That was over a million Dagonite hucks. Enough to pay off his family debts. To own his farm. To go *home*.

"I can do this," he whispered through trembling lips. "Just like the mazes I'd solve with a pencil back home."

He even allowed himself a smile.

That was when he stumbled over something, wobbled, and nearly crashed down. He leaned against the brick wall, catching his breath, and looked at what had tripped him.

A bone. A femur. A human femur.

Two Crows blenched. His head spun. "No. No, it's just a dinosaur bone. Just a dinosaur. It's . . ."

Then he saw them nearby. More bones. A human skull. A foot still in its boot. A skeletal hand still clutching a rusty rifle.

Oh gods above. Two Crows leaned over and gagged. He was going to die here.

He should never have come. What a fool he was! But the offer had been too good to refuse. The mysterious woman had approached him at the racetrack, her face hidden behind a silver mask. He was having a bad night. He had spent most of his life savings on a starship ticket from Dagon to Mintari. Now he was losing whatever remained at the Dino Derby. He had come to this planet to bet on dinos, to make his fortune, to raise enough money to buy his farm. He found himself destitute, too poor to even afford a flight home.

"A hundred thousand mints," the masked woman had told him. "Just to solve a little maze. You in?"

Yes, he was in. He was in deep. And now he could not get out.

He stumbled onward, kicking through bones. More bones. More skeletons. One with a shattered rib cage. One skull had holes the size of golf balls. They had died holding their guns.

Kill the dinosaur or escape the dinosaur, the masked woman had told him, handing him his rifle. *Either way—you win.*

Two Crows quickly abandoned any thoughts of grand heroism. There was no killing this monster. In this case, the choice between fight or flight was obvious. Flight it was. His only hope was to solve this labyrinth and emerge from the other end alive. So he ran onward. The brick walls rose high, too smooth to climb. There was no ceiling. When Two Crows glanced up, he could see the blue sky. Drones hovered overhead, filming his despair. Beyond them, Two Crows could see the sun. Funny. Different planet, same sun. Mintari orbited a little farther from Nyx, but the star seemed just as bright here.

He was hoping Nyx could give him a sense of direction. Perhaps he could follow the sun out of the maze. But the star shone directly overhead now. Not much help. Two Crows was still utterly lost. He ran aimlessly, trying to navigate by the stench of the dinosaur, by the sound of its grumbles. But the creature seemed to be everywhere at once. An eternal presence, omnipotent and omniscient. A god of hunger.

His eye caught more footprints ahead. Human footprints! Fresh ones. Hope swelled in Two Crows. Was somebody else trapped in here? Somebody who could help?

He raced toward the footprints, and he recognized the pattern of the sole. His own footprints. He was moving in circles.

The rumble rose again. And this time Two Crows could tell where it was coming from.

Directly behind him.

Two Crows didn't turn to look. He just ran. He ran in a panic. No map. No plan. All he had was his terror.

But that's not true. I have a gun.

The rifle trembled in his hands. He had fired a gun only once in his life. It was years ago. He had shot into the air, scaring away a pack of prairie devils, furry predators no taller than his knee. The gunshot had sent them running, and Two Crows had felt strong, a protector of his pasture. Now he was prey.

He banged against a wall, careened, ran onward. He tripped over a skull, skinned his knees, shoved himself up, and kept running. The rumble grew closer behind. The stench. Oh gods, the stench of it. A smell of rotten meat and oil and urine.

He could hear the dinosaur breathing now. Hear the heavy footfalls slamming against the ground.

The ground was just soil here. The labyrinth was located out in the wilderness. A place of terror. A place of death. Yet he was not alone here. The drones kept hovering above, filming everything, and in the distance rolled muffled cheers like the waves of the sea. Two Crows could not see them from here. But he knew they were watching. Some sat in bleachers. Others watched on screens, peering down through the eyes of the drones. Some sat in astrolites that hovered above like merciless angels.

These were his life's final moments. A show. Entertainment for vampires.

The crowd roared louder. The monster was near.

Two Crows shut his eyes as he ran, and he imagined himself back there. Back on Dagon, the grass giant, the huge farming world that fed the Nyx system. He was running through fields of barley, and his beloved skipped at his side, her blue eyes bright in the sun, her golden braids bouncing. They fell onto a pile of hay and kissed, and the sun winked between the clouds.

"One day, Dancing Leaves," he told her. "One day I'll buy you this farmland, and I'll buy the farmhouse from the bankers, and we'll be free. We'll be free, Dancing Leaves, and we'll be together."

She smiled in his memory, sparkles in her sky-blue eyes.

I will make it home, he thought. *I will find my way out of this maze. For you, Dancing Leaves.*

He opened his eyes, whipped around a corner, and there he saw it.

The dinosaur.

There it stood before him. The terror in the heart of the labyrinth.

The dinosaur was enormous. Two Crows stood shorter than its legs. The arms were comically small. Like little chicken wings glued onto a monster. But there was nothing funny about this dinosaur's jaws. They were huge. Muscular. Jaws like an excavator. Jaws designed to crush bone and rip through flesh. Brown scales covered the beast, and two crimson horns grew from its head. Devil horns.

Two Crows recognized the species. Here stood a carnotaurus. Its name meant "flesh bull" in Latin. With those horns, it was indeed somewhat bullish. A terrible bull. A flesh-eating bull. A minotaur.

Two Crows skidded to a halt. He stared at the dinosaur, not daring to retreat, not even to breathe. The reptilian predator narrowed his eyes. His nostrils flared. The carnivore seemed to be savoring the scent. His scaly lips peeled back, revealing rows of teeth. He was salivating, and a hungry grumble bubbled up his throat.

Two Crows dropped his rifle.

"Please," he whispered. "Please. Mercy."

He knelt before the carnivore. When he begged, he was begging the people watching through the drone. Maybe the woman with the silver mask was among them. But perhaps he was also begging the dinosaur. The shamans of Mintari worshipped dinosaurs as gods, and today Two Crows understood why. Gods were real. And they were hungry.

The dinosaur stepped closer. His gargantuan feet tore through the ground. They looked like the feet of crows. They were talons. Those who named the carnotaurus had been wrong. This was not a bull. It was a bird. A huge bird covered with scales, horned and clawed. A terror bird. A death bird. Birds had heralded Two Crows's life. With caws birds had welcomed him into the world. And now this ancient bird placed his talon upon him, holding Two Crows in place as the mouth descended, and a growl heralded his death.

As a child, Two Crows had once entered a corn maze, had run laughing with his brothers. He had become frightened when he could not find his way out, had called out to his father, and at night his mother had cradled him in her arms, rocking him to sleep. As the teeth sank into him, Two Crows shut his eyes and thought of home, of his family under the sun, and one more time his mother rocked him to sleep.

An astrolite hovered above the labyrinth. Its floor was transparent, giving a perfect view of the show. Several similar astrolites hung in midair nearby. Jurassic Maze, the brainchild of Amissa Triplehorn, was the newest tourist attraction on Mintari. The astrolites served as boxed seats, letting the wealthy view the labyrinth from above. Velvet couches, a minibar, and a robotic servant filled each flying vehicle, adding a touch of luxury. The poorer folk sat on bleachers around the labyrinth. They couldn't see much from there, only the labyrinth corridors nearest to them. But they could watch the entire action on hovering screens. In the future, Amissa planned to build higher bleachers, giving the masses a better view.

"Marvelous!" Amissa cried, on her feet and cheering. "Marvelous show. Look at that kill!" She turned toward her father, beaming. "What do you think, Dad? And remember—it's all my vision. I designed the labyrinth, oversaw construction, everything."

Chief Tobias Triplehorn shared the astrolite with her. He sat on a cozy velvet armchair, but his body was so stiff he might as well be sitting on an ankylosaurus. A spiky one. His long, narrow face remained emotionless, its usual state. He sipped his wine, his eye twitched, and he lowered the glass. To Tobias Triplehorn, an eye twitch was like a full-blown grimace.

"I will tell you what I think." He put down his cup. "The wine is swill. The gladiator did not fire a single shot. And your dinosaur should be mounted and stuffed!" His lip twitched. "I sent you here to hunt dinosaurs, Amissa. Not to put on a sideshow! Did you drag me all the way from Cloventia for this?" He rose to his feet, and his voice rose with him. "For this *circus*?"

"Whoa, whoa!" Amissa took a step back. "Cool it, pops. This is only a prototype! I plan to expand the labyrinth. To fill it with more dinosaurs. To get real gladiators, give them swords and tridents, maybe toss in a few booby traps—then you'll see a *real* show. Imagine it, Dad!" She gripped his arm. "Just *imagine it*! A labyrinth ten times this size, full of carnivores of every kind. Raptors. T-rexes. Pterosaurs flying above, swooping down to capture their prey. We could charge a fortune for tickets—and people will pay it! They'll fly in from across the galaxy to see it. The greatest show in the universe. The ultimate battle between human and dinosaur!"

Tobias looked through the astrolite's glass floor. He studied the admittedly humble labyrinth, a hastily constructed thing with only a single dinosaur in the middle. He shook his head. "Pathetic. I thought you were a killer, not a carnival barker. I sent you here to hunt."

"This *is* hunting!" Amissa said. "This is the *ultimate* hunting experience, a crucible pitting man against monster. Hunting in the field has become stale. The guns are too big. Poachers today fly in skyslayers, firing machine guns from above, mowing down thousands of dinosaurs in an afternoon. Where's the fun in that? Ha! It's like shooting fish in a barrel. Might as well nuke the dinosaurs from orbit and be done with it. But this, Dad!" She gestured down through the glass floor. "This is the true spirit of the hunt. Just two predators, one against the other. Mano a dino. It will be our legacy on Mintari. This labyrinth will—"

Tobias backhanded her. Hard across the cheek. A stroke that rattled her jaw.

"Our legacy will be the destruction of dinosaurs!" he roared. "I did not send you here to debase yourself, to become some carnival barker, entertaining the hoi polloi with these antics. I sent you here for revenge! Dinosaurs killed your grandparents. You were meant to kill them all. Not feed them farmers in a glorified corn maze!"

Amissa clutched her cheek. She glared at her father with burning eyes.

She wanted to strike him back. She could. She was thirty-four, strong, fit, a powerful huntress in her prime. He was an old man, thin and lanky, used to waging all his battles in boardrooms. She could defeat him with her superior strength. But standing here, she felt like a little girl again. A girl beaten. A girl scolded and shamed. He still had that power over her.

Amissa lowered her head and clasped her hands behind her back. "I'm sorry, Dad," she whispered.

"You wasted family money on trifles," Tobias said. "You are the heiress of Clan Triplehorn. But you've not proved yourself worthy of this burden. I want a dinosaur species extinct by winter. Is that understood?"

Amissa dared raise her eyes. "I'll give you one extinct species, and you let me keep building this labyrinth."

He barked a laugh. "You try to bargain with me?"

"Always. Even as a girl. You remember our chores-for-ammo deal."

He snorted. "Very well. It's a deal."

"You mean it?" She inhaled sharply. "I kill off a species, I get the labyrinth of my dreams?"

Tobias nodded. Amissa squealed and hugged him. Her father stiffened at first, but then his body loosened, and he wrapped his arms around her. He stroked her hair.

"You're a good girl, Amissa. A good girl. Spiteful, boastful, yes. But a good girl."

She found tears in her eyes. It was so rare to hear compliments from him. Amissa had never known her mother. Lifa had abandoned her. She had grown up with Tobias—cold, elegant, always so critical. So many times she had tasted his bitter fists. His praise was like honey. It melted over her, and she savored the sweetness. What else did she have in this galaxy? She had no husband, no children, no friends. Even her fans were now gone. Simone—that wretched, horrible Simone—had deleted Amissa's QuickFame account. Her fans had kept her going; Simone had ripped them away.

But I still have my father's love, Amissa thought, feeling safe in his arms. He was not a fighter like her. But in his own way, he was the strongest man in the galaxy.

"I return to Cloventia tonight," Tobias said. "The business does not tolerate my absence for long. Besides . . ." His mouth twisted into a humorless smile. "I'm a wanted man on Mintari. I believe the Rangers have designated me a traitor."

Amissa laughed. "Let them. Half this planet belongs to me now. My hunters have become an army. The Rangers are in shambles. Soon enough, all of Mintari will be ours. Let them call Clan Triplehorn traitors. In time, they'll call us masters!" She felt rather proud of that diabolical speech. She considered adding an evil cackle but decided that would be too much. If only she had a mustache to twirl!

Unimpressed with her villainous grandiosity, Tobias looked again through the glass floor. Feeling rather deflated, Amissa followed his gaze. The carnotaurus finished devouring the farmer, licked his chops, and belched. The dinosaur resumed prowling the labyrinth, searching for another meal. Amissa had named him Asterius. A marvelous beast.

Soon enough, I'll find you more victims, my beloved Asterius, she thought. *You will devour them all. You could devour the world.*

"One more thing, Amissa, before I leave," said Tobias.

"Anything, Father."

"It concerns your niece. Figaro Triplehorn."

Amissa snorted. "*La petite enfant sauvage?* What's she to us?"

"Family," Tobias said. "And family is everything. Listen carefully, Amissa."

He leaned closer and whispered into her ear. He could have said anything. He loved her. He needed her. For her father, she would pluck every star from the sky and slay every monster in the labyrinth of the world.

CHAPTER FOUR
Creatures of the Wild

Mintari was at war, and Joe was a soldier. But this weekend he did not fight. This weekend he spent with his daughter. Dinosaurs were dying. Mintari needed him. But right now Figaro needed him even more.

For a moment, Joe felt torn between loyalty to his duty and to his daughter. But only for a moment. Joe loved dinosaurs with all his heart. He had dedicated his life to protecting them. But Figaro meant more to him than every dinosaur on this planet.

The room they rented upstairs was small and humble. That day, Fig asked to stay downstairs in the common room. They watched the Dino Derby, and Fig cheered when Gallimimus Gil finished second from last, his personal best. Joe played the piano for her. He warmed up with "Don't Fear the Raptor," which earned (and deserved) only a modest reception. But when he played the chords to "Don't Stop Evolvin'," everyone in the bar sang along. He taught Fig how to play "Twinkle, Twinkle, Little Asteroid," a simple tune, and she smiled so brightly when she finally played it perfectly by herself. Joe savored that smile. Mina's smile. A smile that lit Fig's eyes and lit his heart ten times brighter. He even let her taste wine. Just one sip, which she promptly spat out.

At night, when they went upstairs to their room, she said she was scared. Joe tucked her in, sat at her bedside, and kept her safe until she slept. He gazed down at her, his precious daughter, this miracle girl who survived against all odds. She was so beautiful. So brave. He brushed her dark hair back from her forehead. She closed her eyes, smiling softly.

"You ran with dinosaurs, you survived the savage wilderness, and you stared down a mosasaur," he whispered. "But you're still my little girl. I don't know what I would do if I lost you."

She opened her eyes, still tucked in neatly. "I . . . feel . . . bad. Da kids . . . died. But I . . . live. Not . . . right. Not right."

He kissed her forehead. "Don't blame yourself for surviving, Figaro. Don't feel guilt for living. We can mourn the dead and still celebrate your life."

Fig nodded, closed her eyes, and slept. Joe knew it would take more than a few words to heal her soul. It would take a lot of time, a lot of love. He didn't always have time for her. But he had all the love in his heart.

On Sunday morning, he took Figaro for a ride out of the city. It was just him and her, riding Dozer across the grasslands. As soon as they were outside the city walls, Joe breathed easier. Fig took a deep breath, and the tension in her shoulders eased. They had both been carrying tension for long months. Trapped inside Dinovia, they had been like animals in cages. Most Mintarians lived inside the city, rarely daring to venture into a wilderness swarming with dinosaurs. But Joe and Fig were rarities. They were creatures of the wild.

They needed this trip. Not just to bond. But to escape the maddening crowd and find solace in nature. There was savagery on Mintari. There was predation and despair and danger. But there was healing here too. A deep healing that went down to the soul.

Dozer was clearly content. He perhaps missed the city's petunias, but he found plenty of cycads and bushes to devour. Ultimately, for a triceratops, quantity beat quality. Goodbye fine dining, hello buffet. Vinnie too had joined the expedition. The little velociraptor raced ahead through the grass, scattering autumn leaves, hunting insects and lizards and having the time of his life.

Simone had stayed behind. "Travel into a hellscape full of dinosaurs? No, thanks."

Joe missed the crazy redhead. But this was daddy-daughter bonding time.

Fig took a deep breath. "I missed dis. Air."

Joe ruffled her short black hair. "Your talking is so much better. It gets better every day."

She grinned. "When I'm he-ppy . . . I . . . tok beda." She scrunched up her face. *"Bet-ter."*

He took her to Neraka Gorge, a four-hour ride from the city. It was a long time to spend on the back of a dinosaur. Not nearly enough time to spend with his daughter. On the way there, they admired a brontosaurus herd rumbling across the grasslands, watched a pack of raptors take down an iguanodon (they were careful not to get too close), and even spotted a stegosaurus family in the distance, ambling across the plains.

"Stegosaurs should live in the forest," Joe said, watching the spiky dinosaurs roam. "They usually feed on ferns and other shade plants, not the grass and shrubs of the sunny plains."

"Look." Fig pointed, and her eyes softened.

One of the stegosaurs was wounded. Those looked like bullet wounds. Another stegosaur's scales were charred black.

"They're fleeing poachers and fire," Joe said. "Amissa and her hunters are out there. Burning. Killing." He took a deep breath, trying to calm his rage. Today was not about the war. It was about Figaro.

But even Fig was clenching her fists. "When am big, I . . . wi-wi-will be . . . a Wanga." She tried again. "Wan . . . gerrr . . . *Ranger.*"

They dismounted Dozer and approached the stegosaurs slowly, calmly. Joe wanted to treat their injuries, but the dinosaurs fled. Joe shook his head sadly. They were multiton dinosaurs armed with deadly spikes, yet when two little humans approached, they fled like elephants fleeing mice. Amissa had put that fear of humanity into them.

Fig shed a tear. "Poow bebies."

Joe put a hand on her shoulder. "Come on, Fig, let's keep going."

They reached Neraka Gorge by afternoon. It was a natural wonder of Mintari, twice as deep as Earth's Grand Canyon. Countless pterosaurs made their homes upon the cliffs, filling the gorge with life. They ranged from the grand quetzalcoatlus, pterosaurs the size of airplanes, to humble pterodactyls, flying reptiles no larger than seagulls. Fig stood on the edge, marveling at the sight. Whenever a pterosaur dived down to the river, then rose with a beak full of fish, Fig cheered.

"Teash me to fly?" she asked Joe. "S'mone ses you knao hao to fly."

Joe smiled thinly. "Yes, I know how to ride pterosaurs. But only at an hour of utmost need. The animals of Mintari are not here to serve us. We're here to serve them." Dozer grunted, and Joe patted the beast. "Yes, yes, Dozer, I know. You're hungry."

"As e'ways," Figaro quipped.

The triceratops had found only thorny shrubs along the gorge. He turned his beak up at them. Fig plucked some wildflowers and fed them to Dozer. He gulped them down, then licked the girl. His tongue was nearly as large as her entire body. Fig was left slimed but giggling.

On the way back home, they ran across a herd of dinosaurs. Fig gasped. "Look! Baby twifewataps!" Her face softened. "Aww. Dey didn grao harns yit."

Joe smiled. "Those aren't triceratops. They're protoceratops."

They belonged to the ceratopsian clade of beaked, frilled herbivores. Same as Dozer. But unlike giant triceratops, the protoceratops were tiny, only about the size of wild boars. Like Dozer, these diminutive ceratopsians had bony frills that protected them from predators. But they had no horns. These animals were all about defense, not offense.

"Dey cute," Fig said.

Vinnie squawked, flapped his flightless wings, and pawed at Dozer's leg. The little velociraptor looked up at Joe with puppy-dog eyes.

"What's wong wit him?" Fig asked.

Joe understood. He chewed his lip, considering. "I dunno, Vinnie. There are a lot of them. And only one of you."

Vinnie squawked louder and beat his wings. "Pree pree pree!" he cooed.

Joe smiled. "All right. Go on. Just be careful."

At once, Vinnie was off. He kept low in the grass, hiding as he drew nearer and nearer to the protoceratops herd.

Fig gasped. She understood. "V-v-vim-nie has no pack!"

"We'll keep watch, and if Vinnie gets in trouble, we'll help," Joe said. "He's a velociraptor. A wild animal. And he wants to hunt. Not just bugs and lizards but big game. He's doing what's in his nature."

For all his frequent chattering and squawking, Vinnie could move remarkably quietly when he wanted to. He slunk through the tall grass, inching toward his prey. His feathers blended among the brush. His powerful legs were tense, ready to pounce. Sickle claws rose on his feet, ready to slice. His scaly lips peeled back, revealing his teeth. He was salivating already.

The protoceratops did not even notice. They grazed obliviously, munching on ferns and reeds. Joe and Fig remained at a safe distance, sitting on Dozer, watching the drama unfold. Joe had seen Vinnie hunt before, but Fig tensed. She clutched Dozer's frill, leaned forward, and narrowed her eyes. The girl was utterly fascinated.

Vinnie inched closer. Closer. He was only a few steps away now. The protoceratops grazed without a care in the world. Vinnie froze, just watching, scouting a potential target. Protoceratops were small for dinosaurs, but they were still larger than Vinnie. An adult protoceratops tipped the scales at four hundred pounds. Vinnie weighed maybe fifty pounds after a big meal. Even Fig was heavier than that.

A hatchling wandered off from the herd, chasing a butterfly. The protoceratops looked a year old, maybe two. Old enough to be independent, still too young to be dangerous. The dinosaur was about Vinnie's size. The perfect prey.

The hatchling's mother looked over. She brayed. *Get back here!*

The juvenile ceratopsian looked at her, then back at the butterfly, debating whether to obey his mother or follow his curiosity.

Vinnie took his chance. The velociraptor pounced.

The feathered predator vaulted off a boulder, stretched out his feathered wings, and caught the air. Velociraptors could not fly, but they were decent gliders. Before the young protoceratops realized what was happening, Vinnie landed on him. The herbivore had thick, scaly skin. But Vinnie had sharp sickle claws, and he dug them into his victim.

The hatchling squealed. It was a terrible sound, shockingly loud for such a small animal. The little herbivore bucked and tried to shake Vinnie off, but the raptor clung on, slashing through the skin. Vinnie reached his jaws toward the protoceratop's neck, prepared to finish the job.

But like the triceratops, their (much) larger cousins, protoceratops had incredibly agile heads. The hatchling spun his head around like an owl, bringing his frill into the path of Vinnie's jaws. Instead of flesh, the raptor chomped down on bone. One of his teeth clattered to the ground.

The other protoceratops brayed. They looked around nervously. Were any other raptors here? Was this an ambush? Normally these feathered predators moved in packs, but they saw no others. Could it be? Was this crazy little velociraptor here alone, taking on a herd? He must be suicidal!

The hatchling's mother found her courage first. She rumbled forth, beak open in a furious cry. Vinnie should have run. But he stubbornly clung to the hatchling, tugging its frill, trying to reach the neck. Too late did he see Mamatops approach.

The adult protoceratops had no horns to gore prey. But her heavy frill slammed into Vinnie like a riot shield. The raptor flew through the air, hit the ground, and rolled. Watching from a distance, Joe winced. His beloved pet seemed fine. Bruised, yes. Mostly his ego. But otherwise fine.

Vinnie could have retreated, his pride broken and his body intact. But the plucky (or was it foolhardy?) velociraptor wasn't ready to throw in the towel. With a screech, he lunged back at the hatchling, prepared to claim his meal. By then, Babytops was already racing back to the herd, tooth marks on his frill.

Vinnie gave chase. The larger protos were having none of it. Mamatops charged, rammed her head into Vinnie, and the raptor flew through the air again. More protos lumbered forward, surrounded Vinnie, and cut off retreat. Mamatops rumbled, knocked Vinnie onto his back, then stomped down hard. Vinnie rolled aside. The herbivore's foot hit the ground, shattering rocks. One proto bull swung his tail, clobbering Vinnie and stunning the poor raptor. Mamatops raised her foot again, prepared to crush Vinnie's skull.

All right, that's enough, Joe thought.

He aimed his sleep-or-die. It was loaded with a tranquilizer dart. He hated to intervene with nature, but for Vinnie, he would. He aimed at the mother protoceratops. The enraged cow still had her foot over Vinnie's head, ready to flatten it.

Joe was about to pull the trigger when Fig let out a deafening cry.

"Ayeee! Yip yip yip!"

Eyes alight and teeth bared, Fig leaped off Dozer and ran across the grasslands. Her dress billowed in the wind. She kicked off her shoes and ran barefoot. Her cry shook the sky.

"Ayeee! Yip yip!"

The protoceratops turned toward her, giving Vinnie a delay in execution. Joe watched with wide eyes. He lowered his rifle. Fig was blocking his shot.

"Figaro!" he cried.

She ignored him and kept running. The protos reared. The adults moved ahead, forming a defensive line, protecting the juveniles. It had taken the herd a while to gather their bearings, but they were now moving like disciplined soldiers. A row of frills locked together, forming a shield wall. Poor Vinnie disappeared into the clouds of dust. He was stuck somewhere within the herd, a hostage.

With a battle cry, Fig ripped off the thong she wore around her neck. On the leather strap hung her sickle claw. The claw of an achillobator. It was the length of a man's hand, curved, and sharp.

The protos stomped the ground and snapped their beaks, trying to scare Fig off. Who was this new predator? What species was she? Well, whatever the case, she didn't look very dangerous. No armor, no fangs, just one claw. They could handle it. They would bite her little legs off!

With an ear-piercing "yip!" Fig leaped toward the wall of dinosaurs. The protos brayed and raised their open beaks, ready to bite off her toes. But Fig jumped too high. Their beaks snapped below her. She danced atop their heads, kicked off their frills, and vaulted even higher.

"Figaro!" Joe cried, kneeing Dozer. The big triceratops began rumbling closer.

Meanwhile, Fig landed among the herd. She spun, lashing her sickle claw in a wide arc. Blood sprayed. A protoceratops screamed, a gash on his flank. The herd rumbled and brayed and stomped their feet, raising clouds of dust.

Joe kneed Dozer. "Faster, faster!" He couldn't see much from here, only chaos of frills and dust and flying grass.

"Ayee!" Fig cried from the fray and lashed her sickle claw again. More blood flew. Something heavy thumped down hard. Joe couldn't see what.

Finally Dozer reached the herd. Adult protoceratops were the size of boars, but beside Dozer, they might as well be hamsters. The burly trike lumbered between them, knocking his smaller cousins back. Protos tumbled down like bowling pins. Their defensive lines crumbled. Why was their big cousin attacking them? The herd lost heart. First a velociraptor, then a crazy little mammal, and now this—betrayal. Braying, they retreated, fleeing across the plains toward the distant ginkgos.

They left one of their herd behind.

The hatchling did not make it.

His mother gave a few heartbreaking cries, then moved onward with the herd. She had other hatchlings to protect. She could not serve them by dying here. She must leave her fallen child behind.

That fallen child had a sickle claw in his neck. Fig's sickle claw.

The girl pulled it free, licked the blood, looked up at Joe, and grinned. "Good hunt!"

Vinnie lay beside her. He rose to his feet, ruffled his dusty feathers, and raised his head. Aside from a few bruises, scrapes, and missing feathers, he was uninjured. Mostly his pride was hurt. He did not even look at the hatchling Fig had hunted.

Fig licked her lips, leaned down, and bit into the dead protoceratops. She yanked out a chunk of flesh and chewed hungrily. Blood dripped down her chin. She thrust her head into the wound, bit off another chunk, and kept eating. Blood covered her face and hair. She didn't seem to care.

"Figaro!" Joe shouted. He dismounted Dozer. "Stop that!"

She looked up at him, strips of raw meat dangling from her teeth. She tilted her head, splattering blood. "Hur?"

He stomped toward her. "You are not an animal! Spit that out! Step away from that carcass!"

She snarled and wrapped her arms over the carcass. "Mine!" She snapped her teeth. "My hunt! My food! Mine!"

Joe's stomach churned. He had never seen Figaro like this. Wild. Savage. He took a step closer. She snarled at him, slashed her sickle claw through the air, and snapped her teeth. Then she stuck her head into the carcass, ripped off more meat, and gulped it down.

"Figaro, I told you to stop that!" Joe thundered. "You are a girl, not a dinosaur." He grabbed her shoulders and pulled her away from the carcass. "You are not an achillobator!"

She yowled and wrenched herself free. "I hunt! I hunt'ess! My hunt. My food!"

"Not like this, tar it!" Joe said. "Not raw! Not like a wild animal." He grabbed her again and shook her. "You are not a dinosaur. You are my daughter."

She pulled herself free again. Her eyes blazed. Her upper lip peeled back in challenge. "Hoo-mans hunters! Hoo-mans eat meat."

Rage burned through Joe. "Not like this we don't, tar it. Sticking your head into a carcass? Eating meat raw? That is how a wild beast behaves, not a human."

Fig laughed mirthlessly. "Yes, I sa'. I sa' in city. Hoo-mans buyin meat in gro-sorry s'ores." She snorted. "Let-ting other hoo-mans hunt fo you. I hunt ma' own meat."

"Do you know who you sound like?" Joe said in a low voice. "You sound like Amissa."

Fig froze. She took a step back from the carcass. Pain filled her eyes. "Amissa kill Red S'ar. Ma bes fren."

Joe took a deep breath. "I know," he said softly. "I know, Fig. I'm sorry. I was angry. Your mother always did say I have a temper."

He looked at her, at his precious little daughter. Blood covered her face and hair. She was dirty and scrawny and savage. But yes, she was his daughter. *Their* daughter. His and Mina's. And she was wild at heart. Perhaps hers was a heart that could never be tamed.

Joe heaved a deep breath. "I'm not like other humans. I don't fit well into society. I've been called a loner. A misanthrope. An eccentric. Truth is, I just find solace in the wild, and among humans I feel caged. You're like that too. It's not a bad thing. Perhaps I just hoped you could integrate into human society better than I did."

She loped toward him and embraced him, placing her cheek against his chest and smearing blood across his shirt. He wrapped her in his arms.

"I love you, Dad," she whispered. She had spoken those words perfectly.

He kissed the top of her head. "I love you too, Figgy."

She looked up at him, tears in her eyes. "I don like school. I . . . I hate it! I wanna live here. In wild. Wit you. An' Vinnie an' Dozer." She thought for a moment. "An' S'mone. If S'mone wan come."

Joe couldn't help it. He laughed. "If Simone never saw another dinosaur, I think she'd be happy. She's a city girl." Joe mussed Fig's hair. "I didn't like school much when I was a kid either. But you said you wanted to be a Ranger, right?"

She nodded. "Like you."

"Then you must graduate high school first. I know it's hard. I know other kids can be cruel. But you're strong. You're intelligent. You're a Triplehorn, tar it. And you make me proud."

"Sowwy fo' eating like a pig."

Joe laughed. "You're my daughter all right."

She grinned. "Still neater den when Merl eats."

They both looked at the carcass. Vinnie was tucking in. He was not too proud to eat somebody else's leftovers.

Fig washed herself in a stream, and they rode onward, finally returning to Dinovia by nightfall. The stars shone as they rode Dozer down the cobbled street to the Fossil and Firkin. The kitchen was closed, but Barnum warmed up dinner for them. Shepherd's pie, of course. And, miracle of miracles, Fig actually used cutlery. In just five hours, Joe had to be back at Fort George, training Ranger recruits. But he had time to tuck Fig into bed. She yawned, tuckered out after a long day.

"I had fun, Dad," she said, yawned again, and fell asleep.

Joe tiptoed toward Simone's bed across the room. She was asleep, her red hair spread across the pillow. Joe sat on the bed and caressed her hair. She did not awaken. He missed her. He wanted to talk to her before returning to the base. He would not be back for another six days and nights. He stroked her hair again, a little less gently this time, hoping to "accidentally" wake her up. But she did not stir. She lay diagonally across the bed, leaving him no room.

Joe checked the time. Just past midnight. He must wake up his recruits at four forty-five. He left the room, walked across town, and entered the fort. He missed Simone and Fig already.

The week seemed to last for years. Joe woke up before dawn every day, shouted at recruits, made them run, taught them how to clean guns, how to fire, how to fight. He had to scare them. To break them. Then rebuild them. And he hated it. He wanted to be out in the field, battling Hell's Hunters, but his leg was still too weak. He missed his family so much it ached.

Sunday at dawn, he raced back home (insofar as the Fossil and Firkin was home), eager to see the people he loved. Fig was already up, waiting for him in the common room. She wore a safari outfit, complete with a ceratop hat. Simone must have bought her the outfit, and while Fig was sixteen already, she was so small they must have shopped in the child's section. Her eyes alight, Fig jumped onto Joe, knocking off his own larger ceratop.

"Dad! Can we go riding Dozer 'gain?"

He laughed and lifted his hat. "Of course. Just let me say hi to Simone first."

He went upstairs to her room, but Simone was still asleep. He contemplated waking her but decided against it. Would she be mad if he woke her? He knew Simone was something of a night owl. Instead, he went downstairs to the common room, ordered coffee, and decided to wait for Simone to wake up.

"Dad, Dad!" Fig tugged on his shirt. "Les go. Nao!"

He sipped his coffee. "We're waiting to say good morning to Simone."

Fig snorted, blowing back a lock of her hair. "Mornin'? S'mone never wake up in mornin'. She sleep till noon ev'er day."

Yes, Joe remembered that from their days together in the Last Home Hollow. Simone was definitely not an early bird.

"Dad, Dad, ca' we go? Ca' we go nao?" Fig practically dragged him toward the batwing doors.

"All right!" Joe said, laughing. "Time for another daddy-daughter day."

He had been laughing a lot around Figaro. And this was Joe Triplehorn, the man famous for never laughing. For his fifteen years as a hermit, he had not laughed once. He called them his shadow years. His years hiding from pain in the dark. But now Figaro brought him new life, new joy, love that had always been denied him. Simone did too, and Joe missed her with a physical pain. He would make sure to return early tonight and spend time with her.

He and Figaro left the city, riding Dozer as usual. Vinnie loped alongside them.

"Where we goin' dis time?" Fig said.

"To the crystal caves," Joe said. "They're full of crystals the size of dinosaurs, and glowworms live on the ceiling, making the entire cave glow. I think you'll love the place. I love it."

"Den I will too."

They rode northward across the grasslands. Forests the color of sunrise rustled to their east, and dry leaves like beads of dawn fluttered on the wind. It was autumn in Mintari, and the morning air was brisk. Fig shivered and pulled on her coat. Sitting behind her, Joe wrapped his arms around her, keeping her warm. He wondered how Fig had survived for so long in the wilderness. Had she been cold in winter? Had there been someone to keep her warm?

What have you been through, my sweet child? he thought. But he left the question unasked. In time, when she was ready, Fig would tell him her story. Sometimes she shared a few details. That she had run with achillobators. That her pack had kept her safe. But had she been lonely? Had she been scared? Had she wept at night and wondered who she was? Those questions Joe did not know how to ask. Perhaps in time she would reveal the answers. And if she kept the memories locked forever inside, Joe would understand and respect that. His own heart was home to many ghosts he dared not set free.

They were halfway to the cave when—

Boom.

A gunshot rang out.

Dozer grunted, pawed the earth, and swiveled his head from side to side. Joe shouldered his sleep-or-die and searched for an enemy. Fig hissed and grabbed her sickle claw.

They saw nobody.

"Duck behind the frill," Joe whispered, leaning down and pulling Fig with him.

They dared not move, barely even breathe.

Again a gunshot boomed. Joe cursed and tensed his hands around his sleep-or-die. The rifle had two barrels, one for shooting tranquilizer darts, the other for bullets. Joe flipped the switch from "sleep" to "die."

He peered over Dozer's frill, scanning the area, ready to kill. Nothing! He saw nobody. No bullets had flown their way.

Fig pointed her sickle claw toward a copse of ginkgos with orange leaves. "Came fram der."

Then they heard it. Dim human voices from among the trees, barely close enough to make out.

"Good shot, Rattlesnake! You got him! Right in the neck."

"You slowed him for me, boss. Your shot to the leg doomed him."

Fig bared her teeth. Her face twisted with anger. She suddenly seemed less human and more raptor.

Rattlesnake. Joe knew that name. The name of a notorious poacher. One of the men who had attacked Dinovia City last spring. And Joe thought he recognized that second voice too. Rage flared through him.

"Fig." He spoke through stiff lips. "Dismount now and hide in the grass. I'll come back for you."

"I go wit you!" she said. "Imma warrior! I kin fight!"

Joe wanted to argue. To insist Fig stay hidden. But the girl was sixteen. In just two short years, she'd be old enough to join the Rangers. Maybe she did need this experience in the field. Joe had been teaching recruits for months now. Making them jog, do push-ups, clean guns. One day of battle experience would teach Fig more than a year of boot camp. Yet could he truly put her in danger? She was not a recruit! She was a girl, *his* girl, a *little* girl. He—

"Ayee!" she cried. "Yip yip yip! Dozer, go!"

She kneed the trike, and Dozer burst into a gallop.

Joe pursed his lips and clung on, riding behind Fig. His dear daughter was not one for subtlety.

The voices ahead fell silent.

Dozer charged toward the trees, his horns pointing the way, ready to gore anyone in his path. Vinnie ran alongside, squawking for battle. Fig raised her sickle claw overhead. "Ayeee!"

Dozer ran closer. Closer.

A gunshot rang out.

A bullet slammed into Dozer's frill.

Bits of bone flew, and Dozer howled, but the trike kept running.

Joe aimed his rifle at the trees. He couldn't see a target, but he could lay down suppressive fire. He pulled the trigger. His bullet streaked between the trees. He didn't know if he hit anyone.

A cry from ahead: "Whoa, whoa! Hold your fire! Calm down, dinoboy!"

"Dozer, halt!" Joe cried.

Dozer reared, kicked the air, and brought his front legs down hard. The trike lowered his head, horns pointing forward, frill raised. His muscles remained tense, and steam rose from his nostrils with every breath. He was ready to charge on command.

Joe stared at the autumn trees. He could smell fresh blood and exhaust.

"Who goes there?" Joe called out.

An engine roared. A jippi came rumbling out from the forest. Jippis were a symbol of Mintari, almost as famous as the planet's dinosaurs. Kids bought plastic jippi toys on Cloventia (sometimes with Jurassic Joe action figures inside). The jippi from the forest was enormous, just as large as Dozer, and that triceratops outweighed a mammoth. Six monstrous wheels rolled over logs and boulders, flattening the land. A cowcatcher thrust out from the front, forged of black steel. It wouldn't shame the largest locomotive. Triceratops horns—they looked real—were mounted onto the hood.

A cargo hold stuck out the back. When Joe saw what was inside, his heart sank. He cursed and clenched his fists. A parasaurolophus. A dead one. The duckbill dinosaurs were highly valued by poachers for their head crests. The crests were as long as elephant trunks, brightly colored, and hollow. Parasaurs could blow air through them, creating eerie sounds. Foreigners turned them into musical instruments, hung them on their walls as trophies, or ground them up into supposed aphrodisiacs. Over the past year, poachers had hunted staggering numbers of the parasaurs. They were now an endangered species.

Oddly, when Fig saw the parasaur, her stomach growled. She licked her lips.

Poachers filled the jippi, heavily armed. Rattlesnake was driving. The rawboned hunter wore a long brown coat, a wide-brimmed hat, and bandoleers. His long face seemed made of old leather, brown and deeply lined. Yellow teeth peeked from behind his thin lips. Some said he was an Earthling, a veteran of the slum wars. Others claimed he crawled out from the gutters of Cloventia's underworld. Whatever the case, he was bad news. He stared at Joe with eyes like coals. There was no white to his eyes, just black all around. The eyes of a shabu addict. The drug made you strong. Let you keep fighting long after other men would collapse. It also painted your eyes, shriveled your internal organs, and seared out all humanity.

Several other poachers stood in the cargo hold around the parasaur. They were rough men, bearded and tattooed, armed with grenades, dinosaur guns, and blades. The kind of men you crossed the road to avoid. The kind of men who could drive dinosaurs to extinction. They were perhaps smaller than dinosaurs, but these were predators more dangerous than any on Mintari. They stared at Joe, eyes hard. One man licked his lips, a lurid mockery of Fig's gesture. But he did not hunger for food. He hungered for death.

The jeep halted. It stood on the crushed grass, pumping out exhaust. Dozer stood before the horned vehicle. His frill was about the size of the cowcatcher. It was as if two triceratops stood facing each other, one of flesh and one of metal.

"Where is she?" Joe said. "Where is my sister?"

A grumble sounded from the forest.

A dinosaur emerged.

Joe inhaled sharply. Dozer grunted and pawed the earth. Fig gulped.

It was a massive dinosaur. Almost as big as a T-rex. His legs were powerful, his arms vestigial. Brown scales covered his body, and two red horns sprouted from his head. His jaws opened with a rumble. A carnotaurus. The Killer of the Cretaceous.

A saddle was strapped onto the dinosaur's back. Amissa sat there, smiling and holding a rifle.

"Hello, big brother!" She waved. "Do you like my new mount? I've named him Asterius."

Mirth shone in her eyes. Her chestnut hair spilled out from under her ceratop hat. At first Joe was incensed. A ceratop was a symbol of Mintari. Only Mintarians should wear the hat. Then he remembered that Amissa was Mintarian too, by blood if not by birth. It sickened him. She even wore the Clan Triplehorn crest. A silver triceratops on her lapel.

"You desecrate the symbol you wear, sister!" Joe called from the back of his triceratops.

She laughed. "Same old Joe. Everything with you is symbols, shame, honor, duty. Don't you ever get bored?"

Joe considered his options. He counted six poachers. A lot for one Ranger to handle, even for him, even with Fig helping. He had Dozer. Amissa had a jippi and a carnotaurus. He had one sleep-or-die, and Fig had a sickle claw. The poachers had dozens of guns and grenades. Joe would have loved to arrest them here and now, caught red-handed with a hunted parasaur. But he was outnumbered and outgunned.

He raised his communicator to call for backup.

At once, before the comm even reached his lips, the poachers aimed their rifles at him. Amissa too. She cocked her weapon menacingly.

"Put that down, Joe. We don't want anything happening to you or my beautiful niece."

Joe's eye twitched. He lowered the communicator.

"Toss it onto the ground."

"Amissa, I will not play this—"

"Toss down your comm, brother. *Now.*"

Fig snarled. She raised her sickle claw.

At once, all the poacher rifles turned toward the girl.

"All right, all right, I'm tossing it down!" Joe said, wanting to draw the attention back to him. He dropped the comm onto the grass. "Look, Amissa. No comm. No backup. Now how about you send away your goons, we climb off our dinosaurs, and we settle this between us. Just you and me."

Amissa tossed back her head, laughing harder. "Oh, Joe. More honor from the courageous dinoboy! Are you challenging me to a duel? Now, brother, why would I do that? For honor?" She snorted. "I have the advantage now. I have five fighters with me. You have one." She glanced at Fig and nodded thoughtfully. "Yes, this little one is a fighter. She's like us, Joe. A killer. It runs in the family."

"I wa kii ya!" Fig shouted. When agitated, her enunciation suffered.

The male poachers laughed but not Amissa. She studied Fig from the back of her carnotaurus and nodded thoughtfully. "Yes, you *are* strong. The old man was right."

Fig tilted her head. She looked at Joe questioningly. He just glowered at his sister, clutching his rifle. If he had the chance, would he shoot her? Yes, he decided. Yes, he would. Even if she was his sister. At least in the leg. Pay her back for how she had maimed him. But it was a moot point. Her posse all had their guns on Joe and Fig, and he could not take them all out.

Gazing at Fig, Amissa seemed lost for a moment in a dream, then blinked, appearing to wake up. She looked at Joe. "It's your lucky day, Joe Triplehorn. I won't hurt this child. You get to go today. But you can't hide behind the girl forever." She tugged the reins and kneed her carnotaurus. *"Dyo!"*

Asterius spun around and loped into the forest, taking Amissa with him. The other poachers spat and glared at Joe. Clearly they had been gunning for a fight. Then Rattlesnake turned the jippi around and followed Amissa, disappearing among the trees.

Joe lowered his rifle. The anger still pulsed through him, fire inside his veins. If Fig were not here, would he have fought? Taken them all on? Yes. And probably died trying.

Fig twisted around on Dozer's back, facing Joe.

"Why didna she attik?" Fig asked.

"We didn't want to risk your life, Fig. Neither of us did. We wanted to save your life. So you ended up saving ours."

She was silent for a moment, lost in thought. Then she spoke slowly, carefully enunciating each syllable. "Aw you a killa, Dad? Am I?"

"You're better than that, Fig. You're a survivor."

She gazed at the jippi tracks and carnotaurus footprints. She shuddered. "Ca' we go home?"

"No. We're going to the crystal caves."

"I wanna go home."

Joe frowned. "We're not going to let Amissa ruin our day. We're going to those caves, tar it."

He kneed Dozer. The triceratops kept lumbering across the wilderness. Fig sat quietly, hugging herself, saying nothing throughout the trip. She remained silent while they toured the crystal caves. The glowworms covered the ceiling, casting turquoise luminescence that reflected in a million crystals. The light danced in Fig's eyes, and Joe saw sadness there.

They rode back in silence. Fig sat on Dozer with her legs crossed, wrapped in her coat. Joe kept one arm around her, keeping her safe. The sun had set when they saw the city walls in the distance.

"Fig, do you want to talk about what happened?" Joe said. "I know that seeing Amissa was unnerving. It unnerved me too. Mintari is at war now. It's hard for all of us."

For a long moment, she said nothing. Then she spoke in a low voice. "I tried ta save 'im. Da boy who died. Grayson. I tried. I pulled 'im." Tears flowed down her cheeks. "I coun't save 'im."

"I know, Fig. I know." He gazed at a family of spiky gastonias feeding on bushes. Several sauropods rose behind them in the moonlight, lumbering toward a copse of ginkgos. "That memory will always be with you. So will the pain. But it will get easier. There are shadows in your past but beautiful light ahead. I'll walk that path with you."

Fig lowered her head. "I was 'ungry. Whe' I saw da parasaur. In da jippi. I waned to . . . h-h-hunt."

He mussed her hair. "No more hunting dinosaurs, Fig. If you want to be a Ranger someday, you'll learn to protect dinosaurs instead of hunting them. I know you're hungry, but if I know Barnum, he's got shepherd's pie waiting for us. You're not sick of it yet, are you?"

She shook her head vigorously.

They reentered the city, headed to the Fossil and Firkin, and indeed the smells of shepherd's pie welcomed them. The fireplace was crackling. Merl was banging out a song on the piano, and everyone was singing. Joe stood for a moment at the door, taking it all in. The smells of food, the sound of music, the laughter of friends—they washed the anxiety away like rain washing away the dirt. Joe had spent so long hiding from people.

But this place of good company soothed him. As a young man, before Mintari had broken him, he used to come here all the time. Once more it was home.

They stepped inside and looked around the common room, seeking Simone. He didn't want to miss her again this Sunday. He spotted her by the hearth. She stood, silent, gazing at the fire. Her hair seemed an extension of the flame, and her freckles were like sparks scattered across her face. She was beautiful. The most beautiful woman Joe had ever seen. All he could do was stand there, staring, awestruck. There was majesty in Mintari. Mountains that soared, capped with snow. Caves that glittered with crystals. Dinosaurs that roamed through the mist and pterosaurs that glided under the sun. But across all of Mintari, Joe had never seen anything as breathtaking as Simone LaRue.

He walked toward her. "Hi there."

She gave him a wan smile. "Hello, mister."

"Join us for dinner?"

"I already ate." Simone yawned. "I'm tired. I'm heading up to bed."

She walked past him and upstairs. Joe remained standing by the fireplace.

"Oh. Good night!"

But she was already gone.

"Dad, Dad!" Fig grabbed him. "Can you play dat song agin? Da one about da trisiratips and da honeycomb?"

He wanted to go check on Simone, but Fig pulled him toward the piano. He played for her, and they ate, and he tucked her into bed. When he checked on Simone, she was already asleep.

Joe shuffled back to Fort George. Another week of shouting began. Another week until he could see his daughter again. And maybe Simone too.

CHAPTER FIVE
Fearless

The sauropods had passed through the forest like a tornado, leaving a trail of destruction. Truly they were a force of nature. Their footprints sank deep into the soil, already filling with rainwater. Those footprints were so large a man could take a bath inside. Mighty conifers, trees taller than any building on Mintari, lay shattered like so many pick-up sticks. It was autumn, and these trees were evergreens, but hungry mouths had stripped them of their needlelike leaves. Most of the forest still stood, spreading across the hills toward the distant mountains. But through this green landscape spread paths of desolation like the tunnels of termites through wood. Sauropods had walked here. The giants had carved their way through the forest, eating and trampling everything in their path.

They also left big, steaming hills of waste. Clubber covered his nose as he rode around one hill. The ankylosaurus he rode groaned and snapped his nostrils shut like a camel.

"Well, at least they're easy to track," Clubber said. He shifted in his saddle and rubbed his neck. He had been riding for days, following the trail. He was tired. Bone tired. But he would not rest until he found the herd. Until he saved the sauropods from the menace that stalked them.

His dinosaur snorted, his breath frosting. He sounded unhappy. The ankylosaurus didn't like walking here. Bumpy was a large dinosaur, weighing more than a jippi. Spiky armor covered his muscular body, and his tail ended with a wrecking ball. But even a living tank felt uneasy around sauropods.

And these were no ordinary sauropods they tracked. Clubber was following a herd of *dreadnoughtus*. Their name meant fear nothing. They made brontosaurs seem puny. They were longer than blue whales. Indeed, they were among the largest dinosaurs on Mintari, animals so titanic they were predator proof. Even T-rex dared not attack them. Even Bumpy, who had slain a tyrannosaur or two in his day, feared these giants.

But there was one predator who could kill even the mighty dreadnoughtus. One predator that Clubber must stop. And her name was Amissa Triplehorn.

And if there was one thing Chief Arban Clubber hated, it was Triplehorns.

His upper lip peeled back in disgust. Just the thought of that name—Triplehorn—sickened him. He commanded the Mintari Rangers, a group of warriors from many clans, a force that united Mintari against a common enemy. But deep in his heart, there was one clan he could not trust. One clan that churned his gut. The Triplehorns.

They killed my sister. And now they're killing everything.

Clubber forced a deep breath. That was not fair. He knew that. It was Ivan, the mutant T-rex, who had devoured Mina, who had stolen his precious little sister. But tar it, if Mina hadn't married Joe Triplehorn, if she hadn't followed him into the forest that night—

Enough! Clubber told himself. He took deep breaths, forcing down the rage and grief. *That was long ago. You're on a mission now. A mission to find this herd before Amissa can slay it.*

Snorting sounded behind him. A Ranger rode up to his side.

"How goes it, Chief?"

Hank Hornhead was a lanky, bearded man of fifty. He rode a kosmoceratops, the dinosaur of his clan. It looked like a triceratops, but instead of only three horns, it boasted an entire crown. No fewer than a dozen horns sprouted from the dinosaur's head, and eighteen more hornlets framed its frill, bringing the grand total to thirty. The Hornheads were stubborn, proud, and loyal. And Hank was a good friend.

"She goes, Hank," Clubber said. "She goes." An old answer he always gave Hank. It had become almost a ritual between them.

Hank leaned over the side of his dinosaur, handing Clubber a thermos. "Coffee? Still warm from this morning."

Clubber accepted the thermos gratefully and sipped. The bitter black liquid flowed down his throat, warming his bones.

"Thanks, Hank. You brew a mean cup."

Hank tapped the flask at his side. "Sure you don't want something stronger?"

"Not on a mission, old friend. And this is an important mission."

The two men were the same age, but they looked nothing alike. Arban Clubber traced his ancestry back to ancient Mongolia on Earth. His skin was olive-toned, his eyes almond-shaped, his body stocky. Hank was tall and slender, his skin pale, his beard platinum. Clubber sometimes joked that Hank looked like a ghost. Yet they were like brothers. They had grown up together. In time, they had taken different paths. Clubber rose to become chief of the Rangers. Hank left the force years ago, retiring to write mystery novels (tarry good ones too, if you asked Clubber). But the ghost was back now, wearing the uniform again. Mintari was at war. They all had to fight.

The two men gazed south. The forest spread across rolling hills and misty valleys. Snow-capped mountains lined the horizon. A flock of pterosaurs glided under the canopy of clouds, heading toward a canyon. From here, Clubber could make out the distant dreadnought herd. He couldn't see the dinosaurs themselves, but he saw the forest shaking, the trees falling. They weren't far now.

"Are you sure she's out there, Chief?" said Hank.

"Oh, she's out there." A chill filled Clubber's belly. "The dreadnoughts are migrating south for winter. This is the best chance to hunt them. A chance she'll seize."

Hank nodded. A gust of wind blew, nearly pulling off his ceratop. Hank grabbed the wide-brimmed hat and steadied it on his head. Both men wore thick overcoats over their tan uniforms, but the cold wind cut through the fabric. For a while, the two old friends rode in silence. The dreadnoughts had carved veritable highways through the forest. Even an ankylosaurus and kosmoceratops, multiton dinosaurs, could walk side by side without their spikes clanging together.

Every once in a while, other dinosaurs peered from the walls of trees at their sides. Some were theropods. Big ones too. Megaraptors and even a lone tyrannosaur. But none dared attack. Ankylosaur tails and kosmoceratops horns were nothing to trifle with. And men rode them. The dinosaurs of Mintari had learned to fear men.

And one woman, Clubber thought.

It was barely a year since Amissa Triplehorn had landed here, and already poachers flocked to her. They had become something resembling an army. Hell's Hunters, they called themselves. And truly they were a force from hell. In one year— so much death.

Hank suddenly gasped. He gripped the horn of his saddle. "Look!"

Clubber nodded grimly. "I see it."

A dead dinosaur, lying right on the trail. Freshly dead, judging by the smell. The powerful jaws hung open, and the bloated tongue draped to the ground like a dead snake. The tail lay crushed across the trail, flattened by a sauropod foot.

Hank leaned forward in his saddle. His kosmoceratops snorted and pawed the soil, nervous around the carcass.

"Easy, Kosmo, easy." Hank patted his dinosaur and squinted at the carcass on the ground. "What is that? Some kinda big raptor?"

"Herrerasaurus," Clubber said. He reached over his saddle to pat Bumpy's armored flank. The ankylosaur was stepping from side to side, raising his tail and waving the club around. Like Kosmo, Bumpy didn't like seeing a dead dinosaur. It triggered his fight-or-flight response.

Hank whistled. "Herrerasaurus, huh? The granddaddy of theropods. Late Triassic, right? The other theropods descended from him?"

"Well, not from this one." Clubber dismounted and stepped closer to the corpse. The scaly carnivore lay across the trail. It was one of the most ancient dinosaurs. At least back on Earth it had been. The scaly carnivore was roughly horse-sized. A dwarf compared to its descendants like T-rex and giganotosaurus.

"Tar it, look at its tail," Hank said. The pale Ranger dismounted too and joined Clubber by the corpse. Hank stood taller than Clubber, but he was thinner and lighter. A gust of wind billowed his white beard. "Those dreadnoughts stepped on him like he was a mouse. Flattened his haunches too, look at that. Ground his bones to dust."

"The dreadnoughts didn't kill him," Clubber said.

Hank raised a bushy white eyebrow. "What else could crush a dinosaur like this?"

"Oh, the dreadnoughts crushed him," Clubber said. "But only after he was dead. Look." Clubber knelt and pointed at the predator's neck. "Bullet holes."

Hank's eyes widened. "Well, I'll be tarred." He grabbed his sleep-or-die with both hands. The traditional rifle of the Rangers boasted two barrels. One fired tranquilizer darts. The other fired bullets. With his thumb, Hank flicked a switch, changing the rifle from "sleep" mode to "die." Sweat beaded on his brow even in the cold, and he swept the rifle from side to side.

Clubber didn't bother raising his own rifle. "The poachers aren't here. If they were, they'd be firing on us. My guess is they flew a skyslayer above the path. Shot this poor fellow from above. Then kept flying." Clubber clenched his fists. "The bastards didn't even bother taking a trophy. They just shot, killed, and flew on. For fun."

Hank lowered his gun. He shook his head sadly. "Killing for fun . . . what kind of person does that?"

"A Triplehorn," Clubber muttered.

Again, he knew that was unfair. Not all Triplehorns were bad. Joe was a Triplehorn. His brother-in-law. And Joe was a loyal Ranger.

Then again . . . was he?

Joe had fought in the great Battle for Dinovia last spring. He had faced Amissa Triplehorn on the hill. Yet she still lived. And again, only a few days ago, Joe had met Amissa in the outback . . . and let her go. Clubber had read Joe's report. Joe claimed he had no choice. That he was outgunned, outnumbered. That he couldn't risk a battle with his kid there. But Clubber still had to wonder. Did Joe pity his sister? Maybe even love her? If the two met again, would Joe do what must be done? Or would he betray the Rangers, betray Mintari?

The Triplehorns were a disgraced clan. A treacherous clan. Tobias Triplehorn had abandoned Mintari. From his glittering skyscraper on planet Cloventia, he led the war against his former world. Amissa Triplehorn commanded his troops on the field,

slaughtering dinosaurs and Rangers alike. Could Clubber really
trust Joe Triplehorn?

He married my sister, he told himself. *He loved Mina. He loves
Mintari. He is a good Ranger. And a good man. He's family.*

And yet, and yet . . . that seed of doubt.

For now, Clubber would keep Joe away from the
battlefield. Keep him in the city. Keep him close. Joe's leg was
almost healed. Soon the man would demand to return to the field.
Clubber could not risk him falling under Amissa's sway. Jurassic
Joe was not just a Ranger. He was a hero. A symbol. If he
switched sides, if he joined Hell's Hunters, it could devastate the
Rangers. Clubber would make sure Joe never fought a battle
again.

And now there was another Triplehorn to reckon with,
Clubber reminded himself. A child. Figaro Triplehorn.

Yes, he had heard of the girl. A feral child discovered in
the forest. Daughter of Joe Triplehorn . . . and Mina Clubber.

My niece, Clubber thought.

He winced. His own niece, his own blood—bearing the
surname Triplehorn! He had refused to meet her. He could not. It
hurt too much. He had seen the photos, seen a girl who looked
just like Mina, just like a Clubber . . . with the last name
Triplehorn.

"Chief, you all right?" Hank put a hand on his shoulder.
"Are you in pain?"

"I'm fine." Clubber hadn't realized he was broadcasting his
emotions so plainly. "It's just this senseless killing. It hurts to see."

Hank nodded. "Sure does." He looked around the forest,
still seeking enemies. "We should have brought more men."

"We have no men to spare," Clubber said. "Everyone is
out in the field. Hank, I command only a few hundred Rangers. A
force that can fit into a high school auditorium. And I have to

somehow protect an entire planet. We need more Rangers. More money. More weapons. Or we will lose this war."

Hank's eyes hardened. He raised his chin. "Then let us end this war today. You said Amissa herself is stalking the dreadnoughtus herd. Let's take her out."

Clubber patted his friend on the shoulder. "Just you and me, old friend. Like in the old days. Let's go cut off the snake's head."

The Rangers didn't have much money. Didn't have much equipment. Before the war, Clubber could view the world from his satellites, monitoring the migration paths, forest fires, and floods. He could fly tricopters to aid dinosaurs in danger, and he even operated three astrolites, vehicles capable of breaching the atmosphere, orbiting the planet, and descending anywhere on Mintari within an hour.

Well, those days were over. Amissa had flown here with a veritable army. She had blasted his satellites from the sky. Shot down his astrolites. Burned his outposts to the ground. With superior firepower and numbers, she was sweeping across Mintari, casting out waves of death.

But Clubber still had the greatest weapon on Mintari. The planet's wildlife. His trained pterosaurs flew across the sky, filming Mintari with hidden cameras. His herbivores roamed the plains, broadcasting what they saw back to Clubber's camp. Even underwater, his aquatic reptiles swam in the dark, monitoring the ocean depths. Hell's Hunters used big, loud machines to ruin Mintari. And the planet itself was fighting back.

The ankylosaurus lumbered down the sauropod trail, stepping over, around, and sometimes through fallen conifers, snapping trunks beneath his armored girth. The kosmoceratops followed, tossing his head from side to side, knocking back branches and tilting trees. The two Rangers rode in the saddles, aiming their rifles ahead. Droppings the size of urban jippis steamed across the path. The sauropod footprints were fresher here. The drizzling rain had not yet filled them. The herd was close.

The two Rangers crested a hill, and there it was.

The dreadnoughtus herd.

For years now, a debate had raged across Mintari: Who is the planet's largest dinosaur? The problem was one of semantics. Was the largest dinosaur the longest one? The tallest one? The heaviest one? And did you go by the largest individual dinosaur per species? Or by the species average? And if you went by mass, how did you calculate it accurately? You couldn't exactly put a sauropod on a bathroom scale. Some claimed argentinosaurus was the largest, while others championed the supersaurus or titanosaurus.

As for Clubber, well . . . he would give the title to dreadnoughtus. The giants who feared nothing.

Dreadnoughts were longer than blue whales. They weighed more than a dozen mammoths. A man could walk between their legs, raise his hand, and still not reach their underbelly. Their necks rose as tall as the tallest conifers. Here were dinosaurs the size of starships. Land animals should not be able to grow this big. Nobody told that to the dreadnoughts. They roamed through the forest, knocking down trees, leaving potholes like craters, masters of Mintari. They could stomp on a T-rex. No other dinosaur dared attack these titans. True to their name, they dreaded naught.

Fifty dinosaurs or more comprised the herd. Bulls walked in front and behind while cows walked between them. Sauropodlets hurried between the adults' legs. Some of the hatchlings were barely larger than dogs. Within thirty years, they would balloon to impossible size. The herd walked slowly, eating as they went. The adults' hungry mouths swiped across branches, hoovering up the leaves. The sauropodlets scampered below, happy as could be, devouring whatever leaves fell from above. After every bite, the dinosaurs took another step. Trees collapsed before them. The land itself shook.

Normally sauropods did not move this much. It took a lot of calories to move bodies this large. But the winds of winter blew, and soon snow would cover these lands. They were heading toward a well-trodden path between the mountains, and beyond the snowy peaks, they would head across grassy plains. Down south the sauropods would find warmer climates, fresh water, and grasslands to vacuum up. Come spring they would breed, and then with a new host of hatchlings, they would return north to the sweet pines and melting ice, a realm far from the punishing droughts, buzzing insects, and heat of the south.

For a moment, Clubber and Hank simply sat on their dinosaurs, silent, gazing in awe. Clubber—chief of Rangers, famous warrior, descended of the great khans of old—had to wipe a tear from his eye.

"It's a beautiful planet we have," he said softly. "It's worth fighting for."

Hank held his ceratop over his heart. "Amen, my friend. Mintari is—"

Engines rumbled.

They burst out from behind the mountains. Three flying machines, heavy with armor and guns, leaving trails of smoke. Skyslayers.

Clubber cursed. His heart burst into a gallop.

They were here. The hunters. The enemy.

The skyslayers screamed across the sky, flying in from the mountains. Clubber raised his binoculars and studied them. Triceratops hood ornaments adorned their prows. The symbol of Triplehorn Incorporated. Amissa's machines.

Skyslayers were a new terror on Mintari. They used to be astrolites—vessels that could fly through air and orbit, too small for interplanetary travel but useful for short dashes in and out of space. Amissa had taken such astrolites, mounted them with armor, covered them with cannons, and renamed them. The skyslayers had become her cruelest weapons, angels of vengeance who rained death on Mintari.

The three skyslayers flew toward the herd. Gears clattered on their wings, and machine guns unfurled.

Clubber gritted his teeth, lowered his binoculars, and gripped the pommel of his saddle.

He banged his heels against Bumpy's flanks. *"Dyo!"*

The ankylosaur burst into a run. Covered with several tons of armored plates and spikes, the behemoth moved slowly. Clubber could run faster on his own. But he wanted Bumpy in this battle with him. Just in case Amissa would spring ground forces on him. He also wasn't sure how the dreadnoughts would react to him. He was a human. The titanic dinosaurs were likely to attack him, mistaking him for another poacher. Bumpy was slow, but Clubber needed a tank for this battle.

Kosmo ran alongside. The kosmoceratops was much smaller than a sauropod, but with his thirty horns, not even the biggest dreadnoughtus would dare step on him. Hank bounced in the saddle, his white beard fluttering like a banner. The old Ranger clutched his rifle, eager for the fight. Good old Hank Hornhead. Clubber could think of nobody better to ride at his side.

Ahead of them, the skyslayers were streaking closer toward the herd. Clubber itched to grab the grenade launcher that hung from Bumpy's saddle. The Thagomizer 3000 would make short work of these skyslayers. But he was still out of range. The two dinosaurs thundered downhill, following the migration trail. The rumbling of the engines shook the sky. Just a little closer. Almost there.

But the skyslayers were faster.

They reached the herd first. Their machine guns swiveled and opened fire. Bullets streaked like brimstone cast from the heavens. The barrage pounded the dreadnoughts. The dinosaurs wailed. Bullets drove into their flesh. A towering bull, likely the leader of the herd, rushed to shield the cows and sauropodlets, taking the brunt of the fusillade. The giant swayed on his feet, bullets bombarding him.

"Tar it, faster, Bumpy!" Clubber said, slamming his heels into the ankylosaur's armor. *"Dyo, dyo!"*

The ankylosaurus was wheezing. He wasn't used to running. But he kept going, rushing downhill, around a cluster of mossy boulders, then uphill between palisades of conifers. Kosmo followed just behind. For a moment, the piny hilltop hid Clubber's view of the slaughter. But he could still hear the bullets. Hear the terrible cries of the dreadnoughts. Smell the gunpowder and blood.

Huffing and puffing, Bumpy reached the hilltop, and Clubber saw the herd again. His heart sank.

Several dreadnought cows lay dead already. They had fallen protecting their hatchlings. The skyslayers rose again, spun in the sky, then swooped and strafed the herd. The barrage caught several sauropodlets. The hatchlings were huddling around their fallen mother. They fell, joining her in death. The big bulls still stood. The leader of the pack was bleeding profusely. The poachers must have filled him with a hundred bullets, but the giant still stood, rumbling, furious, terrifying in his wrath but ultimately helpless to stop the aerial bombardment. Sauropods were the largest, strongest dinosaurs on Mintari, but their weakness was lack of armor. They could not withstand this strafing for long.

This wasn't a hunt. It was a massacre.

Clubber was close enough. "Halt, Bumpy!"

Grateful, the winded ankylosaurus halted on the hilltop. Clubber reached down and grabbed his Thagomizer 3000. Behind him, Kosmo rumbled to a halt, and Hank reached for his own grenade launcher.

They were loading grenades when a skyslayer saw them. The machine turned in the air to face them.

Hank cursed and ducked behind his dinosaur's bony frill.

Clubber kept loading his grenade.

The skyslayer roared toward them, guns blazing. Bullets slammed into Kosmo's frill. The dinosaur roared and buckled, falling to his knees. More bullets hit Bumpy, ricocheting against his thick armor. The ankylosaurus bugled and ran toward the trees.

"Hold, Bumpy!" Clubber said, aiming his launcher.

Bumpy stood still, even as bullets sparked against his armor.

A bullet grazed Clubber's shoulder.

Ignoring the pain, he fired.

More bullets whizzed around him. One scraped across his arm, ripping his shirt, tearing his skin.

His grenade flew and found its target.

The skyslayer exploded above. Fire blazed. The mangled machine spun wildly, drawing a corkscrew of flame, then crashed onto the hillside. The forest rocked. Flame blazed skyward like an erupting volcano.

"Chief!" Hank said, rising from behind his dinosaur's frill. A bullet had punched a hole through his ceratop, narrowly missing his scalp. "We can take cover behind those boulders."

Clubber saw it. A henge of crumbling boulders etched with runes. The work of ancient shamans, now overgrown with moss and vines. The shamans had left Mintari, they said. Only Lifa the Wanderer was said to remain. The wild women no longer danced and sang within their henges, but the stones would offer good cover for battle.

Clubber slammed his heels into his dinosaur. *"Dyo!"*

The ankylosaurus and kosmoceratops ran. Both dinosaurs had taken many bullets, but their armor had saved their lives. One bullet had hit Kosmo's leg, but the horned herbivore could still run. Bumpy's armor had cracked in several places, and no doubt it hurt, but the ankylosaurus was still moving fast.

They barely reached the henge before a second skyslayer stormed toward them.

Machine guns roared again. As Bumpy and Kosmo crouched behind the scrimshawed boulders, the two Rangers aimed their grenade launchers and fired.

This time Clubber missed. His grenade flew wide, landed in the forest, and exploded, shattering several trees. But Hank's hit. The second skyslayer burst into flame. The mangled wreck came diving down.

Right toward the henge.

Clubber cursed. "Run!" he cried.

The two Rangers and their dinosaurs ran toward the trees. The burning skyslayer roared down, leaving a trail of smoke and fire. Clubber and Hank jumped, landed on their bellies, and covered their heads.

The skyslayer slammed into the henge behind them.

An explosion rocked the forest.

Chunks of metal, stone, and burning scraps landed all around. A red-hot shard of twisted steel drove into the ground inches from Clubber, nearly severing his arm. Wincing, Clubber stood up and looked around him.

"Hank, you all right?"

The tall, slender Ranger pushed himself up with a groan. He gripped his leg. "I'm fine. I'm fine! Just a scratch."

A mournful mewl sounded behind them. Bumpy stood a short distance away, poking Kosmo with his snout. The kosmoceratops lay on his side, several shards of metal impaling him. The dinosaur moaned, and then his head thumped onto the ground, and the life left his eyes.

Engines roared.

Clubber looked up.

The third and last skyslayer was flying toward him, skimming the treetops.

Clubber raised his grenade launcher. But the grenades were in Bumpy's saddlebag. Clubber knew he had no time to reach them. The skyslayer unfurled its machine guns, and Clubber burst into a run, and bullets hit the ground, and—

A deafening howl tore through the air.

A dreadnought bull came charging uphill. It was the herd leader. The one who had blocked the barrage of bullets with his body. The giant reared on his back legs and let out a furious, trumpeting cry. He swung his neck through the air, grabbed the skyslayer in his mouth, and hurled the machine aside.

The skyslayer tumbled, slammed into the hillside, and exploded.

Clubber stood still, breathing heavily. The dreadnoughtus stomped up the hillside, moving toward him. By Darwin's beard, the dinosaur was huge. In all his years as a Ranger, Clubber had never been this close to a dinosaur this large. He stood shorter than the giant's knees.

The colossal dinosaur bled from many wounds. Hundreds of bullets must have hit him. Some had perforated his neck, and rivulets of blood flowed between his lumpy scales. He took another step. Another. He lowered his great long neck, bringing his head near Clubber, and man and dinosaur looked each other in the eyes.

"I'm sorry," Clubber said softly. "I'm sorry I got here too late."

The dinosaur snorted, breath frosting in the cold afternoon. And then he fell.

His body thumped onto the hillside, and the forest shook, and trees cracked and fell. The sauropod's head hit the ground before Clubber, and his eyes closed.

Clubber lowered his head and mumbled a prayer for the fallen. "Go back now, child of Mintari. Go back to the soil from which you came. We will always remember you, for you will never die."

All three skyslayers were burning on the hillsides. The herd was licking its wounds. Hatchlings crowded around their fallen mothers, wailing. But most of the sauropods had survived. Most would continue on south. The loss was great. But the battle was won.

Clubber turned toward his friend. Hank stood by Kosmo, stroking the dead dinosaur's frill.

"He saved my life," Hank said, voice hoarse. "More than once. He took bullets for me. He fell for me."

"He gave his life for Mintari," Clubber said. "But even a noble death is a tragedy."

Hank's eyes dampened, but his face remained hard. "I know. I've lost dinosaurs before. Men too. It never gets easier. But this is war, and—"

A dinosaur burst out from the forest behind him.

Clubber took a step back, eyes widening.

The dinosaur towered above the two Rangers. Brown scales covered the predator's powerful body. His arms were vestigial, no larger than toddler's arms, but his legs were long and muscular. His talons shattered fallen branches, and his jaws opened wide, full of sharp, curved fangs. Two crimson horns grew from his head. Devil horns.

A carnotaurus. Smaller than a T-rex but faster. Some would say meaner. With blinding speed, the carnotaurus lunged at Hank.

The bearded Ranger never stood a chance. Never had time to aim his rifle. Hank barely turned around before the reptilian jaws closed around him, ripping into his flesh.

"Hank!" Clubber shouted. He raised his rifle, ready to shoot the dinosaur.

That was when he noticed her. A woman was riding the carnotaurus. A woman with long brown hair and mocking blue eyes, a machine gun in her hands.

"Hello, Chief Clubber!" she cried. "Nice of you to come. Meet Asterius, my beloved, hungry pet. Rangers are not the only ones who tamed dinosaurs."

Clubber fired his sleep-or-die.

A bullet slammed into Asterius's head, chipping scales but not penetrating the flesh. The carnotaurus rumbled and swung his head, tossing Hank into the distance. The bearded Ranger thumped down on the hillside. Clubber did not know if his friend was alive or dead. He had no time to check. He fired again, aiming at Amissa, but his shot went wide.

She wheeled her machine gun toward him.

Clubber leaped. Bullets slammed into a log. Chips of wood flew. Clubber rolled behind a boulder. Bullets hit the rock. Chunks of stone and dust filled the air. Clubber cursed, hunching behind the boulder. He couldn't rise. Couldn't run or she'd mow him down. He was trapped here. Outgunned. Tar it, was all this a trap? Had he fallen right into it?

The machine gun roared, pounding the boulder, cracking the stone. More bullets whizzed overhead. And beneath the storm of bullets, Clubber heard the ominous *thump thump thump* of the carnotaurus stepping closer.

A massive talon slammed down atop the boulder. Two crimson horns thrust overhead. Asterius's terrible jaws opened above, the teeth red with blood, and Clubber knew he was going to die.

A snort sounded from nearby.

Feet shook the earth.

Bumpy charged, swung his tail, and slammed his bony club into Asterius.

Scales shattered. The carnotaurus let out a deafening wail, high-pitched, the sound a dog might make when you stepped on its tail. If that dog weighed several tons, that was. The mighty carnivore wobbled, swayed, and stumbled aside.

Amissa swayed in her saddle, nearly falling. Her machine gun fire died.

Clubber did not waste a second. He rose from behind the boulder and fired his rifle. A bullet slammed into Asterius.

The carnotaurus wailed. Bumpy advanced toward him menacingly, tail swishing from side to side. The first blow had been dealt in haste. The club had hit Asterius awkwardly, glancing off the carnivore, chipping scales, maybe cracking a rib or two. Asterius had gotten off easy. The second blow would finish the job. Both dinosaurs knew it.

Swaying in the saddle, Amissa steadied her machine gun and opened fire, forcing Clubber behind the boulder again. When the fire ceased, and Clubber could emerge again, Asterius was racing downhill. The dinosaur vanished among the trees.

Clubber knew he could not follow. Carnotaurs were among the fastest dinosaurs on Mintari. They had been measured running at forty miles per hour, and many believed they could sprint even faster. That was definitely faster than a human or ankylosaurus, even faster than a jippi on rough terrain.

"Coward!" Clubber shouted, shooting blindly at the trees, hitting nothing but branches.

Amissa's distant laugh echoed across the hills. "Until we meet again, Clubber!"

Even if he was slower, Clubber wanted to run, to chase her. But she was right. They would meet again. Someday. This war was far from over. Right now Clubber had a more important task.

He ran among the trees, but not after Amissa. He ran toward his friend.

He found Hank lying among the conifers on a blanket of fallen leaves. The carnotaurus had bitten deep into his abdomen, piercing the belly and chest. Blood covered the leaves and seeped into the soil. Hank's skin was gray, his lips blue. At first Clubber thought him dead, but no! When Clubber knelt, he felt a pulse. Hank took shallow breaths. The white-bearded Ranger even managed to look into Clubber's eyes, to smile thinly.

"How goes it, Chief?" Hank whispered. Blood dripped from his mouth.

Struggling to hold back tears, Clubber held his friend's hand. "She goes, Hank," he whispered hoarsely. "She goes."

Hank seemed to be gazing far away, and his soft smile reached his eyes, melting away their pain. "I go now, Chief. I go back to the soil. Back into this world we fought for."

A tear fell from Clubber's eye, splashing his friend's cheek. "You'll be all right, Hank. I'll call for help. I'll—"

"No, Chief," Hank whispered, then coughed. His breath was shallow. "I can already see it."

"See what, Hank?" Clubber said, a lump in his throat, gripping his friend's cold hand.

"A golden sunrise over a field of clouds. It's beautiful, Chief." His eyes widened with awe. "It's . . ."

His body slumped. His eyes stilled. His breath died.

Clubber pulled his friend into his arms. And then he did something he had not done in fifteen years. Not since his beloved Mina had died. He wept.

CHAPTER SIX
Pixels and Predators

Simone LaRue had never been pregnant. Never been married. But at thirty-two years old, she suddenly became a mother. Her child was a savage little thing, scrawny and wild, an animal who crawled out from the brush and decided to be human. The child's name was Figaro, and to Simone, she was the most precious thing in the world.

Fig was not her child by blood. Nor by marriage. Simone wasn't even sure what relationship she had with Joe these days. But one thing she knew. She had fallen madly in love with little Figaro Triplehorn, and she would do anything in the world to protect her.

Life was hard on Mintari. The wilderness swarmed with dinosaurs. Simone dared not leave the city walls. Her room in the Fossil and Firkin was cramped, and it was not truly hers. Joe was renting it for her. She missed Cloventia. She missed the floating skyscrapers, the neon sea, the shops of high fashion (she liked clothes, sue her), the restaurants serving delicacies from across the galaxy, the robots who catered to her every whim. She missed her parents. She missed her career.

All that was gone now. Simone was no longer a journalist. Her show, *LaRue's News*, was no more. Her glittering apartment was empty. The life she had once so carefully constructed had shattered like colored glass in a storm.

It was the Triplehorn family that ruined her. It was Amissa Triplehorn who killed Simone's twin. It was Tobias

Triplehorn who'd bought the *Cloventia Gazette*, used her as a pawn, then discarded her as rubbish. Now here Simone was. A woman in exile. Jobless. Penniless. Not knowing who she was, what she could become. A woman of civilization lost on a planet of wilderness and murderous reptiles.

Even Joe, a Triplehorn she had actually learned to like, was not here. Six days a week, he was off soldiering. One day a week, he took his daughter out to the wild while Simone remained behind, trapped in this little hotel room, withering. Her lustrous red hair, once her greatest pride, seemed to dull. Bags hung under her eyes. When she looked at the woman in the mirror, she no longer saw the beautiful journalist with porcelain skin and fiery hair. She saw a pale, weary exile.

But she had found one thing on this world worth living for.

And that thing was named Figaro Triplehorn.

If my life is over, I can still build a future for this girl, Simone thought.

With nothing else to do, nothing else to live for, Simone poured herself into this goal.

"All right, Figgy! Up, up! Outta bed! It's schooltime!"

Fig groaned and pulled the blanket over her head. "No. Mo' sleep."

Simone pulled the blanket off. "Up, Figaro. You're going to school."

Fig hissed and snapped her teeth. "Yip yip arrrr!"

"Don't you yip at me, young lady. You're going to school if I have to drag you there in your pajamas."

That got Fig moving. Simone had bought the girl pajamas embroidered with cute little stegosaurs. The girl did *not* want to arrive at high school wearing those. Reluctantly Fig changed into her school uniform. It reminded Simone of Girl Scout uniforms from old Earth movies, complete with a neckerchief. Fig kept loosening the tie, tugging the uniform, and looking miserable.

"Not comfy!" Fig said. "Can I wear pajamas ta school?"

"No."

"Why not?"

Simone crossed her arms. "Because I said so. Now brush your hair."

Fig shook her head. "No!"

"You can't show up at school looking like there's a raptor's nest on your head."

"Yes I can."

Simone grabbed a hairbrush. "Fine, I'll do it myself."

"Ow, ow!" Fig fought against her, but Simone was stronger. She ran the brush through Fig's black hair, smoothing it out. The girl kept her hair short but somehow still got it messy every day.

"Go on, move move!" Simone said. "Breakfast—eat!"

Fig was usually good with eating. Simone fried eggs in her electric pan, and Fig devoured them, getting yolk all over her face, school uniform, and hair. Simone had to take deep breaths, count down to ten, and take three steps back. Wash again. New uniform. More hair grooming.

"Wa I hav ta loo cla?" Fig whined.

"Speak properly. Enunciate! Like I taught you."

Fig growled. "Arrrrooo yaroooo yip y—"

"Enough! Figaro—talk like a human."

The girl took deep breaths and seemed ready to argue, but all Simone had to do was reach for the hairbrush again. Fig gulped and spoke carefully, syllable by syllable. "Why do I haffff hafff *have* ta' . . . loo'k c-c-clean?"

"Because you are a human, not a dinosaur."

Fig raised her hands like claws and growled. "Rawr! Imma dinosir!"

"You're late to school, that's what you are. Come on, out the door! Move it!"

She all but dragged Fig downstairs. Joe had it easy. Training recruits for war? Pfft. Simone was the real drill sergeant here.

As they passed through the Fossil and Firkin's common room, Fig made a break for it, trying to hide behind the piano. Simone grabbed her and pulled her outdoors.

"Have fun at school!" Barnum cried from the bar, waving.

"Halp me!" Fig cried.

"Anyone who tries to reach Fig will have to get through me first," Simone warned.

She pulled the girl outside. They blinked in the sunlight. The sun was so harsh on Mintari. Simone had grown up on Cloventia, which was farther from Nyx, the star in the center of this system. She was used to neon, not punishing sunlight. Oh, her alabaster skin was not made for this planet. Simone would have given a kingdom for Fig's olive-toned skin. The girl actually tanned. Tanned! Ha. Simone could only dream. All she knew how to do was burn. Thankfully, she had applied sunscreen. *Lots* of sunscreen. She suspected she looked like a clown, but winter was around the corner. Ah, winter! Paradise for the pale.

She looked around her. Even here, a good distance from the city center, Dinovia was bustling. Bakeries were already open, selling brontosaurus loaves with long doughy necks. The town knife-sharpener rode a chasmosaurus down the road, pulling a cart full of sharpening tools. He rang a bell, and people rushed out of their homes with blades to sharpen. City folk stood on balconies, watering their flowers, sometimes pausing to wave aside a curious pterodactyl.

Simone shuddered. When she first arrived on Mintari last spring, few dinosaurs ever entered Dinovia City. The Rangers kept them out. But many Rangers had died in the Battle for

Dinovia, and the survivors were mostly in the outback now, hitting Hell's Hunters. Times they were a-changin' and not for the better, if you asked Simone. Today dinosaurs filled the city. Some were pests. Others served human masters. Like Mintari, Simone had to evolve. She learned to appreciate dinosaurs after a fashion. At least she no longer fainted whenever she saw one, and she could even ride Dozer and pet Vinnie without fainting. Still, given a choice, she preferred her dinosaurs much farther away.

Footsteps thudded. A deep bray rippled down the road. A bell clanged.

"Fig, your school bus is here!" Simone said. "Fig? Oh, for crying out—"

The girl was sneaking back into the Fossil and Firkin. Simone grabbed her by the collar and yanked her to the sidewalk.

The "school bus" came plodding around the corner. The brontosaurus was small for a sauropod. A lightweight compared to the true behemoths like the titanosaurs. But he was still tarry enormous. Simone could have walked between his legs without ducking. The dinosaur barely squeezed down the road. His wagging tail slapped the sides of buildings, which already showed old scars. His feet shook the earth, leaving potholes. His neck kept swaying from side to side, giving the dinosaur access to the flowering balconies. As Simone stood below, watching, the brontosaurus found a balcony blooming with lantanas. The dinosaur vacuumed up the flowers and belched. A woman emerged from the apartment, shouting curses, and whacked the dinosaur's head.

A howdah was mounted onto the dinosaur's back. Schoolchildren sat there, tossing paper airplanes, laughing, fighting. The usual chaos. When Fig looked at them, her face fell.

"Canna sta'y home?" she asked.

Simone sighed. "Figaro. I won't force you to go."

"You a' forcin' me!"

Simone laughed. "I suppose I am. But Joe and I want you to get an education. Now quickly, get on the bus! You don't want to miss it."

Fig looked at the sauropod and shook her head in disgust. "I used ta eat dinosirs like dat."

The girl stood on her tiptoes, kissed Simone on the cheek, then ran off. She stood shorter than the sauropod's knees, but a rope ladder dangled across its flank to the ground. Fig scampered up, quick like a velociraptor, and joined the other schoolchildren on the dinosaur's back.

As the diplodocus lumbered off, Simone remained on the sidewalk for a long while, gazing into the distance. She had caught Fig's expression when looking at the other children. An expression of dread.

Is she being bullied? Simone wondered.

Simone herself had been bullied mercilessly at school. She herself had been an outsider. Oh, she knew what some local Mintarians thought of her. The pampered Cloventian princess, roughing it out here on the frontier, far from her penthouse. They didn't know of her past. Simone had been born below the neon sea. Below the sparkling skyscrapers that floated in Cloventia's sky. She had grown up on the planet's surface, a place of shadows, knives in the back, gangs that roamed among the pipes and power plants and magnetic generators the size of starships. She had not seen the sky until she was thirteen years old. The LaRues were bottom dwellers. No wonder their skin was so pale. On Cloventia, skin tone was a status symbol. The poor lived in the shadows. The

rich lived near the sun. The silk emperors had skin as black as
onyx.

With cracked fingernails, Simone had climbed her way
out. And with her—Elize, her beloved twin. A scholarship to
Clover Heights Academy propelled them skyward. For the first
time in their lives, the twins rose from the murk. They passed
through the haze of shops, bars, casinos, hotels—a luminous layer
of sin and pleasure that hovered between the slums and the
heavens. Above the neon sea, that glowing border between the
haves and have-nots, the sisters found another world. A world of
posh uniforms, not rags. A world of wealth, not a hellscape of
landfills swarming with hungry children. A world without
gangsters but with just as much cruelty. Yes, the others bullied
them. Simone remembered.

"Get back into the gutters, rats."

"You don't belong here."

"Who let this riffraff into Clover Heights?"

"Look at her skin. She's never seen the sun. She's from
down there."

One bully was particularly merciless. An older girl. A
beautiful, wealthy, popular girl. A girl whose father had the very
ears of the silk emperors.

Amissa Triplehorn.

She made my life hell, Simone remembered. *And she stole Elize
from me.*

And now Amissa was here on Mintari, leading an army of
poachers. No matter where Simone went in this galaxy, her
tormentor followed.

And here I am, raising her niece, Simone thought. *Life certainly
took some unusual turns.*

Simone turned away from the road. She reentered the
Fossil and Firkin. The place was homey as always. Edna sat by the
hadrosaur fossil, eating sunflower seeds and spitting the shells into

a bowl. Merl was picking his ear with one hand, his teeth with the other. Old Abernathy sat by the fireplace, whittling a piece of wood into a nasutoceratops (it had begun as a triceratops until Abernathy accidentally whittled off the central horn). Vinnie was curled up on the piano, his usual spot, his feathers rising and falling as he snored. It was a comfortable place. A safe place. But Simone felt foreign here. Trapped.

She sat by the bar and placed her hands on the polished, live-edged wood, seeking some comfort from its coiling patterns and sweet smell. She missed home. She missed her parents, who were back on Cloventia. She missed Joe, who was so close but never here. She missed Cody, her dear cameraman and friend, a victim of this planet's savagery. She missed Elize. And perhaps most of all, Simone LaRue missed the woman she used to be. A plucky journalist on the way up, ambitious and hopeful.

"What am I now?" Simone whispered to herself. "Jobless. Alone. A stranger in a strange land. Who am I now?"

Barnum approached her. The rotund barkeep smiled softly. His bushy white muttonchops, pink cheeks, and kind eyes soothed her. "Here, cheesecake." He gave her a cup of coffee and a slice of cherry pie. "Both fresh. For you. On the house."

And suddenly Simone was crying. Big, gloopy tears that fell into her coffee. Barnum raced around the bar and pulled her into an embrace. She cried onto his shoulder.

"What's wrong, lass?" he whispered. "How can I help?"

She smiled thinly. "Got an army hiding behind the bar?"

"Just myself, cheesecake. But I'm deadly with a kitchen knife."

She laughed and wiped her tears. "Have you ever felt lost at sea, Barnum?"

"Aye, cheesecake, I was lost for many years before I found the Fossil and Firkin and set down roots. You're always welcome here. This is your home. And I'll always have a pot of coffee brewing for you."

She was about to hug him again when the holographic television caught her attention. With a blaring sound, the words BREAKING NEWS hovered above the bar. Simone and Barnum turned to look.

A headline materialized: RYUJIN STRIKES AGAIN. TERROR FROM THE OCEAN CLAIMS FIVE MORE LIVES.

"Boring!" cried Merl from his seat in the back. "Change the channel, Barn."

"Shhh!" Simone said.

She watched the program. Dino Dean, Mintari's most popular broadcaster, appeared in hologram above the bar. His real name, which Simone found amusingly apt, was Dean Irritator. Like all Mintarians, his surname represented his family dinosaur. Dean was a member of Clan Irritator, named after a genus of spinosaurid that came from Brazil. Perhaps understandably, he preferred his stage name. Everything about Dino Dean seemed geared for the stage. Like most Mintarians, he wore a safari outfit and ceratop hat. But Dino Dean added flair to his. Raptor teeth encircled the rim of his hat. A bandoleer of dinosaur claws jangled across his chest. Raptor feathers hung from his earrings.

"Crikey, will you look at that!" Dino Dean was saying to the camera. He was flying in a tricopter, one of Mintari's famous three-rotored flying machines. "This is where it happened. Right below!"

The camera panned down to reveal the churning ocean. Flotsam bobbed on the water. Bits of wood. An empty life jacket. A few plastic bags.

"A fishing boat," Dino Dean said. "Just a few friends out to catch their dinner. And from the depths of Hell's Aquarium . . . the terror arose."

The holographic scene went wild. A creature burst from the water. A massive creature. A mosasaur. The beast was covered with spikes and blades. A red scar shaped like a *Z* blazed on his head. His eyes shone just as red, shooting lasers toward the clouds. His jaws opened, revealing a mouthful of skulls. The monster leaped toward the sun, then dived down, blowing fire. A sailing ship burst into flame—only for the mosasaur to swoop and swallow it whole.

A caption appeared below the animation: DRAMATIZATION.

Merl tottered toward the holo-screen, picking his ear. Peanuts clattered inside his overall pockets. "Do mosasaurs blow fire?"

"Of course not!" Simone said. "This is just tacky cheap journalism. Tabloid schlock." The animation was replaying in slow motion. "I mean look at that. You can see the pixels."

Merl shuddered. "Oh no, it can shoot lasers from its eyes!" The big man whimpered and clung to Simone.

She pushed him off. "Oh, for crying out loud!"

"We don't know why Ryujin craves human flesh," Dino Dean continued on the holo-screen. "He attacked five times in as many days. So far, only one person ever survived Ryujin's wrath. Figaro Triplehorn."

A hologram of Figaro appeared. She wore tattered leopard skins, a bone was slung through her hair, and she stood atop a pile of skulls, gnawing on a chunk of raw meat. The DRAMATIZATION caption flashed so briefly Simone barely saw it.

To be fair, that one's not too far off, Simone thought.

Dino Dean reappeared on camera. He stared at the audience. "Dear viewers, we must ask ourselves some hard questions. How could it be that Ryujin spared Figaro Triplehorn of all people? While the girl's aunt, Amissa Triplehorn, hunts our beautiful dinosaurs? While the girl's grandfather, Tobias

Triplehorn, sells poachers their guns? If you ask me—the problem
is not the mosasaur. It is Clan Triplehorn! A clan of traitors.
Could Ryujin be a machine, a robot the Triplehorns constructed
so that—"

"Bunch of rubbish!" Barnum said, switching off the
holographic feed.

Merl stamped his feet. "I want to know if Ryujin is a
robot!" He tapped his chin. "That would explain the lasers."

Simone fumed. "How dare this Irritator or Dino Dean or
whatever his name is spread such nonsense? No wonder Fig
doesn't want to go to school. The other children must have seen
these shows and . . ." Simone paused and heaved a sigh. "And I
forced the girl to go to school." She froze in terror. "Darwin's
beard. I sent her into the lion's den."

"Now, now, cheesecake." Barnum patted her shoulder.
"The lass has survived living with dinosaurs. She can survive a few
schoolyard bullies."

Simone, who had lost her sister to bullying, was not so
sure. When she had arrived on Mintari, Simone had been terrified.
A planet swarming with dinosaurs seemed like her personal hell.
But there were predators everywhere in this galaxy. They prowled
in the floating skyscrapers and fluttered around the robes of the
silk emperors. They hunted in the wilderness, toppling ecosystems
for fortune and fame. They even lurked in schools, preying on
outsiders. Outsiders like Simone had been. Like Fig was.

And for the first time, Simone truly understood why she
was doing this, why she was staying here, why she was tending to
this girl. They couldn't have looked more different. Simone was a
head taller, her skin pale, her hair like flame. Fig was short and
scrawny, dark and quick. Yet when Simone looked at the girl, she
saw herself.

Simone wanted to help her. She was no Ranger. She was
not particularly brave or strong. But there was one thing Simone

LaRue knew. One thing she had done for years back home. She had lost her job, but tar it, she was still a journalist. And she could speak the truth.

CHAPTER SEVEN
In the Wild and the Rain

Another week went by, dealing with the pain in his leg, molding boys into men, rebuilding the Rangers as the poachers roamed wild. Joe could not wait till Sunday. Not only because he missed Fig. Because he missed Mintari. The real Mintari—the wilderness beyond the walls. Most Mintarians never left the city. How could they stay cooped up all their lives? Joe did not understand it.

Finally Sunday came. The day dawned cold and rainy, and the wind whispered of coming winter. But Joe never let weather stop him. He would often explore the outback for days on end, braving snow, hail, or punishing sunlight. A little rain was no reason to stay home.

"Come with us," Joe told Simone that morning. "We're going to explore the western meadows."

She shook her head, her red tresses bouncing. "I ain't going out there, mister. Not with all them dinosaurs knocking about." She looked out the saloon window. "It's raining. Joe, stay here. We can play board games. Watch some movies."

Fig was already pulling on her boots. She let out a whine. "I wanna go to da meadows!"

Joe looked at Simone and shrugged. "Daddy-daughter time. You sure you don't wanna come with us? We'd love to have you."

"I'll just play solitaire." Simone sat down by the fireplace.

Merl raced toward her, nearly knocking over several tables with his girth. "Ooh, can I play solitaire with you?"

Maybe it *was* a little too rainy out there. Joe wouldn't mind a day indoors, relaxing by the fireplace, playing board games and—

"Dad!" Fig tugged his arm. "You promised! C'mon! C'mon, c'mon, c'mon." The girl had even put on her ceratop, excited to go range in the wilderness like a "real Ranger."

Joe looked at Simone.

"Go ahead," she said, smiling thinly. "Daddy-daughter time."

"Woohoo!" Fig cried, pulling Joe outdoors.

As they walked toward Dozer, Joe realized he was barely limping anymore. This strange autumn was almost over. Once he fully recovered, he could fight again. He could leave this city for good, return to his cave, and from there rain down hell upon Amissa and her poachers.

And maybe he could mend things with Simone. Would she return with him to the Last Home Hollow? Would he see her every day, sleep in the same bed every night? He remembered their time right after the Battle for Dinovia. For two weeks, he lay in the cave, recovering from his wounds. Two weeks with Simone in his arms, with Fig in his life. Heaven. Then Chief Clubber had called him to Fort George, and Joe found himself in hell. And one of his angels was fluttering away.

This won't be forever, he thought as he rode Dozer out the city gates. Fig perched before him on the dinosaur, drumming on Dozer's frill. *My leg will heal. I'll go home. I'll become a fighter again. And I'll have time for the people I love. For Simone too.*

As he left Dinovia behind, he remembered her standing by the fireplace, beautiful in the golden light, and his heart ached.

But the beauty of Mintari soothed him. As it always could. The plains swept toward a cycad forest, and beyond the woods rose mountains draped with pines. Pterosaurs soared over golden cliffs and hills, dipping down every few moments to grab fish from a stream.

Across the nearby floodplains, a styracosaurus herd was roaming. At a glance, they looked similar to triceratops. They had the same bulky body, the same beak, the same bony frill. But styracosaurus was far fancier. Instead of three horns like Dozer had, a styrac sprouted an entire spiky arsenal. Eight horns rose along its frill like the spikes in a crown. More horns jutted out from its cheeks like scythes. A huge central horn rose above its beak, its primary weapon. Joe thought they had the most distinct, decorative face on the planet. No other dinosaur, not even stegosaurs, looked so ridiculously spiky.

Fig sat quietly, watching the herd, while Joe cracked jokes about them.

"Well, at least they don't need can openers."

"Geez, I didn't know cacti could move."

"Hey, when they lean into the river for water, are they spiking their drinks?"

"How is a styracosaurus like an orchestra? They both have a horn section."

Fig groaned at every one. "Dad, pees, stop!" she begged.

"Sorry, Fig, when you moved in with me, I became a dad. Bad jokes are part of the job description."

She rolled her eyes. "I wanna go back t' live wit da dinosirs."

Joe laughed, but in truth, that joke hurt him. They were quiet for a while, watching the herd. Finally Joe spoke again, voice soft. "For fifteen years, you were gone, Fig. Fifteen years, lost out here in the wilderness. I can't even imagine what it was like. I'm so sorry I couldn't be there for you."

She leaned against him. "I had the ach-ach-achii...lloo...batirs." She tried again. "Achillobators." She smiled. "I had dem. And Red Scar. He loved me. I was . . . happy."

115

"Are you happy now?" he whispered.

Fig was quiet for a while, lost in thought. "Yes. Not always. But wit you . . . yes. In city . . . not always. Wit oder humans . . . not always."

He looked into her eyes. "Fig, are the other kids giving you trouble at school?"

She looked away. "I . . . fine."

"Figaro. You can talk to me."

She wiped her eyes. "Dey . . . bully me. Dey . . . push me. Dey say I . . . killed da kids . . . in da boat." Her voice cracked. "I told dem I was sorry. Dey don't care. Dey . . . dey hate me, Dad. Dey call me cavegirl. And bad names." She held his hand. "Can we go bek to Last Home Hollow? To da cave? Pees. Pees, Dad. No more school. No more city. *Pees.*"

Joe forced himself to remain calm. So it was true. Other kids *were* bullying his daughter. He would knock them out! He would destroy the school! He would sue them, beat them, ruin them! How could anyone hurt his precious child? He would have roared and howled, but he didn't want to frighten Fig. She had not seen that side of him. He took deep breaths, trying to calm down enough to speak.

"We're turning this triceratops around, we're going to visit your teachers, and—"

"Dad, no!" Fig cried. "No, it make it worse. Pees. Pees no. Just . . . don't. I can han-han-dle it." She smiled shakily. "I suv-suvvv-ive in da wil-wilda'ness. I c-c-can surv-v-vive high school."

Joe couldn't help it. He laughed. "You're a tough one. You're like your mother. She was a lot tougher than me."

"I wish I knoo her. I—"

Fig froze. She sniffed. Her eyes narrowed. She sniffed again, cocked her head, and frowned.

"Fi—" Joe began.

"Shh!"

She stared into the distance, coned her hand around her ear, and inhaled sharply. She began to tremble.

Then Joe heard it. Distant squawks and squeals and high-pitched cries. "Yip yip yip ayee!"

The styracosaurs heard it too. The spiky dinosaurs looked from side to side, snorting. Hatchlings wailed. Bulls and cows rumbled.

The cries grew louder, closer. "Yip yip yip! *Ayeee!*"

They burst from the tall grass, twenty or more, screeching for meat. They were the size of lions, and their sickle claws gleamed in the sun. Their red feathers fluttered in the wind.

Achillobators.

Fig sat on Dozer's back, watching them run.

A pack of achillobators.

Her pack.

Her family.

For a moment, Fig thought she was imagining it. That her eyes were playing tricks on her. That these were just random bators, not *her* bators. But she rubbed her eyes, looked again, and it really was them. She recognized Crooked Wing, her left wing bent at an odd angle. She had broken the limb in a landslide. And there was Half Tail, who had donated half his tail to a protoceratops beak. Brooding Mother was there too, her hatchlings joining her on the hunt. They had grown so big.

Fig's eyes dampened, and she trembled. No. No, this couldn't be. That old world. That old life in the wilderness. The wild child she had been. Since discovering humanity, those years had blurred so quickly in her mind, becoming something like a dream, like a past life.

Yet there they were. The pack that had sheltered her, nurtured her, taught her to hunt, to groom for ticks, to shelter in winter. The pack that had kept her alive. For so long, Fig had thought she was one of them, just another dinosaur in the pack. Yet now here she was, wearing human clothes, a human hat on her head, watching them as one watches mere animals.

The pack didn't acknowledge her. They must have seen her, definitely smelled her. A girl and her father sitting on a triceratops were hard to miss. But they probably didn't realize it was Fig, *their* Fig. Just three inconsequential animals far away. The pack was far more interested in the styracosaurus herd.

Compared to Dozer, their hulking relative, styracs were small. They were only about a quarter of the big trike's size. But they were still substantial herbivores, roughly the size of rhinos from old Earth. Bigger than achillobators. In a one-on-one melee, a styrac would defeat a bator. More mass. Lots of horns. A bad attitude. But bators were smarter, faster, and hungrier, and they worked as one unit.

Fig chewed her lip. This was wrong. The bators should not be here. The styracs were too big for them, their horns too dangerous. Bators were midsized predators. They should be hunting easier prey like parasaurs.

That was when Fig noticed how thin the bators were. Their feathers were matted. Their bodies withered. A mad hunger shone in their eyes. Were they sick? No.

They're starving, Fig realized. *They're desperate.*

Of course. Amissa and her poachers had been hunting the parasaurs for their crests. The bators found themselves without their primary food source. With winter just around the corner, they had no choice but to attack this horned herd.

Fig wanted to tell all this to Joe. But she couldn't imagine talking so much, fumbling around every syllable. Besides, what could he do? Strong as he was, Joe was one man. They needed more Rangers. More people to fight Hell's Hunters.

This is why I must become a Ranger, Fig thought. *Why I must fight Amissa. For the pack. For all of Mintari.*

Helpless, all Fig could do now was sit on Dozer, watching the drama unfold.

With their red feathers, bators struggled to hide in summer or winter. But in autumn, the reason for their red colors became apparent. Autumn was the most important time in Mintari for dinosaurs. A time when they must fatten up for winter. And in this critical hunting season, bators blended into the red-and-orange landscape. They had been able to creep close, to pounce and yip only a short sprint away.

They could have gotten even closer. They chose to reveal themselves early. Fig understood why. The styracs did not. Foolishly, the horned herbivores began to flee the predators, stampeding westward. They were routing right toward the hill where Fig and Joe sat on Dozer, watching the drama unfold.

"Wair fo' it," Fig whispered to her father.

The herd rumbled across the plains, ripping up soil and grass, knocking down trees. Hundreds of horns rose like an army of pikes, clattering together. The hatchlings ran in the middle. The mothers surrounded them. The bulls protected the back line from the pursuing bators. The predators yipped louder. The high-pitched cries ripped across the air, deafening. Panic spread through the styrac herd. Their formations began to crumble. One hatchling stumbled out of line. A big old bull trampled a cow who was too slow. Soon it was every styrac for itself. They were desperately fleeing toward the hilltop.

That was when the achillobators sprang the trap.

Seven powerful hunters leaped from the brush just ahead of Fig. Just a few steps away! They had hidden in the tall grass for hours perhaps, even masking their scent with mud. The approaching triceratops with the humans on his back had not deterred them. The bators had remained hidden, waiting, ready for the signal. This whole time, they had been hiding right ahead of Fig, and she had been completely unaware.

Her chest swelled with pride. What a pack this was!

The styracs reared to a halt, braying in terror. Bators ahead. Bators behind. Desperately they tried to cut northward, but the pack had cleverly chosen this spot for their ambush. A steep slope, covered with sharp rocks and dense conifers, cut off the northern escape. Even if the styracs made it through, they'd encounter a rushing river. To the south, jagged boulders rose like barricades, and beyond them the land plunged into a misty gully full of bones. The herd was trapped.

Clever bators, Fig thought.

Now they just had to deal with those horns.

The pack fanned out, forming a noose around the styracs. The herbivores stomped the ground, snorted, and lowered their heads, pointing their horns toward the enemy. Even encircled, they were a formidable enemy. Flight was off the table. So a fight it was. The styracs regained their bearings, found their courage, and re-formed their lines. Hatchlings in the center. Then mothers. Bulls on the outside. These herbivores had faced tyrannosaurs and carnotaurs. A pack of achillobators was no fun, but the herd had dealt with worse.

The bators knew it. They eyed those horns nervously. A few bators bore recent scars on their hides. Quick Talons had a fresh gash on his flank, no more than a day old. Clearly the pack had been hunting dangerous prey. Fig had never seen her bators look so rough. When the wind fluttered their feathers, she could see their ribs press against their skin. Desperation shone in their eyes.

Fig clenched her fists. *You did this, Amissa.*

The bators circled the styracs again. This time, with the initial panic dying down, the herbivores did not crumble. They maintained their position, horns pointing outward, forming a ring of pikes. The bators made a few fake charges, trying to scare the styracs into breaking formation, but the armored beasts stayed strong.

Fig knew what the bators were thinking.

We're hungry. But this foe is beyond us. Those horns are sharp. Those frills are thick. We can't reach the young or old. This ambush failed.

That was not unusual. In the wilderness, most hunts failed. More often than not, all predators—bators included—must cut their losses and retreat. No shame in that. You simply waited for an easier opportunity. No harm, no foul. In a normal year, the bators would have retreated now. But calories were the currency of Mintari, and this year they were in short supply. The pack had already spent considerable energy on the ambush—chasing, yipping, circling the herd. These were hard losses to cut. The bators were already short on calories, and they had just spent a fortune. They needed meat. They needed it now.

Crooked Wing let out a frustrated screech. She was the new alpha of the pack, replacing Red Scar, whom Amissa had killed. The big female salivated. She made another fake charge, but her foes held the line. Finally Crooked Wing tossed back her head and cried out: "Yip yip!"

She made her choice. Despite the danger, the pack attacked.

The hunters surged. Crooked Wing led the charge. The huntress lunged toward the styracs. She crouched low, hoping to dodge the terrible beaks and horns. Her jaws snapped, trying to catch a leg.

A styrac bull grunted and bolted forward. He was a burly beast, a machine of bony armor, horns, and a sharp curving beak. He plowed his gargantuan head into Crooked Wing. By miracle alone, the horns missed the bator. But the bony frill slammed into Crooked Wing and tossed her into the air. She flew like some doll woven of matted feathers, then thumped down onto the ground.

The other bators, seeing their alpha so rudely tossed aside, lost heart. They hesitated. Only for a second—but it cost them. More styracs charged. They bulldozed into the carnivores, hurling bators into the air. Red feathers flew like autumn leaves. A horn plowed into White Snout, ripping off feathers and skin and revealing the muscle tissue. A beak closed around Sniffer, snapping his wing bone with a terrible *crunch*. The bator yowled and fell back.

Fig cried out in horror. Her pack was being savaged. She drew her sickle claw, prepared to jump off Dozer, run toward her beloved pack, and help. But Joe grabbed her wrist. He held her firmly.

"Le' go!" she cried.

"No!" Joe growled. "No, tar it. Stay here! Let nature take its course."

Fig yowled and struggled against him, but her father held her firmly. Most likely, Joe did not know these were *her* bators, the ones who had raised her. Maybe he didn't even realize they were achillobators. At a glance, they looked similar to other large dromaeosaurs, such as utahraptors and dakotaraptors, their close relatives. In her flustered state, Fig could not find the words to explain. She must watch from Dozer's back, helpless.

Good Mother lunged toward the herd. She was a brooder, not a huntress. Normally she stayed behind with her hatchlings, but the hunters needed help today. She snapped her teeth and shrieked, driving back a styrac bull with pure ferocity. Then Good Mother leaped, flapped her wings, slashed her sickle claw, and drew blood. Fig cheered. The styrac rumbled, spun toward Good Mother, and thrust his large central horn. That horn was longer than a man's arm, and it drove into Good Mother's flank and burst out the other side.

Fig screamed in terror.

The styrac shook his head, tossing Good Mother off his horn. The bator thumped down.

Fig tried to leap off Dozer, to run forward, to join the fight. But Joe kept a firm grip on her.

"Le' go! Le' go! Ayeee!"

She struggled wildly. Dozer looked over his shoulder, concerned at her distress. Joe's face remained hard. His grip was harder.

"No!" he hissed. "You're staying here, Fig! You're a human, tar it, not an achillobator. We're leaving. Dozer!"

"No!" Fig cried, struggling against her father as Dozer spun around.

At least he knows they're achillobators, she thought. *I underestimated him. Of course he knows. He's Jurassic Joe, hero of Mintari. He knows his dinosaurs.*

Fig looked over her shoulder. With the fall of Good Mother, the bators had lost their courage. They retreated a safe distance, crouched in the grass, and whimpered. Good Mother remained on the ground, bleeding out. Her hatchlings yipped and mewled in despair.

The styracosaurus herd grunted and rumbled off, leaving the achillobators behind. The herbivores could have pressed their advantage, maybe killed another bator or two. But they had no interest in vengeance, only survival. The horned dinosaurs lumbered onward. A few were bleeding, but nobody was dead. They had won this battle.

Fig lowered her head, tears on her cheeks. "I'm sorry, Dad."

Joe sighed. "I know, Fig. I know." He relaxed his grip on her. "I'm sorry too, I—"

Fig bit his hand. Joe yelped.

"Ayee!" Fig cried, wrenching herself free. She leaped off Dozer, landed on the grass, and ran toward her pack.

Yes. Her pack. Her family. Tears flowed down her cheeks as she ran. She kicked off her shoes and raced barefoot, and suddenly she was that girl again, *l'enfant sauvage*, wild and free, wearing nothing but feathers and mud, racing across the plains. She tossed off her hat. She ripped off her bracelets, letting them clatter to the ground. A savage child, she ran, adorned with blood and sunlight and the soil of Mintari, a queen of the wild.

She reached Good Mother and knelt by the bator. Dead. Fig lowered her head, and sobs racked her body.

You kept me warm during that one long winter when I was sick, she remembered. *You let me play with your hatchlings. You taught me how to find the healing maggots that clean out wounds, and you groomed me for ticks. I should have been there, Good Mother. I should have been fighting at your side. I could have saved you.*

Good Mother had raised many hatchlings. The oldest were almost adults already, bigger than Fig. The youngest were so small Fig could cradle them in her arms. Good Mother's brood approached the body, whimpering. A hatchling nudged the corpse with his snout, then let out a mournful wail. The youngest hatchlings jumped over their dead mother, nipping her, begging her to wake up.

Fig remembered their father, a lean male. She had named him Black Stripe due to a crest of black feathers along his back. He was not here today. He must have fallen in this desperate year of war. The orphaned hatchlings whimpered, alone in the world. Their survival was now in doubt. The whole pack's survival was. They had dominated this territory for generations. Was their reign ending?

Fig stroked Good Mother's feathers, pressed her face against the body, and wet the bator with tears. In the city, after the

Battle for Dinovia, she had heard Rangers recite Mintari's prayer for the dying. She whispered it now too softly to hear, probably mispronouncing many words, but in her mind it sounded clear.

"Go back now, child of Mintari. Go back to the soil from which you came. In the warm embrace of the world, you will bring forth new life. The energy in your body will feed the grass that grows and the trees that reach toward the sun. Flowers will bloom where you fell, and the rain will wash your blood away. You will be reborn. Rest now, child of life. We will always remember you, for you will never die."

Fig wiped her eyes and looked behind her. Dozer stood on the hilltop, waiting for her. Joe sat on the trike's back, Nyx shining behind him. He seemed so distant. A silhouette. A dream. Was this really her father?

The bator hatchlings finally left the body, realizing it was only dead meat. They tottered back toward the pack. The older bators were licking their wounds. One lean male stepped toward Good Mother, salivating. His jaws widened. He wanted the meat. Fig had seen famished achillobators resort to cannibalism during hard winters. But Good Mother's largest hatchlings snapped their teeth at him, driving him back. This corpse was sacred. Even in their hunger, they would not feed upon it.

Snouts turned toward Fig. Nostrils flared. Eyes narrowed. For the first time, the pack seemed to truly notice her. A few eyes widened. Bators approached, sniffed, yipped. Was it her? Was it the runt? The one who had run with them, hunted with them, groomed them for ticks? No, it couldn't be! She wore a dress! She was clean! She was a human. A filthy human like the ones who killed the parasaurs!

A few bators drew nearer, teeth bared, fury in their eyes. They licked their chops. Perhaps they had found a meal today after all.

"Arooo!" Crooked Wing cried, leaped down, and blocked the other bators, protecting Fig behind her. The huntress flapped her wings. One of those wings was crooked but still sprouted mean claws. "Aroo arrrooo! Harrrr." *Stand back! She is pack.*

Fig approached the big huntress gingerly. For years, Crooked Wing had antagonized her. And why not? Fig had been a loyal servant to Red Scar, the old alpha. Crooked Wing, who had been gunning to replace him, had often taken out her rage on Fig—snapping at her, screeching at her, shoving her away from food. Yet now Red Scar was gone. Now Crooked Wing had new responsibilities, new wisdom, new fear of the terror that prowled Mintari. The big bator had changed, and in her sad eyes, there was something of Red Scar. The burden of leadership was heavy.

Fig stood before the dinosaur, so small before this big feathered theropod. She hesitated, then placed her hand on Crooked Wing's snout. She stroked the huntress, cooing.

"Prrr prrr." *Yes, it's me. I'm your friend.*

Crooked Wing purred in return. *Welcome home.*

From a distance, Joe and Dozer watched, not interfering. They sensed something was precious here. Something was holy.

Crooked Wing sniffed Fig, nuzzled her, and nickered softly. The breath from her nostrils ruffled Fig's hair. The bator's head was the size of Fig's entire torso, covered with red feathers and faded scars. She was an old bator now, too old to lay eggs, and the fire of her youth had faded to embers. In her amber eyes were entire worlds. In those eyes Fig saw the grief of a barren female. A proud huntress who had broken her wing, who was crippled, unwanted by any mate. An old warrior who had survived over twenty winters and hunted across the plains countless times.

"Mhrrrmmmrr," Crooked Wing whimpered. *Come with us.*

Fig lowered her head and cried. She hugged Crooked Wing's great head, burying her face in the soft red feathers. "I can't."

"Mhrmrrrmmr." *Come.*

Hugging that head, Fig wept. Not only for Crooked Wing. Not only for today. But for her years in the wilderness, running with the pack, a bator among bators. Savage child. Queen of the wild.

Gently, Crooked Wing pulled her snout back from Fig's embrace and took a few steps away. The rest of the pack was already by the southern boulders. They would be heading southward in search of prey, following the old trails of their ancestors.

Crooked Wing took another step toward the pack, then looked at Fig. She gestured with her snout. *Come with us, little one. You are pack.*

Fig wanted to. With every beat of her heart, every nerve in her body, every dream inside her, every memory of cruel children, every scar she had earned in the city, every taunt, every nightmare—they all called to her: *You are not a human. You are pack. Go with them. Go with them . . .*

Crooked Wing looked at her, gestured at the pack, looked at Fig again. "Rmmmmrrrrm!" *Come with us, bator! We will hunt together. We will find meat and we will feast!* Crooked Wing knelt. *Ride me! Ride me like you rode Red Scar, and wield your claw from upon my back.*

The alpha bator took a few more steps toward the pack. The sun was low in the sky. They could not wait much longer. The pack stood in the distance, their red feathers gilded with sunlight, watching Fig. Waiting for her. Their eyes shone like stars. *Come with us. Come with us . . .*

Fig took a step toward them, then stopped. She looked back at the hilltop. Joe was waiting there. He did not call her. He did not charge forward on Dozer's back to grab her, yank her up, and drag her home. He knew this was a choice she must make herself.

On one side—her pack. Running wild. Running free. Once more, she would taste the wind, she would sleep under the stars and feast upon the living flesh of this world. She would be loved. She would be a huntress, proud and strong. She would hunger, yes. She would suffer terrible hunger, and in the winter, the snow would freeze her fingers and toes, and in the summer, the punishing sunlight would peel her skin. She would fight every day to survive. Against illness. Starvation. The cruelty of the elements. Her life would be once more an endless war, but she would be free. She would be pack.

On the other side of this world—another life. A life as a human. There was cruelty in that world too. There was guilt. There was the headmaster with his stinging ruler and youths with words that stung ten times hotter. But ultimately those were trivial things compared to the slings and arrows of Mintari's wildness. In the city, she would live in safety, sheltered behind walls, a roof over her head, food in her belly. Barnum would always be there with his shepherd's pie and homemade ice cream. Simone would be there to hug her, teach her about being a woman. And Joe would be there. Joe who could be so rough—who scolded her, who yelled if she misbehaved. But who loved her. Who only wanted to protect her. Joe would burn down the world for her. That too was pack. They too were pack.

Tears ran down her cheeks, because even now, even after so long, she was torn between two worlds, and she did not know who she was.

She looked from side to side. Two packs. Two species. Two Figaros.

If I go with the pack, I will die with them, she knew. Because now they did not only face winters, droughts, the dangers of the hunt. They faced poachers. They faced Amissa.

This is why I must become a Ranger, Fig thought. *Why I must become a human. Because dinosaurs, powerful as they are, cannot win this war. Not without help. And Rangers can help. I can help.*

She ran toward the pack. She pulled Crooked Wing into one last embrace, weeping onto her feathers.

Goodbye, sister. Goodbye. I love you.

Tears in her eyes, Fig turned around and walked away from the pack.

Behind her, they cried out.

"Haoo haoo."

"Yip yip."

"Haoooo!"

Come back. Come back! Don't go!

"Ayee!"

"Ayee!"

"Ayee!"

Huntress! Huntress! Huntress!

Even now, even as they left her, they celebrated her strength. They gave her heart for the battles ahead. They would be with her always, Fig knew. And a part of her would forever run wild with them.

She returned to the hilltop. Joe had dismounted and stood by his triceratops. He was a tall man, but he looked so small compared to Dozer. The dinosaur's skull was longer than Joe was tall. Fig approached her father and stood before him. She clasped her hands behind her back and lowered her head.

"Dad. I'm sorry."

He frowned. "For what?"

"For . . . bein . . . like dis. Half . . . half dinosir."

His face cracked and broke. He pulled her into his arms. "You have nothing to be sorry for. I'm the one who should be sorry. And I am sorry. For how I yelled at you, for how I held you back. For how I wanted to forget all those years you spent apart from me. All those years in the wild. I thought them lost years. Years that didn't count. Years that were just about surviving until your true life began. But I see now. I was wrong. They were the years that forged you. That made you who you are today. You are not half of anything. You are a sum of many parts. You are my daughter. You are a Triplehorn. And I'm proud of you."

On previous outings, Fig dreaded returning to Dinovia City, to the cramped rooms and crowds. But this evening her anxiety flowed away on the wind. She had always wanted to feel whole, but she was a patchwork of many parts like the dresses of feathers and vines she used to sew. Clad in those feathers, she had survived harsh winters in the wild, and she knew she could survive the oncoming winter too. A winter of war. She was moving away from the pack, but she was still a huntress. And she would hunt to save the world.

When Joe got home to the Fossil and Firkin that night, Simone was already asleep.

He stood by her bed, gazing down at her, the woman he loved. The woman he had barely seen all month. In a few hours, he must return to Fort George for another grueling week of training.

He could not bear to wait a full week.

Fig was down in the common room, having a late dinner. Joe knelt by the bed and stroked Simone's hair. A lantern shone on the bedside, painting her gold. It was a cozy room with two beds, a desk, and a chair, all built of live-edge wood. A temporary home. A cozy nest. They had been living here since spring. With his meager Rangers salary (and some deep discounts from Barnum) Joe was able to afford it, to keep Simone and Fig living comfortably while he stayed on base.

"Simone?" Joe whispered.

She stirred in her sleep, making little mumbling sounds of slumber.

"Simone, I'm sorry. I know I haven't been around much. Can I say goodbye and kiss you before I return to the base?"

Her eyes opened. Whenever Joe gazed into her blue eyes, he thought he would drown.

"What time is it?" she mumbled.

"Just past midnight."

She closed her eyes. "I want to sleep."

"Simone." He touched her arm. "I know you can't join us in the wild. I know dinosaurs scare you. Next Sunday, we'll do something in the city. Something you choose. Something you can enjoy."

She sat up in bed. "Joe. I'm all right. I'm not another child you must entertain."

He winced.

Simone sighed. "I'm sorry. I'm a bit crabby when people wake me up in the middle of the night." She gave him a strange look. "And when I'm neglected."

"I'll make it up to you. Next Sunday, what are we doing?"

Simone took a deep breath. Sitting up in bed, she closed her eyes. For a long moment, she said nothing. She seemed to be struggling with something internally. Perhaps wondering if Joe deserved a second chance. For the first time, Joe realized how close he was to losing her. Fear fluttered in his belly. After so many years alone, he didn't know how to love another woman.

His heart blazed for her, but now the storms he had summoned washed over the fire.

She opened her eyes, and they were soft. He saw it in her eyes: she would give him another chance.

"Next Sunday, let's go downtown." She smiled wistfully. "We'll visit the library, the museum, and every café and chocolate shop between them."

Joe nodded. "That's a great idea. Fig loves chocolate. And her reading is improving. Maybe in the library, she can find kid books to practice with."

Simone's smile wavered. She placed a hand on his knee. "Joe. I was hoping it could be just the two of us. Just you and me."

He frowned. "What?"

"Fig can stay here, hang out with Merl and Barnum and the gang, have a relaxing Sunday."

Joe pursed his lips and tried to calm himself. Tar his anger! It was always inside him, threatening to erupt. Even among the people he loved. Especially with them.

"Simone, I missed the first fifteen years of Fig's life. I only have Sundays to see her. And with the war on, who knows what will happen? I might have to leave for months. I might die out there. I can't miss more time with her."

"I know, Joe, but—"

"So why can't she come?" Joe said, a little too loudly.

"Because I want us to have a date, tar it!" Simone said. She let out a mirthless laugh. "Can't I have you to myself for just one day? You've been away nonstop. I barely see you."

"It's not my fault I'm busy. There's a war on. I took a vow to serve the Rangers. And they need me on that base."

"And I need you!" Simone cried. "I need you too. Am I less important? I guess I am. I guess it's the Rangers that matter. It's your war against Amissa that matters. It's Figaro who matters.

It's the dinosaurs who matter. Everyone and everything but Simone LaRue. I'm just an afterthought, aren't I?"

"The Rangers are my life!" Joe leaped to his feet, that old anger surging through him. "I've been a Ranger for twenty years. What am I to do now? Walk away from them? Tell them I quit because I found a girlfriend?"

Simone rose from bed too. She placed her hands on her hips. "I'm not your girlfriend yet, Joe Triplehorn. Don't assume I'm that easy to get. You take me for granted. Of course you do! I'll always be here, won't I? Waiting here for you. Trapped in this room. Trapped on this planet. Whenever you need me, you can stumble in—past midnight, whenever you feel like using me—and wake me up and expect me to just love you. As if nothing happened. As if I'm a toy you can just take out of the cupboard, play with for a while, then put aside. As if you weren't away all month." Tears stung her eyes. "As if I didn't miss you. But I don't matter, do I? I can't even have one day with you. One day!"

"I said you can have a day!"

"With Figaro! A day so you can bond with her instead of me."

"She's my daughter! I love her! It's not a contest between you. Are you jealous of her?"

"Jealous?" Simone barked a laugh. "Do you hear yourself? Painting me as some possessive woman, consumed with envy. I like Figaro. I *love* Figaro. And I thought I loved you."

Joe opened his mouth to argue back. He shut it. He took a step back.

"I see how it is," he said.

His heart sank. It was true. He had ruined it. Ruined everything. Or maybe there had never been anything there at all. Just a dream. A fantasy. Maybe Simone was right. He had taken her for granted, and now she was slipping away.

"Simone—" he said, reaching out to her.

"Joe, I need to leave now." Her voice was choked. "I need to pack my things, get out of your room, and leave right now."

She packed her things hurriedly. There wasn't much. She had never been planning to stay on Mintari long. Joe just stood there, not knowing what to do, feeling like a fool.

"Don't leave," he said.

Tears flooded her blue eyes. She shoved socks into her bag, zipped it up, and pulled on her shoes. "Goodbye, Joe Triplehorn."

She stepped into the hallway.

He followed her.

"Where will you go, Simone?" he called after her. "You're on a strange planet. You have nowhere else to live. What are you going to do?"

She spun around in the hallway. She looked at him, tears in her eyes. "You think I'm so useless, don't you? You think I'm so dependent on you. And maybe I was. Not anymore. Don't worry about me, Mr. Triplehorn. Goodbye."

She didn't go through the common room. Maybe she couldn't face Figaro tonight. Simone made her way downstairs to the back door. Joe followed silently, not knowing what to do. He watched helplessly as Simone stepped out into the rainy night. And just like that, she was gone.

Joe lowered his head, eyes damp. It was all his fault. He had gained a daughter. But he had lost the woman he loved.

CHAPTER EIGHT
Post and Pastries

Simone stood outside in the rain. It was past midnight. She was on a foreign planet. She was alone. Homeless. Hopeless. The rain soaked her hair and ran down her face, mingling with her tears. She realized she was still wearing her pajamas. She had only pulled on a coat and boots, that was all.

"Look at you," she whispered and barked a laugh. "Simone LaRue. Clover Heights alumni. Star of *LaRue's News*. Standing outside in the rain in her pajamas. How the mighty have fallen."

It was hard to believe that only half a year ago, she had been somebody. She had worn business silks and high heels. She had made a down payment on a condo in a floating skyscraper. She was not a famous journalist per se (nothing like Blake Benway, star of *Benway Tonight*), but tar it, she'd had her own show on *Gazette TV*. She had made something of herself, and since she had come to Mintari on assignment, this planet had stripped her of everything. Her fancy clothes. Whatever money she had. Her lifestyle. Her ambitions. All was laid bare on Mintari. The brutality of this world washed away all her pretenses like the falling rain. She was left exposed and hollow.

"Simone!" Joe's voice sounded in the distance. "Simone, get back here. I'm sorry, all right?"

So he was sorry. So what. People were always sorry. Sorries were like police tape. They did nothing but highlight the crime. Simone walked through the rain, leaving Joe behind.

Leaving the Fossil and Firkin. Leaving a man she had loved. A man she still perhaps loved. A man she only mattered to now as she was walking away.

I wish none of this had happened. A lump filled her throat. *I wish I had never come to this planet to find Jurassic Joe. I wish I never heard of Mintari.*

But was that true? Had Mintari truly brutalized her? Or had it only exposed the lies she had woven around herself? It was not Mintari that had bugged her cameras and microphones. Tobias and Amissa had done that back on Cloventia. It was not Mintari that had ended her career. She had quit the *Gazette* once learning of its corruption. No, Mintari did not destroy. Mintari illuminated. And even in this dark rainy night, Simone saw more clearly than ever. She saw her failures. The folly of her ambitions. The frailty of the image she had constructed of herself. All that was falling to pieces now. But from these pieces, she could build a life.

She walked through the rain. Back on Cloventia, whenever it rained, Simone used to run along the floating walkways, holding a coat over her head, terrified of getting one drop on her. Now she was already soaked, and without the need to run, she realized how beautiful the rain was, how liberating it felt not to care, to accept and welcome the rain, to let the sky weep over her. She laughed. A laughter of joy. Everyone else in this city was hiding in their homes. Hiding from the rain. Or the dark. Or what they deemed as impropriety. But Simone walked through the darkness and the rain, laughing, washing off the broken pieces of her old life like a hatchling shaking off the pieces of its shell. This was her rebirth. This planet was still teaching her so much.

She had nowhere to go. She had no place to return to, no path ahead. For the first time in her life, Simone was free.

At two in the morning, she saw a warm light shining ahead. She followed the beacon and found a café that was still open, likely catering to night shift workers, insomniacs, and other lost souls. A sign hung over the door, featuring a dinosaur drinking a cup of coffee and the words JURASSIC PERK.

Simone stepped inside, blinking in the light. Even at this late hour, a couple of patrons were here. An old man sat by the window, rustling through a newspaper. Actual paper, not even a hologram. How quaint. He tipped his ceratop at her. A teenage girl slept at a table over a pile of homework. Baked goods sat behind glass, little temptresses draped with icing and sprinkles. Fresh coffee was percolating, filling the café with its intoxicating aroma.

Simone was low on funds. But she ordered a cup of hazelnut coffee with two sugars and cream. After resisting for a full ten seconds, she caved to temptation and ordered a strawberry strudel too. She sat down at a table, took a sip of coffee, and pulled out her SmartSphere. While in her pocket, the computer was flat like a coaster. When Simone tapped a button, it bloomed into a sphere. Icons appeared across the screen. Simone got to work, tapping away.

She took a bite of the pastry, scrolled, and typed. She emptied her coffee, tapped some more, waited anxiously, refreshed again and again. Soon she had a fresh cup of coffee and, yes, another strawberry strudel.

"Sue me. I eat when I'm nervous," she told the barista, a pimply teenager.

"Um, sue you, ma'am?" he squeaked and scratched his head. She had forgotten that Mintari had no lawyers.

"Be quiet and give me that cookie too."

It only took a few hours of work. And most of that time was waiting for the signals to travel through space. By dawn, Simone LaRue had sold her apartment in Neotropolis, glittering capital of planet Cloventia.

Her bank account swelled to a cool million clovers. That was seven million Mintarian mints. She was rich! She was wealthy! She was comfortably well off! For an hour, at least. Until, with one fell swoop, she paid off her mortgage. Her funds quickly depleted. She had owned only a quarter of that apartment.

Thankfully, real estate in Cloventia was costly. Even a quarter of her apartment brought in some serious mint. After paying off her debts and commissions and taxes (and buying another cookie), Simone still had over a million mints left. That wouldn't go far on Cloventia. But it was just enough to buy a place on Mintari. Paid fully. In cash. Goodbye mortgage, hello financial freedom! Well, financial freedom with only a few utility bills, property taxes, and miscellaneous home maintenance expenses. Okay, she'd still be broke. But she'd be broke with a roof over her head.

As the sun rose, and yawning crowds entered the café, Simone sat there, holding her third cup of coffee, shocked. Her head spun.

I actually did this. I sold my home on Cloventia. I'm not going back there.

She could have walked by this café. She could have hailed down a dinosaur, rode to the spaceport, and flown home. But what awaited her on Cloventia? No job. Friends? Hmm. Well, Cody had been her friend. Bleakly, Simone realized the late cameraman had been her *only* friend. It had never sunk in how lonely she had been on Cloventia.

But on Mintari, things were different. She cared about people here. There was Barnum and his shepherd's pie. Merl and Edna and the other regulars. There was Fig, of course. Fig who was like a daughter to her. Fig whom she loved.

And there was Joe. Sort of. Was there?

Maybe. Simone sighed. She loved the big old idiot. He was gruff, distant, cold. But she loved him. That didn't matter. Love was great but not enough. She could not continue as she had, living like a maid. What kind of life was that? To live in a saloon room he rented for her? To parent his daughter while he was away? To pace the room, bored out of her mind, while he took Fig on daddy-daughter days? Was that the sum of her ambitions?

No. Simone was worth more than that. She knew her own worth. She would rebuild her life.

And she would rebuild it on Mintari.

Wow. There came that woozy feeling again.

Suddenly she regretted it all. She'd call the apartment's new owner. She'd call the bank. She'd cancel all this! She'd call the *Gazette* and get her job back. She could return home, be the old Simone again, the Simone who lounged on the couch on Saturday nights with ice cream, who owned nice clothes, who had nice things, who . . .

Who was lonely, she thought. *Who was miserable.*

She looked around her at the café. People smiled and nodded to her. A Mintari folk song was playing on the radio. Children ran outside, chasing a feathery microraptor and laughing. And Simone realized that she had fallen in love with this world. That she wanted to build a life here. No longer as an exiled woman. But as a Mintarian.

Simone had only slept an hour last night. But fueled with coffee and strudels, she stepped out into the morning.

She had to leap back as a diplodocus rumbled down the road, carrying sacks of bricks on its back. A dactyl swooped from above, grabbed a bagel from a man's hand, and flew off with the prize. An ankylosaurus plodded along, carrying a Ranger on its back. A group of children skipped along, playfully chasing a juvenile sauropod, while an old woman sat on a bench, feeding stray eoraptors. It was not always like this. Traditionally, few dinosaurs entered the city. But with the Rangers out to war, more and more wildlife invaded Dinovia.

I picked a perfect time to move to Mintari, Simone thought. *A time when Dinovia is swarming with dinosaurs.*

Half a year ago, when Simone was still fresh off the boat, this scene would have made her faint. Today, with a deep breath, she strode down the road, shoulders squared. She paused at an apple cart to stock up, and when a stray sauropodlet approached her, she fed the dinosaur one of her apples. Yes, this planet was changing her.

Munching on an apple, Simone wandered through the city, looking for a new home.

She wanted to stay in this neighborhood. To remain close to her friends at the Fossil and Firkin. And close to Figaro. She would not abandon the girl merely because of her row with Joe. And she liked this area. Dinosaurs notwithstanding.

Her SmartSphere showed her the local real estate listings. Mintari was home to only three hundred thousand people, but housing was in hard demand. Almost the entire population lived in Dinovia, keeping safe behind the city walls. Of course, the walls seemed a bit pointless now with all these dinosaurs roaming along the streets. At least they still kept the big predators out. With everyone crowding to live in the same area, competition for housing could get fierce. But Simone was armed with a million mints (*I'm a millionaire!*), a winning smile, and a good dose of desperation.

Buildings in Dinovia came in two main flavors. Larger buildings were built of brick. The city library, Pangaea Hall, and high street shops were all brick constructions. Some of these buildings could get quite gaudy, boasting porticoes, balustrades, and ornate balconies, the stone engraved with decorative patterns. Most of this architecture was centuries old, dating back to the time of the founders. The style was sometimes called Darwin Deco, named after the *Darwin's Ark*, the first starship to carry settlers from Earth to Mintari.

Smaller buildings were built of clay. They were younger, humbler constructions. The first settlers came to Mintari with wealth and power and science—rich Earthlings determined to create a paradise for dinosaurs and oversee their genetic creations. Since then, the population had expanded. Generation after generation got married, had children, made this planet not a vision but a home. Many Mintarians today still carried the convictions and blazing intensity of the founders. But most were simple folk. Like Simone's friends at the Fossil and Firkin. They cared not for grand architecture or lofty ambitions and simply wanted a cozy home.

Thus were born the so-called Dino Domes. The little houses were built of clay. Many had rounded corners, while some had entirely circular walls. Their windows were round, sometimes their doors too, and tin pipes stuck out their roofs, puffing smoke into the cold autumn day. How quaint. Like something out of a magical forest of gnomes. Cute but nothing for a sophisticated, modern woman like Simone LaRue.

At first, on her hunt for a home, Simone checked a few apartments in the old brick buildings. One apartment was located over a bakery. She could get fresh danishes every morning! Her hips would protest, but her stomach would show them who's boss. Another apartment commanded a breathtaking view of Crystal Park, an oasis of cycads and ponds. Enamored with the view—one never saw plants on Cloventia—she almost bought that one. But she decided to check out a Dino Dome too. What the heck. Might be good for a laugh.

Holding her umpteenth cup of coffee, Simone walked toward a Dino Dome for sale. The home was small. Only one story tall. Probably smaller than the apartment above the bakery. The walls were round, the roof domed. A garden bloomed around the clay house, full of fruit trees and flowers. Even this late in the year, persimmons, apricots, and pomegranates filled the branches.

Laundry hung between the trees on a clothesline, and the smell of baked goods wafted out the round windows.

"Darwin's beard," Simone muttered.

Okay, the house was cute and all. But this was clearly the home of a grandmother. Simone was thirty-two, a worldly and educated career woman. She couldn't live here. The gardening alone would take up half her life. And a house like that demanded that she learn how to bake cupcakes. No. No, this wasn't for her.

She took a step away. She paused.

Cupcakes, eh?

Simone pursed her lips.

No, Simone. No. You're buying an elegant apartment that suits your life as a modern woman and . . . what the heck, cupcakes.

Simone walked back toward the house.

She knocked, and the owner opened the door with a smile. Indeed, a sweet grandmother. And indeed, she was baking cupcakes. She gave one to Simone. Lemon poppy.

It must have been the poppy that addled her mind. Poppy was a drug, wasn't it? Or perhaps it was the sleepless night. Whatever the case, Simone's mind was clearly addled. Because she bought the house that morning. Paid in full with cash. One cool million mints.

It was hers.

She had a home. A home of her own. That she owned. That she had earned.

Simone LaRue was officially a Mintarian. God save her. And God save Mintari.

The previous occupant had been an avid spoon collector. Spoons covered the walls, hanging from hooks or fastened to plaques. Spoons filled drawers. Spoons covered the mantelpiece, and Simone even found a few among the fireplace embers. There were spoons hanging on the bathroom walls and spoons dangling like Christmas ornaments from the trees outside. Many were ornate spoons, decorated or painted or adorned with gems. But most were just ordinary spoons.

When the grandmother finally cleared out her spoon collection (with the help of five hulking grandchildren), Simone realized how roomy the house actually was. With the mountains of spoons gone, Simone found two bedrooms, a living room with a cozy fireplace, and a little den by a round window overlooking the backyard.

Simone had no furniture. Nothing but the clothes on her back. Just her in this empty house full of echoes and the faded shapes of spoons on the clay walls. She was so tired that she simply lay on the floor, placed her head on a pillow, and slept for two hours. She woke up with a crick in her neck and new determination in her heart.

Fig would be coming home from school soon. Simone contemplated returning to the Fossil and Firkin to tend to the girl. But no. Fig was not a young child. She had survived for years in the dinosaur-infested outback. She could survive a day without Simone.

There was so much to do. Simone needed to paint the walls. To buy furniture. To get rid of whatever terrible flowers in the yard were making her sneeze. To fill the fridge with food. To call her parents to brag. To somehow pay for everything (she was broke again, after all). And to bake some cupcakes. Ideally more lemon poppy ones.

That could all wait. There was one thing Simone must do first.

She stepped out into the yard, trying to control her sneezes. She really did need to find out what plant was causing this. The milkman rode by on his chasmosaurus, tipped his hat, and waved to her. Simone waved back between sneezes.

"New here?" he asked.

Simone answered with a sneeze, a goofy smile, and a thumbs-up. The grandmother's late husband had kept some tools and slats of wood in the yard. Simone had never used any tool more complicated than a carrot peeler. But with a bunch of curses, a few splinters, and several band-aids, Simone managed to saw a rectangular piece of wood and attach hooks to the top.

She even found some blue paint and a small brush. Sticking her tongue out in concentration, Simone painted letters onto her makeshift sign. Her hands covered with blue paint, her hair a fright, her nose still runny, Simone stood on a ladder and hammered the sign above the door.

She took a step back, admiring her handiwork. She dusted off her hands and nodded.

"This'll do. This'll do just fine."

With a smile, she stepped into the house and closed the door behind her. One nail came loose, and the sign drooped, hanging crooked over the door. But anyone who passed merely had to tilt their heads to read the words painted in blue.

THE MINTARI POST

While Simone was setting up her new house, Fig sat alone at the Fossil and Firkin, gazing blankly into the fireplace.

She had skipped school today. Nobody had been there to wake her up, to drag her out of bed. Her father was at Fort George. Her grandmother was in the wild, roaming the land, healing the dinosaurs; nobody had seen her in months. Her aunt was leading an army of poachers. Now Simone—sweet Simone who was like family—had left too.

They all left me, Fig thought. *Humans are not like achillobators. They leave you so quickly. They are not pack.*

She had never felt so alone. Even here in the common room. A few of the regulars were here. Barnum was polishing the bar yet again. The tarry thing practically glowed by now. Abernathy sat in his usual rocking chair by the fireplace, whittling a maiasaura (it had started out as a parasaur until Abernathy accidentally chipped the crest off). Merl was slumped in his seat, snoring, crumbs on his overalls. Edna was solving a crossword puzzle, pausing now and then to spit into her spittoon. They were good people. But would they leave her too? If Fig's own family had abandoned her, why would anyone care for her?

I should run away. I should return to the pack. I should become a dinosaur once more.

Barnum approached her, carrying a mug of tea and a slice of apple pie. He set them down before Fig.

"Here ya go, cheesecake." The old man's eyes were kind. He wiped his hands on his apron. "You haven't eaten breakfast."

"Not 'ungry."

"Well, I'll leave the pie here for ya in case you change your—"

"I'll eat it!" Merl rushed toward the bar, wide awake now. He grabbed the pie, returned to his usual seat, and added more crumbs to his overalls. Within two minutes, the pie was gone and the big man was slumbering again.

A loud grunt sounded outside the saloon. Footsteps thumped. Plates rattled across the common room. Hanging above the bar, clay mugs jangled on their hooks. Fig gasped, hopped off her barstool, and raced to the window.

An ankylosaurus was lumbering into the parking lot. And he was a big one, almost as big as Dozer. Fig had seen these armored behemoths in the wild. Achillobators never hunted them. Even the largest predators like giganotosaurus avoided them. Their armor could crack the sharpest tooth. Their spikes could penetrate the thickest scales. Their clubs could knock out tyrannosaurs. Some claimed that T-rex was the most powerful dinosaur on Mintari, while others championed the triceratops. If you asked Fig, it was the ankylosaurus.

A saddle was mounted onto this particular ankylosaurus. Just as Fig reached the window, the rider dismounted, disappearing behind the dinosaur. She didn't get a good look at him, but he was heading toward the saloon doors. Fig returned to her barstool.

A moment later, the saloon's batwing doors swung open. A deep voice boomed through the common room. "Bring me four slices of your famous apple pie, Barnum! And coffee in the biggest mug you got. Black. Industrial strength."

A burly man stomped into the saloon, his spurs jangling. He looked about fifty years old, and he was built like his ankylosaurus. His shoulders were broad, his arms bulging with muscles, his legs like tree trunks, his chest like a barrel. He sported a graying beard, a Rangers uniform, and a ceratop hat.

Barnum nodded. "Glad to see you here, Chief! Been too long. I'm on it."

The big man approached the bar. "Thank you, Barnum."

With a groan, the stranger sat down at the bar, taking the stool beside Fig. His joints creaked, and he barked a laugh. "Yes, I'm creaking. When you're my age, Figaro, you will too."

She frowned at him. "Da a' knao you?" She tried again, more deliberately. "Dooo ayyyy know you?"

She stared at his broad face, olive-toned skin, and almond-shaped eyes. Eyes like hers. Eyes like her mother's.

He looks like me, Fig realized. *He's much older, certainly much bigger. But he looks like me. Like my mother.*

Then she noticed it. A platinum pin shone on his lapel, shaped like an ankylosaurus club. The crest of Clan Clubber. Her mother's clan.

The big man smiled and nodded. "My name is Arban Clubber. Mina Clubber was my little sister." He held out his hand for her to shake. "I'm your uncle."

Fig's head spun.

"I . . . I . . . I didna nao ma moda hadda bruda!" She took a deep breath. More carefully this time. "I . . . dint . . . know my . . . . moda had . . . a brudda. Brothhhffer." She ended up spraying saliva with that last word, and she cursed her clumsy tongue. He must think her a blathering idiot.

But Clubber didn't acknowledge her speech impediment. His eyes dampened. "You look so much like her. Just like her. You could be Mina reborn." Then he blinked, perhaps embarrassed by his tears. "Ah—here comes breakfast!"

Barnum placed four plates of apple pie on the bar, and he poured Clubber coffee into a pint-sized mug.

"Are you gonna eat *four* slices?" Fig asked her uncle, her eyes widening.

Clubber laughed. "No. I'm not a pig. Three slices for me. One for you. And I'll order more if you like."

Behind them, Merl perked up, perhaps hoping to eat Fig's second breakfast too. The big man looked like a puppy when you opened a bag of chips. But this time Fig decided to eat. She felt a little better. Maybe she wasn't so alone after all. Joe, Lifa, Amissa, Simone—they were all away. But she had met another family member. She already liked this Uncle Clubber.

She took a bite of pie. It was good. She sipped her tea. Also good. Clubber was already on his second slice.

That was when Fig noticed something. A brass megalosaurus footprint, symbol of Mintari, shone on Clubber's ceratop hat. She knew what that meant. He was the Chief Ranger. Head of the entire force. Her dad's boss. She remembered Joe talking about Clubber; he often ranted about how the chief worked him too hard. But she had never put two and two together, never realized the same Chief Clubber was her uncle. On hindsight it seemed obvious, but the concept of clans still confused Fig, and she had not made the connection. Why had Joe not told her? Was there bad blood between the two men?

She gulped down another bite of pie. "Sir. Why . . . did ma ded not tell me? Abit you?"

Clubber put down his fork and wiped his mustache with a napkin. "He's still sore with me."

Fig tilted her head. "Why? B-b-because you work 'im so hard?"

Clubber barked a laugh. "That I do. Yes, I suppose it's true. But no. Our beef goes back farther. I admit it, I didn't approve of Joe marrying my little sister. I was protective of Mina. Too protective. When Joe announced his intentions to marry her, I . . . reacted badly."

Fig gasped. "How?"

The big chief winced. "I punched your father in the nose. And . . . sort of . . . broke it."

Fig was struck dumb.

"Don't worry, we're on good terms now!" Clubber said. "Civil terms, at least. But I think Joe still holds a grudge. I don't blame him." He heaved a sigh. "At the time, I didn't approve of Clan Triplehorn. You know the story of your clan, I presume?"

Fig nodded. "My grampa sells w'apons to p'chers."

Clubber nodded. "Yes. Back then, I blamed Joe. I made a mistake. Maybe he hasn't fully forgiven me."

Fig lost her appetite. "Uncle Clubber, my dad . . . I miss him. Can you peese . . . not work 'im so hard? I only see 'im Sundays. Give 'im more time off!"

At once, she blushed. She sounded foolish. She could even see Barnum hiding a smile, busying himself with polishing a mug.

Clubber however did not smile. He stared into Fig's eyes. "We're fighting a war, Figaro. A hard war. A war against your aunt. Amissa is ruthless, and she has amassed an army she calls Hell's Hunters. Your father is one of my best soldiers. Maybe *the* best. But this war won't last forever. We will win!"

Fig lowered her head. Why did her family have to fight? Aunt versus uncle, Triplehorns versus Clubbers, humans versus humans . . . Fig felt caught in the middle. Once she had thought all humans were the same, but they divided themselves into clans and armies and killed one another. Life with the achillobators had been so much simpler. Achillobators were pack. Did humans have such loyalty?

Within ten minutes, Clubber had scarfed down his third slice of pie and emptied his mug of coffee. He wiped his lips. "I have to get back to it now, Figaro. Hell's Hunters do not rest, and neither can we. But I loved meeting you. I hope we can meet again soon."

"I'm here eve'y day," Fig said. "Come for b'ekfast."

Clubber rose to his feet. Fig hopped off her barstool too. She didn't even reach Clubber's shoulders. Almost everyone commented on her height. She expected Clubber to do the same. She braced herself for the usual "Wow, you're short!" But Clubber said nothing, simply shook her little hand in his huge paw.

"Unco C'ubber, before you go, can I pat your dinosir?" she asked on a whim.

"Of course. Bumpy is friendly."

They stepped into the parking lot. Bumpy stood in Dozer's usual spot, feeding on the same garden. Poor Barnum kept having to plant new begonias every week. Fig approached the ankylosaurus hesitantly. He was truly a remarkable dinosaur. A triceratops had impressive armor, to be sure. But only on the head. An ankylosaurus was armored head to toe, leaving not a single inch exposed. The body was a cuirass. The head was a helmet bristling with horns. Spikes as deadly as triceratops horns thrust out across Bumpy's flanks. They looked like scythes on ancient chariots (Fig had recently seen those in a book). Smaller spikes covered the dinosaur's back; the saddle was designed to fit atop them. Fig kept a safe distance from the tail. The club on the end was massive. The entire dinosaur probably weighed close to ten tons. Twice the weight of an elephant (Fig had seen elephants in the same book).

Fearsome as he was, the dinosaur was tame. Bumpy remained calm as Fig approached, step by careful step. She reached out gingerly and patted his head. It felt like patting a statue. Up close, she saw no chinks in the armor, not even thin cracks where the armored plates met. When he blinked, Fig saw that even Bumpy's eyelids were little bony visors. She could not imagine any dinosaur, not even a mutant T-rex like Ivan, piercing this armor.

But guns can, Fig thought. *Humans can.*

And she realized how selfish her earlier thoughts had been. She had worried so much about clans fighting clans, but this wasn't just a war between humans. Dinosaurs were in this war too. Both as victims and fighters. They told Fig she belonged to Clan Triplehorn. That her mother came from Clan Clubber. That she belonged in human society. But standing here, her hand on this dinosaur, she felt that her strongest connection was to Mintari itself, to the majestic animals who lived here. She would do anything to protect them.

She turned toward her uncle. "When I grow up, I want to be a Ranger too," she said. Amazingly, she had spoken that sentence perfectly.

"You will make a great one. You're a Clubber, after all." The chief climbed into the saddle. He tipped his ceratop at Fig. "Until we meet again."

He rode off, and Fig reached for the thong on her neck. Her achillobator claw hung from the leather strap. They said she was a Clubber, clan of the ankylosaurus. They said she was a Triplehorn, clan of the triceratops. But in her heart, Fig was an achillobator.

CHAPTER NINE
Between Rocks and a Hard Place

All that week at Fort George, Joe worried about home.

He shouted at recruits to run faster, tar it, while he remembered Simone storming out into the rain.

He taught recruits to lasso animatronic dinosaurs, and meanwhile he thought of Fig, alone in the Fossil and Firkin.

He guided recruits into the wild, showing them how to survive, and he imagined Simone roaming the streets, homeless and afraid.

He couldn't call them. At the fort, he was too busy. Out in the wilderness, comm signals were spotty at best; Hell's Hunters had been shooting down Mintari's satellites. Worse and worse scenarios danced in Joe's mind all week. Simone must still be homeless, lost on the rough streets of Dinovia. Fig was alone, no one to feed her, to tuck her in, to dress her for school, to make her brush her teeth. Every time he pictured them, his imagination made things worse. By Friday, Joe had convinced himself that Simone had found employment in a brothel and plunged into drug addiction, while meanwhile Fig had starved to death.

A part of him realized how silly that was. Simone was an intelligent, capable woman, and if Fig was anything, she was a survivor. But tar it, how could he not worry? He had caused this mess. He had driven Simone away. Now he was out here in the wild, teaching recruits to follow footprints, disguise their smell, and hunt poachers.

They didn't stray far from the city, thankfully. Not to the battle zones. This was just an exercise before the recruits graduated. But spending time in the outback stirred Joe's blood. It was almost Halloween, an old Earth holiday Mintarians still clung to. Six months since the great Battle for Dinovia. His leg was stronger. Almost as strong as before Amissa had shot it.

Soon it would be time to return to the wilderness for real. Not just on training missions but in battle.

Finally, on Saturday morning, they were back at Fort George in the city. Joe had no time to rest. Soon he must teach another group of recruits marksmanship. But he found five minutes to slip into the bathroom, close the door, pull out his SmartSphere, and make a call.

"Tar it, how do you use these things?" he muttered, fiddling with the device.

He only recently bought a SmartSphere. The latest and greatest model, apparently. Joe missed his old communicator. Heavy, boxy, did what you wanted it to do. Not much more sophisticated than a rock. Perfect. His new SmartSphere boasted all the bells and whistles. It could chart the stars, stream movies, play music, probably wash the dishes. It took Joe half his break just to figure out how to make a tarry call.

Finally he got it working. He called Fig's SmartSphere. Yes, the girl had one too. And despite literally being raised by dinosaurs, she figured out the tech faster than Joe.

"Ahoyhoy," she said. A hologram of Fig appeared inside the SmartSphere. Joe had expected to find her feral, probably crouching in a gorge while chewing on a hadrosaur rib. But she was clean, her short black hair was combed, and she even wore a school uniform.

"Fig!" Joe said. "Are you all right?"

She nodded. "Goin ta school soon." She yawned. "Sao early."

Joe exhaled in relief. "So Simone came back. She's taking care of you."

Fig grinned. "S'mone said I c-c-can stay wit her. In her new house." She waved the camera around, showing a dizzying sweep of a rounded clay living room. "It even nicer den our house!"

Joe's eyes widened. "What? She has a new house? She took you in?"

A voice came from behind the girl. "Calm down, Joe. I'm not claiming custody. The girl is just having a sleepover. She'll be back in the Fossil and Firkin for your day off tomorrow."

She did not appear on camera. But Joe knew her voice. It broke his heart.

"Simone?" he said softly.

"Here she is!" Fig said, turning the camera. But Simone dodged it.

"It's all right, kiddo," came her voice from off-screen. "Time for school."

A pale hand grabbed the camera. The call was cut short.

Joe sighed. Yep, she was still angry. Well, too bad! Joe wouldn't spend the rest of his life blaming himself or pitying himself. What was he, some kinda sissy? If Simone didn't want him around, well—her loss!

Ah yes, there was the famous Joe Triplehorn anger again. Well, it felt better than grief. So he stoked those flames. Part of him knew it was petty, knew this fire only burned himself and those he loved, but he could not resist its heat.

He stormed out of the bathroom. A recruit was waiting outside, holding his crotch, bouncing from foot to foot. The lad rushed into the stall. Joe marched outside and kept working.

Finally next morning—freedom.

He had twenty-four hours to mend things with his loved ones.

He was about to rush home when his SmartSphere rang. It took a while, but Joe managed to pick up. It was a clerk from Pangaea Hall, the seat of Mintari's government. The president wanted to speak with him. Right now.

It was Sunday. Joe just wanted to rush home to his daughter. He had no idea where Fig was, what she was doing, how she was handling everything. But when the president of Mintari called you, you showed up.

The new Pangaea Hall was still under construction. Amissa and her pack of tyrannosaurs had toppled the grand building. Half a year later, it was still a bustling construction site. Centrosaurs moved across the courtyard, digging holes with their long central horns. A brontosaurus stood by a half-completed rotunda, carrying a basket of bricks around her neck. Even Dozer was here, helping out. He was walking in circles, turning a winch, raising and lowering a makeshift elevator. Human construction workers bustled across the site, toiling alongside the dinosaurs.

Joe didn't like seeing this. Dinosaurs should be in the wild, not serving humans as living tractors and cranes. More than once, he had grumbled about it to his superiors, but it fell on deaf ears. Maybe they were right. This was a time of war. And everyone needed to carry their weight. Dinosaurs too. Joe paused to pat Dozer and feed him some apples, then had to leave his dinosaur and find the president.

Part of the new Pangaea Hall was already operational. In time, the government would gather under the new rotunda. Frescoes would adorn the round ceiling, featuring the majestic wildlife of Mintari. For now, Mintari's government operated out of smaller, humbler back rooms, working through the construction noises. Mintari was not like other planets. It had no glittering emperors like Cloventia. No brutal warlords like Earth. The population was small. It needed no tyrant with an iron fist. Mintari was a world beyond time. A world that looked to the past. And from the past, Mintari had taken a system called democracy.

Cloventians mocked it. They fancied themselves more civilized than that. What, to let the unwashed commoners, ignorant and petty, decide the leader? Why, they'd merely vote in fools like themselves! Hadn't those ignorant dinosaur riders learned anything from Earth history? Democracy gave rise to decadence, decay, and finally destruction. Well, the dinosaurs had ended with destruction too. Mintari was all about resurrecting old dead things.

A few Rangers stood guard outside Pangaea Hall, armed with sleep-or-dies. They nodded at Joe. He nodded back. He knew these men. Good men all. He had fought with them in this very city. Past the guards, he walked down a corridor. Clerks ran back and forth, busy at their tasks. A few rooms were missing some walls, allowing the wildlife in. A mononykus, a little bipedal dinosaur with an owlish face, was rifling through a garbage bin. A velociraptor brooded on a clutch of eggs near the watercooler, hissing at anyone who approached to drink. An ankylosaurus wandered outside the window, snorting, carrying a construction worker on his lumpy back.

Joe found the right room. A piece of paper was taped to the door. Somebody had written on the paper with a marker: BOB PROUDFOOT (GEOLOGIST & PRESIDENT).

Joe couldn't help but smile. He knew Proudfoot from way back. In the old days, they were both regulars at the Fossil and Firkin. The Proudfoots (Proudfeet?) were an old and (as their name implied) proud clan. Their house dinosaur was a diplodocus, and the sauropod represented their clan ideals. They were stalwart, strong, and benevolent.

He knocked on the door. A scratchy voice sounded inside the room. "Joe? Joe, is that you? Come in, lad. Come in."

Joe brushed dust off his uniform—with the construction going on, dust was everywhere—and entered the room.

He found rocks. Thousands, maybe millions of rocks. For a moment, Joe thought the room still lay in ruin. But this chaos was intentional. Bob Proudfoot was president now, but he was still a geologist at heart, and he had filled his office with rocks. They covered the shelves, the desk, the floor. They filled crates and baskets. Proudfoot displayed some in shadow boxes and glued others onto plaques. A few were crystals, but most just looked like ordinary rocks to Joe.

"President Proudfoot?" he asked, looking around.

An old man popped up from behind a pile of rocks. He held a stone in one hand, a magnifying glass in the other. He smiled, though his wondrous white mustache hid most of it. Like a typical Mintarian, he wore a safari outfit and ceratop hat, and round glasses perched atop his nose. Mintari was too small for a leader to get a big head and fancy clothes.

"Ah, there you are, my lad!" said Proudfoot. "Sorry if I seem distracted. Just got a new rock for my collection. A wonderful specimen! Cut from the bottom of a canyon. Fascinating composition of minerals."

He tried walking toward Joe but was yanked back. His long white beard was trapped between a few rocks. Clearing his throat, he extricated himself, approached Joe, and shook his hand. Or at least tried to. The old man was still holding his rock and magnifying glass. Flustered, he set them aside, then gave Joe's hand a good shake.

"Good to see you, lad! So glad to have you back in the city."

"Thank you, President Proudfoot, though to be honest, I would prefer to return to the field, to serve in the outback like—"

"Call me Bob! Like you used to. None of this President Proudfoot nonsense. Remember the old days back at the pub? Ah! I miss Barnum's shepherd's pie. Does he still make it?"

Joe nodded, smiling. "And it's still delicious. You should stop by sometime. In fact, I was just heading there."

"A not-so-subtle hint. Yes, yes, I know, lad. I dragged you here on a Sunday. I'm sorry. But these are dark times." His mustache drooped. "Dark times indeed." He shuddered, shook his head, and perked up. "How's your leg, Joe? Feeling better? You seem strong!"

Joe nodded. "It's healed. Almost entirely."

"Ah, good, good. Because I have a mission for you, lad. I'm sending you out to sea!" He slapped Joe on the arm.

At once, Joe saw it in his mind. Ryujin rising. The mosasaur crushing the boat in his mighty jaws. Over the past few weeks, Ryujin had struck six times, devouring swimmers, fishing boats, even one leisure pontoon. Nobody had ever taken footage of Ryujin. None that survived, at least. But the media had been replaying animations over and over, and in each one, the mosasaur was more monstrous. The *monstersaur*, the media had begun to call him.

"You're sending me after him, aren't you?" Joe said softly. "To hunt him?"

"Huh? What's that? No, my lad! No! If you're referring to the mosasaur, by Darwin's beard, no!" Proudfoot waved his hand dismissively. "An urban legend, if you ask me. No different from the legend of the fire-breathing Gojirasaurus, the furry Yetisaur who roams the arctic, or the dinosaur-human hybrids said to live in the sewers. Cryptids, my lad. Nothing but cryptids. Besides, I would never send you to hunt an animal. You're a Ranger. You're here to protect animals, not harm them. I'm sending you on a cruise, my lad!"

Joe blinked. He had certainly not been expecting *that*.
"Bob? *What?*"

Proudfoot barked a laugh. "You're going to love this, Joe.
Come, come, take a look!"

A spring in his step, Proudfoot hurried around piles of
rocks toward the desk. He shoved aside hammers, geodes, and
magnifying glasses. A white cloth covered a lumpy object on the
table.

Proudfoot grabbed the corner of the cloth. "Behold . . .
the *Maid of Mintari*!"

He yanked the cloth off, revealing a model ship. The cloth
snagged on the prow, nearly hurling the ship off the table.
Proudfoot caught the model and placed it back in position.

Joe frowned. "It's a cruise ship, all right."

"The first cruise ship on Mintari! Sorry for the bit of
drama with the unveiling and all. I figured this deserved some
flourish. Some panache! Well, what do you think of her?"

Joe stared at the model. He sighed. Proudfoot often came
up with elaborate schemes like these. The old man built the
models himself. Joe still remembered his model of a train track
through T-rex country, giving tourists a view of the carnivores.
And the pterosaur hang gliding idea. And the dinosaur petting
zoo. Eventually Proudfoot ran out of steam, realized his folly, and
added his ideas to the pile of "maybe someday." Joe would have
to convince him to mothball this idea too.

"To be honest, Bob, I think it's ridiculous."

Proudfoot chuckled. "I know! Isn't it though? A cruise
ship on Mintari! Who would have thought? But we polled the
tourists, and they love the idea. Love it, Joe! You see, my lad, until
now, tourists on Mintari could only see dinosaurs on land. But
what about all the wondrous life in Mintari's oceans? The
plesiosaurs with their long necks, the ammonites with their curling
shells, the—"

"—mosasaurs who would love to eat tourists," Joe said.

"Oh, pishposh! This ship is far too large for a mosasaur to handle. And look at this, Joe! The best part!" He raised the model, revealing a glass floor. "Ha ha! Splendid, isn't it? The floor is completely transparent, allowing tourists to see the underwater drama unfold."

Joe took a deep breath. "Bob, how long have we known each other?"

"Twenty years, lad! Or has it been thirty? I remember when you first became a Ranger."

"And I've always been honest with you. And I'll be honest now. This is a bad idea. Bob, wait! Wait. Before you say anything else, just listen to me. The oceans of Mintari are dangerous. Ryujin is not an urban legend. He's a real mosasaur. My daughter saw him. She survived an attack—barely. And Ryujin is only one of a billion enormous reptiles that live underwater. Sending a cruise ship full of tourists into Hell's Aquarium is a disaster waiting to happen."

To his credit, Bob Proudfoot listened until Joe was done speaking. The old man stepped toward a window. He looked out at the bustling construction. For a moment, the president silently watched a ceratopsian dig a foundation for a pillar. Proudfoot's shoulders stooped. He suddenly seemed so old.

"We're at war, Joe. A war we're losing. And wars cost money. You've been training recruits. How many young Rangers have you gotten ready to fight?"

"Thirty so far."

"We need thirty thousand. We need money, tar it. I never cared much for money. Nobody goes into geology for money. But now I'm president. A wartime president. News of this war is spreading. Tourist numbers have crashed. We need to lure them back. We need to offer an attraction to capture the imagination.

To bring in millions of tourists—and their wallets. We need an army, Joe. And we need to fund it."

Joe crossed his arms. "Well, Bob, how do you think the tourist industry will fare once a cruise ship full of families sinks?"

"It's not going to sink, tar it!" Proudfoot cried in a sudden blaze of emotion. He pounded his fist on the table, rattling the rocks, then took a deep breath. "Sorry. Sorry, my lad. I should not have yelled. I haven't slept. I can't sleep . . . Yes, maybe this idea is crazy. But we need crazy ideas right now." His shoulders stooped, and he looked at Joe, his eyes weary. "I was hoping you'd go on the ship. To protect the tourists. And, yes, to impress them. You're a bit of a celebrity, after all. Razzle dazzle them a bit."

"Bob. Listen to me. Listen carefully. This plan isn't just crazy. It's suicidal. You said we need money. Building a cruise ship would cost a fortune! No. Scrap the plan. Put the money into the Rangers instead."

Proudfoot blinked at him. "My lad. You don't understand."

Joe's heart sank. "Don't understand *what*."

"The ship is already built, Joe. It's waiting in the harbor. The *Maid of Mintari* sets sail tomorrow. And Joe—you need to be on that ship."

For a moment, Joe could just stand there among the piles of rocks, dumbfounded.

"You . . . already built the ship."

Proudfoot's eyes sparkled. The old man seemed positively giddy. "I did! Ha ha! It's wonderful, isn't it? As you know, Joe, I have a habit of coming up with great ideas and never following through. So I plowed ahead with this one before anyone could talk me out of it. The *Maid of Mintari* is waiting at Port Mary, just a two-hour drive away. You can be there for the maiden voyage! You'll love it, Joe. Take the family!"

"I will do no such thing. Tar it, Bob, this ship is a death trap."

The president lost his smile. He blinked. "But . . . but . . . we already sold tickets."

"Refund them."

Proudfoot sighed. "Now now, Joe, I know you have concerns. But a thousand people have already booked passage. That's a lot of mints. We can't just pull the rug out from under them."

"You can and you will. Tar it, Bob! Mintari's oceans are dangerous. They're filled with mosasaurs, pliosaurs, giant squids, armored fish the size of cars, and sharks big enough to swallow fishing boats."

"That's why you're going, Joe. To protect these people. And, um . . ." The president looked sheepish. "I also told the tourists you'd sign autographs."

"Bob." Joe grabbed the president of Mintari by the shoulders. "You're sending these people to die. I'll take no part in this. Goodbye."

He navigated between the piles of rocks toward the door.

Proudfoot's voice sounded behind him. "At least the young journalist is going."

Joe froze, one foot out the door.

Slowly he turned around. "*What* journalist."

Proudfoot's bushy white eyebrows rose. "She hasn't told you? Simone LaRue is going on the maiden voyage. She's covering it for the *Mintari Post*."

"The Mintari *what?*"

"Oh boy. Oh dear." Proudfoot adjusted his safari outfit and fiddled with his hands. "I thought you knew, lad. There's a new newspaper in town. In fact, why don't you ask her?" His face brightened. "Simone is here in Pangaea Hall, covering the construction!" He leaned his head out the window. "Oh, Simone, dear?"

Joe's heart sank to his pelvis. He missed life in a cave.

"What do you mean you're going?" Joe growled. "I forbid it."

Simone gasped, tossed her hair, and placed her hands on her hips. "You do not control what I do, Joe Triplehorn. I go where I please. And I'm going on that ship."

"It's a death trap!"

"So are you!"

They stood in the construction yard. Bumpy the ankylosaurus rumbled by them, a worker on his back. The dinosaur approached a slab of poured concrete and slammed his tail down, flattening the mixture. Other dinosaurs roamed about, busy at their tasks. Dozer was shoving piles of gravel with his frill. A construction worker was climbing a brontosaur's neck, carrying a bucket of mortar. He slipped, hung on his harness, and the bucket overturned. Bricks fell, nearly hitting plumbers who were laying a pipe below. Only by miracle was nobody hurt. Curses filled the construction site as workers bustled about, cleaning up the mess.

"Simone. Listen to me." Joe grabbed her arm and leaned closer. "That ship is heading into mosasaur-infested waters."

She wrenched herself free. "Don't you grab me, mister. I know what I'm doing." She raised her chin. "I'm a journalist again. I work for the *Mintari Post*." She tapped a sticky note on her shirt. "See this? A press badge. I'm done living on your terms. You can't keep me in a little room anymore above a bar, serving as your maid. I'm a career woman."

He blinked. "What? My maid? I never—"

"Yes, you did! You did, Joe!" Her blue eyes flashed, her cheeks flushed, and her red tresses bounced in rage. "For months you kept me cooped up in the Fossil and Firkin, tending to your daughter, while you were off gallivanting with the Rangers. Well, I have my own ambitions."

"Gallivanting?" He laughed mirthlessly. "*Gallivanting?* Simone, there's a war on! I was busting my butt, training recruits, fighting Amissa, while you got to sit at home in safety. Safety I provided! In a home I paid for!"

Her freckled face flushed red. "I don't need your money, O brave, tough Ranger. I have my own job. And my own home now. And my own life. And if you think you can control my life again—tell me where to go, what to do—well, you're in for a disappointment. I'm going on that ship."

"Well, so am I then!"

Simone frowned. She tilted her head. "What? What about the ship being a death trap?"

"It *is* a death trap. Which is why you need me there. To protect you."

She rolled her eyes. "Oh, for crying out loud, Joe! Stop being such a Neanderthal. When will you understand? I don't need your money. I don't need your protection. I don't need *you*!"

"Well, I need you!" Joe blurted out. He instantly shut his mouth. Why had he just said that?

She tilted her head in the other direction. "You what?"

He pursed his lips, cursing himself for his slip. What had he meant? The words had just slipped out.

"I mean—I need to be there. To protect everyone. Not just you. The tourists too. A thousand people." He pointed at her, glowering. "You're nothing special, cheesecake, so don't get any ideas."

"You need to protect us . . . from a mosasaur."

"And sharks."

"Mhm." She nodded. "What are you going to do, wrestle them to submission?"

"I could shoot them," he said stubbornly.

"That's your solution to everything, isn't it?"

"Well, at least it's something. I'm going on that tarry ship, Simone. And you can't stop me."

She harrumphed. "Well, fine!"

"Well, good then!"

"Good for you!"

Joe ground his teeth. "Well, I'll see you there."

She crossed her arms. "I certainly hope so!"

Joe walked away, leaving Simone behind in the construction site, and made his way onto the city streets. Somehow, and Joe still wasn't sure exactly how, he had just signed up for a cruise.

He definitely missed life in his cave.

"Okay, Figaro, let's go over this one more time. What time do you wake up?"

"S'ven," the girl said.

Joe nodded. "Good. And what time is the school dinosaur?"

"Ten in da mornin."

Joe sighed. "Figaro!"

"Oke oke." The girl grinned. "School dinosaur at eight. I wow . . . wow . . . *will* be on it."

They were in the bedroom they rented in the Fossil and Firkin. Without Simone living here anymore, the room felt so empty, so cold. And now Joe was leaving too. Soon only Figaro would be here. Alone. For a full week. Joe couldn't help but worry.

"And if Barnum's kitchen is closed, you know how to find the food in the freezer and operate the microwave, right?"

She rolled her eyes. "Dad! I know bata dan you."

"Better than."

She scrunched up her face. "Better d-d-thhfffffan." She ended up spraying saliva.

Joe sighed and wiped his face. "That's it. I'm staying home. I'm canceling the cruise. You need me here to watch over you."

"Dad!" She laughed. "I s-s-surrrvive living in w-a-ald-*wild* for f-fifteen years. I can survive a week da Fossil an' Firkin." She patted his shoulder. "Go on your romintic cruise wif S'mone."

Joe smiled thinly. "It's certainly not a romantic cruise. I'm sorry, Fig. I think I messed things up with Simone. I know you loved having her around." His voice dropped. "I did too."

Fig hugged him. "She loves you. Yes, you messed tings up. Go fix tings."

He held his daughter in his arms. "If only it were that easy, Fig. I'm not very good at this kind of stuff. Maybe nobody is. But I'll do my best to keep Simone safe. I can do that."

Fig held him tighter. "Keep yirself safe too. I'm scared. Scared of Ryujin."

"I know, Figgy. I know. That mosasaur is still out there. That's why I must go. To keep everyone safe."

She tilted her head. "What you gonna do? Shoot him?"

Joe laughed. "You and Simone! I don't know, all right? I'm best when I think on my feet." He checked the time. "I gotta go. Remember that if you need anything, Barnum is just downstairs. And Vinnie is here to guard you. Right, Vinnie?"

They looked over to the velociraptor. He lay on Fig's bed, curled up, snoring. Some watch raptor. Joe had to remind himself that his daughter was sixteen, old enough to survive a week on her own. But his parental instinct kept kicking in. So did the guilt that once more he must leave her.

He took a step toward the door, then looked back. "And remember. I'm just a SmartSphere call away."

"I know, Dad."

"You know how to work your SmartSphere, right?"

"Better den you."

He nodded. "Well, goodbye then."

Fig waved.

Joe stood still in the door, hesitating. Then he rushed toward Fig and hugged her again. "I'm sorry for all this mess lately, Fig. For not being here. For the trouble with Simone. For everything. Things will get better. I love you."

She smiled shakily, eyes damp. "Love you, Dad. Now go!"

When Joe stepped outside the saloon, Dozer was waiting there for him.

Joe patted the dinosaur's lumpy flank. "Feel like a ride, bud? We're heading to the port."

The triceratops tilted his monstrous head. He gave a questioning little whine. Joe imagined he was asking: "Where are Simone and Fig?"

"It's just you and me today, boy. Like in the good old days."

Dozer snorted and crouched. Climbing onto a triceratops was not trivial. Dozer made elephants seem like runts. From beak to frill, his skull was ten feet long. His horns were a foot wide at the base, and his legs made tree trunks seem like twigs. Joe grabbed one horn and pulled himself up with a grunt. His leg still hurt, tar it. Sometimes Joe thought it would never fully heal. Well, no need for anyone to know about that. He would hide the pain.

Finally he was seated on Dozer's back. He closed his eyes, trying to forget the pain. The dinosaur took a few steps, leaving the Fossil and Firkin's parking lot, then halted.

"Dozer?" Joe asked, eyes still closed. "Why did you stop?"

A sound from ahead—somebody clearing her throat.

Joe opened his eyes.

Simone stood on the road, blocking Dozer's way. She wore a safari outfit with a neckerchief and press badge (the "badge" was just a sticker on her shirt, which she had written PRESS on). Her red tresses spilled out from under her ceratop hat. She crossed her arms.

"Simone? What are you doing here?" Joe frowned. "I thought you were taking a jippi to the port."

She looked away and raised her chin. "I ran out of funds."

"Sorry about that."

He waited. She still stood there.

"Um, Simone?" Joe said. "You're in Dozer's way."

She placed her hands on her hips. "You're going to make me beg, aren't you?"

"I didn't say anything."

"Exactly!" Simone approached Dozer and pulled the dinosaur's beak down. She tried climbing Dozer's head, but she wobbled and fell. The trike nudged her with his beak, sniffed, and licked her, covering her with saliva.

"What are you doing, Simone?" Joe snapped.

She pushed herself up, shook off saliva, and shuddered. "Trying to climb onto your disgusting dinosaur."

Joe groaned. "Well, you don't climb up his beak!"

"That's how I always do it."

"Dozer, kneel!" Joe said. When the dinosaur was crouched down, Joe leaned over and reached down his hand. "Come on then, Simone."

She refused his hand. Instead, she tried climbing by herself. "I don't need your help."

"You literally need me to give you a ride."

"Nonsense." She slipped off Dozer's flank. "Dozer is giving me a ride. Not you. I don't need anything from you, Mr. Triplehorn."

She grabbed Dozer's horn with both hands. Groaning, she tried pulling herself up. Without much success.

"You can't even do a single pull-up, can you?" Joe asked.

She glowered. "Yes, I can." She tried pulling herself up again, then relented. "Shut up. I'm not used to Mintari's gravity."

"Or its strawberry strudels."

She gasped. "How—?"

He pointed at crumbs on her shirt. She quickly brushed them away, blushing.

Joe grabbed her and pulled her onto Dozer's back. He set her down in front of him. She wiggled into position, legs straddling Dozer's scaly back. The dinosaur's horned frill rose before her.

"I didn't need your help." She refused to look at him, and she kept her chin raised. "But thank you."

"Hold on."

She looked over her shoulder at him. "Huh?"

"Dozer—*dyo!*"

Joe kneed the trike. With a happy grunt, Dozer burst into a run, bouncing down the street.

Simone slipped sideways, screamed, and her ceratop fell off. Joe grabbed her with one hand, her hat with the other. He steadied her on Dozer's back and placed the hat on her head.

"I told you to hold on."

She gripped Dozer's frill. "You're loving this, aren't you?"

"You know what I love even more? Not going on cruises."

"So don't."

"Oh, you'd love that, wouldn't you?"

Simone groaned. "I should have hitchhiked."

Dozer slowed down to a steady walk, making his way through the city. They passed by flower shops, small galleries, cafés, and souvenir shops. The streets were quiet. The shops were mostly empty. The president had been right. Tourism was dying down. Who wanted to visit a planet where Rangers and poachers were shooting one another all day?

Tourism funded the Rangers. No tourists, no Rangers. No Rangers, the poachers would run wild. Lots of poachers? No dinosaurs. The logic was simple. Maybe the president was right. Maybe they needed more tourist attractions. Maybe Joe could do more good by performing than fighting. But tar it, Joe didn't have to like it. And he didn't.

Dozer trudged out the city gates, over the drawbridge, past the electric fence, and out into the countryside. Joe took a deep breath. He felt better at once. Whenever he left the crowded city, when he saw the rustling trees and smelled the fresh air, a change came over him. It was as if he remembered his true self. In the city, he was like a trapped predator prowling inside his cage, a withered ghost of the man he had been. Out here he was truly alive.

Simone apparently felt otherwise. She shuddered. "I hate it out there. Dinosaurs are going to eat us. I just know it."

"Don't worry." Joe pulled a bottle of amber liquid from his pack. "I brought T-rex urine. The smell will keep dinosaurs away." He uncorked the battle. "Want some?"

"Put that way! I'd rather risk a dinosaur attack." She paused and bit her lip. "Splash just a few drops. Onto my shoe." She grimaced. "This is disgusting."

"Sorry, cheesecake. You have to drink this kind." Joe began gulping down the liquid.

Simone turned green. "Joe!" She covered her mouth.

He lowered the bottle and smacked his lips. "Apple juice. You should see your face."

She flushed. "Give me that." She grabbed the bottle, drank, then shoved the bottle onto his chest. "Now don't bug me. I'm here for work." She rummaged through her pouch, then froze. She looked at Joe. "I forgot my notebook and pens. Turn this dinosaur around, mister."

"Sorry, cheesecake." Joe braided his fingers behind his neck and leaned back. "This is a one-way ticket."

"You are insufferable, Joe Triplehorn."

"Geez, maybe you should leave me."

"You can't leave somebody who's never there."

Those words cut him. But he deserved that. He said nothing more, and neither did she. They rode onward in silence all morning, heading toward the coast. Toward Hell's Aquarium. Toward Ryujin and his watery domain.

CHAPTER TEN
The Tears of Mintari

Mintari was weeping. Lifa felt it in the rain. She heard it in the wind. She saw it in the floods and fire and hills of carrion. Her beloved homeworld was dying. She was the last of the shamans, a wisewoman of the wild, a woman of medicine and worship, yet she could not heal this hurt.

She was an old woman now. Her back was stooped, her knees bent, her hair as white as trilliums. She limped across the wilderness, leaning on a gnarled staff. When she looked at her hand around the knobby wood, she did not recognize it. Her hands used to be so slender and quick, able to weave dreamcatchers, blend herbs, and heal hurts. Those hands were wrinkled and bent now. As Mintari withered, so did she.

Lifa hobbled along a misty glen. Bluebells whispered around her sandaled feet, and ancient cairns rose on the hills like stone giants, the resting places of ancient shamans. Lifa was the last of them now. The stewardess of a dying flame. The necks of sauropods rose in the distant fog, and the snorts of stegosaurs and ankylosaurs echoed in the valley. Grand as they were, the dinosaurs in the mist seemed like ghosts, flickering in and out of reality. Like this world, they were dying. And so they migrated, fleeing the burnt lands in the east in search of new forests. Lifa too was fleeing. And not just the flames but the horror she had unleashed.

Amissa had burned Lifa's home. She had burned the forests. She had slain the great herds and shot the flocks from the sky.

My own daughter.

Tears ran down Lifa's face, flowing through her wrinkles like rain in canyons.

A girl I abandoned. A girl I made into a monster.

Yes, Lifa had done this. She had started this great death. This extinction event. A spasm of pain crossed her, and she closed her eyes. In her mind's eye, she saw again Cloventia, a world of neon and glass and steel, a world conquered, a world where nature was not only tamed but extinguished. A world where she had languished. A world where a husband had beaten her, taunted her, broken her into a subservient, sniffling wretch. A world where she bore two children. A world she fled, taking one. Leaving the other behind.

Lifa fell to her knees among the bluebells. She wept in the mist.

"I tried to take you with me, Amissa," she whispered. "I tried. I battled the courts. I battled your father. But I was too weak. I abandoned you. And he broke you like he broke me. I was left in pieces. But you—he rebuilt you into a monster."

Lifa was a shaman, and she knew the circularity of life and good and evil. A blessing given returned with fortune tenfold. So did an evil deed multiply in the dark and return with a pack of astral curses. Now Lifa's sin came back to haunt her. And those astral curses took the form of her beautiful daughter.

Lifa kept walking through the mist, leaning on her cane, and came upon a skeletal dinosaur. A brontosaurus. A hill of decay. Little was left but bones, and even the scavenging theropods had abandoned the carcass. All that remained were dactyls who nested among the ribs, pecking at scraps of skin and offal. Lifa limped toward a hilltop, and when a gust of wind parted the mist, she beheld a field of dead sauropods like beached whales.

The skulls were missing. The poachers could not fit sauropods into their jippis. But they could take the heads. Little skulls for such large animals. Meaningless trophies. Senseless killing.

"You drove her to this, Tobias," Lifa whispered into the wind. "Because dinosaurs killed your parents, because I fled you to this world, because you're ashamed of your own Mintarian blood, you send our daughter to do this." A tear rolled down her cheek. "And I'm just as much to blame."

She followed the devastation. The trail of tragedy was always an easy one to follow. She passed by the misty sea of dead brontosaurs. She limped along the edge of a forest where jippis had knocked down the ginkgos, flushing out stegosaurs. Their corpses lay across the wastelands, their dorsal spikes and tails removed, gifts to hang on Cloventian walls. Some Cloventian restaurants used them as dinner plates. Atop a distant cliff, gunfire rattled. Rangers were battling Hell's Hunters in the wilderness. This was open war. As Lifa walked across the grasslands, she saw a tiny figure tumble down the cliff, flip in the air, fall and fall for what seemed like eternities before reaching the ground, and she realized it was a man. Another casualty of this war.

She tightened her hand around her staff, and she walked across the wastelands, moving toward the cliff, passing by burnt trees and dead iguanodons, their thumb spikes severed. She limped by a burnt jippi. Skeletons smoldered inside. For a moment, Lifa worried these were Rangers, that her son might be among them. But scraps of skin still clung to the skeletons, showing the tattoos of hunting gangs. Lifa kept walking. She would not pause to bury poachers. Twisted rifles lay mangled among the rocks, the bores molten and wilted. A dactyl scampered across the ground, playing with a cloven helmet.

Beyond a hill of fallen conifers, she found an overturned jippi, its side deeply dented. A pachycephalosaurus lay beside the abandoned vehicle, moaning in pain. His head sported a bony dome covered with knobs and spikes. The dinosaur was only the size of a horse, but with a powerful headbutt, he had managed to overturn a jippi the size of a triceratops. His domed head was now cracked, and bullet holes bled across his flank.

As Lifa approached the dinosaur, he mewled. He tried to rise and flee, but his legs buckled. Terror filled his eyes. Terror of humanity.

She knelt by the dinosaur. The domehead was too hurt to flee.

"Hush now, darling," she whispered. "I'm here to help. Be calm, child of Mintari. Be calm . . ."

She approached gingerly. Domehead dinosaurs could be deadly. Their thick, knobby heads could fell an allosaurus. But as Lifa approached, whispering soothing nothings, the dinosaur calmed. Lifa gently stroked his lumpy head. Blood trickled from his mouth. The bullet holes were deep. They had penetrated a lung. His breath rattled, grew weaker, slower.

Lifa reached into her pouch, mixed herbs in a bowl, and fed them to the dinosaur. He was so weak he could barely swallow. All Lifa could do now was give him this medicine for the pain, to be with him as he passed. She held his big lumpy head as he took his final breath.

"Go back now, child of Mintari," she whispered, cradling his lifeless head. "Go back to the soil from which you came. In the warm embrace of the world, you will bring forth new life. The energy in your body will feed the grass that grows and the trees that reach toward the sun. Flowers will bloom where you fell, and the rain will wash your blood away. You will be reborn. Rest now, child of life. We will always remember you, for you will never die."

Lifa rose to her feet, tears in her eyes. She walked onward
as ash fell from the sky, mingling with the autumn leaves and her
tears. Her old joints ached. A deep pain coiled through her chest
and wrapped around her heart, constricting her. A terror lurked in
her belly, filling the space in her womb where Amissa had curled
up, a bundle of so much hope and promise. For eight years after
Joe, Lifa had tried to have another child until finally—a little girl, a
miracle baby. She had nurtured the babe with her body and her
spirit, had given birth to a precious child, then morphed her into a
monster. Now—here all around her in this misty sea of
skeletons—her original sin came to claim its due, a
Rumpelstiltskin of rot.

Lifa reached the cliff. She found the man who had fallen.
He lay upon the rocks, gazing skyward. She had expected to find a
sight of horrors, but miraculously, his body was barely damaged.
If Lifa hadn't known better, she might have thought him asleep.
He was a young man in a tan uniform. His hat floated down the
river. A Ranger, probably not yet thirty. So many youths died in
this war while she, the old, lingered on.

She knelt by the corpse and lowered her head. With all her
heart, Lifa loved the life on this world. All life. The fireflies that
glowed at night, the flowers that bloomed toward the sun, the
magnificent dinosaurs who roamed the wild, risen again from the
ancient past like forgotten seeds sprouting after a long winter. She
had parted from many majestic beasts and trees, guiding them
into the beyond, and every one was precious, big or small. But
even she, a shaman of nature who shunned humanity, knew that a
human death was a unique tragedy, for every human soul was a
world entire, and Lifa's own soul tore.

"Why did you come here?"

The voice came from behind Lifa. The shaman had heard
her coming, of course. She kept her head lowered, kneeling before
the corpse.

"Did you kill him, Amissa?" Lifa whispered. "Is this your work? What you've become?"

"Turn around and look at me, Mother. You came all this way. At least look at me."

Lifa rose to her feet. The wind billowed her white hair, scented of wildflowers and death. She turned around slowly and looked at her daughter.

Amissa stood in the grass, the wind in her chestnut hair. Lifa's hair had once been that dark and lustrous. Now Lifa was gray and frail, while Amissa stood in the prime of her youth and strength. The huntress carried a bow, and two spears hung across her back. A chain of raptor teeth hung around her neck, and allosaurus teeth lined her belt. A scar ran across her forehead, and a strange fever filled her eyes.

She had changed. A year ago, Amissa would have worn makeup, not war paint. She would have worn a revealing shirt, not a tactical vest. She had been a queen of QuickFame, the Nyx system's most popular social media platform, broadcasting her kills to millions of adoring fans, as flirtatious as she was deadly. In a daring move, Simone had deleted Amissa's QuickFame account, stripping the huntress of her fame. And also of her persona, the mask she had worn for the masses. Now Amissa was hunting not for fame but for blood alone. She had gone savage.

She got a tattoo, Lifa noticed. A triceratops skull on her arm.

"Do you like it?" Amissa said, noticing where Lifa was looking.

"The symbol of Clan Triplehorn," said Lifa.

Amissa smiled thinly. "And of Triplehorn Inc. My father's hunting supplies company. The empire I will one day inherit. That's all this symbol means now." She bared her teeth. "This is the symbol of a warrior."

Lifa looked at the corpse that lay nearby. "Did you kill him? Did you shove this young man off the cliff?"

"Drove him off, actually. Ah, here comes the jippi!"

An engine roared. An enormous jippi came rumbling down the road, belching out smoke. Its six wheels were taller than Lifa, their deep treads finding purchase even on this rocky land. A cowcatcher thrust out the front, a monolith of metal splashed with blood. This gargantuan machine could knock down a sauropod. Several poachers rode inside, filthy and heavily armed. They stared at Lifa, eyes like stones. Eyes without humanity. Or maybe they were eyes full of humanity. Maybe that was what humanity was—death.

"They will kill anyone I ask them to," Amissa said.

Lifa stared at her daughter and raised her chin. "If that's a threat, I'm not impressed."

Amissa tossed back her head and laughed, but there was no mirth to it. Her laughter was a brittle sound like frozen branches threatening to snap in the wind. "If I wanted you dead, Mother, I would kill you myself. I could have many times. But no. Your life is worse than death. Look at you. Old and bent and homeless, roaming the wilderness like a wild animal. It's pathetic."

"There is wisdom in age and in nature, and the only life worse than death is a life that harms rather than heals. Amissa, I did not come to argue, and I did not come to die. I came to bring you home."

"Home? Ha! You mean your shack of straw and mud? Your home burned to the ground! I burned it!"

"All of Mintari is my home, for I was born of this world, and the blood of Mintari flows through my veins. As it flows through yours. You are of the wild, Amissa, and this world is your birthright. But you've not made it your home. You came here like a burglar in the night, sneaking through the window, while I was on the porch with a light, waiting to welcome you in."

Amissa's face flushed. "You abandoned me!"

"I did." Lifa's eyes dampened. "I abandoned you many years ago. I had my reasons, but none can excuse my sin. I left an innocent baby in the lion's den while I fled for my life, and for thirty-three years since, I've scorned myself and cursed myself and never forgave myself. Yes, I left you! But now I've come to bring you home."

Amissa bared her teeth, clenched her fists, seemed ready to shout. But her eyes dampened. She looked away. "It's too late, Mother. I'm not that innocent child you left behind. I'm a killer. I've killed many. I've killed scores of young men and women. You should not invite a predator into your home."

"It's never too late to heal," Lifa said. "Amissa, whatever you've done, I forgive you."

"You shouldn't forgive me!" Amissa said, fury burning away her tears. "I burned your house, Mother. I killed people. I murdered people." Her fists trembled. "I know what I am. I'm beyond forgiveness."

"Not all sins can be forgiven," said Lifa. "But a mother can always love her child. No matter what. And I love you, Am—"

"It's too late for that!" Amissa said. "Now you come and tell me that you love me? Now, after all this, after what my father turned me into?" She laughed bitterly. "No, Mother. Some sins are too dark and cold. They're like a tumor that can no longer be removed. Some cruelty even family cannot forgive." She narrowed her eyes. "There is no forgiveness for a mother who abandoned her child. And there is no forgiveness for what I've done. We are damned souls, Mother. The two of us."

Lifa stepped closer. "Shoot me then! Shoot me if you believe that, because we are better off dead than damned." She took another step. "Show me that you believe that! Show me that you think our lives no longer have worth."

Tears flooded Amissa's eyes. She raised her bow and nocked an arrow. "Stand back, Mother!"

"I will not. I love you, Amissa. I will not stand back and not deny that." She took another step. "I am taking you home, Amissa. I am—"

Amissa screamed. A terrible scream. A torn, hoarse scream that ripped Lifa's heart. A scream with years of pain behind it.

She fired her arrow.

It slammed into Lifa's walking staff, piercing the wood and jamming halfway through. Had the staff not stopped it, the arrow would have impaled Lifa's heart. She stood for a moment, stunned, shocked that she was still alive.

Amissa walked to the jippi. She hopped into the shotgun seat. A leathery old poacher sat beside her, gripping the wheel, his knuckles tattooed.

"Goodbye, Mother!" Amissa called out. "Fate saved you today. Or maybe it cursed you." She slapped the side of the jippi. "Roll out, boys! We got dinosaurs to kill!"

The poachers howled. The leathery old driver pressed down on the gas. The jippi rumbled by Lifa, splashing her with mud, then rattled off, blowing exhaust over her. From this angle, she saw what was in the cargo hold. Piles of parasaur crests, bundled together with bungee cords. Amissa's catch of the day.

Maybe she was truly lost. Maybe Lifa had been a fool to come here. Maybe they were both truly damned.

But all Lifa could do was continue to atone for her sin. Continue to stay true to her role as a healer of this world. She could not save her soul or the soul of her daughter, but she could still heal. If there was any purpose left to her life, it must lie there. With the last shreds of her being, she would serve Mintari.

So she buried the dead and prayed for him. And then she took the long, winding road around the cliff to the higher ground. By the time she had crested the escarpment, night had fallen. The Milky Way spread above, and countless stars shone. The twin moons of Mintari gazed down upon her. In the east shone Cloventia, a blue jewel, brighter than all lights after the moons. In the sky's zenith winked Sol, just a pinprick of light, the star which Earth orbited. The star that had given birth to all life on Mintari.

Atop the cliff, Lifa walked among dead parasaurs. The poachers had sawed off their crests and left them to rot. Already scavengers filled the night. Raptors and carnotaurs fed on the corpses. In the distant shadows, a black lump in the night, a bulky T-rex was ripping into a carcass. Hundreds of dactyls braved the darkness to swoop and steal chunks of meat. Every scavenger knew that by dawn the feast would end. They would not sleep this night.

Lifa walked among them safely, a little old woman limping between towering dinosaurs with no fear. They would not harm her. Partly because she wore the herbs and charms that kept them away. Partly because she was just a thin, bony morsel, and who wanted to chew on bones when one could dine on fatty carrion?

A whimpering cry rose ahead.

Among the dead of the herd, she found one.

A living parasaur.

The dinosaur was only a hatchling, but the poachers had still sawed off his crest, leaving him to die. And dying he was. His wound was grievous. The hatchling lay on the ground by his dead mother, bleeding from his head, mewling miserably. With his last strength, he was nudging his mother, trying to wake her.

Lifa tended to the youngster as best she could. She sedated him with herbs, fed him medicine, and bandaged the stump where his crest had been. The poachers had sawed right through the bone.

Lifa was not easy to anger. But now rage flowed over her sadness. Had Amissa done this with her own hands?

She let go of that anger, allowing it to flow over her like a storm. All storms eventually ended, emotional ones too. A new type of storm was engulfing Mintari now. A storm of guns and trophies and machines of cruelty. The victims of this storm lay all around, dead or dying. Lifa took deep breaths, reminding herself that all storms passed, but a fear filled her that humanity was not a storm. Humanity was an asteroid. And even the mightiest dinosaurs could not survive that.

She held the mutilated parasaur all night, cradling him in her arms, and Lifa watched the stars wheel by, these lights she had worshipped for so long. The explorers mapped these lights, and the scientists charted their celestial mathematics, but to Lifa they were the million eyes of the gods, watching over her, soothing her as if she too were a wounded child.

"There is more in this life than pain," she whispered to the hatchling in her arms. "Look to the stars, for they tell a story of hope and promise. Terror can come from the stars. Hunters and killers came from the stars and asteroids that struck with fire and ice. But we came from them too. We are star stuff, you and I. We fell from the heavens, and when we look above, we see the celestial lands that spread beyond our darkness. Our suffering cannot diminish them. No darkness can. In the glow of the stars, our pain eases and we see eternal grace."

The hatchling survived the night. On this night of so much horror, Lifa had saved a life. She was not damned, and she was not cursed. She could still heal.

CHAPTER ELEVEN
Maid of Mintari

In late morning, they saw Port Mary ahead. Almost every human on Mintari lived in Dinovia City. But a handful of crazy souls made their homes outside the walls. Joe could sympathize. One of those settlements outside of Dinovia was Port Mary, population fifty-one. Today, however, the coastal village bustled. Hundreds of jippis were parked outside in the field. An electric fence had been erected around the area, preventing a potential dinosaur buffet. An army of tourists chattered excitedly, took photos, and raided Port Mary's single pub.

Dozer made his way along the dirt road, following the jippi tracks. Sitting on the triceratops, Joe looked at the village and shook his head.

"This is a disaster waiting to happen. Look at it. No defensive walls. No moat. No armed patrol. Just a single fence . . . to protect a thousand dinosaur snacks. What will they do if a T-rex pack tears down the fence? Or if pteranodons fly over it?"

Simone smiled and patted his shoulder. "That's why you're here, isn't it, Jurassic Joe? The handsome hero, here to save the day! Well, the adequate-looking hero, in any case. You could use a beard trim and some exfoliation."

"And look like one of those pampered, soft-cheeked Cloventian tourists? No, thanks."

She rolled her eyes. "Typical macho Mintarian. Thinks washing is for sissies."

"I wash!"

"In a proper shower. With soap. Not that bucket and lump of tar you use."

"It's pine tar. It's good for you. Puts some hair on your chest." He shook his head in disgust. "I bet in Cloventia, you bathe in tubs of milk and rose petals."

"I'm a Mintarian now," she said. "Just like you."

"Great! You can start using tar soap."

"I'm moving back to Cloventia."

A few tourist children ran toward them, waving action figures.

"Look, look!" cried a boy. "It's Jurassic Joe!"

"Jurassic Joe!" the other children echoed, brandishing their toys.

Joe felt himself blush. Apparently he was something of a folk hero on Cloventia. Simone had told him about that. Not bad-looking toys, he had to admit. They cut quite the heroic figure.

"You look handsomer in plastic," Simone whispered to him.

"The toys look exactly like me."

She nodded. "Maybe the vacant eyes."

As Dozer walked closer to the village, the children scampered alongside, making their little Joes fight, fire tiny sleep-or-dies, and ride plastic dinosaurs. The president had sent Joe here to impress the tourists. Bring some star power. Maybe it wasn't such a bad idea after all. Was it so terrible to be adored?

"Good morning, children." Joe tipped his hat. "Would you like me to sign some autographs?"

Simone snorted so loudly her hat fell off. She caught it before it could tumble to the ground. But not before her mane of red hair billowed in the wind, a fiery banner.

The children gasped.

"It's Simone LaRue!"

"From TV! Star of *LaRue's News*!"

"She's famous."

"Her show was canceled."

"So? There are reruns."

"Simone, Simone! Can you sign our autographs?"

She beamed. "Of course! Happy to. If *somebody* would have turned his dinosaur around when I asked to get my notebook, I'd have paper for autographs." She said that last part in a low voice for Joe's ears only, then smiled at the children. "Who wants their passports signed?"

"Me, me!"

Simone glowed as she signed autographs, replacing the dots atop the i's with hearts. "Watch and learn, Joe. Watch and learn."

They entered the coastal village. The crowds parted to let Dozer pass. Many tourists reached out to touch the dinosaur and feed him leaves.

"*Torikeratopusu, Torikeratopusu!*" cried a group of delighted Japanese tourists, snapping photos. Before crumbling with the rest of Earth, Japan had built huge, self-sustaining space stations across the galaxy. Living in those floating rings the size of cities, the Japanese maintained their old culture. And they loved visiting Mintari on holiday. Or anywhere with fresh air.

Dozer tolerated the photos and pats. Most triceratops were dangerous. They were surly dinosaurs by nature, aggressive and territorial. A typical trike would likely trample and gore any human who tried patting him. But Dozer was used to humans. He put up with them, even seemed to like them.

A sigh rolled through Joe. He hoped Dozer was not becoming domesticated. This planet needed to be pristine. A place where dinosaurs could live free of human influence. But lately that vision was crumbling. Poachers were an obvious evil. But even the Rangers, humans tasked with protecting dinosaurs, negatively affected these magnificent animals. Dozer was just one example.

There were also the dinosaurs on the construction sites. The dinosaurs who lived along the paths of tourist jippis, inhaling their fumes. And now humans would disrupt Mintari's marine life with this cruise ship. Tourism was essential for funding the Rangers, for protecting the dinosaurs—yes, Joe knew that. But tar it, it still felt wrong. An evil committed for the greater good was still an evil.

Maybe he was being overzealous. After all, these were not *real* dinosaurs. At least not actual dinosaurs from Earth's past. They were echoes. Animals recreated from ancient DNA, grown in labs and set loose on a distant planet. Humans had made them, brought them here. Did humans not have a right to interfere?

No, Joe decided. *We don't.*

Because these weren't just robots roaming around Mintari. They were living, sentient beings, animals with thoughts and feelings and personalities. Humans might have resurrected them. But humans were also harming them. Humans and wild animals simply did not mix. They could not coexist. Earth had proved that. Cloventia proved that. Mintari belonged to the dinosaurs. Joe could not eliminate human interference on this planet. But he could minimize it. That was still a war worth fighting.

They reached the water. Port Mary was built on the coast of a large, semicircular bay. Awning Sea spread to the horizon, deep blue mottled with green. Beyond distant islands, the sea plunged into the deeper, colder waters of the open ocean. Both Port Mary and Awning Sea were named after Mary Awning, a paleontologist from ancient Earth. Over a thousand years ago, she had dug up Jurassic marine fossils. Today many of those ancient reptiles swam in Mintari's seas.

Most people had a more colorful name for this sea. Hell's Aquarium.

A boardwalk, a saloon, a few piers, and a lighthouse comprised the port. Normally this place didn't get much traffic.

On most days, only fishermen, scientists, or the odd adventurer launched off these docks. This was where Fig had come with her friends, a midnight adventure that ended in tragedy. The president should have shut down the port then. Not only had it stayed open—now a huge cruise ship waited in the bay, large enough for a thousand tourists.

Dozer stood by the shore, his nostrils flaring to inhale the salty sea air. Sitting on his back, Joe stared at the cruise ship in the bay. There she was. The *Maid of Mintari*.

"By Darwin's beard, she's ugly," Joe said.

"She's beautiful," Simone breathed. "She looks like a starship."

The *Maid of Mintari* was small compared to the cruise ships of Earth's golden age. But she was still tarry massive, roomy enough for a thousand tourists. And hundreds of crew members. Portholes lined her white hull. Her upper deck featured a pool and potted palm trees. A hundred Mintarian flags adorned her, featuring golden megalosaurus footprints on crimson fields.

"It must have cost a fortune," Joe muttered. "This is an extravagance we can't afford."

"You need to learn the concept of ROI, my friend. Look at all those tourists with fat purses." Simone raised her SmartSphere and began snapping photos. "Joe, lean a bit left. I want to get you and the ship in one photo."

"What?" He frowned. "Why?"

"It'll look good on the front page of the *Mintari Post.*"

He rolled his eyes. Simone snapped a photo.

"A journalist. Great! She's a journalist again." Muttering under his breath, Joe dismounted his triceratops. "She couldn't choose a normal profession. A bricklayer or actuary or something. She has to take photos of me for a living."

Simone didn't hear him—or pretended not to, at least. She had hopped off Dozer and was interviewing tourists along the boardwalk.

The port was too small for the cruise ship to dock. At noon, the *Maid of Mintari* sent over a fleet of boats. From what Joe could tell, they were the lifeboats, and they doubled as ferries.

"Are these all the lifeboats you have?" Joe asked one of the boaters, a pimply teenager. The kid wore an old-fashioned sailor suit, complete with a blue neckerchief and white cap.

"Yep!" the boy squeaked. "We got twenty boats. We'll need to take a few trips to ferry everyone aboard. Take a seat, sir!"

Simone waved at him. "Hey, you're the kid who sold me strawberry strudels. What happened to your job at *Jurassic Perk*?"

The kid blushed. "Um, they found a hair in a strudel, and—"

"Twenty lifeboats?" Joe cried, grabbing the kid's neckerchief. "And you can fit, what, ten people in each one? There are a thousand passengers booked on this cruise! What if disaster strikes? How the tar pit are we going to save a thousand souls with only twenty boats?"

The squeaky-voice teenager gulped. "Um, sir, you'll have to speak to the captain."

"Oh, ignore him!" Simone told the kid, stepping into the boat. "He just gets nervous around boats. And people. Joe, get in here!"

Grumbling, Joe stepped into the lifeboat, rocking the little vessel. He glared at the kid in the sailor suit. "She's a journalist. This is all going into her report."

The teenager's eyes widened. "Whoa, Simone LaRue! It really is you! Can I have your autograph?" He blushed again. "And, um, can you not write about the hair in the strudel?"

Joe was ready to hurl himself into the sea.

A gaggle of tourists leaped into the lifeboat with them. There were eight of them, all young women on a bachelorette trip. The bride-to-be wore a frilly white safari outfit adorned with lace. Her bridesmaids wore purple safari outfits and rhinestone-studded ceratop hats.

"This is a mockery of our culture," Joe muttered. He stood up in the boat, ready to give the women a piece of his mind.

"Sit down, Joe!" Simone whispered firmly, pulling him onto his seat. She smiled apologetically at the tourists. But the young women hadn't noticed a thing. They were busy draining schnapps bottles, taking selfies, and emitting scattered "woos!" and other celebratory noises.

The other lifeboats filled up. Unfortunately, Joe had to leave Dozer behind. The triceratops would spend the week around the port, grazing, relaxing, sunbathing, and maybe fighting other dinosaurs if he found any. Joe was envious.

"Taking a cruise in mosasaur-infested waters," Joe muttered to himself. "What could go wrong?"

The boats puttered toward the *Maid of Mintari*, this garish floating palace. The tourists pointed at the ship and oohed and aahed. Other than the bachelorettes, who emitted more "woos!"

Joe ignored them all. He wasn't looking at the ship. He was looking down at the water, and in those murky depths he imagined the coiling, hungry terrors.

"Out of my way, tar it!" Joe barked at a group of chatting tourists. He elbowed his way down the corridor, trying to find his cabin.

"Joe!" Simone grabbed his elbow. "Calm down! You're a role model, remember? Can you try not acting like a grumpy old pachycephalosaurus?"

"If I were a pachycephalosaurus, I'd use my domed head to clear a path," he muttered.

The corridors of the *Maid of Mintari* were narrow, and crowds packed them. The bachelorette party was squealing louder and getting drunker. Families herded excited children and carried crying babies. A handful of robed pilgrims knelt down to pray. A group of seniors stopped in the corridor to chat.

The walls seemed to close in around Joe. His head spun. He was trapped. He couldn't get out. The ship could sink and he would die here among singing bachelorettes and crying babies. He closed his eyes and took deep breaths, trying to calm himself, but only smelled the perfumes, dirty diapers, and alcohol, and he couldn't keep out the endless noise. He needed to leave this ship! He needed to escape this crowd! He couldn't breathe. He couldn't—

"Joe, it's all right." Simone's soft voice flowed through the cacophony. He felt her hand on his arm. "I'm here. It's all right."

Finally the seniors moved down another corridor, the bachelorettes tottered off to the bar, and the traffic jam eased. Joe took a deep breath and kept walking.

"I'm fine," he said. "I just don't like crowds."

Simone cocked an eyebrow. "Did you spend your life living in a cave or something?"

"Or something," he muttered. "You don't need to look after me, Simone. I'm here for work. So are you."

She flinched a little at his brusque words but then nodded briskly, her red tresses bouncing. "Don't worry, Joe Triplehorn. You do your job. You'll barely notice I'm on this ship."

She walked down a corridor. Joe watched her leave, and once she vanished around a corner, he felt oddly empty. He missed her already.

Oh, grow up! he told himself. *She's over you. Let her go. Stop pining like a boy. And you're on duty.*

Even though he was on a leisure cruise, he was here as a Ranger, tasked with protecting these people from the ocean wildlife. And protecting the ocean wildlife from these people. He wore his uniform, badge, and ceratop hat. He had even brought his sleep-or-die. The double-barreled rifle hung across his back. In "sleep" mode the rifle shot tranquilizer darts. In "die" mode it fired bullets. Joe hoped he wouldn't need his gun on this cruise. But in case he did, his sleep-or-die was a powerful, reliable weapon. It was even waterproof. Useful on a cruise.

Bring it on, Ryujin, he thought, imagining himself filling the brute's head with bullets. Normally Joe did not condone violence toward animals. He would make an exception with the mosasaur.

Putting thoughts of violence aside, Joe checked his ticket. Proudfoot had booked him a cabin. One among hundreds on this ship. Hopefully, Joe could spend most of his time locked in his room, sleeping through this nightmarish cruise. He already regretted coming.

Joe followed the signs, making his way to deck 3, corridor L, cabin 305. He finally found the right door. There was no key. Electronic lock. Joe fiddled with his SmartSphere, searching for the *unlock* app. How the heck did this thing work? He tapped a few buttons, struggling with the tarry device.

"You have to slide the permission toggle over," Simone said. "The app won't work otherwise."

Joe looked up, frowning. Simone was back. She stood one door down, her SmartSphere in hand. She loaded her unlock app, slid a toggle bar, and her door clicked open. She flashed Joe a smile.

He frowned. "*That* is your cabin."

She nodded. "Yep, 304."

"Right beside my cabin."

"So it would seem."

Joe scoffed. "How did this happen? Did you book the next-door cabin on purpose?"

"Joe, if I had my way, we would be on entirely different ships. Cruising on different oceans. On different planets." She shrugged. "I guess fate has a way of keeping us together." She winked, then stepped into her cabin and closed the door.

Joe spent a while longer in the corridor, struggling with the app. He cursed, shook the tarry sphere, and was almost ready to bang the door down with his fist.

"The toggle on the bottom right!" Simone cried from inside her cabin.

Joe finally got it to work. His door clicked, he stepped into his cabin, then closed the door behind him. There was a bunk bed, a desk, and a porthole overlooking the sea. It seemed comfortable enough, and—

He did a double take.

Hang on. A bunk bed?

The cabin door opened again. A man stepped in. He wore a Hawaiian shirt, sported cheap plastic sunglasses, and smoked a cigar. "Ahoy, mate! Whoa. Didn't realize I'd have a roommate. Nice to meet ya!" He held out a hand. "Name's Ehren. From Ehren and Ezra's HAV repairs. If you ever need a furnace fixed, we're your best mates."

Joe stared at the proffered hand. It was covered with moisturizer.

A loud *bang* sounded on the wall.

"Oi, Ehren!" A deep voice came from the cabin next door. "You there?"

Ehren gasped and banged on his side of the wall. "Ezra! Bonza, mate, I can hear you perfectly! We can talk through the wall all cruise long."

"I can see you!" said Ezra. His shaggy, bearded face appeared in the air vent. "You won't believe who I'm sharing a cabin with. Simone LaRue!"

"Whoa!" Ehren said. "Can I get her autograph?"

Simone's face appeared in the vent too. "Um, boys? Would one of you like to switch rooms? I don't think I can handle you two talking through the vent all week."

"Sure!" said both furnace repairmen.

Joe cleared his throat. "Does anyone care what I think?"

"No!" said Simone, then her face vanished from the vent.

Within a moment, the two repairmen were in cabin 304. And Simone LaRue was unpacking her suitcase in cabin 305. Here with Joe.

"I call top bunk!" she said.

Joe sat down on the bottom bunk and heaved a sigh. The ship hadn't even set sail yet, and he missed training recruits already.

With great aplomb, the *Maid of Mintari* set sail on her maiden voyage. Joe wanted to stay in his cabin, but Simone dragged him onto the upper deck.

"I'm a journalist and I must be there."

"Why do I have to go?" Joe said as she pulled him down the bustling corridor.

"Because you're here to protect me from monsters, remember?"

"I don't see any monsters. Well, maybe those bachelorettes." They were drinking and wooing again.

Joe and Simone wormed their way between carousing tourists and onto the upper deck. It was late October (Mintari had adopted the names of Earth months for convenience, though a Mintarian year was slightly shorter). The day was brisk, the sky cloudy, the wind cold. A tarry foolish time to take a cruise, if you asked Joe. Then again, he thought any time was foolish for a cruise. The tourists didn't seem to mind the bad weather. They crowded on the deck, drinking, singing, snapping photos. A few drunken "woos!" sounded from among them. Joe could guess who was responsible.

Simone dragged Joe toward the railing. Many tourists were here, leaning over the rails, seeking monsters in the water. The ship was still inside the bay. Port Mary was just a short swim away. The water here was shallow and green. But the aquatic show already began. Thousands of glowing jellyfish filled the water, purple and pink and bluish. Every once in a while, they sparkled with electricity. Tourists pointed and snapped photos. A dactyl swooped from above, grabbed a sea turtle, and flew off. More oohs and aahs from the tourists.

"See? It's not so bad," Simone said.

"Just wait until we reach deep waters and the mosasaurs and pliosaurs show up," Joe said. "Then there'll be less cheering, more screaming."

She shoved him playfully. "Grump."

Dignitaries lined the Port Mary boardwalk, here to see off the ship. President Proudfoot had come, riding a diplodocus, his clan dinosaur. Several prominent clan chiefs stood alongside the sauropod, old and wise, tracing their ancestry back to the original founders of Mintari. Like all Mintarians, they wore simple safari outfits and ceratops, but there was no mistaking their importance.

Their squared shoulders, raised chins, and straight backs proclaimed their power.

Only Proudfoot had brought his clan dinosaur with him. But even from this distance, Joe recognized the different clans. Chief Greatwing was here. Before eschewing civilization, Joe's mother had belonged to Clan Greatwing. They were an ancient, proud clan who could tame and ride pteranodons. Chief Clubber was not here; he was busy leading the Rangers in war. But the brave and warlike Chief Rex had come, representing the *Tyrannosaurus rex.* The Rexes were an aggressive clan, fierce rivals of the Triplehorns. Chief Sharptail, Chief Headstrong, Chief Longclaw, Chief Hardback, and a dozen others—they all stood along the boardwalk, come to see the *Maid of Mintari* set sail. This was a bigger day than Joe had realized.

They're broke, Joe thought. *We all are. Mintari can't compete with my family's wealth.*

He winced. His family. Clan Triplehorn.

Nobody from Clan Triplehorn had come. The chief of his clan, Tobias, was waging war against Mintari. A traitor. A king of poachers. Clan Triplehorn was disgraced.

Joe tightened his lips.

No. There *was* one Triplehorn here. *He* was here. And he wasn't just on the boardwalk, come for some ceremony, but stood here on the ship, ready to do whatever he could to save Mintari.

"Mistew Twiplehown, siw?" came a voice from below. Joe looked down. A little girl stood beside him, holding a Jurassic Joe action figure. "Can you sign my doll, siw?"

Joe nodded. He signed the action figure's chest. The girl hugged her toy and ran off.

Yes, Joe would do anything for this world. Even go on a cruise and sign autographs. This wasn't the usual way Joe fought a war, but these were strange times.

Fireworks burst above. The crowd cheered. And the *Maid of Mintari* set sail, leaving the bay and entering the vast waters of the open ocean. The ship's engines hummed, rippling the water. From up here on the deck, the tourists could barely hear the sound. But underwater, great propellers spun, churning the ocean, slicing up kelp and fish, casting sound waves into the depths.

Far from the ship, deep, deep underwater, a great reptile stirred. A red eye opened. An enormous mouth gaped in what almost looked like a smile.

The party never stopped aboard the *Maid of Mintari*. Joe roamed the ship, prowling and scowling, a predator in a cage. Everywhere he looked—problems. Not enough lifeboats. No armed guards at all. He was the only one here with a gun, it seemed. It took him an hour to find the life jackets, and there were barely any life preservers. Constantly those tarry engines were roaring, grumbling, and rippling the water. To Mintari's marine animals it must sound like an erupting volcano. Not to mention all the other noises—humans singing, music blasting, and somebody had organized a drum circle on the top deck.

"Look at this." Joe shook his head in disgust. "A scuba diving station? Are you serious?"

A tourist couple stood on the upper deck, zipping up their scuba gear. Their instructor stood beside them, chewing his lip. "Um, sir, who are you?"

Joe tapped his badge. "Joe Triplehorn, Mintari Ranger. Who authorized this scuba station?"

"You'll have to talk to the captain, sir."

"Everybody keeps saying that," Joe muttered.

He had sought out the captain an hour ago, only to find the man in the disco, dancing with three women, downing shots between songs. Joe looked around. And there was the captain again, here on the upper deck. The man was slumped in a lawn chair, sound asleep, his snores ruffling his white mustache. Judging by the number of empty bottles around him, he could probably sleep through a mosasaur attack.

Joe turned toward the would-be scuba divers. "This ocean is swarming with man-eating predators. Stay. Out. Of the water."

The tourists gulped and removed their goggles.

"Simone." Joe approached her by the pool. "This ship is a disaster. Everything here is a liability—both for the tourists and the marine animals. I need your help."

Simone cleared her throat. "Joe, I'm in the middle of an interview."

An elderly Japanese couple stood before her. They wore dinosaur hats and carried big cameras around their necks.

"Blast it, Simone! Your audience doesn't want to hear some tarry tourists blabbering about the buffet. You want a scoop for the *Mintari Post*? How about this scoop—this ship is a death trap, and I can prove it."

The tourists blanched. The husband gulped and nearly fainted. His wife ushered him toward a lawn chair by the pool. They nearly tripped over the captain's empty bottles.

"Good job, Joe." She slapped him on the arm. "Give the tourists heart attacks, why don't you?"

"Better that than a mosasaur attack. Come with me, Simone. We're going to prepare a scathing report about this ship. I'll find the violations. You write them down. Together we'll blow the whistle off this ship."

Simone heaved a sigh. "Joe, do you ever have fun?" She gestured around her. "Look at this place! A pool. A bar. There are mai tais. Palm trees. Real ones too! This is the garden of Eden."

"And we know what happened to Adam and Eve. Now come on, let's go to—"

"Joe, look!"

Simone pointed off the starboard beam. Other tourists were pointing too.

Turtles were swimming alongside the ship. Gargantuan turtles. They were bigger than the lifeboats. If you hollowed out their shells, you could park a car inside. Their beaks were large enough to swallow a human.

"What are those?" Simone whispered, eyes nearly popping out.

"Archelons," Joe said. "Turtles from the Cretaceous era. The largest turtles to ever live."

"They're the size of whales!" Simone said.

"Not quite, but yes, they're big."

One of the turtles reared from the water, opened its beak, and let out a bugling cry. Its flippers smacked the water. Those flippers ended with claws like swords.

Simone gulped. "Do archelons eat humans? Those beaks look sharp." She stepped closer to Joe and held his hand.

"Usually not, but I heard they find redheads irresistible."

"Well, that's something you and they have in common, Mr. Triplehorn."

Tourists were pointing and snapping photos of the turtles. Nobody was at the bar or pool anymore. Everyone was leaning over the railing, marveling at the sight. A pimply teenager in a sailor suit approached. Joe recognized the kid from the boat.

"Sir, ma'am, would you like a souvenir photo taken?" the kid squeaked.

"No," said Joe.

Simone slung her arm around Joe. "Yes. Smile, Triplehorn!"

She grinned. He scowled. The kid snapped a photo and handed it to them. "You two make a lovely couple."

"We're not a—" Joe began when everyone started shouting.

He turned toward the water.

Simone clutched him and let out a deafening scream.

An enormous creature burst from the water. It made even the car-sized archelons seem small. At a glance, it looked like a gargantuan crocodile. It had the scaly skin, the big jaws, the sharp teeth. But this reptile had flippers instead of feet, and a fin like a shark's rose from its back. The sea monster's jaws opened with a ravenous cry.

"What is that?" Simone cried. "Is that Ryujin?"

"No, it's not a mosasaur," Joe said. "Too small. This here is a liopleurodon." He grimaced. "You're crushing my arm. Let go."

She tightened her grip. "Never."

A few tourists gathered around Joe, curious to learn more. Reluctantly he kept explaining. "Liopleurodons lived in the Late Jurassic. They swam in seas that covered what is now Europe. They were the apex predator in their environment. Look at their fins. They're like paddles, and they've got four of them. They're powerful swimmers, able to propel themselves at staggering speeds. They're also ruthless hunters. Look."

Off the starboard bow, the archelons were fleeing. The turtles looked like they could munch on sharks for breakfast, yet now they fled for their lives. The liopleurodon pursued. Its four flippers moved like propellers, shoving the reptile forward so fast it looked like a machine.

The beast's crocodilian mouth opened wide, ready to feed. A fleeing archelon raised its flipper in defense, lashing his claws. The liopleurodon leaped through the air, dodging the attack. The reptile soared over the turtle, revealing its entire body. It was easily the length of a bus. The scaly predator dived into the ocean, raising foamy waves, and vanished into the depths. Water splashed the cruise ship, drenching the tourists. A few people cheered.

For a moment, nothing happened. The archelons slowed down, scanning the water, seeking their tormentor. Had the predator fled?

Then the mighty reptile burst from below, slamming his snout into the underbelly of an archelon.

The car-sized turtle flew into the air, flipped upside down, and slammed back into the water. The turtle floundered, its shell in the water, its flippers in the air. It splashed and snapped its beak, blind with surf, unable to right itself, unable to swim.

It was the opportunity the liopleurodon needed. The carnivorous reptile attacked. It bit the turtle's flippers, dragged the claws underwater, then lunged and savaged the underbelly. Though it lacked a shell, that underbelly was not soft. Thick, scaly skin protected it, covering plates of solid bone. But with powerful jaws, the liopleurodon crunched through the armor.

The carnivorous reptile leaped again, then slammed down hard onto the overturned turtle. The hungry predator shoved the turtle's head underwater, blinding and disorienting it. The reptile kept biting. Eating. Devouring its prey alive.

The other archelons didn't bother helping their friend. Ungrateful lot. They fled into the distance.

Soon more liopleurodons arrived. Smaller ones. Juveniles, possibly the hunter's offspring. They began feeding on the turtle too, ripping out chunks of meat, emptying out the shell, and overall enjoying a nice meal with mommy. A few tourists turned green and covered their eyes. One tourist threw up overboard. Others were snapping photos, loving the show.

"It's a mother," Simone whispered. "A mother hunting for her hatchlings." She shuddered. "And I thought predation on land was gruesome."

"Gruesome but natural," said Joe. "Animals kill to eat. Only humans kill for fun. Now come with me, Simone. We've got a report to prepare. We're going to the bottom of the ship."

The *Maid of Mintari* was full of amenities: the pool, the bars, the buffet, and the Amazing Alfonso Magic Show (Alfonso claimed to be the only magician on Mintari who could saw a woman into thirds, which was likely true, given that he was also the only magician on Mintari period). But the star attraction was the glass floor. These days you could take cruises through space, viewing nebulae, black holes, pulsars, and all the other wonders of the galaxy. But only one cruise ship in the galaxy let you explore marine life, let alone ancient marine life. Most tourists these days had seen a dozen nebulae. Here was something new.

Joe and Simone descended to the lower deck. Hundreds of tourists were already there. Surprise surprise. More crowds. The lower deck was enormous. You could race dinosaurs in there. A glass floor the size of a dinoball court offered a view of the ocean depths. Wisely, the ship designers didn't allow tourists to walk on the glass floor. That would simply hide the view. To buffer the crowds, walkways circled the inner hull, and three bridges spanned the floor, creating more space for lookouts.

There was a line just to get onto a walkway. Joe and Simone waited—her patiently, him anxiously. Finally some tourists left to find the bar, and Joe and Simone squeezed onto a walkway, found a bit of free railing, leaned over, and looked down.

A tour guide stood on a balcony, holding a microphone. The young woman wore a safari outfit, red neckerchief, big ceratop hat, and a bigger smile. She was in the middle of a presentation.

". . . and if you look below, you might get lucky and view a rare bothriolepis. These small fish lived during the Paleozoic era. Paleontologists once thought them to be bottom-feeders, but on Mintari, we discovered that bothriolepis enjoy living among kelp and feeding on plankton."

Joe looked over the railing. He saw only the murk. The ocean was deep here, plunging into blackness. Joe could make out some kelp strands, some unremarkable fish, and below that—only darkness. Underwhelming to say the least. A few tourists yawned. One of the bachelorettes said to her friends, "Let's find the bar," a suggestion immediately rewarded with a chorus of "woos!" The young women left the observatory, much to Joe's relief.

"Where are the sharks?" a heavyset man was shouting, sounding more than a little tipsy. "I paid to see giant sharks, tar it."

The tour guide never lost her smile, though it seemed a bit strained. "Ah, here is an interesting visitor! If you look directly below us now, you'll see a family of ammonites. Ancient mollusks. Look at the shape of their shells."

The tourists peered down. Through the glass floor, Joe couldn't see a thing. Just a few shadows.

"Boring!" said a teenage girl, likely dragged here by her parents. She began playing with her SmartSphere.

"Bloody hell, I thought we'd see some proper sea monsters," said Ehren the furnace repairman. He wore a hat shaped like a shark's mouth.

More tourists were leaving, heading back to the bars, buffet, and magic show. It was Alfonso's time to shine.

The tour guide's smile wavered. "How about we try to stir up some more exciting creatures?"

A few tourists stopped at the door. They returned to the railing, willing to give the glass floor another chance.

The tour guide tapped a hidden button. Spotlights switched on along the ship's underbelly. Beams of light pierced the murk, revealing a kelp forest rich with fish, jellyfish, and trilobites. The animals came in every color of the rainbow. The crowd oohed and pointed and chattered excitedly. Word spread, and within moments, more tourists swarmed onto the deck and crowded the walkways. They stood on tiptoes, pointing at the colorful scene below.

Joe gripped the railing so tightly he almost broke it. "These spotlights are disturbing the wildlife!"

But nobody heard him. Not even Simone. The journalist was leaning over the railing, eyes wide. "Look at that fish, Joe! It's huge!"

A gargantuan fish swam below. It was bulky, the size of a car, and covered with bony armor. Its mouth looked large enough to swallow a man whole. Instead of proper teeth, bony shards thrust out from its jawbone. The fish looked like a giant staple remover.

"Behold the dunkleosteus!" said the tour guide. "We're in luck today. The dunkleosteus is a large armored fish from the Devonian period. It's among the largest fish that ever lived. Yes, ladies and gentlemen, this fish is the size of an elephant. Its jaws are filled with fearsome blades—not teeth but sharp extensions of the jawbone. Our beloved dunky can bite down with a force of six thousand newtons. Enough to bite through a car! But don't worry, the glass at the bottom of this ship is strong enough to resist them."

Tourists pointed and snapped photos.

The armored fish swam closer toward the bottom of the ship.

"Turn the lights off," Joe whispered.

The fish swam closer. Closer. Tourists kept gabbing and snapping photos.

"Turn the tarry lights off!" Joe cried out.

The dunkleosteus gained speed, rising higher and higher toward the glass.

The tour guide glanced at Joe. "Sir, please don't worry. We're perfectly safe here, even with the—"

The armored fish slammed into the boat. The *Maid of Mintari* jolted. The deck swayed. People grabbed onto the railing, crying out in horror. The dunky pounded into the glass again and again. Its bony shards scraped along the glass.

Simone yelped and grabbed Joe's hand. He held his breath.

But the glass held.

The armored fish changed tactics. It swam aside, bit one of the spotlights, and the beam of light died. The plan backfired. Electricity jolted through the water, and the fish flipped several times in the murk, then fled into the depths.

The tourists cheered and clapped. Now *this* was entertainment!

Joe shoved his way through the crowd, trudged across the bridge, and reached the tour guide.

"These lights are disturbing the wildlife!" he said. "These animals are used to living in darkness. You can't shine spotlights in their eyes, tar it. It's dangerous for them *and* us."

The tour guide gulped. She spoke hesitantly into her microphone. "Ladies and gentlemen, we'll be shutting off our spotlights for some repairs. Please feel free to visit the Amazing Alfonso Magic Show, starting at four thirty, and the glass floor display should be fully operational again soon."

"If you need a furnace repaired too, I can help," Ehren said, handing out his business card.

Before the remaining spotlights shut off, Joe saw it on the transparent floor.

Scratch marks. Cutting deep into the glass.

CHAPTER TWELVE
No Pineapples Allowed

A thousand children attended Leakey High School, but Fig felt all alone.

She walked down the hall, eyes downcast. Her backpack felt so heavy today. Her guilt was heavier. Students bustled everywhere, chatting, laughing. Laughing at her. Whenever Fig heard laughter, she assumed it was at her expense. Her eyes stung. She was trapped in here. Trapped like a wild animal in a cage. She had run with a pack of achillobators. She had battled a Tyrannosaurus rex. She had faced a mosasaur and survived to tell the tale. But she had never felt as timid as when walking down this high school hall.

It was especially bad now with Joe and Simone away on their cruise. True, even when they were in Dinovia, they never entered the school with Fig. They did not know of her torment. But she could comfort herself knowing they were at least in the same city, that she would see Simone after school, see her father on Sunday. Now they were off at sea, and Fig felt more alone than ever.

As she passed by the other students, Fig felt the stares. Heard the whispers. The snickers. Wherever Fig walked, she sucked out joy from her surroundings, and she infused those around her with hatred and scorn. She was a disease. They hated her for it. And she hated herself.

"There she is," somebody whispered.

Another kid giggled. "The retard."

"I heard she killed those kids. Drowned them in the sea."

"Probably ate them. Still thinks she's a dinosaur."

Fig kept walking, head lowered, pretending she didn't hear. She felt so small. So weak. Growing up in the wilderness, hungry and wild, had stunted her growth. The other students stood much taller than her. Even the younger students. She barely reached their shoulders.

"Hey, cavegirl!" A tall, blond girl shoved her. Her name was Denise Rex, and a golden tyrannosaurus pin adorned her lapel. Clan Rex was the richest and most powerful on Mintari, even more powerful than Clan Proudfoot, and a Proudfoot was president. Certainly they were more powerful than Clan Triplehorn, the tattered family Fig came from. Unless you counted the rich Triplehorns who lived on Cloventia, which nobody did. Denise was sixteen, same age as Fig, but tall, pretty, and well-bred. Everything Fig was not.

Fig kept walking, head lowered.

"Hey, I'm talking to you!" said Denise.

Her friends laughed.

"She can't understand you."

"She's not even human. She's a Neanderthal or something."

"I heard they shaved a monkey."

"Hey, monkey girl! Ooh ooh ah ah!"

The students laughed all around her. Fig laughed too. A scared laugh. An uncomfortable laugh. Maybe if she laughed with them, it wouldn't be so bad. It would all just be a shared joke.

Fig kept walking. Her classroom was at the back of the hall. It was still a long way, and many students stood between here and there. This was a field of thorns. A path of fire. She who had run across the wilderness could now barely walk down a hallway.

"Where you going, monkey?" said Denise, skipping alongside her. The girl's friends all danced around, scratching their armpits, making monkey sounds.

"Wanna banana?" somebody said. He tossed a banana peel onto Fig. It landed on her hair.

"Aww, look, she's gonna cry."

"You gonna cry, monkey girl?"

Fig stopped in her tracks. She pulled the banana peel off her head. Mustering all the courage in her heart, she raised her head and stared at her tormentors.

"M-m-my name is Fig."

"Okay, Pig," said Denise.

"Pig, pig, pig!" chanted the others, then oinked and snorted.

Somebody placed a finger on Fig's nose and shoved it upward. "Look, she has a snout!"

A camera snapped. "Got a photo! This is going right onto QuickFame. She *is* a pig, and we have proof."

Tears budded in Fig's eyes. She shoved the larger kids aside and ran down the corridor, knocking students aside. Everyone pointed and laughed.

Humiliated, her face burning with shame, Fig made it to her classroom. A little oasis of safety. She stepped inside.

This was not like other classrooms at Leakey High. This was a special classroom. A space for special kids. The official name was the Special Education Room for Extraordinary Children. Other students called it the remedial class. In her mind, Fig called it *the nest*. Nests were places of safety and comfort.

Fig always felt better in here. This was not like the rest of the school. Here she was not judged. The others called them freaks, but to Fig, the children in this class were wonderful.

Students came here with many challenges. A few had Down syndrome. Others had Williams syndrome or autism or other conditions. They all had some form of intellectual disability. All but Fig. She was intelligent, her teachers claimed. Maybe even gifted. But growing up in the wilderness had given her a strange brain. She knew how to track prey, how to hamstring a sauropod, and how to communicate with achillobators with yips, coos, and groans. She could find her way across forests and grasslands, build nests, collect berries and roots, and survive winter. But ask her to solve a basic arithmetic problem, and she floundered. She could not speak properly, could barely hold a pen. She could not understand human body language or express it. Even most facial expressions stumped her; she could not tell the difference between a grimace, wince, or glower. She had the body of a girl but the mind of an achillobator. If you took a dinosaur and dressed it in a school uniform, it wouldn't do any worse than Figaro Triplehorn.

So they put her in the nest. A place for those who didn't fit in. Those who thought differently, learned differently. When Fig entered the class, some of her fellow nesties waved and smiled. Others didn't smile. Didn't talk. Not today, not ever. That was their way, but they were valuable members of the nest nonetheless. Fig had learned that everyone communicated differently. The pack had taught her that.

Fig took a seat beside Abbey, her best friend.

"Hi, Abbey."

The girl ignored her. She kept her eyes glued on her paper, where she was drawing a stegosaurus clobbering a tyrannosaur. Both dinosaurs were purple—same color as Abbey's scrunchy, fingernails, and backpack. Clearly Abbey had a favorite color. She didn't so much as glance toward Fig.

"I like your scrin . . . scrin . . . scrun-chy," Fig said, struggling to pronounce a new word. "Paple is my fav'ite color too. I wish m-m-my hair were long enough for scinchies."

Abbey didn't respond. Didn't even look at Fig. She lifted a red crayon and added splashes of blood to her masterpiece.

Abbey Longspikes came from a proud old clan. The Longspikes had chosen the stegosaurus to represent them. And like their clan dinosaur, they were prickly. Abbey had long blond hair, green eyes, and a silver stegosaurus pinned to her school uniform. She never said hi to Fig. Never asked her about her day. She never spoke at all.

Unless it was about dinosaurs.

"I like yo d'awing," Fig said. "S-s-steg'saurus vs. T-rex?"

Abbey raised her eyes. She didn't make eye contact with Fig, but she managed to gaze somewhere over Fig's head.

"Actually, the carnivore you refer to is not a *Tyrannosaurus rex* but a *Qianzhousaurus*, a genus of tyrannosaurid dinosaur that lived in Asia during the Late Cretaceous period. There is currently only one species named, the type species *Qianzhousaurus sinensis*, which is a member of the tribe *Alioramini* within the group, and most closely related to *Alioramus*, another alioramin."

"Oh," Fig said. She looked at the crayon drawing. It still looked like a T-rex to her. "It's very nice. Looks scary."

"*Qianzhousaurus* is a medium-sized tyrannosaurid estimated at 6.3 meters in length, 2 meters in hip height, and 750–757 kilogram in body mass. The taxon can be differentiated from other tyrannosaurids in having a highly narrowed premaxilla, a pneumatic opening on the upper extension of the maxilla, and the lack of a vertical ridgelike structure on the lateral surface of the ilium. Please try to be more accurate next time."

Fig tapped the drawing of the stegosaurus. "What's dis one? A triceratops?"

She meant it as a joke. But Abbey took her at face value. The girl took a deep breath. "It's a stegosaurus—a genus of herbivorous, four-legged, armored dinosaur from the Late

Jurassic, characterized by the distinctive kite-shaped upright plates along their backs and spikes on their—"

Their teacher entered the classroom.

Abbey went silent. She pulled off her purple scrunchy, letting her hair fall and hide her face. She lowered her head and kept drawing.

Their teacher, Rita Proudfoot, was a kind, gentle woman. She was the president's daughter, but she had chosen a career outside of politics (or geology). Her smile was sweet, her voice soft. One of her own children was in the special education class— Rocky Proudfoot, a boy with Down syndrome. But Rita treated all the nesties equally well, showering them with encouragement and love. She did not judge. She did not yell or punish. With a soft voice and gentle smile, Rita Proudfoot encouraged every student to learn as best they could. And in her classroom, they flourished.

Fig sat at her desk, watching Rita help a boy remove his jacket and open his backpack. His fingers kept fumbling. When the boy let out a howl and began to cry, frustrated with the experience, Rita soothed him until he was smiling.

It was funny, Fig thought. Her old pack would never tolerate a gentle soul like Rita Proudfoot. Nor would they tolerate children like the nesties. Were Rita an achillobator, the others would have ripped her apart. In the wild, there was no room for compassion or gentle encouragement. The meek died. From the achillobators, Fig learned about honor, strength, and ruthless survival. But here in this classroom Fig learned about compassion.

In a sense, compassion was a luxury. Bators faced death at every turn. They must be ruthless. Humans were far safer. They had roofs over their heads, food in their fridges, protective walls around them. In such safety, compassion could grow. But it was not everywhere, Fig reminded herself. These flowers of human compassion were not a sprawling meadow but little secret gardens, hidden away like this nest. Fig glanced at the classroom door. Out there, among the alpha humans, it was a jungle. Those ones were predators.

Fig leaned toward Abbey. "Tank you."

The girl kept drawing, ignoring Fig.

"You're nice," Fig whispered. "You're my friend. Tank you."

For a split second, Abbey's crayon paused over the paper. Then she kept drawing. Yes, she had heard Fig. And on her paper, above the dueling dinosaurs, Abbey drew a heart.

For the next few hours, Fig engaged in her passion. Learning.

She had always loved learning. To survive in the wilderness, you needed to learn a lot. How to foresee the coming and going of seasons. How to find water and shelter. How to track a herd and ambush prey. How to groom for ticks and lice, heal wounds, and rip a carcass apart. She had learned which herbs were edible and which upset her stomach. Which lizards and insects were good for eating and which stung. She had learned how to weave dresses of feathers to protect her from the snow, how to cover her head with leaves to protect her from the sun, how to fish ants from logs using sticks. The pack taught her some of those skills, and others she figured out by herself.

Here in the human world, she learned new things. How numbers worked. How little scribbles on paper could symbolize sounds. How sounds formed words. How words formed concepts. She learned how to read human facial expressions and body language, which was just as complex. Ms. Proudfoot said that Fig was gifted, a quick learner, and would catch up with the "normal kids" someday soon. Fig hoped not. She dreaded the idea of moving to a "normal" class. To study in a class with Denise Rex? No, thanks. Fig would much rather sit beside Abbey with her crayons and encyclopedic dinosaur knowledge.

In the wild, I became a predator, Fig thought. *But I started out as a runt. Here I'm a runt again.*

Ms. Proudfoot approached. "Figaro, would you like to keep working on your pronunciations?"

Fig nodded. "Yes, Miss Pridfi. Pri—Pri-Proudfit." Almost.

They sat for a while, working together to improve Fig's speech. She could understand Nyxian perfectly. She even learned to write her name. But speaking was a different matter. For years, Figaro had used her mouth for yipping, growling, snorting, howling, cooing, and all the other sounds achillobators made. Crafting human syllables was challenging. But she had made progress. Lots of progress. Six months ago, Fig could barely say her own name. Now she was speaking full sentences and getting them mostly right, and she was better every day. Ms. Proudfoot believed that within another few months, Fig would be speaking normally. Assuming she kept practicing.

I'll probably always have an accent though, Fig thought. *The first and only human with a bona fide dinosaur accent.*

Ms. Proudfoot went to help another student, leaving Fig with a math workbook. It was printed for little children, but Fig had to start somewhere. Before diving into *Bruno the Brontosaur's Wonderful World of Numbers,* Fig glanced toward her neighbor. Abbey was busy with crayons, drawing something new.

Fig leaned closer, looking at the crayon creation. A sea monster this time. A huge reptile rising from the sea, crushing a boat.

A mosasaur. A purple one, but a mosasaur nonetheless.

As Fig watched, Abbey crayoned a scar onto the mosasaur's head. A jagged Z.

"Ryujin," Fig whispered.

Abbey looked up. "Mosasaurs are the apex predators of Mintari's oceans. They grow even larger on Mintari than they grew on Earth during the Late Cretaceous. They are larger than sperm whales, and some individuals even approach the size of a blue whale. They are known for their voracious appetite. You're lucky to have survived your encounter, Fig."

Fig took another look at the drawing. Abbey had drawn a stick figure swimming away from the mosasaur. A figure with short black hair.

"Is dat me?" Fig asked.

Abbey nodded. "Yes. I apologize. I'm not as good at drawing humans."

She had drawn a few more stick figures. Other humans. These ones were underwater, their eyes x'ed out, their tongues sticking out.

"Abbey, you shou'n't draw such tings," Fig whispered.

"Yes, perhaps I need to improve my skills before I attempt to draw more humans. I will start a new drawing. Would you mind if I drew a pack of achillobators? I could add you to the drawing, if you don't mind another crude attempt. Achillobators are fascinating. They are large dromaeosaurid dinosaurs that lived in Asia during the Late Cretaceous period in what is now the Bayan Shireh Formation. The genus is currently monotypic, only including the type species *A. giganticus*. The first remains were found in 1989 during a Mongolian-Russian field expedition in Mongolia and later—"

"Wait. Bators are from Mongolia?" Fig asked.

Abbey nodded. "Indeed."

Fig leaned back in her chair, amazed. Her head spun. Since returning to human civilization, Fig had learned about Clan Clubber, her maternal side of the family. The Clubbers had been living on Mintari for centuries, but they traced their ancestry back to Mongolia on Earth.

I lived with dinosaurs from my country, she thought. *What are the odds?*

Fig didn't know. Pretty tarry low. She didn't need to complete *Bruno the Brontosaur's Wonderful World of Numbers* to know that much. And it seemed to Fig that powers beyond her understanding were at work in this world. That some grand storyteller was weaving the tale of her life. She was not alone.

Abbey kept rattling off trivia about achillobators. As she chattered along, regurgitating information, Abbey worked on her new drawing. She gave her achillobators red feathers, and she drew Fig riding one. Tears filled Fig's eyes. She missed that old world.

Maybe I should run away, Fig thought. *Maybe I should leave this human world. Return to the wild.*

What had humanity given her? She was the lowest omega in this great human herd. She was nothing and nobody.

But that was not entirely true. She was a daughter. And she was a friend.

She hugged Abbey. "Tank-tank-ttfffthank you for being a friend." She wiped spit off her lips.

Abbey did not hug her back, did not say a thing. After all, Fig had not spoken about dinosaurs. But Abbey drew a new drawing. A drawing of two stick figures, one with short black hair, one with long blond hair and a purple scrunchie. They were holding hands.

The bell rang. School ended. A thousand children ran outside into the crisp autumn afternoon. Red and golden leaves glided through the air and fluttered along the cobbled roads. Fig stood among the crowd, thinking of autumn in the wild. A time of great urgency. A time when they hunted the hardest, hoping to fatten up before winter. Autumn was a time of danger in the wilderness, a herald of hardship. Here it was a time of beauty.

Outside of school, she crossed the road and stepped onto the sidewalk. Clay houses rose around her, adorned with fake skeletons, cobwebs, and spiders. (Last week, Fig had nearly fainted, thinking them real skeletons and real giant spiders, and Simone had to explain the concept of Halloween decorations.) Pumpkins stood on patios, grinning their terrible grins. Halloween was not until tomorrow, but many children wore their costumes already. The idea of a holiday still perplexed Fig. Especially this holiday. In the dinosaur kingdom, if you had a skeleton outside your nest, it was a real one.

Several sauropods lumbered onto the road, barely fitting. Schoolchildren climbed rope ladders and entered howdahs on their backs. The living "school buses" plodded off, carrying the children home.

Fig hefted her backpack. She decided to walk home today. She had tried riding with the other children, but it never felt right. A dinosaur should not have seats, ladders, and a bridle. A dinosaur should not be lumbering down city streets, feeding from flowering balconies. Fig shut her eyes and remembered riding Red Scar through the wilderness. She had needed no saddle, no bridle. She would simply squeeze her legs around the dinosaur, grab fistfuls of his feathers, and ride on the hunt, the wind in her hair. She missed it. She missed it so much that her eyes dampened. Sometimes she dreamed of sneaking into the wilderness just for a chance to ride again, bareback and free.

She walked down the cobbled road. The autumn leaves swirled around her feet. How did the wind make them swirl in funnels? She would ask her father when he came home. He would be gone for a week, Simone too, and Lifa was wandering the wild beyond anyone's reach. But Barnum waited back at the Fossil and Firkin. He would bring her a plate of his famous shepherd's pie, and maybe Merl would play the piano. For a man with sausage fingers, he sure could tickle the ivories. The Fossil and Firkin was like the remedial class. An oasis of kindness in a cruel world. A home.

"Hey, Pig."

A group of teenagers stepped out from an alleyway. Denise Rex led them. A pack of friends stood behind her.

Fig froze. Her heart leaped into a gallop. Denise was smiling. Ms. Proudfoot had taught Fig that smiles were friendly, smiles were good. But Fig had spent enough time in the wilderness to recognize *this* smile. It was the smile a predator gave its prey before biting.

Fig hissed, bared her teeth, and reached for her sickle claw. Then she remembered. She didn't have her sickle claw with her. The school forbade weapons, and they had deemed her claw a weapon. Fig raised her fists instead. They were small fists, but they would have to do.

Denise and her friends laughed.

"Look at her!"

"She thinks she's a boxer."

Denise raised her own fists, laughing. "Are you challenging me to a bout of fisticuffs, Pig?"

They all laughed. Tears burned in Fig's eyes. She snapped her teeth and yowled. That only made them laugh harder.

"She oinked!"

"She *is* a pig, she really is a pig!"

Fig could not defeat so many. Sometimes a predator knew when she was beat. Fig turned to walk the other way. But more students blocked the sidewalk. Ten or more, all much taller than her. A crowd gathered along the road, surrounding Fig. So that's how it was. An ambush. Fig had seen many ambushes in her life, but never from the prey's point of view.

Somebody began a chant. "Fight, fight, fight!"

Soon a hundred children or more were chanting along. "Fight, fight, fight!"

Somebody shoved Fig from behind. She stumbled closer to Denise. The faces all swam around her, jeering, laughing, screaming.

"Look, she's crying."

"Fight, Pig!"

"Fight, fight, fight!"

Somebody shoved Fig again. She jolted forward and slammed into Denise.

"Get off me, Pig!" Denise said. Her eyes blazed with fury. No. Not fury, Fig realized. It was something worse. It was disgust.

Grimacing, Denise backhanded Fig. She stumbled back, cheek stinging. Everyone cheered.

Fig snarled. Rage flared inside her like a fire. She would teach this soft, pampered girl a lesson! Fig had battled dinosaurs before. What was a girl? She lunged toward Denise, fists flying.

But Denise blocked the blows. She backhanded Fig again. Everyone laughed.

Fig stood there, shocked. How was Denise winning this? Fig was a predator! A girl raised by bators! She had slain parasaurs! How could she lose to some pampered city girl?

Then she understood.

In the wild, I had the bator pack with me, Fig thought. *I had my sickle claw. Here I'm just a runt. Alone.*

Denise came bearing down on her. Up close, the size difference between them was striking. Denise was tall, athletic, healthy. Fig was scrawny, short, her growth stunted by years of want.

Denise attacked again and again. She wasn't punching Fig. Not even hurting her much. She was slapping her. Hard, stinging slaps meant to humiliate, not injure. Fig tried lunging, tried to claw and scratch and bite, but hands grabbed her from behind.

Students gripped her arms. Clutched her legs. And Denise just kept slapping her, and tears flowed down Fig's burning cheeks.

A gunshot *boomed.*

Everyone jumped and gasped. At once, the hands released Fig. Denise paled and took a step back.

The crowd parted. Fig stood there on the sidewalk, humiliated, tears on her stinging red cheeks. Somebody had ripped her clothes, she noticed. With everyone else, she looked toward the source of the gunshot.

A woman stood there. A tall, beautiful woman in her midthirties. Her chestnut hair flowed in the wind, and her blue eyes shone like daggers reflecting the moon. She wore camouflage clothes and carried a smoking rifle.

"I shot that bullet into the sky," the woman said. "The next time somebody picks on my niece, I shoot them in the head."

Denise's cheeks flushed. Her eyes flooded with tears.

"My father will hear of this!" she said and fled down an alleyway. Her friends followed. The crowd dispersed.

Fig stood there, cheeks stinging and uniform torn, staring at her savior. She recognized the woman.

"Amissa," she whispered.

The last students wandered home. Fig remained on the sidewalk, facing her aunt.

Where were the Rangers, tar it? Why weren't any Rangers showing up? Amissa was a wanted woman! She was a poacher— the queen of poachers! She had fired a gun right here in the city! Fig glanced around, seeking help.

219

"I know what you're thinking," Amissa said. "No Rangers will show up to arrest me. They're busy fighting my men in the field."

Fig blushed. Did she broadcast her thoughts that obviously? To her, human body language and facial expressions were still mysterious. Fig could interpret a little of it. Not a lot. It reminded her of her time in the pack. She could smell a little. Not a lot. Meanwhile, the achillobators sensed entire worlds with their noses. What humans lacked in pheromones they made up for with expressive faces.

"What d-d-do you want?" Fig said.

Amissa raised an eyebrow. "Must I want more than to help my niece? I saw you were in trouble. I stepped in to help." She *tsk*ed her tongue. "They fight dirty, those ones. All good predators do, you know. They're a pack. And you stepped right into their ambush."

Fig's cheeks flushed again, this time with anger. "D-d-don't talk to me of p-p-packs! You killed him!" Tears burned in her eyes. "You killed Red Scar!"

The memory flooded her. The Battle of Buckland Hill. A hot spring night. Fig had charged with the pack, riding Red Scar, holding her sickle claw high. She had yowled and yipped for battle. With her fellow bators, she had mobbed the terrible T-rex, cut his legs, stabbed his eye, brought the great beast down.

Then Amissa had shown up. From the shadows. A stalking predator. And fired her gun.

Even now, six months later, Fig could still hear the sound Red Scar made. A sound like a hatchling when you stepped on its tail. For long years, Red Scar had protected her in the wild. Nurtured her. Fed her. Kept her warm and safe. And at the end, she had been there for him. She had held his head in her arms, a scaly head as large as Fig's body. He had died gazing into her eyes.

And now here before her stood the killer.

Fig spotted something on the ground. A rock. She ran, grabbed the rock, and raised it. She stared at Amissa.

"I will crush your face!" Fig said. Interesting. She spoke better when violent.

"Ah, there's the spirit!" Amissa smiled. "That's the niece I like to see. Some fire in you at last! Where was that spirit when that girl was slapping you?"

"Go away!" Fig shouted.

Amissa sighed. "Fig, I didn't know that Red Scar was your friend. I didn't even know who you were. I saw a pack of achillobators in the city. I saw blood on their teeth. So I fired my gun. And I killed your friend. For that I'm deeply, deeply sorry. Had I known . . ." She shook her head. "I'm sorry. It's tormented me since that day. But my guilt is nothing compared to your grief."

Fig tilted her head. Was Amissa sincere? Tar it! Fig couldn't tell. Amissa was making the right facial expressions. Her body was slumping. Her eyes were downcast. On paper, that all meant remorse. Could she be faking it? Fig didn't "speak" human body language well enough yet to know.

She lowered the rock, but she kept it in her grip. "Why are you here? In this city?"

Amissa took a step closer. Her blue eyes were soft. Her smile seemed sincere. "I came to see you. I heard your father was away on holiday. That means we could talk. Just you and me. You've never heard my side of the story. I'm your aunt, Fig. We share blood. At least hear me out."

Fig could turn and run. She was small and weak, yes, but she was fast. Why wasn't she running?

She's a murderer! Fig thought. *She's evil! A poacher! A madwoman! And . . . she saved me.*

Fig pursed her lips and nodded.

Amissa smiled. "Good. But let's not talk here. Come with me. I'll buy you dinner. Anything you like."

"Pizza," Fig blurted out before she could stop herself. She loved Barnum's cooking, but one could only eat so much shepherd's pie. Half a year of the stuff was getting a bit rough. Pizza though—now there was a food Fig could eat every day for the rest of her life. She had only tried it once before—a treat at Simone's new house. But just that one time had convinced her. It was her favorite food. Her stomach growled and she salivated.

Amissa laughed. "I like pizza too. I know a good place a few blocks away. Let's go."

The poacher walked down the road, her gait quick and confident. Amissa didn't even turn to see if Fig followed. Fig stood for a moment, watching the woman. She had thought Denise and her posse tall, strong, and mighty, but they were nothing, they were weaklings and runts compared to Amissa. Her aunt was striking, powerful both physically and mentally. A true warrior. She didn't need to turn to see if Fig followed. Amissa Triplehorn walked like a leader, always facing forward. She gave Fig the choice. Follow or remain behind.

She's like my father, Fig thought. *She has the strength of a triceratops. My clan is strong.*

She imagined Amissa in a fight with Denise. Oh, how the blond bully would cry! Amissa would make chopped meat of her. Even without a gun. Denise was only a baby T-rex, and Amissa was an adult triceratops, furious and mighty. She would bulldoze over the girl. The thought made Fig smile, and she hurried after her aunt.

Amissa had long legs and a quick stride. With her little legs, Fig must jog and skip to keep up. They made their way down the road, passing by clay houses, shops, and bistros. Autumn leaves glided through the air, and pumpkins winked and laughed and made silly faces. The smell of pumpkin spice and apple pies wafted from the windows of cafés. Ghosts and skeletons hung from trees, and one family's yard boasted tombstones and a smoke machine. Fig decided that pizza was her favorite food and Halloween was her favorite holiday.

And who is my favorite Triplehorn? she wondered, looking at Amissa.

She chided herself at once. *Stop it, Figaro! Amissa is a poacher. A killer. The enemy. Don't you forget that. Even if she buys you pizza.*

They reached Paleozoic Pizza, a little hole-in-the-wall. A wooden sign hung above the door, featuring a pterodactyl eating a slice of pizza. If Joe were here, Fig suspected, he would grumble about how pterodactyls didn't live in the Paleozoic era. Thankfully he was not here. Aunt and niece stepped inside. This was nothing like the warm, welcoming Fossil and Firkin. This joint was greasy, shadowy, and crowded. Fig froze in the doorway, recognizing some teenagers from her school. The kids glanced her way, whispered among themselves, and somebody snickered. Had they seen the fight? Would they torment her?

Fig stepped closer to Amissa. She felt so small; her head barely reached Amissa's shoulder. Beside her aunt, she felt safe. She glared at the teenagers. They lowered their eyes, pretending not to notice her. They knew who Amissa was. Everyone knew Amissa Triplehorn. Nobody would harass Fig while her aunt was here. Maybe nobody would harass her ever again.

Fig raised her chin, glaring at her tormentors. *That's right, kids. You mess with me, you mess with Amissa Triplehorn!*

All the tables were taken. But Amissa walked confidently to the back of the room. She approached the teenagers, rapped her knuckles on their table, and gestured with her chin toward the door. She didn't even need to speak a word. The kids leaped to their feet and scrambled over one another, fleeing to the street.

Amissa held out a chair for Fig. "I believe there's a free table."

Fig hated to admit it. She was starting to like her aunt.

She sat down. Amissa smiled and sat down across the table.

"What pizza would you like?" Amissa said. "My treat."

"No pineapples!" Fig checked the menu. She pointed. "Dis one. Meat lovers."

The pizza (the most expensive one on the menu) included meatballs, sausage, bacon, and pepperoni. Mintari had no farm animals. Farming damaged the environment. It was strictly forbidden on this planet-sized nature reserve. A few eccentrics like Granny Lifa raised chickens (or at least she had before the forest fires), but that was about it. This meat had likely come from planet Dagon, frozen and shipped across space. Not fresh. But in Fig's experience, even this meat from another world was delicious. It worked for Barnum's shepherd's pie.

Amissa grinned. "You *are* a Triplehorn. I know our clan dinosaur is a triceratops, but we human Triplehorns are carnivores. I'm getting a large one for us to share. Wait—*extra* large. And some beer."

Fig bit her lip. "My dad said I cin't drink beer. I'm too young."

"I won't tell him if you don't." Amissa winked. "Come on, Fig. I'm the black sheep of the family. The cool and dangerous aunt. Let me be a bad influence."

Her aunt smiled, but Fig did not return the smile. Instead, she lowered her head.

I shouldn't be here, she thought. *What am I doing? She's a poacher. My dad would kill me. I'm meeting with the enemy!*

But was she? Was this really Fig's war? Or was she simply caught between her father and aunt? They were all one family. All Triplehorns. Why must they fight? Why must Fig choose sides?

She killed Red Scar! cried a voice inside her. *Now you sit with her here? You desecrate the memory of your friend!*

It was an accident, said another voice.

An accident? And you buy that?

She saved my life!

Oh please. Denise wasn't going to kill you.

Well, she saved me from dying from humiliation. That's something, isn't it?

"A penny for your thoughts," Amissa said, interrupting Fig's internal dialogue.

"You know what I'm tinking."

"Maybe I do." Amissa nodded. "But slow down. First pizza. Then heart-to-heart. *Garcon!*"

Soon the pizza was on the table, topped with meaty goodness. The waiter placed down two mugs of beer. He made some noises about checking Fig's ID, but when Amissa tossed him a silver coin, his eyes widened, he bowed, then brought them two more beers.

"It's good to be rich." Amissa winked.

"My dad says dat p-p-poverty is better dan blood money."

Amissa laughed. "Sounds like Joe all right. Noble, honorable, not too bright." She sprinkled chili flakes on her pizza. "Figaro, I know what they say about me. That I'm a monster. An evil, cackling villain. That I just need a mustache to twirl. That's what they say. So what? You know what it's like when people talk."

Fig placed down her half-eaten slice. "You *are* a killer. I saw you shoot pe'ple."

"Did you? You saw me shoot a dinosaur, which I believed was a menace. You saw me shoot into the air to scare off Denise Rex and her friends. Did you ever see me shoot a human?"

Fig hesitated, then shook her head.

"Even when you and Joe interrupted my hunt in the outback, did I harm you?" Amissa continued.

Again Fig shook her head.

Amissa leaned across the table. "Figaro, I heard what those girls were saying about you. Calling you a pig. A cavegirl. An idiot. Let them talk. They talk about me too. Let them call us names. We don't care. Do you know why?" Amissa inhaled sharply and grinned, and her eyes lit up. "Because we're strong! Because we're Triplehorns! They demonize us because they fear us. Remember something, Figaro. You can't make people love you. But you can make them respect you."

Fig chewed that over for a while. She hated to admit it, but Amissa was making sense. Most of the human world wasn't like the Fossil and Firkin or the Nest. Most humans weren't sweet like Simone or honorable like Joe. Even here, within the city walls, the laws of nature reigned. There were predators and prey. There was violence and survival. The rules were different, but ultimately it was the same game.

Amissa reminded her of Crooked Wing, the new alpha female of the pack. Both were brutal, violent, and hostile. But also strong. Survivors. And fiercely defensive of those in their packs.

When Fig looked at her father, she saw a triceratops. Powerful. Dependable. Amissa belonged to Clan Triplehorn too. But when Fig looked at her aunt, she didn't see a triceratops.

She saw an achillobator.

And once more, Fig felt torn between two worlds.

Amissa reached for another slice of pizza. "I'll give you a tip, Fig. Because I can't always be around to protect you. Those kids are gonna come after you again. Easy to see why. You're smaller than they are. You're weaker. You look, sound, and act different. They're gonna come back, again and again, and make your life hell." She leaned forward, a strange light in her eyes. "So you're not going to let them. You're smaller, so you gotta be fiercer. You're weaker, so you gotta be meaner. If they push you, you bang their heads into the wall. If they slap your cheek, you punch out their teeth." Her voice rose. "If they attack you, they are the enemy! You are a huntress. And you will destroy them." Amissa leaned back, took a deep breath, and smiled. "Now how is that pizza?"

Fig reached for another slice. She ate it silently, lost in thought.

CHAPTER THIRTEEN
Onesies and Tragedies

Joe walked through the engine room, wincing. The engines were roaring. Pistons were pumping. The deck vibrated.

"It's awfully loud!" Joe shouted.

The ship engineer, a stocky man with white hair, tilted his head. "Eh?"

"I said it's loud! Tarry loud!"

The engineer smiled and nodded. "Yes, we *are* proud! The *Maid of Mintari* is a fine ship." He patted a rattling pipe.

"No, I said it's—Oh never mind," Joe muttered. He turned toward Simone, pulled her close, and spoke into her ear. "If it's loud here, then for the animals below—"

She pushed him away, wincing. "Stop shouting in my ear!"

He pulled her between two pipes where the sound was dampened a bit. He still had to speak up. "Sound travels louder through water than air. And marine animals have sharper ears than we do. This must be excruciating for the wildlife."

Simone nodded. "Getting it into my report. We're blowing the lid off this joint. President Proudfoot expected me to give his cruise ship a glowing review. Wait until he sees my ruthless investigative journalism. Once I bite into a story, I never let go. Back at the *Cloventia Gazette*, they used to call me the bulldog." She thought for a moment. "Actually, that might be because somebody brought her bulldog puppy to work once and I fainted. But that's in the past. I work for the *Mintari Post* now. And this will be the *Mintari Post*'s biggest story."

Joe frowned. "How many stories have you printed so far?"

"This will be the first. But it's a big one." She laughed suddenly.

"What's so funny?"

"You know, I used to fear animals. Somehow I've become an animal rights activist." She shuddered. "I feel so dirty."

"You are. It's all the tarry smog in here."

Joe walked through the room, examining the different engine components. Simone kept taking notes. She had bought a notebook in the ship's gift shop. Actual paper. And she used an actual pen. Antiques. Mintari was rubbing off on her. Joe turned away from the machinery for a moment and watched Simone. She stood there, writing diligently, her red tresses dangling around her freckled face. He remembered her coming into his life last spring—a Cloventian in a tattered high-fashion outfit, barefoot, terrified, completely helpless on this world of dinosaurs. Today she wore Mintarian clothes, she was strong, confident, in her element. Over these past few months, she had changed, and Joe had learned to love her. Looking at her now, he realized that he loved her with all his heart. That he was broken without her.

She glanced up at him and blinked. "What?" She touched her cheek. "Is there smog on my face?"

You're beautiful, he wanted to tell her. *You're perfect. I love you.*

But Joe just cleared his throat, pushing away those thoughts. What use were they? She had walked out on him. Pining would only hurt him.

"I wanted to show you something. Come with me."

While they were talking, the hard-of-hearing engineer had wandered into his office. As they passed by his window, they saw him eating a cinnamon roll, sipping coffee, and reading a comic book.

"Hey, they got cinnamon rolls!" Simone said, making a beeline to the office.

"Not now, Simone." He held her hand and pulled her along. "Come with me."

"What could possibly be more important than cinnamon rolls?"

"Our lives? The lives of everyone aboard? The very survival of this planet?"

Simone considered. "Depends. How much icing is on those rolls?"

With a sigh, Joe led her across the engine room. He pointed. "Look."

Copper tubes rose from the deck toward the deckhead, filling the room like a tree trunk. Pistons rose and dipped across the floor like groundhogs—up and down, up and down. Each piston held a magnet. The magnets moved up the copper tubes like elevators, then detached, sank to the floor, and repeated the motion.

"What is it?" Simone said, watching the towering machine work.

"It's delivering electricity from the ship's reactor. The magnets propel the current through the tubes."

"Fascinating!" Simone said. But she wasn't taking any notes.

"This machine is generating a powerful electric field," Joe said.

"Riveting!" said Simone. She tapped her foot. "Joe, if the science lesson is over—"

"It's not over. Magnetic fields interfere with marine life. The underwater animals of Mintari can sense the planet's magnetic field. That's how they navigate. It's how they orient themselves. For them, magnetism is an important sense. Just as important as sight, smell, or sound. This ship isn't just deafening them with its rumbles. The magnetic field must be driving them crazy."

"Ah, got it. So it's like you playing piano at the saloon." Simone tapped her chin. "Maybe that'll keep them away from us."

"That armored fish attacked the ship. I thought it was because of the spotlight. What if it hated the magnetic field?"

Simone shuddered. "How far can this magnetic field travel underwater?"

"Far," Joe said. "Imagine sticking a blowhorn into a koi pond."

"You'd get some pissed-off koi."

"Pissed-off koi don't rip the hulls off cruise ships. Mosasaurs might."

Both Joe and Simone turned toward a porthole. The engine room was located underwater. The porthole revealed the ocean depths. Sunlight cascaded through the water, illuminating fish, eels, and ammonites. In the distance, a great shadow moved through the water, long and black and jagged. For an instant, Joe glimpsed jaws full of teeth. Jaws large enough to devour a lifeboat. When he blinked, the apparition vanished, and all he saw was swaying kelp. He must have imagined it. But when he looked at Simone, she was pale, and she clutched his hand.

A few hours later, Joe stood in the shower, eyes closed, and let the hot water wash over him. It had been a long day. He and Simone had compiled a list of problems aboard the *Maid of Mintari*. Maybe enough to shut the ship down. At the very least, it was bad press. Joe had to admit—it was nice to have his own journalist to sic on his enemies. As they said, the pen was mightier than the sleep-or-die.

Standing under the hot water, Joe let those vengeful feelings wash away. He just wanted to go home. He hated this ship. Hated being trapped here. Hated the crowds.

And he hated being so close to Simone yet unable to hold her. Unable to love her. Seeing her here, staying in the same cabin with her, yet knowing she was no longer his . . .

He turned the tap until the water nearly froze him. He shivered, but it doused the fire in his blood.

Why had he come here? Was it really to protect the people on this ship and the animals below? Or to be near her?

He had promised to go to dinner with her. She had insisted. He had agreed. More foolishness! He should stay in the cabin. Eat some crackers. Go to sleep and forget about her. Survive this week. Go home. Move on with his life.

But she was everywhere. Even when she wasn't with him, she haunted his mind. Her crooked smile. Her freckles. Her bright blue eyes. Her red hair. There was even a long red hair on the shower wall. Joe shuddered. He could have done without *that* reminder.

Finally he stepped out of the shower, a towel around his waist, to find a triceratops in his cabin.

Or at least—Simone in a triceratops costume. She wore a fluffy green onesie. The hood was pulled low, hiding her face. That hood sprouted a fabric frill, a fuzzy snout, three yellow horns, and googly eyes.

"What the hell is this?" Joe said.

"I'm a dinosaur!" Simone raised her hands menacingly, mimicking claws. She kept her head lowered, displaying the triceratops face on the hood. "Rawr!"

"I know you're a dinosaur!" he snapped. "Why?"

"I'm Dozer! It's my Halloween costume." She pushed back the hood, revealing her freckled face, and grinned. "Happy

Halloween!" Her eyes traveled up and down his body. He was still only wearing a towel. "Oh my, is that your costume?"

Joe tightened the towel around him. "I'm not wearing a costume."

"You're not wearing much of anything."

"It's not even Halloween. Not until tomorrow."

Simone shrugged. "It's Halloween Eve. I figured I'd get dressed up for dinner."

"I'm not taking you to dinner dressed like that."

"Why not? I thought you liked triceratops." She pulled the hood back over her face, dropped to all fours, and walked round the cabin, grunting in her best imitation of Dozer. The onesie even sprouted a tail, which Simone kept wagging.

"How old are you?" he snapped.

She looked up from munching a houseplant. "Thirty-two. But you're never too old for Halloween." She grabbed his towel. "Now get your costume on!"

Cheeks hot, he clutched the towel before she could rip it off. "I'm on duty. I'll wear my uniform."

Simone made a face and spat out leaves. "These are disgusting."

Twenty minutes later, they sat at Maison Megalodon, one of several restaurants aboard the *Maid of Mintari*. Joe had refused to visit Brontosaurus Buffet one deck down (despite Simone's hope that they served cinnamon rolls) or Gallimimus Grill on the upper deck. Those were far too crowded for him. But even Maison Megalodon was packed tonight. Joe and Simone couldn't get a table by a porthole, and they contented themselves with sitting by the doorway.

Joe ordered the fish 'n' chips. Simone ordered steak, lobster, and a mai tai.

"Things must be going well at the *Mintari Post*," Joe said, eying her expensive meal.

She raised her eyebrows. "I thought you were paying tonight."

"I'm no longer your boyfriend, remember? I'm off the hook."

She snorted. "As if you ever took me out for dinner." She sliced into her steak. "I'm not sharing. Enjoy your fish fingers."

She was about to take her first bite. Just then, her triceratops hood fell over her face. Joe found himself staring at googly eyes and fluffy horns. She pushed the hood back, blushing.

"Why did you have to wear this tarry costume?" Joe muttered. He looked around. "Nobody else is wearing a costume."

"Sure they are! That girl over there is wearing a witch hat."

"She's seven years old!"

"The waiters are wearing sailor suits," Simone said. "Sailor suits are costumes."

"It's their uniform. They wear that every day."

"And I can't be Dozer one day a year? Come on, Joe." She batted her eyelashes. "Admit it. You think I'm cute."

He snorted. "Stop flirting."

She gasped. "*Moi?* How dare you! Don't get a big head, Mr. Triplehorn. I'd sooner flirt with the waiter."

Just then, the waiter showed up to check on them. It was the same pimply, squeaky-voiced teenager from the lifeboat. The kid blushed. "Um, I brought you your crab cakes, Ms. LaRue."

He placed them on the table and fled for his life.

"Hey, do you serve cinnamon rolls?" she cried after him, but he was already gone.

For a while, they were quiet and focused on eating. Joe had to admit it. Yes. He did think she was cute.

He pushed those thoughts aside. It was over between them. It was only a twist of fate that brought them together aboard the *Maid of Mintari*. In a week, they'd be home. He would serve at Fort George, spend Sundays at the Fossil and Firkin, then once he was healed, he'd fight from the Last Home Hollow. Simone would live in her new house, focusing on the *Mintari Post*. And they would likely never see each other again. At that thought, his heart ached.

Simone looked up at him. "Why are you looking at me? I told you I'm not sharing my lobster and steak."

"You've got sauce on your horn."

"Clean it."

"I'm not cleaning your horn."

"I can't see my own horn. You have to clean it. Do it! Or I'll gore you."

Begrudgingly, he dabbed sauce off her horn, then leaned back, looking at her. She was busy eating, alternating between her steak, lobster, and crab cakes, sipping wine between bites. At one point, she paused, gulped, and looked up at him.

"Why are you looking at me now?" She touched her horn. "Is it dirty again?"

Joe had barely touched his food. He spoke softly. "I missed this."

"What, eating proper food instead of whatever slop they serve on your base?" She reached for another crab cake.

"You," he said. "Us. Just sharing a meal together."

Simone heaved a sigh. She put the crab cake down. "Joe, I don't want to do this now."

He stiffened. "Do what?"

"Talk about our relationship."

His upper lip twitched. "We're not in a relationship anymore. Remember, Simone? You left."

She snorted and bit into her crab cake. "All right."

"What?"

"I said all right."

"You snorted!"

She slammed the cake down. "Fine. You want to do this now, Joe? *Fine.* I didn't leave. You left! Weeks before me! You checked out long before I moved out."

He leaned forward, jaw clenched, struggling to keep his voice calm. "I was busy at work."

"And with your daughter. And with your boss. And with everything and everyone else. Other than me. I don't blame you, Joe! I'm not angry at you. I know you have big things going on. But I was tired of being your lowest priority."

"You're not my lowest priority! I love you, tar it!"

Simone froze, hand over her steak, going pale.

Joe cursed himself. Why had he blurted that out?

The waiter, who had just come to check on them, squeaked and backed away.

"Joe." Simone put her hand on his. "I'm sorry if I gave you the wrong signals tonight. I just wanted dinner. As friends."

Joe nodded. "Mhm."

She frowned. "What?"

"Nothing."

She slammed her cutlery down. "What, Joe?"

He pointed at her. "You've been following me nonstop. Coming to Pangaea Hall when I had a meeting there. Coming on this ship I was sent to. Booking the cabin next door. Swapping beds to be my roommate."

"Those were all coincidences!" Simone said. "What are you suggesting? That I'm some lovestruck girl playing a game?"

"You regret walking out on me. Admit it."

She raised her chin. Her hood fell back, revealing hair like furious fire and eyes that burned even hotter. "You admit that you're a megalomaniac who doesn't know how to treat a woman. Or anyone!"

"Fine, I admit it."

"Fine!" Simone said.

"Fine then!"

The waiter returned, holding a dessert tray. He gulped. "Maybe just the bill?"

"I'm getting the chocolate cake," Simone said. "I'm staying and eating dessert. Joe Triplehorn can go back to his room, hide from society, and sulk."

Joe ground his teeth. His rage blazed through him. He hissed at the waiter, "I'm having the apple pie." He glared at Simone. "With ice cream."

They ate their desserts silently, eyes shooting daggers at each other, each spoonful like another blow in a boxing match.

Finally that night, they returned to their cabin. They stood for a moment by the bunk beds, staring at each other.

"I know what you're thinking," Simone said. "And it's not happening."

He frowned. "What am I thinking?"

"That you can seduce me. That I'll join you on the bottom bunk."

He barked a laugh. "Is that what I was thinking?"

"If you want me, Mr. Triplehorn, you can climb onto the top bunk." She grabbed the ladder and climbed.

"As if that'll happen!" He sat down on the bottom bunk. "If *you* want *me*, I'll be on the bottom bunk. How do you like them apples?"

She tilted her head over from the top bunk. "Keep dreaming, buster. You'll be up here in no time." She pulled her head back.

"In your dreams, cheesecake!" he said.

"Fine then."

"Fine!"

Joe plonked himself down, grabbed a pillow, and closed his eyes. On the top bunk, Simone angrily dropped onto her back, crossed her arms, and pursed her lips. For a moment they lay there, silent and stewing.

Finally Joe spoke softly. "Good night, Simone."

She was quiet for a moment. "Good night, Joe."

Joe closed his eyes. He began drifting off to sleep when—

Bang!

His entire body jolted. It was like an electric shock pulsing through him.

At first he thought it a dream. Sometimes, just as he was drifting off to sleep, he would dream that he was falling, and his body would jolt awake. But this was real. A crack echoed through the cabin. Cups and books fell off the bedside table.

"What was that?" Simone cried.

For a moment, everything was quiet. Joe stepped out of bed. He stood there, listening. He could hear only the humming of the engine, a creaking in the deck. Simone climbed down from the top bunk and stood beside him.

He frowned at her. "You went to sleep in your triceratops costume?"

"It's comfy." She looked him up and down. "You sleep in your Ranger uniform?"

"I'm still on duty. I—"

A massive *thunk* reverberated through the deck. The cabin bounced. Objects fell off the shelves. Simone swayed and grabbed onto Joe. Screams sounded from other cabins.

Another *thunk*.

The deck shook. The bunk bed tilted over, and Joe had to push it back against the wall. Shouts and running feet sounded from the corridor.

Joe and Simone stared out the porthole. The window was so small they had to press their cheeks together.

The ocean was black. Clouds hid the moon, but the *Maid of Mintari* cast lights through her porthole. In the dim glow, Joe discerned a shadow rise. A massive shadow. A creature that would make Moby Dick look puny and send Captain Ahab fleeing. The ship's lights glinted on rows of teeth. Then the shadow vanished underwater.

Simone clutched Joe's arm. "What was that?"

The ship jolted again. Cracks and booms sounded from the lower decks. Joe and Simone fell, and the shelves and bunk beds collapsed. Joe placed himself over Simone, protecting her with his body. Mattresses, blankets, and the bed frame slammed onto his back. He grunted with pain. Thankfully the beddings had softened the blows. He found himself lying above Simone, staring down into her terrified eyes.

"Ryujin," he answered her. "That was Ryujin."

They ran through the ship. Hundreds of people—tourists and crew alike—ran with them, clogging the corridors, scrambling over one another, crying out in fear.

Another jolt shook the ship.

Through the portholes they saw it. The long, scaly body of the beast. A sea monster. A mosasaur. A god. It swarmed alongside the *Maid of Mintari*, larger than the great sperm whales of old and far more powerful. The ship rocked again. People fell, slamming into a bulkhead. A pipe burst, unleashing steam. The lights flickered.

"He's ramming us!" somebody cried.

"He's trying to tilt us over!"

"Run!"

The ship righted herself, knocking people over. A man thumped into a bulkhead, bloodied his head, and slumped to the deck. People ran over him, trampling him. Through a porthole,

Joe saw the mosasaur retreat, swim lower, and then another jolt shook the ship. This time from below. People flew through the air. Joe grabbed Simone, pinned her against a bulkhead, and protected her with his body. Elbows, knees, and chins slammed into his back. He nearly crushed Simone against the wall.

"We're all going to die!" somebody cried.

"Oh God, he's knocking us over."

"We're trapped!"

Most people didn't even bother with actual words. They were just screaming.

His arms around Simone, Joe turned his head toward the crowd. "Calm down, everyone! Listen to me! Calm down! The hull is thick. We're still safe. But if you panic, then—"

A *boom* rolled over him.

A blast of kinetic fury tore through the ship.

The lights died. Battery power kicked in, and red strobe lights filled the corridor. Klaxons wailed.

Everyone looked around. The screams died. People were weeping.

"What happened?" Simone whispered, her arms around Joe.

For a moment—silence.

Then another blast. Another. Then a gurgling, terrifying sound. Joe looked down at his feet. Water was bubbling up from the lower decks.

"He bit through the hull," Joe said. "This ship is going down." And his heart was sinking with it.

Everyone started screaming and running again. An old man fell. Tourists trampled over him, racing toward the staircase. Finger bones snapped. A child, separated from his mother, was crying. The water kept bubbling up. Simone rushed toward the old man and helped him to his feet, then soothed the child.

"Everyone stay calm!" Joe shouted. "Form neat lines. Lines, not mobs! Slowly and confidently, head toward the stairs and climb to the upper deck. Remember—be nice and calm and we'll all—"

"Run for your lives!" The pimply teenager came splashing through the water, eyes bugging out. "Run!" he squeaked again. "It's every man for himself!"

Joe grabbed the kid and shook him madly. "Listen to me. You are a sailor aboard the *Maid of Mintari*. Lead these people to the upper deck and into the lifeboats!"

The kid was barely listening. "We're doomed! We're all going to die, we're all going to—"

Joe slapped him. "Get a grip!"

The kid gulped. "Right. Right. To the upper deck!"

To his credit, the kid collected himself. He began leading people down a corridor and up the stairs.

Scales flashed across the portholes. A rumble shook the *Maid*. Joe glimpsed a huge tail coiling backward, then lashing toward the ship.

Thunk!

The ship tilted and shook and creaked and cracked. Water came rushing in through a bulkhead. People screamed and fell, but amazingly, the kid kept leading them on.

"Simone, go with them," Joe said.

Her eyes widened. "What about you?"

"I'm heading to the lower deck. There are people there too. They need me."

Her eyes nearly popped out. "It's flooded down there!"

"Not yet. Water is leaking in—but slowly. If the lower decks were flooded, we'd all be on the ocean floor by now. Go to the upper deck and get into a lifeboat!"

Joe turned and elbowed his way toward a hatch. Simone followed. "I'm going with you."

"Like hell!"

She raised her chin. The googly eyes on her hood rattled. "Not your choice, Mr. Triplehorn."

Joe pulled open a hatch, revealing a staircase. People came racing up from below, pale and drenched. When Joe glanced down, he saw water sluicing the deck. A lot of water. And more people panicking.

"Everyone—this way!" Joe cried. "Simone, these people need help. Stay here and lead them onward. I'm going deeper."

She seemed ready to object again, then nodded. She understood these people needed her. She held an old woman by the hand, began leading her upward. More tourists followed, praying and trembling.

Joe moved against the crowd, plunging deeper into the ship.

The damage was worse down here. Cracks spiderwebbed across the bulkheads and hull. Water came rushing in through a dozen holes. The water was already up to Joe's knees. The engine room, observation deck, and warehouses were one deck below. Those might be completely flooded, which meant this ship was going down fast. Thankfully, no tourists would be down there at night.

Joe waded through the water. Many cabin doors were closed. Tourists were shouting, banging on the hatches. The weight of the water kept the doors jammed. Joe splashed toward one cabin. People were screaming inside, begging, pounding the door. Joe took a step back, then shoved himself against the hatch. Again. Again. Finally the door ripped open. Hands reached out from inside, scratched and bleeding, like the hands of those buried alive reaching from their coffins.

Joe recognized the trapped tourists. The bachelorettes. They weren't *wooing* now. He grabbed their hands, pulled them out, and led them toward the staircase. Simone was beckoning from above, guiding them to safety.

As Joe approached another cabin, he passed by a porthole. The mosasaur slithered alongside the ship. For a terrible moment, the eye of the beast filled a porthole, staring right at Joe.

Joe stared back. He saw intelligence in that eye. He saw malice. It was an eye the size of a dinner plate. And it craved flesh.

The mosasaur recoiled, then slammed his scaly head against the hull. The ship tilted. Bulkheads cracked. Water came gushing in. Doors jerked open, spilling out tourists. The backup generator died, plunging the lower decks into darkness. Some dim lights came from the upper deck, where apparently the power was still on.

"Everyone—this way!" Joe said. "Come on, move through the water! Swim if you can't feel the deck. Here, toward my voice!"

The beast slammed into the ship again. The deck cracked. The water rose up to Joe's waist now. In the darkness and chaos, he kept moving through the cold water, pulling tourists from cabins, herding them toward the staircase where Simone was waiting.

He couldn't save everyone. Corpses floated around him. He had to nudge them aside and focus on the living.

He wanted to rage. He wanted to grab President Proudfoot and strangle the man. He had told them! He had warned them! But he couldn't let these feelings control him. He was here now. He had come to help. Right now all he could do was work to save whomever he could.

Joe kept going back to the cabins, again and again, pulling out more people. It seemed like he spent hours at the task, though it might have been only minutes. The water kept rising. Soon it reached his shoulders. He kept swimming deeper, pulling out survivors, leaving the dead behind. As he toiled, the *Maid of*

Mintari began to tilt. Water flooded one side of the deck, hiding half the bulkhead. Wildlife came gushing into the ship with salty torrents. Fish with sharp teeth bit Joe. Eels slithered in the dark. Mollusks clung to the walls.

And outside the mosasaur kept swimming. Kept beating the ship with his fins. Kept gnawing on the hull, punching holes with his teeth. The roars of the beast vibrated through the hull and shook the ship and pounded Joe's bones.

"Joe, get outta there!" Simone cried from the upper deck. "You'll drown!"

Joe looked around him. He was swimming now. His feet didn't even touch the deck. Within moments, the deck would be flooded, but half the ship was still above water. Joe swam up the staircase, knocking aside bodies. Simone reached down, grabbed his hand, and pulled him up.

This deck was flooding too. Holes pierced the hull. The ship kept tilting, and streams of water gushed in, thick with fish and algae. The last few tourists were racing toward the top deck and open air. Soon it was only Joe and Simone down here. Along with the dead.

"Come on." Joe grabbed Simone's hand. "Let's get you into a lifeboat."

"And you!"

He ignored her and pulled her upstairs.

They emerged into the open night. Hundreds of tourists and crew stood on the upper deck as the *Maid of Mintari* slowly sank below them. The twin moons glowed behind the clouds like stains of luminescent mold.

The deck tilted farther. The pool was spilling out. Lawn chairs, bottles, and bodies piled up against the starboard balustrade. A handful of spotlights still shone, illuminating the scene with eerie white light. People were leaping into the first few lifeboats, which were still strapped to the gunwale, dangling several feet above the water.

"They shouldn't be going into the water," Simone whispered. "Oh God. Joe. Look."

She pointed. Joe stared at the water.

The ocean churned. A scaly spine ridge emerged, then vanished underwater. The mosasaur was circling the ship. Stars above, the size of him! His head breached the water, and his jaws opened wide. His teeth gleamed. His furious rumble shook the night. Joe saw it on his head. A scar shaped like the letter Z. There could be no doubt now. It was him. The mosasaur that had nearly killed Fig. Ryujin, god of the ocean.

People were pointing. Screaming. Weeping. Praying. A few tourists were already in a lifeboat, but they hesitated, not lowering the boat to the water. Understandable. They were trapped between a sinking ship and a hungry mosasaur. Made a rock and a hard place seem lovely in comparison. Would they choose drowning or digestion? An impossible choice.

The mosasaur rose higher from the water. His mighty fins pounded the ocean, propelling his body into the air. He rose higher and higher, exposing more of his scaly girth. Soon only his tail was in the water. Joe stared in silent horror. He had never seen a carnivore this huge. Not in all his years on Mintari. Ryujin made even Ivan, the mutant T-rex, seem like a runt.

The mosasaur balanced on his tail, tilted forward, then came swooping down toward the *Maid of Mintari*.

"Run!" Joe shouted.

"Run *where?*" Simone cried.

He grabbed her hand. "With me!"

They ran together, and the crowd followed. A great shadow hid the moons, and the air whooshed like a man's breath fleeing stabbed lungs, and barnacles hailed, and seawater rained, and a rumble filled the sky like the engines of gods, and still they ran—ran across the deck, ran through the storm of salt and foam, ran as the mosasaur came plunging down and—

Ryujin slammed onto the deck.

His tail was still in the water. His upper half plowed through the balustrade, destroyed the tiki bar, pulverized the water slide, and finally shattered the wooden deck, crushing tourists. The blow just barely missed Joe and Simone. The deck shook so wildly they fell. Tourists fell around them. Simone screamed, clinging to Joe as the ship tilted more and more. Everyone and everything began sliding down what remained of the deck.

Joe lay on his stomach. He could barely see, barely tell up from down. He clung to Simone's hand as people slid around him, tumbling toward the sea.

In the chaos, Joe turned his head, managed to look below.

Ryujin's gargantuan head, upper body, and flippers lay on the deck. The rest of him was in the ocean. His girth had shoved the starboard railing underwater. The deck sloped at a dizzying angle. Everything from tables to tourists was sliding downward.

The mosasaur opened his mouth. A tourist slid into the waiting gullet, and Ryujin chomped down, chewing, swallowing. His head moved from side to side, snatching up tourists, crushing them, and gulping them down. A few people tumbled into the water, avoiding death in the jaws of the beast. But Ryujin lashed his tail from side to side, breaking their bones, hurtling them into the distance.

Joe and Simone slid down the steep deck. Joe scrabbled for purchase while Simone screamed so loudly she deafened him.

"Can you stop screaming and grab something?" he snapped.

"I am! I'm grabbing you!"

Finally Joe's hand found and grasped something—a hand rail at the edge of the swimming pool. It was bolted onto the deck, and Joe clung on. Simone held a second rail. Just below their kicking feet awaited the monster's snapping jaws. Joe felt like a marble in a game of Hungry Hungry Hadrosaurs.

The ship sank lower. Ryujin beat his flippers, climbing higher on the deck. His mind addled with terror, Joe had the bizarre image of some obese, scaly merman trying to climb onto a raft, only shoving it deeper into the water. Joe shook his head, banishing the ridiculous thought.

Stop thinking of mermen and Hungry Hungry Hadrosaurs, he chided himself. *Reality is horrific enough.*

Ryujin's maw quivered just below Joe's feet. Corpses jiggled inside. The mosasaur thrust his snout closer, eager to feed. Joe and Simone pulled their knees toward their bellies. The mouth snapped shut, missing their legs by inches.

"Simone, hold me!" he cried.

"I'm scared too, but now is not the time for cuddles."

"Stop with the jokes and hold me, tar it! I need both hands!"

She nodded. She gripped the pool's handle with one hand, held him with the other. Joe managed to aim his sleep-or-die. He flipped the switch to "die" and fired.

A bullet pounded the mosasaur. Joe fired again. Again. And again. Bullets bombarded the reptile.

"Die, you bastard!" Joe shouted, emptying his magazine into the beast.

His bullets chipped scales. Blood spurted. The mosasaur closed his mouth, slipped off the deck, and vanished underwater.

The ship rocked, but even with Ryujin's weight removed, the *Maid of Mintari* did not right herself. She had taken on too much water. She kept sinking. Half the upper deck was now underwater. The survivors scrambled to the other half, grabbing onto whatever they could. Many were floating in the water.

Only a triangular chunk of the ship still rose above the ocean. And the *Maid* kept sinking, sinking deeper into the abyss.

There was no choice now. No hope to still save the *Maid of Mintari*. It was the lifeboats or join the *Maid* underwater.

The survivors realized this. They were leaping into lifeboats and rowing away. Joe spotted the captain of the ship, his cheeks flushed, his white mustache disheveled. He was already in a lifeboat, rowing into the distance. There were several empty seats in his boat. Many people were simply swimming, desperately trying to keep afloat. A few people were fighting in the water for broken scraps of deck. They reminded Joe of flies bustling in blood.

Suddenly great fountains of water splashed. Tentacles emerged from below. A bizarre creature rose from the water. Its shell was shaped like an ice cream cone. Tentacles stuck out from the top like wriggling serpents. The animal was the size of a bus.

"What the heck is that?" Simone cried.

"An orthocone," Joe muttered. "Terror of the Triassic. It was once an apex predator."

"Terror of the Triassic, great," Simone said. "Everything on this planet is the Butcher of the Jurassic or the Killer of the Cretaceous or the Murderer of Mesozoic. Can't we ever meet anything cute and fluffy?"

The monstrous mollusk wrapped its tentacles around a swimming man. The swimmer screamed and struggled, but the tentacles constricted him, then began reeling him in. The orthocone opened a sharp beak, bit down hard, crushed the man, and gulped him down.

More tentacles flailed across the sea. An entire pod of orthocones had come to feed. They snatched swimmers, pulled them into their ravenous beaks, and feasted. Screams and blood filled the water.

"Where is Ryujin?" Simone said, clinging to Joe. "Did you kill him?"

They both still lay on the sinking deck. Their feet were almost in the water now.

"No," Joe said. "He's still alive. I hurt him. He's licking his wounds."

"Hopefully he licks them far, far away for a long, long time."

A deafening *crack* tore through the ship. Simone clutched Joe tighter. Was that Ryujin? No. Joe could not hear the mosasaur's grumbles.

"The hull is cracking underwater," Joe said. "We need to get everyone into the lifeboats."

Simone nodded. "Hopefully those giant squids don't like the taste of wood. Or gingers."

They wobbled across the sinking deck, moving toward a waiting lifeboat. Several tourists and crew members were climbing inside.

"Get in there!" Joe said, leading Simone toward the boat. "You first."

Joe shook his head.

"Joe!" She stared at him reproachfully, but then her expression softened and tears filled her eyes. "Tell me you're getting on this boat."

"Not until all the women and children are safe," Joe said.

Tears rolled down her cheeks. "Stop being so honorable." She clung to him. "I'm staying with you."

"Simone, you have to go. To survive. To be there for Fig. Please. Live." His voice cracked on that last word.

Simone nodded and sobbed. "I love you, Joe," she whispered, her own voice choking.

A lump filled his throat. His eyes stung. "I love you, Simone. Even if you look ridiculous in that sopping wet triceratops onesie."

She laughed through her tears.

The deck sank another meter underwater. Their feet vanished into the murk.

Simone grabbed his cheeks, pulled him closer, and kissed him on the mouth. Their tears mingled. Then Simone climbed into the lifeboat, weeping. She joined mothers, children, and elders. The survivors were pale, huddling together, praying.

Joe untied the rope. The lifeboat drifted across the dark water. Simone stood among the survivors, looking back at Joe, tears on her cheeks. Behind her, a dozen lifeboats were bobbing on the water, and hundreds of people were swimming, trying to reach the boats but sinking, drowning. Several men swam toward one lifeboat, tried to climb in, but the survivors inside kicked them, stepped on their fingers, and the men sank. Every moment, another orthocone rose, and tentacles grabbed survivors, grabbed boats, and the predators feasted.

Joe stood on the *Maid of Mintari*, gazing upon hell. Below him, the ship sank deeper and deeper. And somewhere far below, a bellow rolled.

CHAPTER FOURTEEN
Polar Opposites

Joe stood on the deck of the *Maid of Mintari*, watching the lifeboats sail away. Watching Simone on her boat moving farther into darkness until he only could glimpse her red hair. The ship sank lower below him. The water touched his feet. And Joe knew he was going to die.

Most of the cruise ship was underwater now. Only the port balustrade, a few chimneys, and a narrow crescent of deck were above the surface. A hundred survivors or more clung to what remained.

There was one lifeboat left. Just one. It could hold ten, maybe twenty survivors at most. Hundreds were trying to reach it. The ship kept sinking, and the water rose above their ankles.

Joe splashed through the water toward the survivors. They were scrambling for the lifeboat, shoving one another aside. One man almost grabbed the lifeboat. But tentacles rose from the water. An orthocone came scraping across the submerged deck, grabbed the man, and devoured him. Joe reloaded his rifle and fired. The mollusk squealed, retracted its tentacles into its conical shell, and vanished underwater.

"Women and children first!" Joe shouted, climbing toward the lifeboat. It was strapped to the port gunwale, still held above the water. Everyone was reaching toward it, but they kept sliding down, and more tentacles emerged from the water, grabbed ankles, and pulled victims into waiting beaks. The lifeboat seemed unreachable like a loaf of bread held tauntingly above starving children.

The deck began to splinter. People screamed. Joe kept climbing. He leaped upward, grabbed the balustrade, and pulled himself higher. He found himself beside the last lifeboat, which was still tied to the railing.

The people cried out below, reaching toward him.

"Women and children first!" Joe repeated.

"What do you mean first?" cried a man. "There's just one boat left! You mean only women and children!"

"Then only women and children!" shouted an old man.

"Easy for you to say. You're half already dead!"

"I want to live, I want to live," whimpered a young man.

Somebody handed Joe a toddler. He placed the wailing child in the boat. A young mother climbed the submerged deck. Joe grabbed her, pulled her up, placed her into the boat. As he worked, the orthocones kept rising from the dark water, kept feeding. For every survivor Joe placed in the boat, another fell to the tentacles.

Finally the boat was full. By now, the ship had sunk so much the port balustrade was touching the water. Joe cut the knots, and the lifeboat drifted into the chaos, carrying a handful of survivors.

Screams filled the night. Hundreds of survivors filled the lifeboats or swam in the water. Hundreds more were gone already. Corpses slapped against the sinking hull. A severed arm floated by. Again and again the water splashed as the creatures from below came to feed. More than orthocones feasted now. Other monsters joined the banquet. Aquatic scorpions the size of seals grabbed people with their claws. A scaly green reptile swam between the boats, its neck ridiculously long. Longer than its entire body. Longer than four or five giraffe necks. A vicious little head topped that hose-like neck, full of sharp teeth. The head kept swinging from side to side like a tetherball, grabbing people, pulling them off boats, biting, eating.

An albertonectes, Joe thought, watching with a mix of wonder and horror. He had heard of such animals. They had the longest necks in history. He never wanted to see one again.

He knew he was going to die tonight. The lifeboats were full. There was barely room for half the passengers. Ancient monsters filled the water. It would take the Rangers hours to get here. Joe knew the Rangers had only a few small boats and tricopters, enough to only rescue a few people at a time. It could take days to pull everyone out of the water.

Joe would not last this night. He only hoped that the women and children survived. That Simone survived.

I'm sorry, Figaro, he thought, a lump in his throat. *I'm sorry I never got enough time with you.*

The ship sank lower below him. Only a bit of twisted balustrade now rose from the water, the mangled hand of a drowning titan. The boats bobbed on the water. People were swinging oars, trying to knock back the predators. They swatted tentacles aside. Batted at toothy little heads on long necks. They were not Rangers, not trained to fight. They were mothers protecting their children, and that made them the fiercest warriors on Mintari. They gave Joe hope that some would survive. That some would make it ho—

A monster burst from the ocean.

Enormous jaws opened wide, grabbed a lifeboat from below, and snapped shut.

The boat shattered.

People fell overboard, screaming. They were the lucky ones. Others ended up inside that terrible mouth.

The beast rose higher, rearing from the water, fins held out in triumph. The reptile towered over the boats around him. Ryujin was back.

Survivors began swimming toward the remaining lifeboats. But the other boats were full. And no boat seemed safe now.

Joe aimed his sleep-or-die. He only had a few bullets left, but maybe he could hurt the monster, scare him away. Before he could fire, Ryujin sank underwater again, taking several people with him. He left behind the shattered scraps of the lifeboat, blood in the water, and screams.

Joe looked around from side to side, seeking signs of the beast. The water did not stir. He heard no rumbles.

He looked up toward one of the lifeboats. In the darkness, Simone's pale skin and red hair stood out like a beacon. She made eye contact with him across the void.

Then Ryujin rose again.

He came from below. Another surprise attack. His jaws closed around a lifeboat. The boat right beside Simone.

Again the jaws snapped shut, shattering the boat, crushing people. When Joe had been a child, he had seen a video of a hippo eating a watermelon. The animal had crushed the entire fruit in its mouth, scattering red juices everywhere. That was what Ryujin chomping on the lifeboat reminded him of.

He fired his gun. His bullets hit the reptile's scales. Ryujin rumbled and sank underwater. The bullets stung him but apparently did little damage.

This isn't going to work, Joe thought. *I can't kill him. He'll keep coming back. Eating and eating. Until we're all gone.*

But no. There must be hope. Figaro had encountered this mosasaur before. And she had survived.

Ryujin rose again from the water. This time he didn't bother shattering a lifeboat. He simply scooped up two swimmers, then dived down, pulling their bodies underwater.

How did you survive him, Fig? Joe thought.

The ship's balustrade sank deeper. Joe could no longer feel the deck below his feet. The *Maid of Mintari* was sinking toward the ocean floor.

Frantically, Joe thought back to Fig's stories. She had been in the water, she said. Wearing a life jacket. Her friends had been in the rowboat. Ryujin had only attacked the boat, not her. Why? Did he only hate boats? No, Ryujin was attacking swimmers now too. What repelled him about Fig?

Then it snapped into place.

Her life jacket.

Joe had seen it. A life jacket with magnetic clasps.

"Magnets," he whispered.

Joe dived underwater.

He must reach the engine room. Rip the magnets off the generators. Carry them toward the lifeboats.

Magnets! he thought. *You might have just saved us, Fig.*

But the engine room was deep underwater. And Joe's lungs were already aching for air. Then a memory flashed through him—standing on the deck, scolding scuba divers, warning them against entering the water.

There was scuba gear on the ship! Right below the top deck! That wasn't too deep. If Joe could just reach the scuba gear . . .

His lungs cried out in agony. Ignoring them, he kept swimming deeper, deeper. Air. He needed air! Where were those oxygen tanks? He reached the *Maid*'s deck, scrabbled across the wood for a hatch—

He couldn't do it. Joe rose to the surface. His head burst out into the cold night. He gulped down air and coughed.

Ahead of him, the mosasaur rose again. The reptile scooped three more swimmers into his mouth.

Joe took a deep breath and dived again. This time he moved faster, with more purpose. He reached a hatch on the deck, dived into a cabin, and yanked open the closet. There! Jackpot! The scuba gear.

He grabbed an oxygen tank, a mask, and tubing. He wanted to grab goggles and flippers too. No time! No time! He had to breathe! He fiddled with the scuba gear. He couldn't get it to work.

He swam upward, dragging the gear with him, his lungs screaming in pain. Bubbles rose from his mouth and nose. He was going to die. To drown. But he clung onto that oxygen tank. Stars ignited across his vision. He rose higher and his head burst over the surface. He gulped down air. The stars faded. Cold night air filled his lungs.

With frigid blue fingers, he untangled the scuba gear, attached the tubing and straps, and placed the mask on. Oxygen flowed into his lungs. And he dived again.

He plunged through the dark, bloody ocean. Only his flashlight illuminated his way. The *Maid of Mintari* was sinking fast now toward the ocean floor. The water churned in vortexes, buffeting Joe, but he swam hard, staying on course. He shoved aside debris, reached the upper deck, and swam through a hatch.

As he dived through the innards of the *Maid of Mintari*, the ship kept sinking around him. He had to keep pace. Fish, eels, and squids moved around him. Perhaps they were seeking leftovers from the apex predator who feasted above; mosasaurs were messy eaters, scattering meaty scraps everywhere. Aiming his flashlight downward, Joe kept diving. A bulkhead tilted and bumped against him. A deckhead thudded against his back. The water churned everywhere, and the eyes of eels, carnivorous fish, and squids shone in the darkness.

Joe began breathing heavily. His heart pounded. He felt trapped. This was worse than being in a crowd. He was lost in the dark, predators all around, he couldn't breathe, he was going to suffocate.

Calm down, he told himself. *Deep breaths. Keep going. Simone needs you.*

The anxiety cleared. He kept swimming, moving down staircases, entering the bowels of the ship. Corpses floated around him. Finally Joe reached the engine room. The schools of fish parted. The engines were dead, but perhaps the fish could still sense the magnetic field in this cabin.

He noticed that his teeth were chattering. That his fingers were blue. Tar, it was cold down here. Hypothermia could kill him as easily as any sea monster. But he had no choice. He had to ignore the cold, keep moving, keep going.

He swept his flashlight around. There, just as he remembered them—the magnets. They were attached to the turbines, designed to run across the copper rods, generating electricity. Joe swam toward one magnet. It was the size of a dinner plate. He tugged at it, but it was screwed onto the piston. Tar it!

Joe looked around for tools. Nothing. Finally he found a chunk of metal pipe. He wielded it like a club, banging it against the magnet again and again. A magnet came loose. It fell off a piston. Success!

He swung the pipe once more, knocking off another magnet. Then a few more. He stacked them together, snapping them into place. Above the surface, they would be cumbersome and heavy. But underwater he could carry them with ease. He found some cabling, wrapped it around the magnets, and dragged them through the flooded engine room.

He was about to swim upstairs when the hull shattered.

A creature burst into the engine room, jaws wide open, baring sharp bony shards. The beast looked big enough to chomp down on a mammoth. Armored plates covered it from head to tail. Blazing white eyes the size of melons glared at Joe.

A dunkleosteus.

Joe had seen the enormous armored fish—maybe the same one—attack the ship before, ripping off a spotlight. It was the magnets. The creature hated them. But instead of fleeing, the ill-tempered fish wanted to crush the magnets. The dunky's jaws came thrusting toward Joe, opening wide, lined with bony blades. The fish was like a staple remover the size of an elephant.

Joe hurled the metal pipe at the monster. The dunkleosteus snapped its jaws shut, shattering the pipe like it was a toothpick. The armored brute swam closer to Joe, intending to do the same to his bones. Joe swam backward, fumbling in the water for his rifle. His back hit a bulkhead. The dunky swam closer, mouth opening wide, revealing a hungry gullet.

A furious cry pierced the water.

A diver rose above the fish.

Red hair billowed in the water like the fins of a goldfish.

Simone! Joe thought.

An oxygen tank hung across her back. In her hands, she held a trident. She drove the weapon down hard, piercing the dunky's eye.

The fish squealed. Joe hadn't even realized fish could make that sound. Or any sound, for that matter. But squeal the dunky did. It turned tail and abandoned ship, the trident stuck in its head.

Simone waved at Joe. He had a million questions, but he couldn't talk with his scuba gear on. They swam together, dragging the magnets on a rope. They swam out a hole in the hull, into the open water, then rose above the surface.

Joe ripped off his scuba mask. "Simone! That was a dangerous stunt!"

She nodded. "So dangerous it saved your life."

"Where did you get that trident?"

She smiled shakily. "A woman on my lifeboat lent it to me. She got dressed up as Poseidon. It's Halloween, you know. The scariest Halloween of my life." She shuddered. "Tar it's cold, did you notice?"

A rumble sounded behind them. Joe turned to see the mosasaur rise again, scooping up another swimmer in his massive jaws.

"Simone, these magnets might repel Ryujin," Joe said. "I think that's how Fig survived."

"If they didn't repel that fish, how would they repel a mosasaur?" Simone said.

"Well, elephants fear mice, right? Maybe giants have phobias. It's worth a try. Help me distribute the magnets among the lifeboats."

Simone nodded.

They swam between the lifeboats. The orthocones parted before them, tentacles recoiling into their conical shells. The long-necked albertonectes hissed and sank underwater. These animals didn't like the magnets either, it seemed. Joe looked around for Ryujin, but the mosasaur was currently underwater, perhaps chewing his most recent mouthful of tourists. All night so far, Ryujin had kept rising again and again for more. Most likely, Joe didn't have much time before the next assault.

They reached one boat. Survivors stood inside, women and children all. The stronger women held oars, pipes, and other weapons. One nearly smacked Joe on the head, perhaps mistaking him for a sea monster.

Joe leaned over the edge of the boat. He dropped a heavy magnet onto the deck.

"Hold on to this magnet. It might keep the sea creatures away."

They swam between the other lifeboats, distributing magnets. A few men joined the effort. They swam alongside Joe and Simone, armed with knives or just their fists, ready to knock back any threat that approached.

None did. No squids. No eels. Not even little snapping fish.

The magnets were working.

Until now, the magnets had been clustered together deep inside the ship. Now, with them distributed among the lifeboats, a magnetic field spread across the scene like an invisible shield. It protected both those in the boats and those who swam among them.

Deep underwater, Joe heard the rumbling of the mosasaur. But Ryujin seemed farther now.

They had banished the dark god.

"It worked," Joe whispered, waves of relief flowing over him.

He allowed himself a few deep breaths. He couldn't stop shivering. His teeth kept chattering. Simone's lips were blue, her skin ghostly pale.

"Get into a boat and warm up," he told her.

She shook her head. "I'm staying with you." Her teeth too were chattering. "It'll warm up soon. Dawn is rising."

In the early-morning light, Joe looked around him at the scene. Ten lifeboats remained, crammed with survivors. Some survivors still swam in the water. Not many.

The water roiled.

People screamed and pointed.

"He's back! Ryujin is back!"

The enormous scaly head rose from the water. But the mosasaur kept his distance from the boats. He did not open his jaws to feed. Across the distance, Ryujin stared. With malevolent red eyes, he stared right at Joe. And Joe stared back.

And Joe had the terrible feeling that this creature was sentient. That Ryujin was sizing him up.

"What the hell are you?" Joe whispered.

Without a sound, the mosasaur dipped underwater and swam away.

Joe closed his eyes. The monster was gone but not forever. Joe knew this war was not over. He had seen that promise in the eyes of the beast.

But this battle was over, and it had been a hard one. They had sailed here with a thousand people. Perhaps three hundred still lived. The sea had taken the rest.

At noon, help finally arrived. Three Ranger ships. Salvation was here.

The next few hours passed in a haze. Joe kept slipping in and out of consciousness. Vaguely he was aware of Rangers pulling him from the water. Wrapping him in a thermal blanket. Putting an oxygen mask on his face. He was not wounded seriously—nothing but an assortment of scratches and bruises. But the cold had run deep through his body. Hypothermia had come close to doing what Ryujin could not.

Through the shivering haze, Simone remained at his side. She too got the same treatment. The blanket, the mask, the cake.

Joe frowned. The cake?

"Where did you get that?" he moaned.

She sat beside him on the deck of a rescue ship, eating heartily. "I asked if they had cake. They brought me a slice. Coffee cake. I prefer cinnamon rolls, but beggars can't be choosers."

They sat on the upper deck in the open air. It was a small ship, but a hundred survivors covered the deck and filled the lower cabins. The three rescue ships raced across the sea, leaving churning wakes. Armed Rangers stood at the gunwales, aiming cannons at the water. The captain of the *Maid of Mintari*, still half-drunk, was telling the Rangers how he had saved hundreds of lives.

"Oh, you might hear some talk of how I got into the first lifeboat," the captain was saying. "I was leading the way to safety! Cutting through the enemy!"

The Rangers nodded, clearly not buying any of it.

"I'll go join the watch," Joe said. "My gun still works, I think."

He started to rise, but Simone grabbed him and pulled him down. "You're not going anywhere, mister. You've earned a day off." She leaned against him. "And I need you to snuggle me and keep me warm."

He bristled. "I'm a Ranger, tar it. Rangers don't snuggle."

"You do now." She cuddled against him.

With a sigh, he slung an arm around her. They sat huddled together under the blankets, and Simone forgot all about her cake and wept onto his shoulder.

"Hey Joe," she finally whispered, drying her eyes on her sleeve. "What is a mosasaur's favorite meal?"

He frowned. "What?"

"Fish and ships."

Joe stared at her as if she were crazy. Then he guffawed.

Simone smiled shakily. "Hey Joe. Why do mosasaurs live in salt water?"

"Why?"

"Because pepper makes them sneeze."

"That's awful, Simone."

"Hey." She nudged him. "Why did the mosasaur cross the ocean?"

"I don't care."

"To get to the other tide."

"Simone, please, I beg you, stop."

She nuzzled against him. "Did you hear about the mosasaur who fell in love? It was love at first bite."

"Please shut up."

She kissed his cheek. "At least if a mosasaur eats me, I'll taste funny."

He put a finger on her lips, finally shushing her. Then he held her close, never wanting to let her go again.

CHAPTER FIFTEEN
The Bite Fight

Dawn rose. It was Halloween on Mintari.

In her room in the Fossil and Firkin, Fig woke up alone. Joe and Simone were still on their cruise. For long moments, Fig lay awake in bed. The morning light fell between the shutters, dancing across her face. She did not want to leave the warm blankets.

It was funny. This city was home to three hundred thousand people, more if you counted the tourists. But since moving here, Fig had never spent so much time alone. An achillobator was never alone. Their packs were small, usually including only twenty dinosaurs. But with her pack, Fig always had somebody to hold, feathers to nuzzle, a warm heartbeat to listen to. Humans lived in great herds, but they must be the loneliest animals on Mintari.

It was almost time for school. Fig didn't want to go. She should stay in bed all day. Hide under the blankets. Or better yet—run away. She would flee into the wild, find her bators, and live among the pack again.

But that scared her. Winter's winds were mustering. Soon the hosts of snow and ice would fall upon the land. Fig remembered those long winters, huddled in a nest, nuzzling under the feathers of her pack, shivering and not knowing if she would live to see spring. She had survived then, but barely. The thought of winter in the wild chilled her. Perhaps the wild was no longer her home. Perhaps the pack would not welcome her back.

Perhaps, after only half a year in Dinovia, Fig was domesticated, merely a caged animal, no longer able to survive in nature.

She rose from bed.

Come, Figaro, she told herself. *You survived winter in the wild. You can survive another day at Leakey High.*

She examined her feelings, and she realized what she feared most. Denise. Fig feared a million things, but Denise Rex loomed atop the pyramid of her horrors. The cruel laughter. The staring eyes. Those hurt more than the slaps. Fig had suffered many injuries in her life—the sting of fangs, the scrapes of claws, the bite of winter's winds—but none hurt more than humiliation. Whenever Fig walked the halls of Leakey High, she wished she could disappear.

But wait a moment! The proverbial light bulb appeared over Fig's head. This was Halloween. She didn't need to disappear. She just needed a costume.

She checked the clock. The school dinosaur would be here in a few minutes. Normally, Simone would be shoving her out the door by now. Fig glanced around the room, looking for something—*anything*—she could turn into a costume. Joe had left some of his Ranger uniforms here. Perhaps she could dress up like him? He had even left a spare ceratop hat. No, that was ridiculous. She was half his size. His uniform would drape across her body like a sheet.

"A sheet, eh?" Fig muttered.

The light bulb shone again.

Fig pulled the sheet off her bed. With a pair of scissors, she cut two eyeholes. She draped the sheet over her and looked in the mirror. Fig became what she wanted to be every day. A ghost.

She flounced downstairs into the saloon's common room. Dozens of pumpkins filled the room, alongside fake cobwebs, wreathes of autumn leaves, and plastic dinosaur skeletons. Barnum was already awake, waxing the bar as always. A few of the locals were up, drinking coffee. Merl was eating baked beans from a can, dripping tomato sauce onto his overalls, while Old Abernathy sat by the fireplace, whittling. The old man waved at Fig, scattering sawdust.

"See ya later!" Fig said, rushing to the batwing doors. She could already hear the school diplodocus outside.

Merl whimpered. "A ghost! The saloon is haunted!" He clung to Abernathy.

Fig was only half-sure he was kidding. Merl was a giant of a man, but when they watched *Curse of the Zombiesaur* last night, he had shivered and hid behind Fig.

She rushed out the doors and onto a cobbled sidewalk strewn with autumn leaves. The diplodocus lumbered to a halt. The massive dinosaur was draped with cobwebs and plastic spiders, and somebody had placed a witch's hat on his head. Fig felt sorry for the proud old dinosaur. Nobody deserved to be humiliated like this. But then again, she had been a huntress in the wild, and she was wearing a sheet now, so she was not one to talk. She scampered up the rope ladder and joined the other pupils in the howdah.

She sat beside Abbey. The girl wore a plush stegosaurus onesie. It looked similar to the triceratops onesie Fig had helped Simone choose at *Frankie's Costume Emporium* last week.

"Nice cos-toom, Abbey," Fig said as the diplodocus plodded down the road, heading toward the school.

"Thank you, Figaro." Abbey glanced down at her onesie and sighed. "Though I'm afraid the costume makers got stegosaurus morphology completely wrong. I counted only ten cloth triangles along the back, while real stegosaurs have seventeen dorsal plates, and they weren't even triangular. The thagomizer is wrong too. Only three spikes. Three! There should be four. And the color is completely wrong too. I ask you, Figaro, have you ever seen a purple stegosaurus? I do love purple, but I love anatomical authenticity more. I asked the storekeep to aspire to higher scientific accuracy with his wares, but he only gave me a strange look. I truly wish more people understood dinosaur biology, especially since we live on Mintari."

"I tink da cos-toom looks nice," Fig said.

Abbey heaved a sigh. "Well, it matches my clan crest at least." She tapped the silver stegosaurus pinned to her chest. "I figured a stegosaurus costume behooved me. I can't say I approve of your costume, Figaro. It has nothing to do with dinosaurs."

"I'm a dinosaur ghost," said Fig.

"Ah. Which species?"

"Um . . . triceratops," Fig said. "Like my clan."

Clans were still a strange concept to Fig. They were like packs within the larger human herd. But why did dinosaur species represent them? Fig apparently belonged to Clan Triplehorn. Her clan lived by the ideals of the triceratops—strength, stubbornness, stability. Yet Fig still felt like an achillobator, quick and deadly. She wondered if she could start her own clan. Clan Achillobator. Yet she also felt loyal to her family. To her father.

And to my aunt? she wondered.

Meeting Amissa still haunted her. Her aunt was a poacher. A villain. A terror. Yet when Fig remembered her scaring away Denise, remembered sharing a pizza with her, she smiled. The woman had killed Red Scar! Yet Fig had felt safe around her. Felt she was with family. That Amissa truly cared about her. Joe was a triceratops, yes, tough and cranky. But with Amissa, Fig felt like she did among bators. Amissa was a Triplehorn on paper, but in her heart, that woman was a predator.

Like me, Fig thought.

The diplodocus halted outside Leakey High. Fig sat on the dinosaur's back, gazing at the schoolyard. Everyone was in costume. She saw witches, skeletons, dinosaurs, monsters, Rangers, space fighters, silk emperors, and countless other mimicries. Fig had known animal mimics in nature—insects that looked like leaves or sticks, snakes that resembled branches or vines, toads that seemingly turned to stone. It was a tool for survival, but humans made it a game. The variety of colors and shapes overwhelmed Fig. One never received this much sensory input in the wild. She wanted to stay on the dinosaur, ride him into the wild, and never return.

But I want to become a Ranger someday, Fig thought. *A real Ranger.*

For that she must graduate high school. Once she was a Ranger, she would leave this city, she decided. She would live in the Last Home Hollow with her father. From that cave, they would protect the dinosaurs together. Far from the crowds of Dinovia.

She climbed off the dinosaur. At least she had her disguise.

Like a true ghost, she glided through the school halls, her sheet rustling. The costumes surrounded her, spinning her head. An alien leaned toward her, blinking multifaceted eyes, and waggled its antennae. A skeleton cackled and clattered its jawbone. A zombie tapped Fig's head, searching for brains. She kept walking. Normally people avoided her. But nobody recognized Fig like this. They actually approached her. Actually interacted with her. Even the normal kids. She had wanted to be invisible. Instead she became . . . normal. Hidden under the sheet, Fig smiled.

There they were.

Her smile faded at once. Her heart burst into a gallop. There—right ahead. Denise Rex and her friends.

Denise wore red silken robes trimmed with gold. A tiara of golden teardrops adorned with rubies topped her head of blond hair. She had dressed up as Princess Al-Sadai, daughter of Magin IV, the mightiest of Cloventia's seven silk emperors. Al-

Sadai was not only a famous imperial but an infamous socialite, known to frequent dance clubs across Cloventia, often falling headfirst into scandals (figuratively and sometimes literally). A year ago, the princess had even visited Mintari on safari. According to the tabloids, she had stayed in Rex Manor, the ancestral home of Clan Rex. Clearly Denise Rex had been smitten.

Her regular posse was with her. Their costumes were less striking. Fig spotted a witch, a vampire, and a giant pumpkin. Fairly pedestrian, but well, they couldn't eclipse their queen's splendor. They stood a step behind Denise, subservient to her.

Fig approached them. She didn't know why. But she could not resist. Hidden in her sheet, she glided toward the princess and her coterie.

"Boo!" Fig blurted out.

Denise raised an eyebrow. "Um, what?" She snickered.

"Cool, a ghost!" said one of her friends, a witch.

Fig raised her arms and made spooky noises. Denise rolled her eyes, but her friends laughed.

"Who's under that sheet?" said the vampire. "Lia, is that you?"

Fig dropped her voice, speaking in a rumbling baritone. "I . . . am da ghost . . . of Denise's future . . . dead . . . dead . . ."

Everyone burst out laughing. Everyone other than Denise, who paled with fury.

"Denise, dude, she totally owned you!" said the giant pumpkin.

"Who is that?" Denise cried, reaching for Fig's sheet. But Fig stepped back, dodging the silken princess.

"You can't . . . touch . . . a ghost!" Fig waved her arms, speaking in a deep, spooky voice. It helped disguise her speech impediment. "I . . . curse you!"

A hand grabbed her shoulder from behind. "Come on, Figaro. We're late to class."

Fig's heart nearly stopped.

It was Abbey Longspikes, wearing her plush stegosaurus costume. She began pulling Fig down the hall.

"Figaro Triplehorn!" Denise cried, pointing at Fig under her sheet.

Fig laughed and hurried with Abbey down the hall. Denise tried to chase them, but with her elaborate costume and high heels, she was too slow. Fig and Abbey made it into the remedial class, shut the door behind them, and collapsed into a fit of giggles.

Suddenly Fig realized something. She lost her smile and gaped at Abbey. "Back in da hall, Abbey. You t-t-talked! And it wasn't 'bout dinosaurs!"

Abbey blushed, pulled her stegosaurus hood over her face, and hurried to her desk. She began scribbling dinosaurs, gripping her crayons so tightly she snapped one. Fig sat beside her, smiling again. They were both making progress.

It was almost a good day. Almost her best day yet.

Until the headmaster called her into his office.

Fig had been to Headmaster Rex's office several times already. It never ended well.

His full name was Victor Rex, and he was a gray-haired, gray-skinned lump of a man, his nose deeply veined, his eyes black and beady. Yes, he hailed from Clan Rex. Same as Denise. Same as many across the city. The Rexes loved positions of authority. They worked as judges, Rangers, lawyers, and—to Fig's misfortune—headmasters.

"Figaro Triplehorn!" Headmaster Rex boomed. "Again you find yourself in my office. What are the odds?"

"You c-c-called me here," Fig said, instantly regretting her words.

The headmaster grabbed a ruler from his desk. Fig knew the sting of that ruler all too well. Rex swung it, slapping Fig across the cheek. She was still wearing her ghost costume. But that blow stung. She yelped and raised her hand to her face.

"You will not talk back to me, insolent girl!" he roared. "Every day, it's something with you. Growling in class. Hissing like an animal. You no longer live in the wild, girl. You live among humans. Act like one!"

Fig raised her chin. "Y-y-yes, sir." Tears budded in her eyes.

"What was it I heard? Getting into fights outside of school? Tormenting Denise Rex, one of our finest pupils?"

"Your niece?" Fig said.

He swung the ruler again, this time stinging her shoulder. The ruler actually ripped the sheet. She yelped.

"Hold out your hand, girl!" the headmaster boomed. "I thought I punished you enough last week, but I see you need more. Hold out your hand!"

Fig remembered last week. Somebody had shoved her in the hallway. Fig had stumbled into another pupil, causing him to drop his lunch. The headmaster had dragged her into his office by the ear, commanded her to hold out her hand, then rapped her hard across the knuckles. Multiple times.

Trembling, she held out her hand again.

The headmaster slammed the ruler onto her hand. Pain flared. Fig yowled.

He raised the ruler for another strike.

And something broke inside of Fig. Too much pain. Too much torment. Amissa whispered in her mind. *Fight back!*

Fig reached out and grabbed the headmaster's wrist, holding back his blow.

His eyes bugged out. "What do you think you're doing, girl?" He splatted her with saliva.

Fig snarled, baring her teeth. "You will not hurt me."

He tried to wrench his arm free. Fig held him fast.

"You will not hit me," she said. "If you hurt me again, if you hurt anyone again, I will make you pay!"

Fear filled his eyes.

She released his arm, and he retreated behind his desk.

I spoke those words perfectly, Fig realized. *I didn't even stutter.*

She began to shake. Her head spun. Her knees knocked. She fled the headmaster's office. She heard him shouting something. Calling her to come back. Saying she would be expelled. Be beaten. Let him yap.

She kept walking, leaving the office behind. In her mind, Amissa smiled. Her aunt would be proud.

It was a victory. So why was Fig shaking?

She did not think this day, this year, this life could get worse. Until she was walking home from school and Fig's life changed forever.

Denise was waiting for her outside of school. Same place as yesterday. Say what you like about Denise Rex, the girl appreciated a good routine. She still wore her Princess Al-Sadai costume, and her goons were with her. The witch. The vampire. The pumpkin. A zombie and demon had joined the posse.

Fig stood before them, still wearing her ghost costume. Abbey stood beside her in her plush stegosaurus suit.

"Well, looky what we have here," said Denise. "Two stegobrains from the remedial class."

Abbey Longspikes cleared her throat. "Actually, I'm a stegosaurus. You know, a genus of herbivorous, four-legged, armored dinosaur from the Late Jurassic, characterized by the distinctive kite-shaped upright plates along their backs, though you'll have to excuse the costume, which portrays them as triangular."

Denise and her friends burst into laughter. Abbey blushed and closed her mouth.

"They're idiots," said the pumpkin.

"Losers," said the vampire.

"Look at her." The witch tugged at Abbey's costume. "Wearing a onesie like a baby."

"I don't care about that one," Denise said. The tall, blond girl never removed her eyes from Fig. Those eyes were shooting daggers. "This is the troublemaker. Right under that bed sheet. Figaro Triplehorn."

She grabbed Fig's sheet and ripped it off.

Everyone stared at her. Not just Denise and her friends but other kids along the road.

Denise gasped. The others guffawed.

"She's wearing pajamas!" Denise whispered, eyes wide.

Fig glanced down at her body and blushed furiously. In her mad dash that morning, scrambling to catch the school dinosaur, Fig had forgotten to change. She still wore the pajamas Simone had bought her. They were embroidered with little cartoonish dinosaurs.

Everyone laughed at her. Everyone pointed. More pupils gathered around. Jeering. Mocking.

"Look, she's gonna cry!" Denise said. "Cry, Pig. Cry for the camera!" She pulled out her SmartSphere and began filming

Fig. "This is going straight onto QuickFame. Millions are going to see you, Pig."

The camera pointed at her. Everyone laughed at her.

"She's crying."

"Look at the loser."

As Fig stood there, Amissa's words returned to her.

You're smaller, so you gotta be fiercer.

Fig swung her hand and knocked the SmartSphere from Denise's grip. The apple-sized computer clattered onto the ground. Fig stepped on it, crushing it under her boot.

The crowd oohed.

"Fight fight fight!" somebody chanted.

Denise stared down at the smashed computer. She looked up at Fig, her eyes wild. The tall blonde balled her hands into fists.

You're weaker, so you gotta be meaner.

Fig didn't wait for Denise to land the first blow. With a battle cry, Fig shoved the larger girl. Denise stumbled back. Her friends caught her.

"Why you pathetic little worm!" Denise cried. She reached into her purse and drew a switchblade. "I'm going to cut off your face!"

If they push you, you bang their heads into the wall. If they slap your cheek, you punch out their teeth. If they attack you, they are the enemy! You are a huntress. And you will destroy them.

The knife lashed.

Fig sidestepped, dodging the blade, and caught Denise's wrist. She twisted. Denise screamed and dropped the knife.

Fig could have stopped then. She knew it. She had already won this fight. She could walk away.

Instead, she let out a deafening cry. The cry of an achillobator on the hunt. "Ayeeee! Yip yip yip!"

Suddenly she was in the wild again. She was a predator. And here was her prey. She leaped onto Denise, grabbed her tightly, and bit her ear. Fig yanked her head back, ripping out a chunk of flesh. Blood filled her mouth. She spat out Denise's earlobe.

Pupils screamed.

"Darwin's beard, she bit off her ear!"

"Somebody call the Rangers."

"Call an ambulance!"

"Figaro!" Abbey grabbed her. "Figaro, what did you do?"

In the chaos, Denise was quiet. She stood there, stunned, and reached up to touch her ear. She winced. A chunk of her ear was bitten clean off.

Fig took a shaky breath, shocked, not believing what she had done. Tears flooded her eyes.

"I'm sorry, I . . . I . . ."

She turned and ran.

She did not get far.

Most of the Rangers were out in the field, battling the poachers. But some remained in the city. And many belonged to Clan Rex. Apparently they didn't like it when you bit a fellow Rex's ear off. Who knew?

They caught Fig only two blocks away. She thought they would toss her into jail. Maybe just toss her out of the city. But oddly enough, they dragged her back to school.

Classes were over. The pupils were gone. But four burly Rangers pulled Fig down the corridor. She tried to escape—kicking, wriggling, even biting. But they handcuffed her, and they grabbed her arms, and fierce as Fig was, she could not fight four grown men. Finally she relented and marched with them, head lowered, tears of shame in her eyes. She never found her ghost costume. She walked in pajamas. A few pupils peered through the windows, snapping photos of her humiliation. She still tasted Denise's blood in her mouth.

Headmaster Rex was waiting in his office. The Rangers shoved Fig into the room, then slammed the door shut.

Fig stood before the headmaster, cuffed and bruised and terrified.

The headmaster stared at her from behind his desk. A deranged smile danced on his warty face. "Now now. Figaro Triplehorn. You're in serious trouble now. I could have you locked up for years."

Fig raised her eyes, blinked away her tears, and stared at the man. "My fadder is Joe Triplehorn! He is mo' important den you. *You* will end up in jail! You!"

The headmaster laughed. "Big words from a runt."

He raised his dread ruler.

Fig hissed.

He struck her. Again and again. She leaped at him, trying to bite him, to kick him. But with her hands cuffed, she could not fight properly. Whenever she lunged at him, he swung his weapon. It moved so fast the air whistled. Again and again the ruler struck her, leaving welts, drawing blood. Finally Fig fell to her knees, defeated.

Headmaster Rex stared down at her. "You're right, Ms. Triplehorn. Your father is a prominent Ranger. I can't have you locked up for long. But this school is my domain. And you are never to enter these halls again. You are expelled. Not only from my school. But from every school. The headmasters of the city are with me. It's over for you, Figaro Triplehorn."

Expelled.

Fig gasped. That meant—she would not graduate. She could not become a Ranger.

She leaped toward the headmaster again, ready to bite his face off. But the Rangers entered the office, grabbed her, and dragged her out. They tossed her onto the street, battered and weeping.

Most of the pupils had wandered home by now. Abbey Longspikes was still outside, her stegosaurus onesie muddy. She approached Fig and hugged her, and Fig wept bitter tears into the arms of her friend.

Fig did not return to the Fossil and Firkin that day. Barnum, Merl, Abernathy, Edna—they would all be there. They would see her torn clothes. The welts. The tears in her eyes. She could not face their questions. Maybe they had already seen it all on QuickFame. Fig could not bear to see them, to expose her shame. Their eyes would be full of pity, and that would destroy her.

She didn't want anyone to know. Anyone to see her ever again. She was impure, broken, shamed.

Why did I ever come to this city? she thought, sobbing. She walked down the streets alone, aimless, blood and tears on her face. *Why did I ever leave my pack? There is nothing in this human world for me! Nothing but pain!*

She had been such a fool. There was no future for her here. How would she become a Ranger? She couldn't even survive high school. This human world wasn't for her. This terrible city trapped her. Stones and bricks all around! Staring eyes and laughter and mockery! Shame. Nothing but shame. She was shameful here, more a runt than she ever was among the achillobators.

She would go back. Back to the wild. Back to being somebody who mattered. If her pack no longer welcomed her, she would find a new pack. Mintari was large and many achillobators roamed her wilderness. And if no pack would welcome her? She would wander the outback alone. Sometimes bators left their packs, became lone predators. Their lives were hard, but they survived. Fig too would survive. She would live on her own terms, cold, hungry, scared—but proud. And if she died in the wilderness? Better to die free than live in a cage.

Suddenly Fig wanted to see her father so badly. She wanted him to hug her, comfort her. But he was still away at sea. She wanted Simone there—funny, quirky, nurturing Simone, a mentor and mother figure. She even wanted to see Amissa. Proud, strong Amissa.

But no. Fig shook her head. Amissa had caused this! Amissa had told her to fight! Fig had listened. What a fool she had been.

Fig knew she should wait for her father. Say goodbye. At least leave a note. But she could not stand to spend another moment in this city. He would understand. If anyone could understand the need to escape a crowd, it was Joe Triplehorn.

An idea struck Fig. A good idea. She would travel across the wilderness until she reached Mudge Mountain. It was only three days away, two if she hustled. There she would find the Last Home Hollow, the cave where Joe used to live. A cave full of supplies. He would know to look for her there. Fig would wait for him, safe and warm, and someday soon they would be reunited.

There. She felt better already. A plan of sorts. A short-term plan at least.

A wall surrounded Dinovia City, protecting the people from the predators who roamed this planet. With the war on, more and more dinosaurs found their way into the city, but thankfully only tamer herbivores. The great wall of Dinovia still kept the more aggressive beasts outside. Fig made her way toward the city's eastern gate, the same gates Amissa and her poachers had smashed last spring. The towering doors had been rebuilt. The old doors had been made of wood; the new ones were solid steel. They were closed and barred. Beyond them, the drawbridge was likely raised, and past the moat, the electric fence was probably crackling. But all Fig must do is hide in the shadows and wait. She tucked herself between two rain barrels, shooing aside a few stray eoraptors. Oh, if only she still had her ghost sheet! She could have hidden inside it. Hard to blend into shadows when you wore purple dinosaur pajamas.

Soon enough she heard the call from above the wall.

"Rangers returning! Rangers returning!"

Fig peeked from behind the barrel and craned her neck back. Rangers stood atop the wall, armed with sleep-or-dies. In her dreams, Fig had often imagined herself manning those battlements, a proud Ranger protecting this city. So much for that.

Her eyes dampened. But before she could cry, an engine rumbled outside. A jippi was coming home.

The Rangers turned winches, lowering the drawbridge. From here behind the barrels, Fig could not see the drawbridge, but she felt the ground rattling. Then the towering metal doors creaked open.

A jippi rolled into the city. It was an enormous machine, easily Dozer's size. Its cowcatcher led the way, splattered with mud and pocked with bullet holes. The windshield was shattered. Arrows stuck out from the tires. Five Rangers sat inside the jippi, bruised and bloodied. One man sat in the cargo hold, wrapped in bandages. Clearly they had seen battle, and not against dinosaurs. Fig wondered if Amissa herself had fought on the other side. Had she fired those bullets, those arrows?

I hope she's all right, Fig thought. And the thought surprised her. She crushed that thought. Where exactly did her loyalties lie?

Before the doors could close, Fig leaped from behind the barrels and ran. She vaulted between the open doors, landed on the wooden drawbridge, and ran. The bridge was already rising.

"Hey!" shouted a Ranger from the wall. "Hey, stop that! Stop!"

Fig kept running. The drawbridge rose higher. She reached the end and jumped. Her legs kicked in midair. She vaulted over the moat, hit the far bank, and rolled through the grass.

She made it! Well, almost. One more obstacle. At once, she bounded up and ran again. The electric fence rose before her, but the power was still off. At least Fig heard no crackling. A good sign, she hoped. She shoved the fence's metal gateway, swinging it open, and she didn't die. Another good sign.

And then she was out in the wilderness.

She was free.

She was free!

She kicked off her shoes and ran barefoot like in the old days. She needed to feel the ground beneath her feet. As the Rangers cried out behind her, calling her to return, Fig ran through the tall grass, and the wind blew the tears from her eyes.

CHAPTER SIXTEEN
A Night at the Races

Fig had been planning to head straight to the Last Home Hollow. It was a three-day walk, two if she pushed herself. She could hunt and gather along the way, and once she reached the cave, she could pick the lock, step inside, and find Joe's stores of food. The man had collected enough canned goods to feed a triceratops. There she could wait for him. And if necessary, wait out the winter.

That was the plan, at least. Until Fig heard the distant cheering.

She frowned. Cheering?

She paused in the tall grass, tilted her head, and listened. She heard crickets. Rustling grass. The grunts of a few protoceratops on a hilltop. That was it.

But then the wind gusted, and she heard it again, carried on the air. Definitely cheering.

Fig's eye widened. Of course! It was Halloween. She knew what that meant.

"The Dino Derby Halloween Eve Spectacular," she whispered to herself. She muddled most of those words, but in her mind, she heard them perfectly.

For half a year now, Fig had been watching the Dino Derby religiously. Barnum played it over the bar. Fig knew all the jockeys. All the dinosaurs. All the stats. The dinos raced almost every day right after school.

"How can you watch that stuff?" Joe had muttered one time while Fig was watching the races. "It's immoral! Riding dinosaurs?"

"You ride a dinosaur," Fig had told him.

"That's different!" Joe had snapped.

"How?"

Joe had closed his mouth, thought, and finally grumbled, "No more Dino Derby!"

But Fig kept watching. And sometimes she even caught Joe watching the derby from his table (only when he thought nobody noticed, of course). Fig had begged to go see the derby in person. But Joe would hear none of it. Fig had even asked Simone to take her, but the woman was terrified of dinosaurs. Seeing scores of them stampede along a track would probably give her a heart attack. So Fig—without money to afford a ticket—had always contented herself with watching the holograms racing above Barnum's bar.

But tonight was special. The derby had been building up to this event. All month, Derbyniks (as folk called them) had stood on street corners, handing out flyers. Holographic ads floated across the city. Somebody had even hired a tricopter to pull a banner across the sky. And now it was here. The Halloween Eve Spectacular.

This wouldn't be a normal race. Tonight many champions from previous years would race for charity. Even old retired jockeys and their dinosaurs would race. The Dino Derby was raising money for the Mintari Rangers. Normally, the Rangers and the Derbyniks were enemies. Most Rangers did not approve of racing dinosaurs for sport. And most Derbyniks thought the Rangers were a bunch of party poopers. But Mintari was at war. And war made for strange bedfellows. If anything could unite Mintarians, it was their shared hatred of Hell's Hunters.

Derbyniks and Rangers—allies! What next? T-rexes and triceratops living together?

A trembling smile touched Fig's lips. Maybe this day wouldn't be so horrible after all. She was free now. Free of school. Free of the city. She could go. She could sneak in. She could see the Dino Derby with her own eyes. And not just any race but the Halloween Spectacular!

Her spirits lifted. All the grim thoughts of shame, exile, and the coming winter fled. This was something exciting. Just for one night—she would forget her troubles and escape into a world of wonders.

She had been running east. Now Fig changed directions and followed the sound of the cheers. The Dino Derby was located outside the city walls. There was simply no room to race dinosaurs inside Dinovia. It also made it easier for the Rangers to turn a blind eye. Leaving the city was dangerous, of course. Lots of predators roaming about. That made the Dino Derby even more appealing. It was borderline illegal. It was definitely dangerous. There was gambling, drinking, mayhem, and lots of very fast dinosaurs. It was the best show on Mintari.

Fig saw a dirt road stretching north. Electric fences lined the way. Civilian jippis were rumbling down the road, raising clouds of dust, heading to the races. The sun had not yet set. Right now probably only the rookies were racing. Or maybe the dinosaur pantomimes were playing. The big races had not yet begun. Fig had time.

She crawled under the fence and stuck out her thumb. A jippi slowed down. An old man and his wife sat in the front. A gaggle of grandkids bounced around the cargo hold, wearing dinosaur hats.

"Hop in," said the old man.

Fig soon found herself sitting among jumping, laughing children, sharing their peanut butter crackers, rattling down the road toward the races.

Soon enough, they reached it. The Dino Derby arena.

Fig had seen it countless times in a hologram. Seeing the real thing was an entirely different experience. The arena was massive. You could probably fit Port Mary inside. From out here, Fig could not see the dinosaurs, only the exterior walls. But even the walls were spectacular, sporting murals of past champions.

So far, every champion was some type of ornithomimid. Multiple ornithomimid species lived on Mintari, but they were all pretty much the same—slender, bipedal, feathered, and fast. They had no teeth, no sharp claws. Everything about them was designed by evolution for one purpose. Speed. Superficially they looked like ostriches, but they were larger and even faster.

Every year, a few non-ornithomimids joined the races. Raptors, mostly. Sometimes dilophosaurs. Once a four-legged chasmosaurus had joined the derby (and finished last). About a century ago, a carnotaurus had once finished ninth place, the best result ever for a non-ostrich. Try as they might, these other species never won. Not even close. So far, only the ostrich-dinos got the trophies. Every year, people hoped to end the reign of the ornithomimids, but bookies always gave them low odds.

Fig paused to admire a mural of Strutter, a struthiomimus (a type of ornithomimid). He was her favorite. He had won the Christmas Cup last winter, the third trophy of his career. Many fans, Fig included, believed he would win the Halloween Spectacular as well. Strutter looked like a typical ostrich-dino, but while most ornithomimids had dull brown colors, Strutter boasted shimmering blue feathers, green eyes, and bright yellow legs. He knew he was pretty, and he was proud of it. That dino liked to strut.

The murals depicted the jockeys too. Sometimes the jockeys took a back seat to the dinos, but to Fig, they were heroes too. Like her, the jockeys were small. Most were no taller or heavier than Fig, and she was the smallest girl at Leakey High. Yet on the walls of the arena, the jockeys were painted as giants. To Fig, they were heroes. Not as heroic as Rangers maybe. But almost.

There were four entrances to the arena. Crowds were lining up. Fig made her way toward the nearest entrance, drowning in the crowd. Everyone but the children stood head and shoulders taller. Fig noticed that few people here wore safari outfits. They wore garish Hawaiian shirts, silk robes, camouflage outfits, space trucker coveralls, or neon coats that nearly blinded her. At first Fig thought these were Halloween costumes. Then she realized these were tourists. Many spoke Nyxian, like Fig, but they had accents like Simone did. Cloventian accents. Others spoke languages Fig did not recognize. Perhaps they had come from Earth, Dagon, the Japanese habitats, maybe even the frontier systems beyond Nyx.

When first integrating into human society, the concept of locals and tourists had confused Fig. They were all humans, equally weird to her. But she had learned that they were different. Roughly half the humans on Mintari were locals. They wore tan and brown clothes (Simone called them "safari outfits") and ceratop hats, and they tended to be outspoken yet friendly. The other half were tourists, and they kept coming and going like migratory dinosaurs. They were louder, cruder, more colorful. They did not respect the wilderness like the locals. It was no wonder that the Dino Derby, which raced dinosaurs for sport, would appeal more to tourists. Not many locals wanted to see this.

My dad would be furious to see me here, Fig thought.

But her dad was still on his cruise. Her school had expelled her. Her mother was dead. Fig was alone. She could do what she wanted. She was free. Freedom was the most valuable prize in the world.

So why were tears flowing down her cheeks?

I bit off a girl's ear, she thought. *I can still taste the blood.*

She blinked her tears away.

No. Stop that! You did nothing wrong. You are a huntress. You won a battle. Now enjoy this night!

Fig skipped the ticket booths. She had no money. The very concept of money still seemed ludicrous to her. Could you imagine if bators had to pay for meat or shelter? Instead, she directly approached the southern entrance. She would have to sneak in with the crowd, perhaps by blending into a large group of tourists. She was small enough. It could work. And if any usher gave her trouble, she would bite them! She was a huntress. An achillobator. A wild child. She feared nobody.

I bit a girl's ear.

Her eyes stung.

I'm not human. I don't belong. They were right. I'm a monster.

She sniffed, knuckled her eyes, and searched for a group of tourists to hide among. She found a good group. Several friends, probably in their twenties. Young enough to blend in with. And tall too. Much taller than Fig. Good for hiding behind. She slipped close to them, hovering at the perimeter of their group.

"Tickets please, tickets—" said the usher.

The friends stepped forward as a group, displaying their tickets. Fig clung to them, sneaking through the doorway into the—

"Ticket please!"

A hand grabbed her shoulder.

Fig cringed. She turned to see an usher gripping her. At first Fig wanted to attack, to claw and bite. But she hesitated. The usher was a burly, bearded man, twice her size. Fig knew she was fierce. But she had learned that even she, for all her ferocity, could not defeat large, powerful humans in battle. Not without weapons. Defeating Denise Rex in a fight was one thing. Defeating a strong adult man was quite another.

"Leggo o me!" Fig said.

"Have you got a ticket?" the usher said.

The group of friends was looking over, perplexed. Then they shrugged and entered the arena. From here, Fig could glimpse thousands of spectators inside and even a hint of the track.

"I lost it." She tried to shake herself free, but the usher's grip was iron.

"Trying to sneak in, huh?" He began dragging her off. "Well, we got holding cells for sneaks like you. You can spend the night underground, and—"

"She's with me."

The familiar voice came from nearby.

Fig looked up, and there she was, standing in the crowd. Auntie Amissa.

As usual, Amissa wore camouflage clothes, clawed boots, and a crooked smile. Her chestnut hair flowed from under her ceratop, and handguns framed her hips. She sauntered forward, and people parted to let her through, bowing their heads. Everyone knew of Amissa Triplehorn, heiress to the clan fortune, dinosaur huntress extraordinaire. And even if they didn't know— Amissa exuded so much confidence she practically oozed importance.

"Pardon, ma'am." The usher lowered his head.

Amissa grabbed Fig and pulled her close. "She's my niece. She was supposed to meet me at the VIP line. She got confused and stood with the commoners. I got our tickets here." She flashed two holographic barcodes, then palmed them.

"Of course, ma'am." The usher nodded. "I'll escort you to your boxed seats myself."

"No need. Stay here and keep the riffraff out." She winked and tossed him a silver coin. "For your trouble. If you're a betting man, bet on Frankie Lightfoot. I hear good things."

Fig glanced at a holographic betting board that hovered above the line. Frankie Lightfoot was fifty to one. Strutter was the favorite to win. As usual.

"But Frankie is—" Fig began.

Amissa grabbed Fig's hand and pulled her into the arena. Her grip was tight, her gait long and quick. Fig had to hop and skip to keep up. She was stunned silent—both by Amissa showing up and the grandeur of the arena. As Amissa dragged her along, Fig gaped at the wonders all around.

The arena was gargantuan. Twenty thousand people filled the seats. Fig had heard that on Cloventia, they had stadiums that could hold the entire population of Mintari. But for Mintari, this was a stunning crowd. People were cheering, chatting, chanting. Drones hovered about, selling popcorn, hot dogs, and dinosaur toys. Huge holographic screens hung everywhere, displaying contests, racing stats, and spinning 3D models of race dinos and jockeys.

The racing track formed a huge circle. The track was two kilometers long. A fast dinosaur could race a loop in under two minutes. A dinosaur named Jurassic Steed (sometimes billed as Steed McQueen) still held the Mintari record for fastest lap. Sixty-seven seconds. A record that had stood for a century now. Many thought no dinosaur would ever beat it, though Strutter had come close a few times. Most races involved several laps, and they sometimes included obstacles to make things more interesting.

Broadcasting stumbling dinos in slow motion always fascinated the crowd. Especially if the dinos stumbled into one another.

The sun was setting, but the racers weren't out yet. Half the seats were still empty. As more people streamed in, the pantomimes were entertaining the crowd. The circular racetrack enclosed a grassy field. Five styracosaurs were lumbering across the grass, their scaly bodies painted to look like skeletons. Their long nasal horns were painted to look like candy corns. Acrobats stood atop the elephant-sized dinosaurs, juggling pumpkins. Fig remembered seeing a herd of styracosaurs bravely face her achillobator pack. They were fierce dinosaurs, yet here they acted like clowns, balancing on balls, dancing in circles, and standing on their back legs on command. Among them, three velociraptors were leaping through flaming hoops, while an oviraptor bounced on a trampoline.

But the star of the pantomimes was, without a doubt, the albertosaurus. He was an imposing predator. At a glance, he looked like a T-rex, though he was only a third of the size. That still made him big enough to tower over his human handler. The dino-trainer wore a rhinestone-studded tuxedo and top hat, and he cracked a flaming whip. The albertosaurus (who wore a matching top hat) obediently fell to the ground, rolled over, and kicked his feet in the air. The crowd cheered at this supposed victory. But Fig noticed that the dinosaur's claws had been removed, and his jaws were tied shut.

Maybe my dad is right, Fig thought. *Maybe this is disgraceful.*

The dinosaurs reminded Fig of herself at school. Trapped. Forced to be someone they were not. Then again, was nature any less cruel? Fig had seen triceratops gore predators to death. She had seen ticks reduce dinosaurs to skin and bones, worms borrow into their eyeballs, and snakes stop their hearts. She had seen winters freeze them, summers burn them, floods drown them, droughts desiccate them. Was jumping through a flaming hoop really that bad?

Most of the seats were cheap plastic, crammed together so closely the audience barely squeezed in. Some of the wealthy Cloventians, their silken robes doing little to hide their ample haunches, had needed to buy two seats. Little plastic seats were fine with Fig. She would easily fit. But Amissa flashed her holographic pass, which opened a hidden door under the tiers of seats. Still pulling Fig along by the hand, Amissa climbed a staircase between holograms of racing dinosaurs. After climbing for a while, aunt and niece entered a luxurious balcony overlooking the track.

Fig's eyes widened. This balcony was nothing like the crammed seating areas below. Instead of plastic seats, there were five plush leather armchairs. Instead of drones selling popcorn and hot dogs, a waitress—a living human—smiled and bowed and handed them a menu. It featured steaks, grilled salmon, fine wines, and decadent cakes.

"Whoa!" Fig blurted out.

Amissa smiled. "Nice, huh? Boxed seats are a luxury not everyone can afford. I booked the whole box for the night. I'm proud to share this place with my niece."

Fig gasped and skipped around the balcony. The pantomimes were still going on below, but Fig didn't notice. She grabbed a fistful of complimentary peanuts, jumped on three of the leather seats, and bounced toward the menu.

"I want da steak and da wings and . . . do you have pizza?"

The waitress nodded. "Of course. Which pizza would you like?"

"Meat lovers!" Fig and Amissa said at the same time, then both burst out laughing.

As the waitress left to get the food, Fig looked at the five leather armchairs. "Who is joining us?"

"Nobody," Amissa said. "Sometimes I bring friends here. Tonight it was just going to be me. Until I saw you in line. I would love to share this night with you."

Hmm. Really? Fig thought for a moment. It all seemed too coincidental. There were twenty thousand people here. Fig was short and had taken pains to hide herself. It dawned on her.

"You've been following me!"

Amissa nodded. "I admit it. I'm a huntress, after all. I'm good at remaining hidden. You, my dear, still need some work."

Fig considered. Then a shocking possibility occurred to her. Fig had not gone home after school. Amissa must have been following her since . . .

"You were there?" she whispered. "After school? You saw?"

Amissa nodded. "I saw."

Tears budded in Fig's eyes. "Why didn't you help?"

Amissa grabbed her arms and stared into her eyes. "I wanted to see how you would handle things yourself. It was your trial by fire. And you were *spectacular*. When Denise attacked you, you savaged her! When the headmaster struck you, you lashed back! I'm so proud of you."

"I was beaten!" Fig cried. "I was expelled! You coulda helped!"

"And crippled you? No." Amissa shook her head. "You are a predator, Figaro! Same as me. You know what happens in the wild. The young hatchlings must learn to hunt for themselves. They must! It's like that with achillobators. You know this. The human world is no different. Joe has been sheltering you. I will not."

Fig wrenched herself free. "You're not my mom!"

"Your mother is dead, Figaro. But I'm the next closest thing. Your aunt. And I love you."

Fig frowned. She took a step back. "Love me? You barely know me."

"You mean I haven't known you for long. Neither has your father." Amissa sighed and sat in an armchair. The leather creaked. "Fig, I've never had children of my own. Never saw much use to them, to be honest. But believe it or not, family is important to me. I know—funny to hear from a woman who's been at war with her brother. But this war between Joe and me . . . I don't want it to ruin my other family relationships. And I want to have a relationship with you. We had fun that time at Paleozoic Pizza, didn't we?"

Fig nodded hesitantly.

"So come." Amissa patted the armchair beside her. "Let's have fun tonight too. A girls' night out."

The waitress returned with the pizza, and the delicious smell tickled Fig's nose. Part of her wanted to run. Nothing about this place seemed right. But it was a cold night. She had no pack anymore. No warm, feathered bodies to cuddle with. Here on this luxurious balcony she had shelter, delicious food, and an aunt who loved her. And of course—her heroes would soon race before her very eyes. It seemed a no-brainer. Why was she still hesitating?

Amissa reached for a slice. "Well, I guess I'll have to eat this entire pizza by myself."

"No way!" Fig hopped into the armchair beside Amissa and grabbed a slice of her own. "I'm eating it all."

"No way, share!" said Amissa.

"Nuh uh. Mine!"

Horns blared. The hovering screens lit up. The crowd cheered. Fig leaned forward in her seat, elbows in the railing, eyes wide. The pantomime performers slunk away. Speakers thrummed, blasting the song "Speed Racer" by the Rex Pistols, Mintari's favorite rock band.

An announcer's voice boomed over the crushing guitar riffs: "Ladies and gentlemen, welcome to the Dino Derby!"

Fig forgot about her troubles. For tonight, she put it all aside. Her past with the pack. Her father being away. Simone leaving. Her grandmother lost in the wild. The bite fight. The expulsion. All of it—she placed it into a box inside her and sealed it up. Tonight was about fun.

"Woo!" Amissa cried, raising her beer.

"Woo!" Fig cried in imitation. It was almost like an achillobator sound. She could speak this language easily.

The lights across the arena all shut off. Only the stars lit the night. Everyone hushed. All twenty thousand spectators.

Then a single spotlight illuminated a gate.

Rock music began to blast. Fig recognized the song. "Permian Rhapsody" by Ronnie James Dino, a legendary rocker. And the first racer stepped into the arena.

"Let's hear it, ladies and gentlemen, for Gallimimus Gil!" boomed the announcer.

A few people clapped politely. The racers entered the arena according to ranks established in previous derbies, starting with the slowest. Gil didn't have many fans. He was awkward, even for a Gallimimus, and those dinosaurs made ostriches look graceful. He wobbled his way into the arena, tripped once, and wandered toward a concession stand before an usher shoved him the right way. Gil's jockey held a bottle of booze. The little man was already hiccuping and swaying in the saddle. Good old Gil. Tonight his betting odds were eight hundred to one. Not bad for him.

A new song began to play. "Sweet Home Dinovia" by the Gratefully Extinct. Another ostrich-dino stepped into the arena. Frankie Lightfoot was his name—a rookie but a confident one. The dinosaur pawed the earth and snorted and bounced around. He couldn't get to the races fast enough.

"That's my boy!" Amissa said. "Keep a close eye on that one."

The song "Lucy in the Sky with Dactyls" by AC/BC blared from the speakers, and a raptor stepped into the arena, snapping his jaws and hissing and clawing the dirt. Bandages covered his jockey. People didn't often race raptors, and for good reason.

More intro songs played, and more and more dinosaurs entered the arena. Amissa and Fig cheered for each one, getting louder and louder as their favorites arrived. Each dino-and-jockey pair circled the grassy field, bowing to the audience. Fans threw down flowers and plush dolls.

"Ooh, look at Speedy Bandito!" Fig said. "He's looking strong this year. I saw him race only two days ago, though seeing him in real life is *so* much better, and—"

A new song began to play. Fig caught her breath. She knew this music. "Born to Roar" by Guns 'n' Raptors. It was her favorite song. She leaned forward, eyes wide.

The gate opened again.

"There he is, there he is!" Fig cried, jumping up and down.

"Ladies and gentleman, let's hear it for our reigning derby champion—Strutter!"

The crowd roared.

A struthiomimus strutted into the arena, his little head held high. His feathers were shimmering blue, his legs yellow. His jockey wore an outfit of red sequins. A laser show burst to life above the arena, lighting the night, while fog machines competed with the pyrotechnics. Even some of the jugglers and acrobats returned for a quick reprise.

Fig was jumping so much she nearly fell over the railing and tumbled down to her death. Amissa had to grab her and pull her back. But Fig couldn't contain her excitement. This was nothing like sitting in the Fossil and Firkin, watching a little hologram (while trying to ignore Merl picking his ears, Abernathy scattering wood chips everywhere, and Edna spitting into her spittoon). This was real. This was more exciting than anything Fig had experienced. There, just below—her heroes in the flesh!

The dinosaurs arranged themselves in position. A gun fired.

And they were off!

The dinosaurs ran, and Fig's eyes nearly popped out, and she could barely breathe. They raced along the track at breakneck speed. All but Gallimimus Gil, who wandered toward the grassy yard and began to graze.

"Strutter is in da lead!" Fig cried, jumping and pumping her fist. She even forgot about the pizza. Amissa stood at her side, smiling and enjoying a cup of wine.

Strutter ran faster. Faster. Moving ahead of the pack. Hovering screens displayed his speed. Sixty-eight kilometers per hour, and he was still accelerating. His jockey leaned forward, eyes narrowed. Speedy Bandito ran just behind him, his snout grazing Strutter's feathery tail. The other dinosaurs were gaining speed too. This would be a race to remember.

I bit a girl's ear off.

The thought just popped into Fig's mind. She shoved it down.

Focus on the race!

Strutter widened his lead. Frankie Lightfoot was moving into fifth place. Gallimimus Gil finally found the track, but he was running the wrong way. Lightfoot moved into fourth, and Strutter and Speedy Bandito were soon tied for first place, running neck and neck. The dinosaurs raced around the curving track, and then they *whooshed* right under Fig. They were so close! She could almost reach down and touch them! The screens clocked Strutter's speed. Seventy-two kilometers per hour.

Everyone cheered as the dinosaurs raced by. Amissa howled, fist in the air.

The mosasaur nearly devoured me.

And Strutter completed his first lap! And Speedy Bandito ran just behind him! The dinosaurs raced on, moving faster and faster, soon clocking speeds of eighty kilometers per hour. The lasers beamed overhead. The music pounded the arena. The crowd was on their feet, cheering wildly. And Frankie Lightfoot moved into third place! The judge gave Gallimimus Gil a do-over, and the plucky dinosaur restarted his first lap, leaning forward and determined, not realizing he had dropped his jockey at the starting line.

They died, Fig thought. *The others all died.*

They raced below her again. Strutter's jockey even looked up and winked at Fig.

But I lived. Why did I live?

The dinosaurs raced onward, and Amissa wrapped an arm around her. Fig realized that tears were falling down her cheeks.

"I know how it hurts," Amissa whispered into her ear as the crowd roared. "I know how the pain never leaves. I'm here for you, Figaro. I love you."

Fig hugged her aunt, crying onto her shirt. "I love you too, Auntie Amissa."

Holding each other close, they watched the race. Strutter kept his lead for another lap. And another. Whenever he passed under Fig, the jockey winked at her. Several dinosaurs fell far behind. The raptor bit Gil's haunches and was disqualified. Gil went off with the medic. The others raced on. It was only in the final lap that Frankie Lightfoot suddenly gained an enormous burst of speed. He hit ninety kilometers per hour and kept accelerating. Ninety-five. Ninety-nine. He reached a hundred kilometers per hour and passed Strutter, and everyone screamed. Fig included.

Frankie Lightfoot widened his lead. Strutter raced close behind, then caught up. They were in a dead heat. Snout to snout. Racing forward, forward, and the finish line was just ahead, and Lightfoot gave a final burst and hit a hundred and twenty kilometers per hour and roared past the finish line, beating Strutter by a full two seconds.

The crowd went wild.

"This is incredible, ladies and gentlemen!" the announcer screamed. "Absolutely incredible! A new speed record for the derby, and after three years of Strutter supremacy, our Halloween cup passes to Frankie Lightfoot!"

Lasers flashed through the air. Pillars of fire blazed skyward. Confetti flew and fireworks exploded overhead.

Fig gasped, arms hanging limply at her sides. Strutter lost? Her favorite race dino, no longer champion?

Amissa was leaping and cheering and laughing. "Lightfoot, Lightfoot!"

Fig looked at her aunt. She was waving a betting chit.

"Fifty to one odds." Amissa winked. "I'm rich. I mean— richer than before. Paid for our box seats tonight."

"How did you know?" Fig narrowed her eyes. "Did you fix da race?"

Amissa laughed. "Do you think so poorly of me? I may be an outlaw, Figgy, but I'm not a cheater. I've spent years hunting animals. I know how to spot the fast ones."

As they left the arena that night, Fig leaned against her aunt. She was exhausted. It had been one of the longest, weirdest days of her life. Amissa had also let her drink a beer, which was spinning her head. But her aunt supported her as they stumbled along a dirt pathway toward the parking lot.

"Did you have fun tonight, Fig?"

She nodded. "Yeah. I did." She yawned. "I'm tired."

"I'll take you home."

Fig stopped walking. She suddenly remembered her decision. To return to the wild. The Fossil and Firkin still scared her. If she went back there, the others would know. About the fight. About Fig biting Denise's ear off. About her expulsion. Her father, when he returned, would be furious. But worse—he would be disappointed.

Fig looked at her aunt entreatingly.

"What's wrong?" Amissa said.

"I . . ." Fig sighed. "Can I maybe stay wit you tonight?"

Amissa tilted her head. "Trouble at home?"

"Trouble eve'ywhere."

"Don't I know it. Of course. You can crash with me. For as long as you like. Until we figure things out. I have a camp outside the city. Don't worry, we have a fence and armed guards. It's safe." Amissa laughed. "Look who I'm talking to. The girl who survived for fifteen years in the wild. Come on. We'll take my jippi."

The jippi rattled through the wilderness, headlights piercing the night. Amissa sat in the driver's seat, holding the enormous steering wheel. Fig sat beside her, feeling so small in the huge vehicle. She almost drowned in her seat. A blanket was pulled up to her chin, and she kept yawning. Soft Mintari folk music played on the radio.

For a long while, they drove in silence. There were no roads out here, but Amissa drove confidently across grasslands and rocky fields, following her satellite map. Every once in a while, the headlights illuminated the eyes of a nocturnal dinosaur. But the animals all moved aside. No dinosaur in its right mind would take on a jippi with a massive cowcatcher and steel horns thrusting out the front.

Finally Amissa broke the silence. "That was some race, huh?"

Fig was quiet for a long moment. Finally she dared to speak. "I bit off her ear, Amissa. I don't know if I can ever go back to da city."

Amissa shrugged. "I've done a lot worse. And I'm fine."

"I wanted to be a Ranger."

Her aunt looked at her, then burst out laughing.

"What?" Fig said.

Amissa struggled to compose herself. "A Ranger? Oh no, child. You're no Ranger material. Nobody spends fifteen years running with bators, then becomes a Ranger. No. You're stronger than that. Wilder. You're a huntress, all right. You're just young. Only fifteen. A child."

"Just turned sixteen, actually."

"Sixteen! Wow. You're small for your age. Not a bad thing. Small hunters are often the deadliest." Amissa patted her thigh, rattling the blades and guns she had strapped there. "I wish

I were a bit smaller. You'd think camouflage pants would be more slimming."

Fig hung her head low. "I was expelled from school."

Amissa put a hand on Fig's shoulder and smiled. "I'll share a little secret with you. So was I."

Fig gasped. "You? *You* were expelled from school? But you're rich!"

"I was seventeen. Almost eighteen. Close to graduating from Clover Heights Academy. I got into a little tiff with your friend, Simone LaRue. A fight."

"No way! S'mone was in a fight? Wit you?"

"Mhm. Much like your fight with that Rex girl. She instigated it. I won it. So I was kicked out. And look at me now. I'm richer than ever. I got my own jippi. My own astrolite. My own apartment back home on Cloventia. And a job I'm passionate about. There's still a future for you, Fig. Even if it's not among the Rangers."

Fig heaved a sigh. "Maybe I should just become a derby jockey. I'm small enough."

"So do it."

Fig laughed. "Yeah. Great idea."

"I mean it." Amissa swerved around a herd of iguanodons, waking up the slumbering giants. "You love the derby. You're small. You have experience riding dinos from your years in the wild. You'd make a darn good jockey."

Fig's mouth dropped open. Was her aunt actually serious?

"I can't just become a jockey!"

Amissa shrugged. "Why not?"

Fig sputtered. "Well . . . first of all, I'd need a sponsor."

"Easy. I'm rich. I'll sponsor you."

Fig could not believe what she was hearing. Was her aunt actually, truly serious? She would spend all that money?

"I . . . also need a dinosaur!" Fig said.

"So find one. In case you haven't noticed, Fig, we live on Mintari. A planet that's home to billions of dinosaurs."

"It's not dat simple!"

Amissa squeezed her shoulder. "Nothing is, baby. But we do it all the same. We're Triplehorns, after all. We—"

A rumble shook the night.

Eyes flashed in the headlights.

A huge scaly dinosaur thundered toward them. Fig screamed.

A theropod. A big one. Longer and taller than this jippi. *A T-rex!* was Fig's first thought. But no. Similar, but no. The arms were longer. The claws sharp.

"A torvosaurus," Amissa said, yanking the steering wheel.

The dinosaur lunged toward the jippi, jaws open wide. That mouth could swallow Fig with a single bite. Amissa swerved around the dinosaur. The jaws snapped shut on empty air. Amissa floored the accelerator. The jippi roared across the field. The torvosaurus howled and followed.

Amissa laughed and accelerated. "The derby is on!"

The torvosaurus ran faster. Faster. Fig watched the dinosaur in the rearview mirror. It was a thin female, almost skeletal.

"She's starving," she whispered. "Why else would she attack a jippi?"

This was strange. It was almost winter. Predators should be plumping up now, building up fat reserves to last the long winter. This torvosaurus was emaciated.

Something is different this year, Fig thought. *This is wrong.*

The jippi roared down the field. For all its horsepower, it was probably slower than the ostrich-dinos in the derby. But it was fast enough to escape a weak, starving torvosaurus. Finally the scrawny predator gave up and wandered off, defeated. After spending precious calories on a failed chase, the dinosaur was weaker than ever.

"Is it sick wit tick disease?" Fig wondered.

Then she realized something. On the drive through the night, they had barely seen herbivores. A few sleeping iguanodons, that was all. Where were all the herds of parasaurs? Normally they slept across the land like little hills, with a few parasaurs awake to guard the camp. Probably Fig just couldn't see them in the darkness.

The jippi rode onward, and Fig sat silently, hugging her knees.

Finally Amissa smiled and broke the silence. "Ah, look! There's our camp."

The headlights revealed a metal fence. An electric one, judging by the humming generator. Armed guards stood at the gates and atop steel towers. Fig leaned forward, squinting. Seeing armed guards was nothing new to her. She had seen many back in Dinovia City. But Dinovia's guards were always Rangers, clean-cut do-gooders in tan uniforms. *These* guards wore shabby camouflage, bandoleers of grenades and rifles, and an array of tattoos and war paints. Fig hissed and bared her teeth.

"Poachers!" she said.

Amissa arched an eyebrow. "In case you haven't noticed, Fig, you've been spending all evening with a poacher. But we prefer the term hunters. Hell's Hunters, we call ourselves. *Poachers* is a slur the Rangers use to discredit us."

"Discredit you?" Sudden anger rose in Fig. "You hunt dinosaurs!"

"As did you for most your life. How many did you kill in the wild?"

Fig raised her chin. "Hun'reds," she boasted.

Amissa mussed her hair. "We're not so different, Fig. Two huntresses."

Somehow this all felt wrong to Fig, but she was exhausted, scared, still traumatized by the bite fight, the headmaster beating her, and her escape from the city. To make things worse, the beer swirled around her head. So she only nodded. She would make sense of things tomorrow. For now, she had no future in Dinovia City, no more home in the wild. But she had her aunt. And Amissa loved her.

They rolled toward a metal gate. A bearded guard stood there, draped with bandoleers of bullets, holding a rifle. He nodded at Amissa.

"Interesting catch tonight," he said. "Who's the shrimp?" He gestured at Fig.

"My niece. Anyone here even looks at her funny, I gouge their eyes out."

The guard looked away at once. "You're the boss, boss." He pulled open the gate, and Amissa drove her jippi into the camp.

"Welcome, my dear niece, to Fort Devana. My home."

The Hell's Hunters camp was like a village. Jippis stood in the mud like buildings. Roofs were pulled over their cargo holds, forming makeshift homes. Tents and trailers rose between them. Cooking fires were scattered throughout the camp, generators hummed, and lights hung overhead. Cooked parasaur crests hung from a rope, sizzling with sticky red sauce. A massive triceratops skull stood in the center of the camp, a lurid monument.

"You killed a triceratops?" Fig whispered as Amissa parked the jippi. For a terrible moment, she thought it might be Dozer, but this skull looked too small. It was still much larger than Fig.

"He charged into our camp. A loner without a herd. See the fence there?" She gestured. "See how it's welded together? The trike barged right through it. Killed two of my men too. So we took its skull. Maybe it'll warn the others off."

Fig bit her lip. She knew Dozer well. He would never harm anyone. Were other trikes different?

A yawn interrupted her thoughts. This had been the longest day of her life.

Amissa mussed her hair. "Bedtime, little one."

She yawned again—a huge yawn that rolled through her entire body. All the fear, trauma, and pain—they drowned under her weariness.

"I have a proper bunk set up in my astrolite, but it's a mess right now, and the heater's on the fritz," Amissa said. "I sometimes sleep in the back of my jippi instead. It's cozy."

"Right now I'd sleep on a bed of raptor claws." Even in her weariness, Fig noticed how much better she was speaking. Her accent was still thick, but she could pronounce nearly every word now.

Amissa tapped a button, and a roof pulled over the cargo hold of her jippi. She rolled out blankets and grabbed a few pillows. They lay side by side. It was a cold night, but when they pulled heavy blankets over them, Fig felt warm and safe.

"Tank you, Auntie Amissa," she whispered. She bit her lip, tried again. "*Th*ank you."

Amissa kissed her forehead. "We're blood. I'm always here for you."

"I love you, Auntie." Again her tarry tears fell.

"I love you, Figaro."

She drifted off to sleep, but she found no rest, and in her dreams all night, Fig was biting ears off her classmates and racing, racing around a track with blood in her mouth and scars on her body.

CHAPTER SEVENTEEN
Family Reunion

After returning to shore, the docs wanted to keep Joe overnight in the hospital. Maybe for several nights. He refused. Figaro wasn't answering her SmartSphere, and more than he needed medical care, Joe needed to find his daughter.

So he headed straight to Dinovia City, where he now rode Dozer down the streets, moving toward the Fossil and Firkin. He tried calling her again.

Nothing.

"The tarry girl!" he said. "Why isn't she answering?"

Simone rode before him, holding Dozer's frill. They had wanted to keep her in the hospital too. She had insisted on joining Joe. Her skin was even paler than usual, which Joe had not thought possible, and a plaid blanket wrapped around her. Only yesterday, they had survived a mosasaur attack and nearly drowned. They should be recovering, but they were rumbling through the city astride a dinosaur, heading toward the Fossil and Firkin.

"I'm sure she's fine," Simone said. "She's a teenager. Teenagers don't answer their spheres."

Joe took a deep breath. "I know. But with everything going on, how can I not worry? Fighting at school. Biting a girl's ear. Getting expelled." He shook his head. "And now she's not answering me."

"Oh, the worst crime of them all!" Simone quipped.

He had heard the news that morning. Chief Clubber had told him in person.

"And you don't know where she is?" Joe had asked the chief, eyes wide.

The burly Ranger had shaken his head. "We let her go. No reason to arrest the girl."

"No reason to arrest her, tar it?" Joe muttered under his breath, riding through the city. "She's not answering her sphere! That's grounds for arrest." Joe kneed his triceratops. "C'mon, Dozer, faster."

The trike rumbled down the cobbled road, squeezing between merchant shops and clay homes. A microraptor fled from his advance, flapping four colorful wings. A few Japanese tourists pointed and snapped photos. "*Torikeratopusu! Torikeratopusu!*" Finally Dozer reached the Fossil and Firkin. Joe leaped off the dinosaur and ran into the saloon, knocking one of the batwing doors off its hinges.

"Is she here?" he panted.

Everyone looked up. Merl rose so quickly he spilled his can of beans. Barnum's rag froze over the bar.

"Joe!" The portly barkeep waddled toward him. "We heard about the *Maid of Mintari*. Thank the stars you're all right."

"Is Figaro here?" he said.

Barnum shook his head. "She didn't come home last night. I thought maybe she was with you."

Joe's heart sank.

"She might be at my house," Simone said. "She knows where I hide the spare key."

Joe nodded. "We'll go right over."

Barnum cleared his throat. "Hold on, hold on there! Have you tried tracking her SmartSphere?"

"Of course," Joe snapped. "She has tracking turned off."

Barnum smiled. "Well, there are ways around that. Good thing we have a hacker here." He turned his head. "Merl! Get over here. Never mind your spilled beans! Get over! We need your skills."

Merl stumbled toward them. With his big hands, the giant was wiping baked beans off his overalls. "Sure thing, Barn. Just show me to the right toilet. I can get any toilet unclogged. Just gimme a sturdy pair of gloves and—"

"Not your plumbing skills, man," Barnum said. "Your hacking skills! We need to track down Fig."

"Sure thing, Barn." Merl sat down at the bar. "You know I work for peanuts. Literally." He reached for a bowl of salty nuts.

"We don't have time for this," Joe said, heading toward the doors.

Merl cleared his throat. "Does she have the new model Y3K SmartSphere or the older StarSky model? Also what sat-nav data relay protocol is she on? If you got her SSIM number, that's a good start, otherwise just her plain ID code will be dandy. I can log into the geo-live databases to link up her telemetry profile." The big man pulled his own SmartSphere out of his overall pockets, summoned a holographic keyboard, and began to type. "Well? Do you at least know her number?"

Joe sat beside the big barfly. "Yes. I'll give you what I know."

Within ten minutes, Merl tracked Figaro down.

"Thar she is!" The big man pointed at a floating map. "Just two hundred klicks out of the city. Right there in the heart of Hell Valley."

Joe rose from his stool. "She headed back into the wild. I'll go get her." He took a step toward the door, then paused and looked back at Merl. "Thank you, buddy. If there's anything you ever need, just—"

"Go get her, man!" Merl said.

Joe nodded and rushed out the door.

He was mounting Dozer when Simone came running out the saloon. "Wait! I'm coming with you."

"Not a chance," Joe said. "Too dangerous."

She snorted. "Mr. Triplehorn, I just survived a shipwreck. I can handle a field trip. Make room!"

Joe sighed. "I'd have to tie you up to keep you back, wouldn't I?"

She grabbed one of Dozer's horns and began pulling herself up. "You really need to install a ladder on this dinosaur of yours, mister." She wobbled and flipped upside down, losing her hat. With a sigh, Joe pulled her onto the triceratops. Soon she was sitting in front of him, holding Dozer's frill.

"Hold on tighter," Joe said.

"You might have to tie me to my seat." She yawned. "I haven't slept in two days. When you install the ladder, can you add seat belts?"

"*Dyo!*" Joe said. The triceratops burst into a run, rumbling toward the city gates. Simone yelped and nearly fell off.

They thundered over the drawbridge and into the wilderness. A cold wind blew. Simone's hair billowed, covering his face. Joe shoved the red tresses aside, leaned forward, and stared over Simone's head into the distance. The grass rustled and the distant trees swayed. Storm clouds were rolling in from the east.

What madness drove you out here, Fig? he thought.

But he knew. She was hurting. Sometimes when pain grew too great, people ran, hoping the pain would not follow. Fig's encounter with Ryujin still haunted her. Then Simone and him separating. The fight at school. Getting arrested. Getting expelled. The poor girl was probably too ashamed to show her face in the Fossil and Firkin again.

"I wasn't there for her," Joe said softly, speaking more to himself than to Simone. "When she needed me most, I wasn't there."

Simone spun around on Dozer to face him. She leaned against the dinosaur's frill and put a hand on Joe's knee. "We're going to find her. She'll be all right."

"I thought she was heading to the Last Home Hollow." Joe held out his SmartSphere, which was locked onto Fig's position. "But look. Her tracker is north from here, not east. Where the tar pit is she going?"

Simone squinted at the spherical screen. "She's been there all night. She's not moving much. Just a few steps back and forth."

Joe pursed his lips. Was Fig hurt, abandoned in the wilderness, perhaps with a broken limb?

I'm coming, Fig. I'll be there soon.

Dozer kept trundling through the wilderness, stomping on grass and shrubs. It was late afternoon, and the sun hung low in the sky, peeking between cycad fronds and casting shadows like blades. Fig had been out here for twenty-four hours now. Joe wouldn't relax until he held her in his arms.

So this is what parenting is like, he thought. *Always worrying. But always knowing it's worth it. Figaro, I missed most of your life. I won't miss the rest.*

Joe could have taken a jippi on this journey. In the rumbling behemoth, he could have reached Fig within an hour or two. Clubber had even offered Joe a tricopter. The slender flying machines made even jippis seem slow. But Joe had never liked machines. Anything more complicated than his sleep-or-die was too much technology for him. Besides, he didn't want to pull valuable equipment away from the battles. The jippis and tricopters, once used to rescue dinosaurs and lost tourists, had become machines of war.

So here Joe was, riding Dozer. Strong, steady, and very slow Dozer. To be honest, Joe began second-guessing his decision. Was technology truly so terrible? Yes, he felt better with his stalwart companion here. In the wilderness of Mintari, you wanted a Dozer at your side. But the dinosaur was just so tarry slow. And Fig still seemed so far.

He tried calling her again. No answer. But the tracker showed her moving, pacing within a small area. She was alive. Maybe hurt. Maybe trapped. But alive.

Simone wrinkled her nose. "What is that *smell*?" She gagged and waved the air. "Dozer, is that you? Did you get into Merl's beans again?"

Joe sniffed. "Carrion. Just north of us. Old carrion."

They traveled north, and the smell grew stronger. After traveling for about a kilometer, they saw it ahead.

Carcasses. A dozen or more. Dead parasaurs, by the looks of it. It was hard to tell for sure; the scavengers had already gotten to them. Raptors and dactyls covered the corpses, squabbling for what remained. Even a massive mapusaurus, among the largest and rarest carnivores on Mintari, had come to the feast. He was feeding on his own private parasaur. Nobody dared share a meal with that giant. The dinosaurs raised their heads as Dozer approached, but they didn't bother attacking. Why risk a fight with a triceratops (a questionable activity at the best of times) when free meat was lying all over?

Simone covered her mouth. "What the heck? Did they hunt all these parasaurs?"

Joe shook his head. "No. Humans did this. Poachers. Look. The crests were sawed off. Poachers sell them on other planets. People turn them into musical instruments. Or grind them up and drink them as aphrodisiacs. Sometimes people just hang them on the wall. The poachers take what they want, then leave the corpses behind."

"How horrible," Simone said. "What can we do?"

"Today—nothing. But tomorrow—we keep fighting."

They rode onward, leaving the macabre feast behind, heading north in search of Figaro.

The smell of death faded behind them. They headed northward as the sun dipped in the sky. Soon night would fall, and they would continue in the darkness. Joe didn't like the thought of Fig out here alone in the dark. He knew she had survived for years in the outback, but he still hated the thought.

With a sigh, he tried calling Fig again.

Amazingly, this time she answered.

Joe gasped. "Figaro!" he called out.

Her face appeared in the SmartSphere. She lowered her eyes. "Dad, I'm sorry. I . . . I should have called."

"Are you safe? Are you all right?"

Fig sniffed. "Yes, I . . ." She glanced behind her. "I gotta go. I'm fine. Outta batteries."

"Wait, Fi—"

She hung up.

"Tar it!" Joe cursed.

He tried her again. Nothing.

He clenched his fists. "Tar it all, what the hell was that?"

Simone chewed her lip. She sat on Dozer ahead of Joe, one knee pulled up to her chest. "She was scared of something. Did you see how she glanced behind her?"

"Yes. I couldn't see her surroundings though, tar it. What got her so spooked?"

"Not dinosaurs," Simone said. "Our Figaro doesn't fear any dinosaur. Definitely not one overhearing her SmartSphere conversations."

"Humans then." Joe's belly soured.

"We don't know that," Simone said. "I suppose we shouldn't get ahead of ourselves. Maybe she's just upset about the fight at school, and—"

A grumble shook the land.

A theropod burst out from the brush.

Joe slung his rifle over Simone's shoulder. The redhead screamed and ducked behind Dozer's frill.

Joe sized up the dinosaur, not yet firing. If possible, he would avoid sedating the carnivore. Most predators steered clear of hale and hearty trikes like Dozer. Even the grand Tyrannosaurus rex feared triceratops horns. Unless they were desperate.

This predator was desperate.

"A torvosaurus," Joe said. "She's starving."

"Put her out of her misery!" Simone cried, sheltering behind Dozer's frill. "Shoot her! Shoot her!"

Joe still hesitated, not pulling the trigger. Sedating a healthy dinosaur was safe, but sedating a sick dinosaur could push the animal over the edge, potentially stopping its heart. This torvosaurus looked near death. It was like somebody had shrink-wrapped her. Her scaly skin clung to her skeleton. Her long, powerful arms dangled at her sides. She opened her mouth, grumbling, desperate for food.

Dozer grumbled, hunched forward, and assumed a battle stance. His horns thrust out, a foot wide at their base, tapering to deadly points. The dinosaur grunted and pawed the earth, eager for a fight.

The torvosaurus slowed down, hesitated, and hissed. She did not back down. She was a large predator. From snout to tail, she was as long as a bus. If Joe stood on the ground, his head would barely reach her knees. Her mouth could swallow him whole. Even in her emaciated state, the torvosaurus probably weighed four tons.

But Dozer was bigger. Stronger. He stood closer to the ground, perhaps, but he probably weighed three times more (Joe would never know for certain until somebody invented a scale big enough for a dinosaur). Most likely, Dozer could plow over this torvosaurus and gore the beast with his horns. The trike grumbled and stamped the ground, just waiting for Joe's approval. He snorted again and again, eyes rolling back to glance at Joe.

C'mon, boss, lemme fight! he seemed to be saying.

Joe patted the gargantuan dinosaur's frill. Just his skull was longer than Joe was tall. The big old boy loved to brawl.

"Easy, Dozer, easy," Joe said. "We might not have to fight."

Dozer whined. *But I love fighting!*

Joe patted the trike's frill. "Hang on, Doz. Just defend, don't attack."

Dozer groaned. *But I love attacking!* He stamped his feet. *Fine.*

The starving torvosaurus inched closer, growling. Normally, a lone torvosaurus would be mad to attack a healthy triceratops bull. But this one needed food. She needed it now. The animal seemed to be thinking, *I can attack and probably die by horns, or I can retreat and probably die of starvation.* Not an easy choice.

Finally the torvosaurus inched closer, sniffing, salivating. Simone whimpered and cowered behind Dozer's frill. The triceratops grunted and pawed the earth, just waiting for the command to charge. Despite the dread horns, the torvosaurus crept even closer, teeth bared.

She's suicidal, Joe thought.

The torvosaurus sidestepped, lunged toward Dozer's flank, and snapped her jaws. But it was a desperate, pointless attack. Dozer swiveled his massive head, bringing his horns to bear on his attacker. A triceratops head was unique. Most skulls in the animal kingdom connected directly to the spine. But a trike's was mounted onto a perfectly spherical ball joint. That allowed the dinosaur to wheel his head in every direction at speeds that would normally break an animal's neck. And a massive head it was. Dozer's head was ten feet long from beak to frill, and it easily weighed one ton, maybe two. The torvosaurus, impressive as she was, took a step back and whimpered.

Dozer grunted and snorted and scratched the earth, shattering rocks. Normally he would have charged by now, ending this impudent predator's life. But he obeyed Joe. He showed mercy.

This situation was unusual to say the least. Joe had never seen anything like this. Not even during the bad drought seven years ago. Sometimes predators looked this scrawny after a long winter. But in the autumn? This torvosaurus should be plump and happy.

Joe knew why. Amissa was why. She was killing the parasaurs for their crests, depriving many predators of their food source. Raptors were forced to hunt larger prey, competing with the apex predators. The apex predators, once the undisputed kings of Mintari, suddenly found themselves battling swarms of raptors. The entire food chain was collapsing. And Joe could see the results before him now. A starving predator near the end of her life. This animal should be strong, healthy, ready to lay eggs next spring. Instead, she might not survive the winter.

But there was something Joe could do today, a little way to help this world he loved.

"Fig is alive and well enough to walk around," Joe said. "We have time for a quick detour. Dozer! Turn back south."

The triceratops tilted his head, glanced at the torvosaurus, then back at Joe. He gave a grunt that sounded almost like a "huh?"

Dozer patted the trike's lumpy skin. "Go on, boy. Turn south but move slowly. Let's see if our hungry friend follows."

The trike hated nothing more than running from a fight. But this was hardly even a "fight." A thorny bush was more of a threat. So Dozer trotted south, and the starving carnivore followed. Every once in a while, the torvosaurus made a half-hearted attempt to lunge at Dozer from behind, maybe catch a juicy mouthful of tail. But Dozer was fast enough to always stay out of bite range.

Night had fallen by the time they returned to the parasaur carcasses.

The aroma of rotting meat filled the air. Most predators would have smelled it from miles away. But the torvosaurus had been upwind, unable to detect the stench of rot. Now the dinosaur perked up. Most predatory dinosaurs disliked rotting meat. They preferred a fresh kill. They liked to hunt, not to scavenge. But beggars couldn't be choosers, and the torvosaurus lunged toward the carcasses, using her last bits of strength for a final dash.

The twin moons of Mintari illuminated the scene. Not much remained of the parasaurs by now. Little more than skeletons. But to a starving carnivore, this was a feast. The torvosaurus crunched bones and cartilage between her jaws. She ripped off bits of skin and gizzards, guzzling them down along with the maggots. She even found a few rotten chunks of meat along the ribs, and she scarfed them down. She moved from carcass to carcass, feeding. Most of the other scavengers had fallen asleep in the field, bellies full. The torvosaurus enjoyed the leftovers.

Simone gagged. "That. Is. Disgusting."

"This is not natural," Joe said. "This is what Amissa created. She's turning Mintari into a macabre stage of death and decay. And my father is pulling her strings."

Dozer made unhappy noises and stuck out his tongue. He began to cough and gag.

"What's wrong with him?" Simone asked.

"He doesn't like the smell."

"Dozer complaining about smell?" Simone snorted. "Pot calling the kettle black. But I agree. Let's get outta here."

They resumed their journey north, leaving the sordid scene behind. Joe's body already ached from riding Dozer for so long. Most folk didn't realize that riding was hard work. Joe rode bareback on a lumpy, scaly dinosaur, and chafing was an embarrassing yet very real problem. It didn't help that he had barely slept since his trauma at sea. His entire body ached, and he longed to sleep, but concern for Fig kept him riding through the night. Simone leaned back against him. The poor woman had been through just as much, and she had borne it with grace, humor, and courage. Joe wrapped his arms around her and kissed the top of her head. She slept as Dozer trudged onward.

Joe could not sleep. He had nobody to lean against, and he would likely slip off Dozer if he slumbered. Besides, the pain and anxiety kept him awake. Holding Simone in his arms, he looked at the night sky. Hypnos and Thanatos, the twin moons of Mintari, both shone tonight. Beyond them spread a field of stars. Joe sought out Cloventia, and he could see the planet shining above, blue and bright.

You're there, Father. You're watching. You're pulling the strings. I will cut your strings and smash your marionette.

At dawn, after a long night of hard riding, Fig's signal brought them to a Hell's Hunters camp.

From miles away, Joe had seen the jippi tracks, smelled the cooking fires, heard the distant clangs and rumble of machinery. He had dared to hope Fig was just near the camp, not inside it. But as he approached, the signal flashed brighter on his SmartSphere, and there could be no doubt.

Fig was in that camp.

"They took her captive," Joe said. "We're going to break her out."

Simone stared at the fenced camp ahead. She narrowed her eyes and her cheeks flushed. "I'll wring Amissa's neck myself."

Joe loaded his rifle, then handed Simone a handgun. "No need to wring necks. This is a time for bullets."

Simone winced, staring at the gun. "I don't know how to use one of these. I'm a fiend with a makeup kit. Guns are less my style."

"Take it," Joe said. "You need to be armed."

Simone took the handgun. She grimaced as if holding a sea cucumber. "Did you buy this from a T-rex?"

"Huh?"

"I figured he's your small arms dealer."

Joe groaned. "How long were you waiting to use that line?"

"Since arriving on Mintari. Want to hear another one?"

"No." Joe patted his dinosaur. "Dozer, you'll finally get to fight."

The triceratops snorted and tossed his head in approval. His breath frosted, and his horns sliced through the frozen clouds.

They rode closer. Dozer moved at a slow, steady gait. The morning seemed unusually quiet. The wind did not blow. The insects did not chirp. The last few leaves on the trees did not rustle. The only sound was Dozer's steady footfalls and grainy breaths. Joe kept his rifle lowered, but he also kept his finger on the trigger.

As they drew nearer, Joe studied the camp, sizing out the enemy force. An electric fence. Eight jippis. A few trailers and tents. Guard towers, and there would be armed men in them. Normally Hell's Hunters operated in groups of three or four. This was a sizable outpost. Probably a good fifty poachers, maybe more. And one little girl.

A safe distance from the camp, Joe signaled Dozer to stop. Silently they stared. The sun had not fully risen, and shadows still cloaked the land, but Joe could make out figures in the guard towers ahead. Armed men. Just waiting to shoot.

The silence stretched. Joe and his foes stared across the distance, fingers twitching on their triggers. A gust of wind blew. Dry leaves rolled across the land.

I can't win this, Joe knew.

He was outnumbered. He could not take on this force. Not even with Dozer and Simone here to help. Keeping one hand on his rifle, he reached for his SmartSphere to call for backup.

"Put down the SmartSphere, brother!" came a voice from the camp. "Or I'll shoot it from your hand."

She leaned out a guard tower, a crooked smile on her lips. Her chestnut hair billowed in the wind. Leisurely she balanced her rifle on the railing, aiming the muzzle at Joe.

Simone hissed and raised her handgun.

A rifle boomed.

A bullet streaked overhead.

Dozer grunted and reared.

Simone tried to fire her gun, but it didn't work. She had forgotten (or didn't know how) to flip the safety switch.

"I don't have to miss next time!" Amissa shouted from the guard tower. "I said lower your SmartSphere. And put a leash on that animal of yours. And I don't mean the triceratops."

Dozer thumped back onto all fours. Joe dropped his SmartSphere back into his pack. Simone kept her gun pointing at Amissa, her lips tight and her eyes blazing with blue fire. Amissa kept her smoking rifle aimed at her.

"It's all right, Simone," Joe said. "Lower your gun. Keep holding it. But lower it."

"It doesn't work anyway," she whispered, voice shaking.

Hands trembling, Simone lowered her gun. Joe kept his rifle aimed at the ground. He stared at Amissa in her guard tower.

"Hand my daughter over, Amissa!" Joe cried. "And we all walk away."

Amissa tossed back her head and laughed. "Hand her over? Oh, dear brother. Your daughter goes where she pleases."

Joe's fingers flexed round his rifle. He yearned to aim, to fire, to blast her down. His fury surprised him. This was his sister! His own blood! Could he actually shoot her?

She shot me, Joe thought. The pain in his leg blazed again. *She could shoot me again.*

Yet even if he got off a shot, even if he killed her—he was dead. An army of poachers was here with her. And they had Fig. They would kill Fig if he took that shot.

"Let me see her!" Joe called.

Amissa shrugged. "If she wants to talk to you."

"Stop playing games, Amissa!"

She laughed. "Life is a game, brother. Here she is. Your little girl. Come, Fig! Your father is here."

Fig climbed onto the guard tower. She was too short to see over the railing, but Amissa shoved a crate of ammo into place, creating a makeshift stool. Still Fig hesitated.

She wanted to see her father. More than anything. But she feared him too. He would be angry, but that was not what Fig feared. She feared to see the disappointment in his eyes. She stood beside Amissa, hands clasped behind her back, and looked up at her aunt.

Amissa looked down at her, eyes soft.

"You don't have to talk to him, Fig. Not if you don't want to. Whatever you choose, I'm here for you."

Fig chewed her lip. "I'll talk to him."

She stepped onto the ammo crate and looked over the guard tower railing. And there was Joe, sitting on Dozer. Simone had come with him. The journalist looked up at Fig, compassion in her eyes.

Fig blushed. Shame filled her.

They all know. How I bit a girl's ear off. How the headmaster beat me and expelled me. Now they see how I joined a Hell's Hunters camp. They hate me.

She felt humiliated. Disgusted with herself. Yet when Amissa touched her shoulder, Fig felt better at once.

She glanced at her aunt. Amissa was staring off the railing, eyes narrowed, body tense. Amissa understood. What it was like to be violent. What it was like to be rejected, dangerous, a monster.

She's wild like me, but she's not ashamed. She's proud of who she is.

"Figaro!" Joe called from below. "Are you all right?"

She returned her gaze to him. "Yes." Her voice was so soft he probably didn't even hear. She lowered her head.

Joe took a deep breath. He slumped, seeming relieved and exhausted. "Fig, I'm going to get you home. Amissa! Let her go."

The tall huntress shrugged. "I told you, Joe. She's not a prisoner. And she's not a child. She's old enough to go where she likes."

"She *is* a child, tar it, and she's *my* child. Let her go!"

Amissa rolled her eyes. "Dear Lord, Joe, are you that thick? You don't listen."

"I'm warning you, Amissa," he growled, flexing his fingers around his rifle.

Amissa tensed at once, aiming her muzzle at him. Simone whipped her gun up. On the other guard towers, poachers cocked and aimed their weapons. Dozer snorted and pawed the earth, ready to charge.

"Stop!" Fig shouted.

Everyone turned to look at her.

"Stop fighting!" Fig said, tears budding in her eyes. "Stop. Both of you. All of you. Just stop!" A sob fled her lips. "I'm not worth it. Not worth blood spilling! I . . . I'm staying here, Dad."

Joe climbed off his triceratops. Simone remained on Dozer, crouched behind his frill, aiming her gun over the bony barricade. Joe took slow, careful steps closer to the camp. He let his rifle dangle on its strap, and he held out his open palms.

The poachers in the towers placed their fingers on the triggers.

"We got him now," rasped Rattlesnake, a leathery-faced poacher with yellow teeth.

Amissa waved them down. "Hold your fire."

Joe kept approaching, hands held open. Soon he stood directly below the guard tower.

"Fig, I know what happened," he said. "The fight at school. Everything. I'm not angry. I love you, Fig. I love you more than anything. I just want you home and safe."

Her tears fell.

"What home?" she blurted out. "A room in a saloon? You're always away. Always. And Simone left." She trembled. "She left and I was scared."

Simone kept her gun pointing at Amissa, but her eyes softened.

"Fig, I'm sorry," Joe said. "I'm sorry for everything. For missing the first fifteen years of your life. For missing most of the sixteenth. I'm not the perfect father. But to me you are the perfect daughter. No matter what. I love you unconditionally. Come home, Fig. Come home."

Fig looked at Amissa.

"Auntie Amissa," she whispered, "what do I do?"

Amissa heaved a sigh. "I want you to stay with me, Fig. But more than that, I want you to be your own woman. To make your own choices. If you like, you can live here with me. I'll look after you. Teach you. Train you. You'll become stronger, independent, proud. But I'm just your aunt. He's your father." She put a hand on her shoulder and looked into her eyes. "What do *you* want?"

Fig looked up into Amissa's blue eyes. Strong eyes. The eyes of a huntress. Not just a huntress but a poacher. But in them, she saw true compassion.

"I want to stay with you," Fig whispered. "But I can't. He's my dad. I want to go home."

Amissa nodded and hugged Fig, holding her tight in her strong arms. "I understand." She smiled and mussed Fig's short black hair. "So go to him, kiddo."

Fig nodded and turned to leave, but Amissa held her arm.

"Auntie Amissa?"

"One more thing, Fig. Think about what I said. If you want to become a jockey, I'll sponsor you. When you're ready, I'll be there." She smiled her crooked smile. "You just need to find a dinosaur."

Fig kissed her aunt on the cheek, climbed off the guard tower, and stepped out of the camp.

Joe ran toward her and pulled her into his arms. She leaned her head against his chest. She knew that she loved him. That she had made the right choice. Yet as she climbed onto Dozer, ready to head back home, she knew something else.

She would become a jockey. And she would see Amissa again.

Amissa stood on the guard tower, watching Joe, Simone, and Fig ride south.

There he was. Right there. Joe Triplehorn. Her brother. Her nemesis. Her white whale.

She clutched the railing so tightly her knuckles whitened.

Rattlesnake climbed the guard tower, stood at her side, and aimed his rifle. The weathered poacher sneered. "I got a clear shot. I can take out his head." His finger twitched on the trigger. "Just say the word."

Amissa was tempted. Stars above, she was tempted. She could end this now! She would win this war! Her own hands itched to raise her rifle, to put Joe's head in her scope, and pull the trigger. Then take out Simone next.

But no.

She did not raise her rifle. And she pushed Rattlesnake's gun down.

"No. Not like this. Not in front of the kid."

Rattlesnake turned his black eyes toward her. The eyes of a shabu addict. Eyes without any white to them. He hissed. "She makes you soft."

"That girl will win us the war," Amissa said. "But first we must win her trust."

Rattlesnake licked his sharp, stained teeth. "You have a plan?"

"Always," Amissa said.

Rattlesnake snorted. "You're a devious woman, Amissa Triplehorn."

"Don't you forget it."

The leathery old poacher climbed off the guard tower. Probably going to his jippi to snort his drugs. Amissa remained on the tower, gazing south as Dozer became smaller and smaller and finally disappeared into the distance.

Let Rattlesnake think that she was vicious. Let him think she was merciless. Let him think she planned far greater torment for her enemies. The truth was—she liked her niece. In Fig, she saw herself. She would kill Joe someday, yes. And Simone too.

But not like this. Not with Fig watching. Not until Fig's heart was hardened. The girl was still too innocent, too hurt.

"You'll come back to me, little one," Amissa whispered. "And I will harden you. You will be even stronger than me. And we will kill your father together."

CHAPTER EIGHTEEN
The Good Old Kois

Joe had only been home for two hours before his SmartSphere beeped. A message from Chief Clubber.

Joe. Come see me right away. HQ. Bring LaRue.

Joe read the message twice.

Tar it.

"Can't the man give me a single day off?" he muttered.

He was sitting in the Fossil and Firkin, waiting for his shepherd's pie to arrive. Fig and Simone sat beside him, munching on bread rolls. Dear Vinnie, their beloved velociraptor, ran around their feet, hunting crumbs. Life was almost normal. So of course it couldn't last.

Just that morning, Dozer had carried them through the gates into Dinovia City. It had taken two days to ride home from Amissa's camp. Those had been two good days. Days Joe got to spend with those he loved most—his sweetheart, his daughter, and his dinosaur. He only wished his mother could have been there, but Lifa was still missing, wandering the wild, healing Mintari's hurts. Joe missed her. But he knew her journey was as important as his. Maybe more so.

He looked at Simone. At her freckled face, red tresses, and intelligent blue eyes. He looked at Figaro. Her tanned skin, short black hair, and fierce dark eyes. He had almost lost them both. He would do anything for them. He would move mountains and conquer storms and drain the ocean to keep them at his side.

"I'm sorry," he said. "Stars above, Fig, I'm sorry, but—"

"You have to go to work." Fig nodded. "I un'erstand." She lowered her head and played absentmindedly with her cutlery. "I saw da-da—*th*e devastation outside. The carcasses. The despair." She looked up and met his eyes. "You fight for Mintari, Dad. I know."

He reached across the table and held her hand. She was expelled from school. They would likely never let her back. Clan Rex controlled the schools, and they held the Triplehorns no love. It wasn't Fig's fault. The girl was caught in the cross fire of these petty clan wars. Joe didn't know what the future held for Fig. But he knew he'd be there to guide her. She smiled softly. She understood, and it comforted her.

Joe turned toward Simone. He showed her the message. "The chief wants you too, LaRue."

She heaved a sigh, rose to her feet, and smoothed her safari outfit. "Of course. Whenever dinosaurs are in trouble, you call Simone LaRue, heroine of Mintari." She placed her ceratop on. "I just hope this isn't the time those dinosaurs eat me."

Just then, as Joe and Simone were stepping away, Barnum arrived at their table, carrying three plates of shepherd's pie. The old man's eyes widened. "But I just brought lunch! Must you go so soon?"

Joe smiled. "Give all three servings to Fig. She'll eat 'em."

Fig was already devouring her first helping. "Gimme." She snatched the other two plates.

Simone knelt beside her and kissed her cheek. Joe mussed her hair.

"Bye, kiddo," he said. "I'll be back soon." He looked out the window. "You ready, Doze?"

The triceratops stood just outside the window, working his way through several bales of hay. The dinosaur belched, rattling plates across the saloon. Joe still hesitated, looking back at Fig. Leaving his daughter hurt too much.

Fig noticed his hesitation, and she paused from eating. She touched Joe's arm. "I'll be fine. I promise." She lifted Vinnie and hugged him. "And Vinnie is with me."

The velociraptor nuzzled her and licked her cheek.

Joe nodded, kissed Fig's forehead, and left the saloon. His heart broke to leave her again, but maybe Amissa was right. Fig was not a child. Maybe the girl had to make her own choices, had to find her own path. Yet would she take the right path without his guidance? Joe felt himself torn between two wars. The war against his sister. And the war to save his daughter. Or maybe those two wars were one and the same.

Right now he must go to Chief Clubber, because in the war for Mintari, Joe was a soldier, and he would obey his commander.

Joe and Simone rode Dozer down the cobbled streets of Dinovia City. Construction workers bustled everywhere. The necks of sauropods rose across the city like cranes. Six months after the worst battle in Dinovia's history, the city was rising again. Joe was proud of this city. Proud of these people.

"We Mintarians are hardy folk," he said, looking at the people building, sweeping the streets, or just going about their daily lives. "Nothing can keep us down."

Simone, who sat in front of Joe, leaned back against him. He was surprised to feel Simone's hand slip into his. She looked over her shoulder at him, kindness in her eyes, and smiled.

"I'm proud to be a Mintarian now. At least—I hope I qualify as a Mintarian."

"We're happy to have you."

"We?" She raised an eyebrow.

"I am." He held her hand tightly. "I'm happy you're here. With me."

He didn't know where he stood with her. On the sinking *Maid of Mintari*, they had confessed their love. They had also been terrified, hurt, dying. Now in the sunlight, safe in the city, Joe wasn't sure what would happen. Would they live together again? Were they friends or something more?

Ah, tar all this mushiness! he told himself. *I have a war to fight. I can't get bogged down in lovey-dovey tar pits.*

He told himself this. But he still held her hand, and it still felt tarry good.

They reached Fort George, headquarters of the Mintari Rangers. The armed guards nodded, saluted, and waved them in. Dozer rode into the barracks, where he joined a handful of other dinosaurs in the yard. Eddie the edmontosaurus was here as usual. The towering herbivore, whom the Rangers rode for riot control, was lying on the dirt, sunbathing. Even lying down, he was an imposing dinosaur, a veritable hill of scales and muscle. Dozer walked around his languid friend, heading toward the bales of hay at the back of the yard.

Joe looked around him. Fort George. It had become his home. Joe had spent months here, training recruits. His leg was healed now. He was ready to get out there and fight. He hoped Clubber had realized this, which was why the chief called him here today.

He's been sidelining me for months, Joe thought. *I need to fight again.*

As usual, Clubber was not in his office. Joe had known the man for twenty years. He was never in his office. The burly Ranger lived for the outdoors, God bless him. Joe could sympathize. He found the chief here in the yard, waxing his ankylosaurus. Bumpy snorted and purred, enjoying the royal treatment. The dinosaur was almost as big as Dozer, every inch of him covered with armor, and his tail ended with a wrecking ball. Yet he still purred like a kitten when his master waxed his armor. Clubber ran the oiled cloth over the bumps and spikes and horns that covered his ankylosaurus. He was as bad as Barnum with his bar.

Joe saluted. "Chief, reporting for duty!"

Simone looked at the polished ankylosaurus and squinted. "Sir, your dinosaur is shining." She covered her eyes. "Finally someone who reflects more light than me."

Clubber dropped his rag and walked toward them. He was shorter than Joe, but he was so beefy he practically waddled. His dark eyes narrowed.

"Joe. Simone." He saluted them. "Thank the stars you're all right. What happened at sea . . ." He shook his head with a sigh. "What a tarry travesty. You saved hundreds of lives out there. Both of you did. You're heroes. And I'll be tarry sure that everyone on Mintari knows it."

Joe nodded, his throat constricting. "Thank you, Chief. But seven hundred souls died on my watch." His eyes stung. "I couldn't save them."

"Tar it, man, you saved three hundred lives. Without you, they'd be gone too. Tarry foolish thing, a cruise ship on Mintari." Clubber pursed his lips and clenched his fists. "I'm Chief Ranger. I can't criticize my president. But by the moons, I could break that Proudfoot's nose." He clenched his fist, then loosened it and shook his head. "Never mind that now. I'm just glad you two are alive. I wanted to tell you that in person."

Joe, whose own nose had suffered the wrath of Clubber, nodded. "Thank you, Chief. And yes, good idea to spare Proudfoot's nose. Mine is still a little crooked."

Simone narrowed her eyes, studying the burly chief. "But that's not why you called us here, is it? There's something else."

Clubber nodded. "You're astute. No wonder you became a journalist. Yes, there's something else. Something big. Something secret. The fate of Mintari itself depends on what I show you today. Come with me."

Clubber led them into his office—the first time Joe had seen it. Judging by how the office looked, it was the first time Clubber had seen it too. There was still plastic wrapped around the office chair. The desk was bare aside from dust and cobwebs. A little feathered microraptor was sleeping in the corner. Clubber had to shoo it out the window. The diminutive dinosaur hissed at the humans, flapped its four wings menacingly, but then hopped outside to hunt bugs.

"Just moved into a new office?" Simone asked, brushing aside cobwebs. "I'm sure it'll look fine after you clean and unpack."

"Been here five years," Clubber said. "Don't use it much. I'm not an office type."

Joe pointed. "There's a nest in the corner."

Clubber nodded. "Yeah, I think those are microraptor eggs. I let 'em be."

Then Joe noticed something. A photo of Mina hung on the wall. It was perfectly dusted. The only clean thing in the room. He stared at his late wife.

Clubber came to stand beside him. "Not a day goes by that I don't think of her. I loved her so much."

Joe patted the chief on the shoulder. "She thought the world of you. You were her hero."

Clubber's face hardened. "Now then. I didn't bring you here to see my office. I want to show you what's *below* my office."

The burly chief knelt, removed a few floorboards, and revealed a trap door. He pulled it open with a shower of dust. Simone sneezed.

They climbed down a ladder into a shadowy basement. A handful of lanterns cast an orange glow. Tools, cables, and electronic scraps topped wooden tables, and dusty science books covered rickety shelves. The skull of a sea monster—it seemed to be an ichthyosaurus—hung from the ceiling on chains, its mouth full of melting candles. Generators hummed and twenty SmartSpheres hung in the air, scrolling through scientific formulas and graphs. Electric cables and pipes ran across the floor like the roots of an old forest.

"What is this place?" Joe said. "I've been a Ranger for over twenty years and I've never seen this."

Clubber lit a few lanterns. "Welcome to the Mintari Rangers Laboratory. This is where we're developing the technology to save our planet."

Several scientists were moving through the room, fiddling with vials, levers, and winches. They wore brown leather aprons, helmets with thick goggles, heavy gloves, and steel-tipped boots. Gears and vials hung from their belts, and tools stuck out from their pockets. They were working on big machines whose purpose Joe could not divine.

"Darwin's beard!" Simone whispered, reaching toward a cylinder full of blueish liquid. A dinosaur fetus floated inside, curled up like a human baby. Pipes ran from tanks into the incubator. When Simone placed her fingers against the glass, the fetus inside moved and blinked.

"Ah yes, I see you've met Debbie," Clubber said. "Our new baby iguanodon. She'll be larger than a jippi when fully grown."

The chief pulled a lever. Lamps thudded on, flooding the back of the laboratory with an orange glow. The light revealed twenty more cylinders full of blue liquid and dinosaur fetuses. Joe recognized raptors, parasaurs, even something that looked like a juvenile T-rex. A blackboard rose behind the incubators, scrawled with mathematical formulas and DNA strands.

Joe turned toward Clubber. "What are you creating here, Chief? Are you cloning dinosaurs? That hasn't been done on Mintari in five hundred years."

"And Mintari's dinosaurs haven't faced the possibility of extinction in five hundred years," Clubber said. "Not until your sister showed up."

Joe pursed his lips, trying to calm down. He spoke slowly and carefully. "I'm handling Amissa."

"She nearly wiped out the entire population of parasaurs," Clubber said. "Within only six months. Imagine what she can do over the next six years."

"She won't live for six years!" Joe said.

Clubber snorted. "Are you going to shoot her, Joe? Your own sister?"

Joe bit down on his words. He didn't know. He could have shot her outside her camp. He had not.

"So this is your plan." Joe gestured around the room. "To replace Amissa's kills with your little lab creations."

"This is one of my plans," Clubber said. "But there's more. The next part might be . . . shocking. Come with me."

They walked between the incubators. The eerie orange light danced around the blue liquid. Pipes thrummed and bubbles swirled inside the cylinders. Simone couldn't resist her curiosity. She approached another incubator and leaned toward the glass, squinting at the fetus inside. She tapped the glass. The fetus—a raptor—opened its eyes and lunged at her, tiny jaws snapping. The embryonic dinosaur hit the glass and bounced back in the liquid. Simone yelped and grabbed Joe's arm.

"Don't tap the glass," he growled.

Simone gulped. "Sorry."

Clubber led them into a back room. Cables stretched everywhere like cobwebs. Electronics flashed and gears moved along the walls. Piles of odd equipment rose on a desk. Joe saw helmets, wires, electrodes, and components he didn't even recognize. An aquarium dominated one wall, full of fish. A toy castle, a treasure chest, and a sunken ship stood among plastic algae.

"Another incubator?" Joe asked.

"Just a regular aquarium," Clubber said. "But take a closer look at those fish."

Joe and Simone both stepped closer to the aquarium. At first Joe saw nothing unusual. Just a run-of-the-mill aquarium, full of large orange fish. Goldfish? No, too big. Koi, he thought. Then he noticed it, and his eyes widened. The fish had flashing electronics attached to their heads.

"What did you do to them?" Joe said, squinting at the electronics. "Are those tracking devices?"

"Neural implants," said Clubber. "They send signals directly to the brain. They allow us to remotely access and control the animal."

Simone gasped. "You created remote-controlled fish!"

"Even better," Clubber said. "Basic remote control is easy. We've created something far more sophisticated. With these implants, an operator can control the movement of the fish, yes. But also see through its eyes. Hear through its ears—and yes, fish do have ears, though you can't see them. In essence, this technology allows a human to become the fish."

"Like a demon possessing a body," Simone whispered.

Clubber smiled sourly. "We think of them more as avatars than demonic possessions. Would you like to try it?"

"Yes!" Simone said. "But test it on Joe first."

"Hold on," said Joe. "Chief, what is all this about? Why are you developing this? And what do Simone and I have to do with it?"

"All will be answered in time, Joe," said Clubber. "First try the technology. See how powerful it is. Then you'll understand."

The chief lifted a helmet from the table. Cables, electrodes, and flashing lights covered it.

"What is that?" asked Simone, eyes wide.

Clubber hefted the helmet. "The scientists call it the Generalized Host Observation, Sensation, and Takeover helm. GHOST helm for short."

"Not creepy," Simone said.

"With this helmet, you can observe what your host observes. Sense what it senses. And even control its body." Clubber held out the helmet. "Still want to try it?"

Joe frowned. "I don't know about this."

"Try it on first!" Clubber said. "To believe what I'll tell you next, you must experience how powerful this technology is."

Joe begrudgingly took the helmet. It was a flimsy thing, kludged together. Cables flowed out the top, and electrodes filled the inside. Some parts were held with tape. The helmet was designed to cover the ears and hide the eyes behind a visor.

"Go on, try it on," Clubber said.

Joe glanced at Simone. "You wanna go first?"

She shook her head. "I'm good."

Clubber patted Joe on the shoulder. "Joe, we're family. You can trust me. Try it."

Joe grumbled, removed his ceratop hat, and pulled on the helmet. The visor was opaque and blinded him. Earmuffs locked in place, deafening him.

I'm deaf and blind, Joe thought.

But wait. He could hear something faint.

"Hold on!" Clubber cried. He was yelling but his voice seemed miles away. "Let me turn it on. And I mean hold on! Ms. LaRue, give him your hand. He'll need support."

"Wait, wh—" Joe began when he suddenly plunged underwater.

He jolted. What? What happened?

Water flowed around him. Bubbles rose from his mouth. He held his breath, panicking, looking around in confusion.

He was under the ocean again. Massive sea monsters swam around him, covered with orange scales. They were as large as him. A ruined castle lay below him on the ocean floor.

Wait a moment. He had seen that castle. A little plastic thing at the bottom of Clubber's aquarium, though it seemed huge now. Those sea monsters around him were koi fish. Giant koi fish the size of dolphins.

Joe suddenly understood. No. Impossible!

He looked down at his body, but he saw nothing. He held out his hands. Nothing. He didn't have hands. Didn't have arms. Instead, flippers moved on his scaly body. He swam toward a pane of glass, looked out into a laboratory, and saw himself standing there, a helmet on his head.

"I'm taking this tarry thing off!" Joe said. He heard his voice coming from outside the aquarium. The man outside the aquarium was speaking. At the same time, Joe's fishy mouth moved, releasing bubbles. Who was he? Who was speaking?

"Wait, Joe, wait!" Clubber said. He grabbed Joe's wrists, pulling his arms down. "Don't just yank off the helmet! You'll give yourself brain damage, man! Power it off first. Here, let me help you."

Looking through the koi's eyes, Joe watched the scene. Clubber turned some dials on Joe's helmet. The flashing lights dimmed. Joe blinked and—

He was back in his human body. He swayed, grabbed the table for support, but his legs still buckled. Simone caught him.

"Whoa, steady there, dinoboy," she said. "Deep breaths. You all right?"

Joe took deep breaths. He realized he had been holding his breath the whole time. "That was tarry strange." He shuddered. "Chief, enough experiments. I'm not a guinea pig. I want answers." His legs still shook, and pain throbbed in his head.

"Of course," said the chief. "I owe you that. It's a doozy, isn't it? Most of us were dizzy the first time. I'll grab you a tea or coffee. Or something stronger, if you prefer?"

"Something stronger."

Clubber laughed. "Thought so. I've got a bottle of good Mintarian whiskey. We'll drink and I'll explain. But let's drink in the yard. I need to feel the sun on my skin, tar it. Being trapped down here underground . . ." Clubber shuddered. "I feel like a Cloventian down here. Those folk live like mice in holes." He looked at Simone. "Oh, sorry about that, cheesecake."

"No worries. I'm no longer Cloventian. I moved to Mintari and bought a house. You'd like it. Big yard."

"Excellent!" Clubber slapped her on the shoulder. "Have you joined a clan yet?"

"Nope. Waiting for Joe to propose so I can join Clan Triplehorn." She laughed. "Look at his face! I scared him half to death. Shocked him more than your science experiment."

Clubber laughed too. "Come on, both of you, into the sunlight. Mintarians belong outdoors."

Simone sighed and reached into her purse. "Thankfully, I brought a lot of sunscreen. If I run out, can I borrow Bumpy's armor polish?"

They returned to the rangersaur yard. Dozer raised his head from his bales of hay, snorted a greeting, then returned to eating. Bumpy the ankylosaurus was eating from a trough, his armor gleaming. Eddie the edmontosaurus was still sunbathing. The big dinosaur seemed to have fallen asleep. It was wrong to keep dinosaurs here like this, Joe knew. To turn wild animals into rangersaurs—domesticated dinosaurs. They should be in the wild, not serving the Rangers. But he had to admit that these three seemed happy enough in the city. A carnivore would be miserable here, but herbivores were happy so long as they had food and shelter. It wasn't natural. But at least it wasn't cruel.

Clubber poured three cups of whiskey.

"Aren't you boys on duty?" Simone asked.

Joe and Clubber stared at her, perplexed.

She sighed. "Mintari customs. I get it. All right, here's to being a Mintarian." She raised her cup. "What shall we drink to?"

Clubber raised his cup high. "To those who fell in this war, humans and dinosaurs alike."

"To the fallen," Joe said.

"To the fallen," Simone said softly.

They all drank, somber. The amber liquid burned down Joe's throat and warmed his belly. It almost tasted too good. He should not drink again. It would be too easy to fall back into that tar pit.

"Now that you got some booze in you, Chief, spill your secrets," Joe said. "Don't make me beat 'em out of you."

Simone raised an eyebrow. "You talk that way to your boss?"

"When my boss is also my brother-in-law, yes," Joe said. Though maybe the booze was already spinning his head, making him speak too hastily. Tar it, he needed to stop now. He had spent enough years lost in his cups.

Clubber overlooked Joe's flippant tone. "Very well, Joe. No more games. You've been out there in the field. You've seen what's going on."

"Death everywhere," Joe said. "Fields strewn with dead parasaurs, their crests sawed off. Food chains collapsing."

"It's even worse than you know," Clubber said. "Poachers have been hitting Mintari everywhere. Across the entire continent. An area too wide for us Rangers to patrol. They're organized into a gang now. Some would call it an army. They have spaceships. Astrolites. Jippis. They have better tech, better weapons, more money. And over the past few months, we've noticed a disturbing trend. At first Hell's Hunters engaged in trophy hunting. They went after the big, famous dinosaurs. The kind collectors want mounted. Stegosaurs. T-rexes. Triceratops."

Dozer whined and looked up from his bales of hay.

"Not you, Dozer!" Joe said. "Get back to eating, you fat lard."

With an offended snort, Dozer returned to his food.

Clubber continued, "The poachers began targeting parasaurs. Almost exclusively. Methodically. This isn't just trophy hunting. It's on an industrial scale."

Joe nodded. "They sell the crests on the black market. People turn them into musical instruments. Grind them up into aphrodisiacs. Or just hang them in their homes."

Clubber's eyes darkened. "Either intentionally or simply due to greed, the poachers are driving the parasaurs to extinction. To me, this looks less like trophy hunting, more like a purposeful extermination campaign."

"Wait a minute!" Simone said. "Hold on, Chief. Hold your hadrosaurs. Extinction? There must be millions of parasaurs on Mintari!"

"And they're killing them all," Clubber said. "Hell's Hunters are devastating entire herds. Cutting off communities of parasaurs. Forcing carnivores to compete for the survivors. If the parasaur population drops too low, the entire ecosystem will collapse. Entire species of raptors and even larger theropods will die off. We must save the parasaurs to save the food chain. To save the *planet.*"

Joe nodded. "So that's why you're breeding dinosaurs from DNA down there. You want to breed more parasaurs." He frowned. "But why the remote-controlled fish?"

Clubber seemed to be gazing inward. He spoke softly. "Because we need to find her. After five hundred years, we must finally do the impossible. Find *Darwin's Cradle.*"

Joe spat out his drink. "Chief! You can't be serious! Are you drunk already?"

"That's too far, Joe." Clubber glowered at him. "You're still speaking to your superior officer. Whether we're family or not."

"I'm sorry, Chief, but the *Darwin's Cradle?* C'mon. It's a fairy tale."

Clubber shook his head. "No fairy tale, Joe. She's real. We're going to find her. *You're* going to find her."

Joe was shocked silent.

Simone frowned. "What is going on? Will one of you boys fill me in? What's the *Darwin's Cradle?*"

"An old Mintarian legend," said Joe.

"An old Mintarian fact of history," Clubber said.

Joe heaved a sigh. He turned toward Simone. "Do you know how Mintari was founded?"

She bit her lip. "Um . . . a mentally ill explorer found a planet of dinosaurs, decided to land, and five hundred years later, a redhead was doomed?"

Joe smiled thinly. "Dinosaurs aren't native to Mintari. Five hundred years ago, scientists invented time-casting. They discovered how to send very small objects, no larger than beans, back in time. So they sent back electronic mosquitoes, which collected blood from dinosaurs. The mosquitoes then burrowed underground, froze the DNA using advanced cryogenics, and waited for millions of years. Finally the scientists could track their beacons and retrieve the blood. Eventually the scientists collected the DNA of hundreds of dinosaur species. And they decided to recreate them."

"The darkest day in history," Simone said.

Joe's smile widened—but just a little. "Those scientists decided to recreate their dinosaurs but not on Earth. On a world that would be dedicated to those magnificent animals. Mintari was perfect. A habitable, empty world. A nature reserve for dinosaurs. So they sent a starship over. A starship full of dinosaur embryos and the scientists who will grow them."

"Right," Simone said. "*Darwin's Ark.* I saw the starship on Buckland Hill. Ivan bit a chunk out of it. Probably because you charge fifty mints to step inside."

Joe frowned. "If you know about *Darwin's Ark*, why did you play dumb?"

"Because I'm suffering from tarry heat stroke! I only became a Mintarian a few months ago. I'm not used to all this sunlight." She applied another layer of sunscreen.

"Every Mintari child learns about the *Darwin's Ark*," Joe continued. "The ship landed on Buckland Hill, and the city of Dinovia grew around it. Most Mintarians today are descended from those original scientists. But legend has it that Earth sent two ships to Mintari. The second was named *Darwin's Cradle.* Supposedly she carried thousands of dinosaur embryos. But she crashed into the ocean and vanished."

"*Millions* of embryos!" Clubber put in.

Simone cocked an eyebrow at Joe. "What makes you so sure it's just a legend?"

"Many cultures have some myth of a sunken wonder," Joe said. "In some legends, it's a sunken city like Atlantis, Mu, or Ys. In other legends, it's a sunken palace, temple, or ship. This is just Mintari's version of the age-old legend."

"Not a legend, Joe," said Clubber. "Our drones have recorded real evidence of two starships in Mintari's sky. And evidence of one crashing into the ocean."

Joe frowned. "What do you mean—recorded evidence? This all happened—supposedly—five hundred years ago!"

Clubber nodded. "Exactly. And we filmed it. Using time-casting!"

Joe's eyes nearly popped out. "Time-casting! The Rangers have a time-caster?"

Clubber stepped closer, frowning. "This remains between you, me, and Simone. Yes. We've built a time-caster. We sent tiny drones back in time. And we captured images of the *Darwin's Cradle* crashing into the ocean."

"Impossible," Joe said. "Time-casting only works in units of a million years. You can't send something back only five hundred years ago."

But Simone understood. "You sent drones back a million years. And they waited. For a million years. Poor things. I wonder if they got bored."

Clubber pulled a SmartSphere from his pocket. "Here is the footage. Filmed from low orbit. See? Two ships! *Darwin's Ark* landed here on Buckland Hill. See this dot and slender line of light? It's not a comet. That's *Darwin's Cradle*. Crashing into the ocean." He closed his SmartSphere. "Joe, Simone—that ship is still underwater. And I want you two to find it."

Joe felt woozy. He stumbled toward Dozer and leaned on the triceratops. "Why?"

"The embryos aboard her might still be viable," Clubber said. "And if the embryos are dead, the ship will still have DNA records. Maybe even live DNA strands. That ship might have thousands of individual parasaur embryos. And the embryos of many other species. Enough to replace the lost populations. To rebuild what the poachers are stealing from us. They're killing our dinosaurs, so by God, I say we make more."

Joe furrowed his brow. "Chief, this planet is full of DNA. Dead dinosaurs still have their DNA in their carcasses. Why not collect that DNA?"

Chief raised an eyebrow. "Do you fancy spending a few years traveling the planet, moving from body to body, collecting millions of DNA samples? And then collecting millions of egg cells, hollowing them out, and attempting to create viable dinosaurs? Because that's what we've been doing so far. And we managed to build ten baby dinosaurs. We need millions."

Joe heaved a sigh. "All right, I get it. We need a lot of embryos and we need 'em now. So let me get this straight, Chief. You want us to remote control koi fish, swim them under the ocean, and retrieve the lost embryos?"

"No, my friend. The koi are only for testing the technology. For your actual mission, well . . . I have something a bit bigger in mind. I'll show you. Feel like taking a drive?"

They rode their dinosaurs out the city and west across the wild. Clubber led the way, riding Bumpy. The ankylosaurus left a deep, wide path in the tall grass. His tail swung from side to side, shattering shrubs and small trees, and his powerful armored mouth devoured bushes and wildflowers. Dozer followed, carrying Joe and Simone on his back. Behind the triceratops, five Rangers rumbled along in a jippi. Their security detail.

Along the way, they encountered no poachers. But they did see the destruction they had wrought. Parasaur carcasses rotted in a field. A pack of velociraptors lay dead on a hilltop, riddled with bullets. Perhaps the raptors had attacked the poachers. More likely, the poachers had simply killed them for sport.

Good thing Vinnie isn't here to see this, Joe thought.

After riding all morning, they reached the coast. Joe expected Clubber to lead him to Port Mary. But instead, the chief took them north of the seaside village. They finally stopped atop a cliff that overlooked Awning Bay. The rocky wall plunged down toward the gray, foaming sea.

Bumpy and Dozer busied themselves eating the sparse bushes atop the cliff. Their human riders dismounted. The Rangers in their jippi parked farther back, keeping watch.

Joe looked around him. From up here, he could see for miles across the ocean. Hell's Aquarium, they called it. A sea full of terrors. A cold wind from the bay cut through his beard to sting his cheeks. Simone's hat blew off, and her hair billowed. Bumpy caught her hat and began to chew it, leading to a tug-of-war between the hungry ankylosaurus and the irate journalist.

"What's here, Chief?" Joe asked. "Surely you didn't invite us here for a romantic walk along the beach."

The burly chief snorted. "If I had time for romantic seaside walks, I'd be here with Mrs. Clubber, not you. We have to be careful, Joe. To keep things hidden. Secret. Your sister has spies everywhere. Come with me. I'll show you."

The two men walked along the top of the cliff. Simone followed, a half-chewed, saliva-covered hat on her head. Their security trailed behind, guns loaded and ready. Dozer and Bumpy ignored the humans. They were busy eating and enjoying a well-earned break.

Clubber tested the ground a few times, kicking aside rocks, tapping the dirt. Finally his wide, lumpy face lit up with a smile. "Ah, here we are! Found it."

He kicked aside dirt and parted shrubs, revealing a handle.

"Another trapdoor!" Simone breathed. "How many of these things do you have hidden across Mintari, mister?"

Clubber paused, hand on the handle. He looked at Simone. "Ms. LaRue, this installation is top secret. Do not report about this location in the *Mintari Post*."

She raised two fingers to her forehead. "Scout's salute."

Clubber opened the trap door, and they climbed down another ladder into shadows.

They climbed down and down into darkness. They descended deeper than Joe had expected. The temperature plunged. He could hear a deep murmur through the stone walls. He realized that they had descended below sea level. He was hearing the water.

Finally they reached another underground lab. Joe remembered the lab beneath Clubber's office back in the city. This place was far larger, cleaner, and more impressive. The room had been dug into the living rock of Mintari. Huge glass panes revealed the ocean. Joe could see fish, kelp, and patterns of light dancing over the seabed. His eyes widened. The observation pane was enormous—larger than an old-timey movie screen.

"Look at this place!" Joe approached the glass windows, gazed out at the ocean, then looked back at Clubber. "It must have cost a fortune."

Clubber nodded. "Paid for by the tourism industry. I know you don't like tourism on Mintari, Joe. I don't care for it either. But it's how we can afford our projects."

Two big pods stood in the center of the lab, full of water. They looked like bathtubs with pull-down lids. Cables and monitors surrounded them. Sophisticated helmets hung beside them, attached to beeping machines.

Simone approached the pods. She ran her hand along the rim of one, then looked up at Clubber. "These are sensory-deprivation tanks, aren't they?"

The chief nodded. "Yes. They're used with advanced neural controllers. Similar to the crude helmets back at my personal lab. These are more sophisticated machines for the same purpose. The pods are used to remote control larger animals."

Joe stood by the glass pane, gazing out into the sea. He turned toward the chief. "What larger animals?"

Clubber joined him by the observation window. The glass pane rose three times their height. The chief pointed.

"There they are. They're coming closer."

Two enormous reptiles came swimming through the kelp, heading toward the glass pane. They were long animals, almost as long as a T-rex. But most of their length was in their necks. Their bodies were relatively small, sprouting flippers and stubby tails. Their slender necks stretched out, longer than giraffe necks, tipped with vaguely crocodilian heads.

"Elasmosaurs," Joe said, watching them approach. They were fearsome predators. Not apex predators. They were smaller than giants like mosasaurs and megalodons. But they were still impressive beasts.

"But can you tell what species?" Clubber asked, a twinkle in his eye. "Let's see if the famous Jurassic Joe gets it right."

Joe grunted. *Elasmosaur* was not a specific species. It was a diverse family of aquatic reptiles. Multiple species of these long-necked fish-eaters swam in Mintari's oceans. Joe leaned closer to the glass and squinted.

"Styxosaurus?" he asked.

"Close!" said Clubber. "These are tuarangisaurs. A bit smaller and tamer. Good for our purpose. At least that's what our biologists say. If you ask me, all elasmosaurs are pretty much the same."

Simone stood a few steps back. She shuddered. "To me they're all just sea monsters."

The two elasmosaurs regarded the humans through the glass. One was male, slightly larger, with deep green scales. The other was female. Her scales were blue, and dozens of red spikes rose across her head.

Simone gasped. "She's a redhead! Like me!" She finally stepped closer and placed her hand against the glass. "My spirit animal."

The female elasmosaur bolted forward. Her jaws opened wide. Rows of sharp teeth scraped the glass. The reptile seemed to be trying to bite Simone's hand off. The journalist yelped and scurried behind Joe.

"She's a monster, kill her!" Simone cried.

Clubber chuckled. "They can get aggressive sometimes. But they take well to neural control. We considered several marine reptiles. Ichthyosaurs are too wild. Megalodons are too dangerous to capture. Mosasaurs, well . . . you've seen what those brutes can do. This pair of elasmosaurs took to it perfectly."

Joe noticed it then. Flashing electronics embedded into their scaly heads. Same as the koi had.

Joe forced a deep breath. "This is immoral. Domesticating dinosaurs in Dinovia is bad enough. But to turn Mintari's wildlife into zombies? I'll have no part in this."

He turned to leave. Clubber grabbed his arm. "Tar it, Joe, listen to me. They're the only way we can reach *Darwin's Cradle*."

"Send divers," Joe said.

"That deep? The sea would crush them."

"Send drones."

"It would crush them too."

"Submarines then!" Joe insisted.

"We have none. And no facilities or money to build any. We aren't rich like Cloventia, you know that. This is the best way, Joe. You and Simone will remote control these animals from sensory-deprivation tanks. You'll guide them underwater to retrieve the lost embryos."

Joe looked at the liquid-filled pods. Then he turned back to Clubber. "Why us? Why Simone and me?"

Clubber stepped closer to the observation pane. He placed his palm on the glass. The two elasmosaurs swam nearer. Their huge scaly snouts came together, touching his hand.

"Neural remote control is a delicate art," Clubber said softly. He seemed almost to be speaking to the aquatic reptiles. "It's not about seizing brute control and forcing the animal along a path against its will. No. Neural control requires a handler to understand the animal. To mold with it. To experience reality with it." He moved his hand along the glass, and the two scaly snouts followed. "These two are a mated pair. We need a mated pair of humans to control them."

Joe looked at Simone. She looked back. They both turned toward Clubber.

"We're a mated pair?" they asked together.

Clubber raised an eyebrow. "Aren't you?"

"Well, um . . ." Joe stumbled over his words. After all, Clubber was Mina's brother. Her very protective brother. How would the man feel about Joe finding new love? How did Joe himself feel about it? "I mean, we kind of are. Sometimes. I think. I'm not sure. I . . ."

Simone grabbed him and pulled him close. "Yes." She took a deep breath. "We'll do it."

Joe closed his eyes, and pain rolled through him.

So back we go into Hell's Aquarium, he thought. *Back into the darkness. Back into the realm of the monsters.*

CHAPTER NINETEEN
Hands Off!

Amissa walked through Dinovia City, wrapped in a cloak and hood. She could have revealed her face, walked confidently in the open, let everyone see that she was Amissa Triplehorn, that she owned this planet. She did not fear the Rangers. But fighting them was such messy business. Last time she had walked here in the open, a Ranger had spotted her. Amissa had put a bullet between his eyes. Too much noise. Too much hullabaloo. Today called for some stealth.

She hefted her heavy rucksack. The little dinosaur squirmed and struggled inside.

"Soon, my friend," Amissa said, patting the lumpy sack. "I know you're hungry. Patience."

The dinosaur whimpered but stopped struggling. Amissa had been starving him. But soon he would feed.

It was a cold November morning, and most of the autumn leaves were gone. The pumpkins were rotting on the patios. Some fake cobwebs, tombstones, and skeletons still adorned the houses. A few overeager residents had already hung up their Christmas lights. If you asked Amissa, it was ridiculous to celebrate ancient Earth holidays on Mintari. Tar it, even reusing Earth month names was silly. The Mintarian year wasn't even the same length. But the Mintarians still couldn't cut the umbilical cord of Earth. That was not a flaw Cloventians possessed. Most Cloventians denied their ancestors even came from a hellhole like Earth.

It's strange, Amissa thought, walking among the remnants of Halloween decorations. *Dinovia seems almost peaceful.*

The city seemed to forget the battle that had raged here six months ago. But Amissa had not forgotten. She had failed then. She had shattered half this city but fell short of annihilating it. Let them enjoy their antiquated holiday season while they could. They would not live to see Christmas.

Not if Amissa got the girl on her side.

"You will change everything, Figaro," Amissa whispered. "My beloved niece. You will be the greatest huntress who ever lived. We will fight our enemies together. We will take them down."

Amissa made her way toward Leakey High. The school rose among trees. A few dactyls glided overhead while a diplodocus stood in the yard, a howdah on its back. Children played and laughed. Amissa stopped and closed her eyes. Pain jolted through her. Suddenly she was a girl again. A pupil at Clover Heights Academy.

The two schools could not be more different. Clover Heights floated above the neon sea of Cloventia, a school that hovered among skyscrapers and skylanes, a place of glass and metal and air and technology. But the sound of laughter and playing children was the same. The hopes of youth were the same. The pain was the same.

"I was weeks away from graduating when you got me expelled, Simone," Amissa whispered. "I could have been somebody. Somebody educated. Somebody who mattered. You made me who I am."

Now Fig too, her beloved niece, had been expelled. Now Fig felt that same pain.

"But you have something I did not, Fig," Amissa whispered, eyes closed. "You have an aunt who loves you. You have me."

She took a deep breath, calming the storm inside her, and stepped into Leakey High.

The children were outside in the yard, enjoying recess. Amissa strutted down the hallways without anyone stopping her. There was no security. No teachers walking around. A few children ran by, not even pausing to give her a glance. Silly Mintarians. She had savaged their city only last spring, and they were still so complacent.

Her backpack whimpered and wriggled again.

"Soon, friend, soon," Amissa whispered.

It was easy enough to find the headmaster's office. A big door with the word HEADMASTER on it caught her eye. Ha! If Amissa were beating little girls, she wouldn't advertise her location so brazenly. She didn't bother knocking. She stepped right inside, ready to raise hell.

Ah, a waiting room. A secretary stood up, eyes wide.

"Who are—?"

Amissa raised her pistol and fired. The secretary slumped back into her chair, a tranquilizer dart in her neck.

Weeping sounded nearby. Amissa followed the sound to another door. She kicked the door open and entered an office.

The headmaster stood there. A pasty man with quivering jowls, big meaty hands, and pulsing veins on his forehead. He was holding a wooden ruler. A girl stood before him, her hand covered in welts, tears on her cheeks. The girl turned toward Amissa, eyes damp.

"Get out," Amissa whispered to the child.

The girl nodded and fled the office.

The headmaster stood there for a moment, shocked and sputtering. He hid his ruler behind his back. His cheeks flushed. Amissa noticed teardrops on his desk. And a drop of blood.

"Ma'am, parents are required to fill out a form before—"

"Nice place you got here, Mr. . . ." She squinted, reading his diploma on the wall. "Rex? Ah, another Rex! Like the girl who lost her ear. Your clan's spawn is all over this planet."

The headmaster flushed an angry red. "Who are you?"

Amissa leaned against his desk, lifted an apple she found there, and took a bite. "Mmm. Honeycrisp." She gulped. "Amissa Triplehorn, at your service. I'm Figaro's aunt. I know you brutalize many children, but I trust you remember Figaro Triplehorn?"

The headmaster glanced at her rucksack, which Amissa had dropped onto the floor. It was wriggling again.

"What the devil have you got in there?"

Amissa continued eating the apple. It *crunched*, filling her mouth with juice. "Not bad. I'm normally something of a carnivore, but I must admit, I do enjoy a good piece of fruit now and then." She tossed the core onto the headmaster. "Now, you bloated toad, let's talk business. My understanding is that my niece was defending herself from one of your little Rex miscreants. Off school property, I might add. And your reaction was to beat her and expel her."

The headmaster stared at the apple core on the floor, then back up at Amissa. "Claire!" he shouted. "Claire, call security!"

"Claire is taking a nap."

The headmaster reached toward his SmartSphere, which stood on his desk. Amissa reached it first, snatching the round computer away.

"Uh uh uh, Rexy! Naughty naughty. No calling the Rangers." She collapsed his SmartSphere and tucked it into her pocket. "I'm confiscating this. We'll work this out between us. Just you and me. And the little friend I brought along." She glanced at the wriggling sack.

Rex gripped the edges of his desk. His eye twitched. A vein throbbed on his forehead. "I won't readmit your degenerate niece. She bit off a girl's ear, tar it! She's a wild child. An animal. She doesn't belong in civilization."

"Oh, I agree, Rex. I don't want her to come back to your school. Or to this so-called civilization of yours. But you see . . . you hurt her. You struck her hand with a ruler. Same as you were doing to that other girl when I walked in. Same as you likely do to many children. Do you enjoy inflicting pain, Rex?"

"Of course not!" he barked. "I'm an educator. I discipline errant children. I do it for their own good. To return them to the right path. I do not *enjoy* inflicting pain."

"Well . . ." Amissa smiled. "I do."

She reached out, quick as an asp, and grabbed his wrist. She yanked his hand down, slapped a handcuff around his wrist, and bound him to his desk. It was done before he even knew what was happening.

Rex gasped. He tugged on the handcuff. The desk rattled. It was a heavy wooden desk that likely weighed more than him. He wasn't going anywhere.

"What the devil!"

"Don't worry, Rex. You'll be free soon enough." She leaned toward her rucksack. "Have you ever heard the phrase an eye for an eye, Rex? It's from the Bible. Old justice. An eye for an eye. A tooth for a tooth. And a hand for a hand."

She opened her rucksack. The velociraptor growled inside, bound with leather straps. The dinosaur was no larger than a goose, but he was far, far deadlier. Velociraptors were vicious little things, their powerful jaws full of shark teeth. The dinosaur struggled to open his mouth, but a leather belt kept it shut.

The headmaster paled. He pulled his hand again. The table scratched across the floor. Amissa sat on it, using her weight to keep the table—and headmaster—in place.

"I'm sorry!" the headmaster said. "I'm sorry. I'll let Figaro back into school! I'll—"

Amissa unstrapped the velociraptor's snout. Gripping the dinosaur firmly under his wings, she held him forward.

"*Bon appétit*, my pet."

The headmaster screamed.

Blood sprayed the office.

Amissa smiled as the dinosaur enjoyed his meal. Then she placed him, content, back into the rucksack. She looked around her and sighed.

"You Rexes," she said. "You just keep losing body parts. First an ear, now a hand. Be careful, Rex. I still own many hungry dinosaurs."

She strutted down the hallway, covered in blood, a grin on her face. A few teachers saw her, gasped, and fled back into their classrooms. Amissa twirled the souvenir she had kept from Rex's office. A long wooden ruler.

Joe put one foot into the sensory-deprivation pod. The water was lukewarm. He had stripped down to his boxer shorts, and electrodes covered his body. A GHOST helmet topped his head, its visor raised. This helmet was far more sophisticated than the one back at Clubber's personal lab. Before placing another foot into the pod, Joe stared at his chief.

"You sure this'll work?"

"You tried it with the koi," said the chief. "Same thing."

Joe looked out the lab's glass wall into the ocean. The two elasmosaurs were still there, watching him through the glass. The electronic components blinked on their temples. Joe would be merging with the big green male. The aquatic reptile made eye contact through the glass. The animal seemed to know what was coming. It had gone through this before with another human handler.

"You boys could have offered me a proper bathing suit," Simone said. "This wetsuit you gave me isn't exactly flattering." She stood beside her pod, wearing a skintight white suit. Electrodes and cables draped across her, and her helmet hid her mane of red hair. "Joe, how do I look?"

"Like a sea monster," he said.

She stepped into the pod and sat down in the water. "Watch out." She snapped her teeth. "I bite."

Joe just kept one foot in the water for now. He turned toward Clubber. "Chief, what happens if the elasmosaurs are hurt? Or if they die? Would that affect us?"

Clubber shifted his weight from foot to foot. "You'd be perfectly safe."

"Should I listen to your words or your tone? Because the tone said I'm toast."

The chief winced. "All right, I'll admit it. In the past, we've had some issues. With the old helmets. Like the ones you tried in my lab back at Dinovia. The death of a host could deliver a shock to the controller. It could even cause brain damage. Even . . . deadly brain damage."

Simone leaped out of her pod as if stung by jellyfish. "So if the hosts die, we die?"

"Only with the old helmets!" Clubber said, raising his palms. "That's why we developed these sensory-deprivation pods and state-of-the-art GHOST II helmets. If something happens to the elasmosaurs, our team here will have time to power down your helmets, wake you up, and you'll be fine."

Joe pursed his lips. "Chief, all this talk about brain damage . . . it's not encouraging."

"I told you this because I'm honest, Joe. And I'm honest now. You will be reasonably safe with these pods."

"It was *perfectly* safe a moment ago," Simone muttered.

"We tested everything," Clubber continued as if he hadn't heard her. "We put controllers into animal hosts. We killed the hosts. And we woke up the human controllers without incident."

Joe's eyes widened. "You killed hosts? You killed living animals? You treated the wildlife of Mintari like guinea pigs?"

"We had to," Clubber said. "This is war. We must make sacrifices in war. We must bend our morals."

"For the greater good, huh?" Joe said, bitterness draping his voice.

"Yes, tar it!" Clubber said. "For the good of this planet. For the good of the dinosaurs who live here. If I must sacrifice the few to save the many, I will. That is my duty as chief. That is a moral dilemma the Rangers in the field don't have to face. I do. I made my choice. And I would do it again."

Joe pulled his visor down. He lay down inside the pod. The salty water enveloped him, leaving only his face exposed. "All right. Turn this tarry thing on."

Simone lay down in her own pod. "See you on the other side, Mr. Triplehorn. Don't bite me."

Clubber's head appeared over Joe's pod, looking down at him. "Godspeed, Ranger." He saluted Joe, then closed the pod's lid.

Darkness enveloped Joe. The sounds of the lab—beeping machines, shuffling feet, conversing scientists—all faded. He floated in the water. He was blind, deaf, senseless. All he had were his thoughts. It felt like being an incorporeal soul. Even his leg, which still ached most days, seemed happy.

Then the water flowed over his head.

He floundered. He was drowning! They flooded the pod to the very top! Even his face was now underwater.

Holding his breath, he squirmed, trying to shove the lid. But he had no arms. No legs. He touched no lid, no pod walls. He . . .

He was staring at the glass pane. From the outside. He floated in the ocean, looking into the lab. Through the glass, Joe could see the two sensory-deprivation pods. They were closed. Clubber and a few scientists stood beside them. Joe was out here in the ocean, underwater, gazing in.

My body is still in the pod, Joe thought. *But my mind is out here.*

Slowly he turned his head around. That head was mounted onto an enormously long neck. The neck curved gracefully, green scales chinking, giving him a view of his body. The torso seemed surprisingly small for such a long neck, and it sprouted four flippers. Joe was able to move them. Pretty easy. They seemed to correspond to the same commands he normally gave his arms and legs. He even had a tail, but try as he might, he couldn't wag it.

"Joe!" came a voice from beside him. "Joe, is that you?"

Joe swung his long neck in the other direction. His head moved too fast, disorienting him. He blinked a few times, and the ocean came back into focus. He found himself staring at another elasmosaur. The one with blue scales and red spikes on the head.

"Simone?" he said. Bubbles rose from his mouth.

"How can we talk?" Simone said. Her jaws opened and closed with every word, releasing bubbles. "Do elasmosaurs have vocal cords?"

A knocking sounded on the glass pane. They turned to see Clubber tapping the glass. The chief lifted a microphone, and a speaker thrummed on the ocean floor.

"Can you hear me, Joe and Simone?"

The two elasmosaurs nodded.

"How are we able to talk?" Simone asked.

Clubber spoke through the speaker. "You're not really talking. You're just grunting and groaning. But your human bodies are talking inside your deprivation tanks, and we can transmit the words to your human ears wirelessly. So it seems like you're talking to each other as elasmosaurs. The illusion should be complete. Pretty neat, huh?"

Joe couldn't help but shudder. His scales chinked. "Neat is one way to describe it. Creepy is another."

"It might take a while to get used to your new bodies," Clubber said. "And remember—elasmosaurs need to breathe air. You're not fish. You're warm-blooded animals. When you feel the pressure to breathe, rise to the surface. Good luck. Both of you."

Joe swung his neck toward Simone, accidentally bumping heads with her. She winced.

"Ow!" she cried. "Watch out, mister! You're an elasmosaur, not a pachycephalosaurus."

Joe grimaced. "Ow is right. One of your spikes scratched me."

"So we can feel pain in these bodies," Simone said, bubbles rising between her fangs. "Great. Why not?"

"We still need some practice to avoid bonking heads," Joe said.

"*You* need practice, mister. I didn't do anything."

They spent a while learning to operate their new bodies. At first it was awkward. Joe was able to move his flippers easily enough, but he could barely steer this long-necked body. He banged his head against the glass several times, slammed onto the seabed, and flipped himself upside down. Simone wasn't doing much better. At one point, she began spinning in mad circles, neck flailing like a lasso.

"Slow down!" Joe said.

"I can't!"

Their bodies crashed together, knocking them both into a forest of kelp. Their necks and flippers tangled in the tall seaweed. Grumbling and cursing, they flailed in the leafy net. They finally had to bite their way out. Not the tastiest thing Joe ever bit into, kelp.

Once free from the seaweed, Joe felt a sudden, overwhelming urge to breathe. He glanced up. The surface of the water glimmered above with beads of light. Sweet air awaited. He flapped his flippers, trying to swim upward. But he pitched forward and tilted toward the seabed.

His lungs ached.

Come on, Joe! he thought.

He worked the flippers again. He craned his neck upward. His lungs demanded air and now.

Don't kill this body, Joe!

He struggled but wasn't rising. He couldn't move. He—

He wagged his tail.

He figured out how to wag his tail!

He propelled himself upward, tail flapping, and his head burst over the surface. He gulped down sweet, sweet air.

"Joe, help!" Simone cried from below. "I can't get up there!"

Joe ducked his head under the water again. "Wag your tail."

"I can't!" She was floundering below.

Joe dived down, slid below her, and shoved her up to the surface. She gulped down air then glided back down. She gave him a toothy, simpering smile.

"Simone, I figured it out," Joe said. "To move these elasmosaur bodies, you need to flap the tail along with the flippers."

"But how? I can move the front flippers like arms. The back flippers like legs. I just use the same neural commands I do in my human body. How do you move the tail?"

Joe felt the blood rush into his scaly face. "You have to . . ." He lowered his voice to a mumble.

"What?" Simone tilted her head.

"You have to . . ." He mumbled something again.

"I can't hear you, Joe."

"You have to wiggle your bum."

Simone's eyes widened. She guffawed, blasting bubbles between her fangs. "Mr. Triplehorn! Did you wiggle your bum?"

"It's the only way this works!" he snapped.

She tossed back her head, long neck swinging backward, and laughed. "Jurassic Joe himself! Wiggling his bum under the ocean. Wait until the *Mintari Post* readers hear about this."

"Don't you dare! This mission is classified."

Simone paused, squinted, concentrated, then wagged her tail. She moved upward in the water. "It *does* work!"

Clubber's voice came through the speaker again, rippling the water. "We've installed a geolocation tracker into your neural chips. It shows your position and the position where the *Darwin's Cradle* crashed. Remember—that crash happened five hundred years ago. Since then, the seabed shifted. You might have to spend some time looking."

Joe turned toward the glass pane and looked at his chief. Funny. Clubber had always seemed like a large, powerful man. Now he looked so small. Joe could crush him between his teeth.

This is how dinosaurs see us, Joe thought. *As small, funny little mammals. No more than naked mice.*

Yet these naked mice had guns, and they were sending the ecosystem crashing down.

"How do we see these maps?" Joe said.

"You have to say the code word," Clubber said.

"Please?" asked Simone.

"The code word, not the magic word," Joe snapped.

Clubber continued as if he hadn't heard Simone. "Say or even just think the word *Magellan* to activate the map. The same code can shut it off."

Joe frowned. "Huh? Magellan?"

His neural implant hummed. A three-dimensional holographic map materialized in the water. It depicted a matrix of the seabed flowing toward a distant trench. Two icons, one green and one red, glowed in the center of the map. They were labeled *Joe* and *Simone*. Farther out, so small Joe could barely see it, flashed a red icon shaped like a starship.

"Follow the red dot," Clubber said. "Remember, it's just an estimated location."

"Chief, once we find this shipwreck, how are we supposed to collect the embryos?" Joe asked. "You forgot to give us luggage."

"The embryos should still be in their frozen cannisters," said Clubber. "You swallow them."

Simone's eyes widened. "Swallow them! We're not cannibals!"

Joe understood. "Elasmosaurs often swallow gastroliths. Stomach stones. They rub together in the animal's stomach, grinding up food and aiding in digestion. Some plesiosaurs can carry rock collections in their bellies that would make President Proudfoot jealous. We should have room for plenty of cannisters." He glowered at Clubber. "You better not cut these animals open to get the cannisters. We'll discharge them naturally."

"Hopefully once I'm back in my human body," said Simone. "It sounds painful."

Clubber saluted through the glass. "Good luck, Joe and Simone. The very survival of Mintari depends on you."

"No pressure," Simone muttered, turning away from the glass.

The two elasmosaurs swam into the distance, tails flapping, seeking a legend.

Chief Arban Clubber stood for a long while by the glass pane. He kept watching the ocean long after the elasmosaurs vanished into the distance. In the glass, when he refocused his eyes, he caught his reflection. His face was stern. His eyes hard. His jaw set. When Joe and Simone had been here, he had forced himself to sound relaxed and confident. Now the mask slipped off. Now all traces of geniality faded. His fists balled at his sides.

He turned toward his security guards. The Rangers stood in the lab, faces as hard as his, their ceratop hats shadowing their eyes.

"Joe Triplehorn is away. It's time."

The Rangers nodded.

Clubber walked down the corridor. For months now, he had been sidelining Joe, keeping the Ranger away from the battlefields. At first Clubber used Joe's wounded leg as an excuse. He ordered the man to stay at headquarters, to train new recruits. Then Clubber convinced President Proudfoot to send Joe on that ill-fated cruise. But Joe Triplehorn just kept coming back, eager to fight Hell's Hunters in the wild.

And I cannot allow that, Clubber thought. *Because he's still a Triplehorn. And I cannot trust a Triplehorn. Not in battle. Not against the one we fight.*

So now, once more, he sent Joe away. This time farther than ever before.

Clubber reached a shaft, climbed a ladder out of the lab, and stepped onto the cliff. His Rangers followed.

Bumpy and Dozer were still atop the cliff, eating bushes. The Ranger jippi was parked beside them. The sea churned below, spreading into the horizon. Clubber knew what terrors lurked under that water. They didn't call it Hell's Aquarium for nothing. He didn't envy Joe and Simone.

But he had a mission of his own. One just as dangerous. One he needed Joe far, far away from.

Because Joe Triplehorn was compromised. Joe was a man Clubber respected, admired, even loved. Tar it, he was family. But Joe was still a Triplehorn. He was still related to Amissa and Tobias, the greatest enemies of Mintari. In battle, if Joe had Amissa in his sights, would he pull the trigger? Would he kill his own sister?

Clubber didn't think so.

"But I will," he grumbled to himself.

He climbed onto Bumpy and sat in the ankylosaur's saddle. His Rangers entered their jippi. They all knew where Amissa was lurking. Joe had been to her camp only days ago to free Figaro. Yes, Clubber knew all about it. He had satellites in space, drones in the air, spies everywhere. Nothing happened on Mintari without him knowing.

"We will rally the troops," he said. "We will mount an attack. Amissa Triplehorn is going down."

CHAPTER TWENTY
On Wings of Fire

Once more, her father was gone. Once more, Fig was alone in this city of three hundred thousand souls. And once more, she headed out into the wild.

She walked through the tall grass, moving east, leaving the city behind. Autumn leaves fluttered in the air. The cold wind ruffled her short black hair, stung her cheeks, and rustled her dress of red feathers. It had been half a year since she had donned this dress. A dress woven with achillobator feathers. Her feral garb. She held her sickle claw, and a smile touched her lips. A predatory smile.

I was never meant to be a schoolgirl, she thought. *I'm a wild child.*

She would not sit idly in her room, wasting away the days. She had no more school. No more hope to become a Ranger. But she had her aunt. And she had a new dream.

The city vanished behind her. Fig took a deep breath of the cold autumn air. The grasslands spread toward distant cliffs, and beyond them rose misty forests. Mushrooms grew around her feet, and dactyls glided among slender clouds. This was right. This was good. This was Mintari. In the city, Fig had languished. There was danger in the wild. There were predators and starvation and ticks and storms, but there was beauty here, a savage beauty that still called to her. She was a human, but her heart belonged to the wild. Her grandmother survived out here without a pack. Fig could too.

The cold wind blew again, and Fig detected the faint hint of rot. Dead animals somewhere in the distance. Walking here, she noticed how empty the land was. Herds of iguanodons did not carve pathways in the grass. Hadrosaurs did not congregate on the rivers. And the dactyls above cawed and dived down to feed on carrion. Mintari was sick.

Did Amissa know? Did she realize she was hunting too much? Fig knew what her father said. That Amissa was a ruthless poacher. A heartless killer. That she would drive the dinosaurs to extinction. Yet her aunt had been kind to her. She had protected Fig from bullies. Guided her. Mentored her. Even offered to sponsor her in the Dino Derby. That wasn't the Amissa Triplehorn the Rangers spoke of.

I'll talk to her, Fig decided. *I'll show her the ruin across the world. I'll teach her to hunt responsibly. Like an achillobator. She can teach me strength, but I can teach her compassion.*

Maybe there was still a way to resolve this war without violence. Her father and her aunt hated each other. But maybe Fig could build a bridge between them.

But that was all for another day. Today Fig had a mission. Today she must find a dinosaur to ride.

She had been watching the Dino Derby religiously for months now. She gobbled up articles, books, and documentaries about the races. And she had even seen a race in person, enjoying the show from the balcony like an empress. That had been the best night of her life.

And Fig had learned some things about the races. She knew that race dinosaurs (which the derby sometimes called derbysaurs) were not wild. They had been hatched in captivity, bred over generations for speed and obedience. They were always some species of ornithomimid, also known as ostrich-dinos. But derbysaurs weren't just any random ornithomimids. Genetic modification was illegal at the Dino Derby, but expensive breeders modified their derbysaurs with meticulous selective breeding. Their dinos were the best of the best, descended of previous champions, masterpieces of speed. They cost more than most houses.

At least the ones who won races. Every once in a while, some crazy (or poor) jockey showed up with a wild dinosaur to ride. Sometimes it wasn't even an ostrich-dino but a raptor. Those dinosaurs were plucked from the wild, given some rudimentary training, and slapped with a saddle. Invariably, they refused to stay on track, disobeyed their jockeys, and sometimes even ate an audience member or two. The Thanksgiving Derby still held a moment of silence every year for the infamous Red Race, in which raptors had devoured fifteen spectators.

Fig also knew about the best jockeys. They trained since childhood in ruthless riding schools. It was whispered that they were half-starved and given puberty blockers to remain small. Many jockeys, even as adults, stood no taller than Fig. And she needed to stand on tiptoes to scratch five feet.

Well, Fig had no access to some fancy and expensive breeding farm. Buying a costly ornithomimid was out of the question. And she certainly hadn't grown up in some posh riding school, nor could she dream of affording one now. But she could turn lemons into lemonade. After years of malnourishment in the wild, she was the right size. And she had years of riding experience.

She had not ridden ostrich-dinos. She had ridden achillobators. And Fig knew they were tarry fast.

And so now she wandered the wilderness, but she was not lost. She was seeking an old friend.

Achillobators kept to distinct territories. They marked their borders with urine and spoor, and they respected pack boundaries. Sometimes border disputes occurred. Sometimes packs migrated. Sometimes alphas died and packs shrank and lost ground. But the territories retained their general shapes, and strong borders could last for years, even generations. Fig's old pack had hunted across a vast territory. Over a thousand square miles of forest and plains belonged to them, and (unless it was mating season) no other bator may enter. They often fought to protect their territory from other dinosaurs, such as the dreaded utahraptors, their mortal enemies.

Fig knew the other packs of achillobators. Sometimes she had seen them from a distance. Normally, the packs gave one another a wide berth. But during mating season, they emitted strong pheromones. During such times, bators could leave their packs, venture into another pack's territory, and seek to mate. Mating between packs kept the gene pool strong. Over her time with Red Scar's pack, Fig had seen seven bators transfer between packs for good mating.

Nobody had ever wanted to mate with Fig. Back then, she had not understood why. She had not realized she was human. Now so much made sense. Why she was smaller. Why she had to collect red feathers instead of grow them. Only in the human world, reading in the library, had Fig learned about pheromones. Her nose could not detect them, but they explained so much achillobator behavior. Only in the human world had Fig learned the mysteries of her pack.

Walking here today, Fig realized how much she had changed. She thought in human terms now. Thought about "square miles" and "gene pools." Back then, in the pack, Fig had simply followed along in the ancient game of survival. Perhaps the achillobators themselves did not understand why they behaved the way they did. Today Fig knew about instincts. The bators simply felt things deep in their souls.

Some achillobators, Fig knew, did not fit into this rigid game of survival. Some bators did not thrive in a pack. They challenged an alpha or lost. Or they went out in search of a mate and found none. Or they were wounded and abandoned, left behind to starve. For whatever reason, such achillobators lost their packs. They became lone dinosaurs, the wildest souls on Mintari.

Fig knew of such an achillobator. A dinosaur she had always feared. A lone predator. A rogue. A savage heart. She whispered his name into the wind.

"Firewing."

The wind seemed to answer, gusting and conducting a dance of autumn leaves.

Fig had seen him hatch. He had been born in her pack, the child of Red Scar, a prince of predators. But he was different from his brood mates. Smaller. Fiercer. When adults tried to guide him, he bit at their wings, ripping off feathers. On hunts, he blew his cover too soon, racing through the grass and scaring off the prey. He tried to mate with females who were already bonded. Once he had tried to smash eggs fertilized by a rival male, but Red Scar had seen and shoved him aside.

Achillobators did not give one another names. But in her mind, Fig invented names for them all. The big alpha was Red Scar because of the mark on his snout—the mark she herself had given him, slashing her sickle claw when he had tried to devour her. Blue Snout had bluish feathers below his chin. Longclaw had the sharpest and deadliest sickle claws in the pack. For a while, Fig had debated what to call the wild runt with the snapping jaws. Little Tooth? Big Anger?

Ultimately, his wings inspired his name. Achillobators sported a coat of crimson feathers. The feathers changed across the body. Underbelly feathers were barely more than fluff. Flank and back feather were thick and short. Feathers on achillobator arms were long and slender, forming wings (flightless but good for gliding), while the tail feathers were the largest of all, used to impress mates. But though their shape and length varied, the feathers were all the same red shade.

At least with most bators. The aggressive little bator was different. His wings sprouted feathers in all the colors of autumn. Crimson, cherry red, yellow, orange, and burnished gold—his wings were like fire. Firewing, she named him. A dinosaur with a flaming heart.

She knew where he lived.

She walked through the tall grass as autumn leaves danced around her on the wind. Every once in a while, a gust would raise the leaves into a whirlpool of red and gold, and it would be like spirits of autumn dancing on the plains. Fig sniffed the wind. She could not smell pheromones, but she could smell carrion. And if you wanted to find a lone predator, you followed the stench of rot. That was the price of freedom. The lone bator might be proud and fierce, but even such a soul of fire could not hunt well alone. Could not set an ambush. Could not surround prey. So most lone bators became scavengers, feeding on death. Freedom was their blessing and the taste of rot their curse.

Following the foul aroma, Fig crossed the grasslands, moving toward Collini Cliffs, realm of the pterosaurs. In the afternoon, with the sun hanging over the cliffs like a slab of butter over bread, Fig reached the killing field. Hundreds of dinosaurs lay dead and rotting. Parasaurs. Again—parasaurs! Once more, their crests had been cut off. The bodies littered the land.

Thousands of pterosaurs had descended from the cliffs to engorge themselves. Pterodactyls fluttered like moths over the corpses. Several imperators with kite-like crests battled over a rib cage. A mighty quetzalcoatlus stood above one dead parasaur, shooing aside a crowd of dimorphodons. The quetzalcoatlus was the size of a tricopter. Its beak was twice as long as Fig was tall, and it ripped into the carrion.

This was wrong. All of it. Pterosaurs should be eating fish, reptiles, sometimes sauropodlets or other small dinosaurs. Not rotting meat. These parasaurs should be fattening up for winter, ready to lay eggs in spring, creating a new generation that would sustain raptors and tyrannosaurs. This scene of rot was a disease on Mintari's flesh. Fig stared, tears rolling down her cheeks.

Amissa must understand, Fig thought. *I must show her. I must tell her that Mintari is dying.*

Fig could not believe the stories. Amissa was not some heartless conqueror who had come to destroy. She was mercurial, yes. Fierce, certainly. But was Fig any different? They were both huntresses. But Amissa was too good a huntress, too deadly, too greedy. Fig must temper her. It would be like taming a wild animal, something Fig knew how to do.

Something she must do today.

She stood on the edge of the macabre feast, tossed her head back, and let out a cry. "Arrorororooo! Ayeooo ayeoooo! Maoooo!"

The mating call of a bator. Sure to attract any male.

She paused to catch her breath. A few pterosaurs looked up at her, shrugged their leathern wings, and returned to their feast. Fig scanned the crowd, seeking red feathers. This was his territory. This was where the lone bator roamed. Was he here? Had the stench of meat not called to him? Or was he too good for scavenging?

Well, it certainly didn't help that Fig couldn't release pheromones. She'd just have to yell extra loud.

She took a deep breath, tilted her body back, raised her hands, and cried out, "Arrooorororooo! Ayeeoooo! Ayeoooo maooo!"

I am female! I am achillobator! Dance me a mating dance!

She breathed heavily, looking around. Where was he? Could he have found a new pack already?

It had been a long time. Three years since she had seen him. She still remembered that day. It had been summer. A hot, dry summer of drought. Food was scarce and tempers flared in the pack. Far Leaper, one of their best huntresses, had died from wasting tick disease, and a hatchling had fallen into a bog. In the chaos, Firewing had made his move, attacking Red Scar, determined to claim the pack to himself. The big alpha male defeated the young upstart in battle. But Firewing tried again and again. Every day, he antagonized Red Scar, nipping at his tail, vying for his crown. One day Firewing danced for Red Scar's mate. A terrible insult. The alpha had banished him that day, casting him out into the cold.

Firewing never joined another pack. He refused to be subservient. Sometimes they ran across him, and Firewing snarled and clawed the earth. He was always alone. He had become a rogue bator, too headstrong and stubborn to work in a pack. A lone bator was a dangerous thing. They killed whenever they could. They were always hungry.

"Arooroororoo!" Fig cried. "Ayeooo maoooo!"

Nothing. He wasn't here. Nothing but pterosaurs and carrion.

Fig heaved a sigh. She would keep looking, though she would probably not find Firewing tonight. Lone bators carved out their own territories, which tended to be small. But they were infamous for encroaching on other territories. He could be anywhere. Fig might have to spend the night in the wild, but without a pack, without a nest or cave, that was dangerous. She could try to rush back to Dinovia before sundown to—

"Haoooooooo!"

A distant cry.

Fig spun around, cocking her head. She searched the landscape. The sound had come from the south, but she saw only the rustling grass, the fluttering leaves, and clumps of cycads and conifers. A few sauropod necks rose in the distant mist. That was all.

Fig had recognized that sound. That was the cry of an achillobator.

She scanned the distance. Nothing!

"Aoorooooo!" she howled, head tossed back. "Aii aii aiiii!" *I'm here! I'm here!*

Nothing. No more bator cries. An ankylosaurus raised his armored head from the tall grass, grunted, then lumbered off. A few pterosaurs clattered their canoe-sized beaks. The wind rustled Fig's dress of red feathers. She heard nothing more. Had she imagined it?

Then he rose from the grass, so close Fig started and stumbled back.

He was only a few steps away, staring at her with keen yellow eyes.

"Firewing," she whispered.

He stood before her, a young, strong male. He was not the largest achillobator, but he was still the size of a lion (an animal Fig had seen in one of Merl's picture books). Firewing's legs were powerful and strong, covered with tiny black scales. Crimson feathers rustled across his body and long, flicking tail. His wings were flightless yet graceful, covered with feathers in all the shades of fire. Mean claws thrust out from his wingtips, sharp enough to disembowel his prey. In his powerful jaws, he held a dead sauropodlet. He had actually raided a sauropod herd and snatched a hatchling.

So much for Firewing stooping to eat carrion, Fig thought. *Wild he was, and wild he still is.*

He took a step closer. His upper lip rippled, revealing bloodstained teeth half-sunk into his prey. His yellow eyes blazed like two suns, and his slit pupils thinned to narrow black lines. His nostrils flared, sniffing her. Within a second, he could rip her apart, Fig knew. A low growl rose in his throat.

"Kah! Kah!" Figaro said. "Kah!" *I am pack!*

He took another step. He let the sauropodlet drop onto the grass, and his jaws opened, revealing his rows of teeth and a quivering red gullet. His growl grew louder.

Who is this strange mammal who claims to be pack? he must be thinking.

He doesn't remember me, Fig realized.

"Kah! Kah!" She crouched. "Essssss. Esssss." *I am pack.* *Think! Remember!*

The achillobator lunged toward her, jaws opening with a deafening screech. Fig cowered, shielding her head with her arms, sure she had only seconds to live.

Firewing froze, his powerful jaws held inches above her. Hot saliva splattered her. He stared, not yet feasting.

He stared at the sickle claw in her hand. The claw she had taken from a dead bator. He sniffed at the red feathers that covered her. Bator feathers. Feathers that smelled like their old pack. The family they had both left.

He closed his mouth, tilted his head. "Aroo?"

Fig nodded, heart pounding, tears in her eyes. She placed a shaky hand on his snout. "It's me," she whispered. "Fi-ga-ro."

At first he did not trust her. When Fig reached out to stroke his feathers, Firewing hissed and raised one of his talons.

His sickle claw was the size of a bread knife. When she tried to press her nose against his snout, he growled, snapped his teeth, and nearly bit her face off.

But he did not bite her. And he did not claw her. He was hurt. He was angry and afraid. He had been alone for so long, and so had she. Bugs scuttled below his feathers. Lice and leeches clung to areas where he could not reach. He was in pain.

When Fig reached for a leech, he screeched and pulled back. But she was determined. She reached out again. He slashed his claws over her head, slicing off strands of her hair. He could have killed her; he had chosen not to. Encouraging. Fig cooed. She huffed. She calmed him. When she pulled off the leech, he yowled. But he let her pull off the second one. And a louse.

He glared at her, eyes narrow with pain, lips rippling with snarls over his teeth. Then he lay down and revealed an underbelly rustling with parasites.

Fig cringed. "Ow." No wonder he was cranky.

She shuddered, pursed her lips, and got to work. Not to brag, but back in her wild days, she had been known as the best groomer in the pack. She was, after all, the only one with fingers. She plucked off bugs of all sorts, small and sharp and big and soft.

She found one tick among them. That one was the most dangerous. Fig had lost bators to ticks before. She watched the bitten bators wither, their feathers fall out, their joints harden as if they were being fossilized alive, until they died in agony. It was a long, torturous death, sometimes stretching over a full year. Not every tick infected a host with their terrible wasting disease. But at least half did. If this tick was diseased, Firewing was not long for this world. She plucked the tick off, careful to remove the legs too, then tossed it aside. More than starvation, more than ice, more than triceratops horns or ankylosaur tails—it was the humble tick that killed the most achillobators.

Firewing looked down at his belly, clean of bugs, likely for the first time in years. He rose to his feet, lowered his big head, and nuzzled her. His eyes closed, and he let out soft whimpers.

It's been so long since anyone was kind to you, hasn't it? Fig thought, cooing to him. *But you're no longer alone. And neither am I.* A shaky smile found her lips. *We are pack.*

As the sun set, she rode him across the plains. She laughed, the wind in her hair. She clung to Firewing with her thighs, and she clutched fistfuls of his feathers. He bounded across the plains and hills, faster than Red Scar had ever been, and the cold wind blew the tears from Fig's eyes.

She was free. She was wild. She was *l'enfant sauvage*, a feral child, riding once more across the world she loved. Mintari.

Who had she been in that school? Who was that girl who had languished in a room where she could not see the grass or sky? Who was Figaro Triplehorn, that mouse in the city? That was not her. She was the wind and the feathers and the sunset over the land. She was the first stars that shone and the moons above. She was the cold air and the turning seasons. She had a human body, but her soul was the soul of a dinosaur.

As night fell, she tossed back her head and let out a cry of savage joy. "Aoooo! Yip yip yip!"

Firewing tossed back his own head and howled at the moons.

He did not tire. He did not lose speed. He swept across the plains like no achillobator Fig had ever seen. He was faster than the great leaders. Faster than the hunters. He was a lone bator. He was a wild child. He was *hers*.

I will race you, Firewing, she thought. *I will race you in the wild and on the track before the crowd. I will race you over the plains, and I will race you to victory. We are pack. We are bonded. We are one.*

That night, Fig did not fear to sleep in the wild. She did not bother returning to the city. She and Firewing found a hollow under overhanging roots, and they lay down on a bed of moss. She curled up in his feathers and hugged his snout, and in her dreams she was riding him over the clouds.

Amissa stood on the battlements, waiting for blood.

"They're coming," she said. "We're ready."

All day, Amissa and her soldiers had toiled, preparing for battle. They dug trenches. They raised barricades. They set traps. They filled guard towers with ammo and guns. Amissa had eyes across Mintari. Cameras hidden in fields, on mountaintops, and on civilian satellites. Whisperers everywhere. She knew they were coming.

She had shown Fig her camp, then let the girl go. The Rangers knew they were here. And they were heading this way.

Amissa leaned over the guard tower railing, staring south. Her body armor clanked. She had donned a helmet, elbow and knee pads, and a bulletproof vest. Magazines filled the pouches of her tactical vest, two rifles hung across her back, and blades and handguns clung to her thighs. Triplehorn Incorporated had armed and armored her. A silver triceratops head—logo of her company, her clan, her army—shone on her chest. This was not a hunt. This was war. She was ready.

"We should have kept the girl," muttered Rattlesnake. "She summoned the enemy."

The lanky poacher stood beside her in the guard tower. Rather than dress for battle with humans, he remained in his usual hunting garb. He wore a wide-brimmed hat, a long dark coat, and bandoleers heavy with bullets. With wiry hands like tree roots, he gripped a rifle, and pistols hung at his hips. When he shifted his weight, spurs jangled on his boots. Among all of Amissa's soldiers, only Rattlesnake dared criticize her. He was her top killer. He knew his worth. So did Amissa.

"Good," Amissa said. "Let them come."

Rattlesnake turned his eyes toward her. There was no white to his eyes, just two pure black orbs. They gleamed in the light of the moons. "Are you so eager for battle? We're hunters, Amissa. Not soldiers."

"We're soldiers now. This is war, my friend." She gave him a crooked smile. "Are you really so scared of the Rangers? You've killed T-rexes."

"T-rexes don't carry automatic weapons."

Amissa smirked. "Maybe they should. We can train a few, replace their useless little arms with machine guns."

"You still think this is all a big joke, Amissa? I spent thirteen years fighting warlords on Earth. I know what battle is like. Battle is dangerous business. Far more dangerous than hunting. Yes, even more dangerous than hunting dinosaurs. If we must fight, let us fight from the shadows. Guerrilla warfare is how we win. It's how the rebels are winning on Earth. Let us disappear into the wild. Let the Rangers find an empty camp. We'll strike them one by one. When they do not expect it. We'll fight on *our* terms."

Amissa considered. Rattlesnake was a ruthless killer, yes, but a cautious one. That was what she liked about him. Amissa had become aware of her own faults in this war. She was quick to anger. Too headstrong. Too impulsive. Her rashness had almost claimed her life several times. Should she listen to the grizzled old hunter?

"No," she finally said. "These *are* our terms, Rattlesnake. Here in this camp, we have the advantage. We have barricades. Vantage points. A knowledge of the land. I might not have your battle experience, but I've learned a thing or two this year. It's always easier to defend than attack. If our intelligence is correct,

Chief Clubber himself is coming on this raid. If we kill him—*when* we kill him—we will cripple the Rangers. We'll never have another chance like this."

"Neither will they," hissed Rattlesnake. "You are here. I am here. The other leaders are here. They can end us tonight."

Amissa nodded. "Yes, they can. But I will stay and face them nonetheless. We will no longer run and hide. We will show the Rangers who rules this world."

She pulled out her new SmartSphere. Simone LaRue had destroyed her old one. Not before deleting Amissa's QuickFame account. That day, Amissa had lost millions of followers. Lost her fame. Lost her reason to live. But here on Mintari, she discovered a new purpose. She no longer had her fame, but she had Hell's Hunters. She no longer inspired the masses with her photos and flirty videos. She commanded an army.

I was vain and weak then, she thought. *I danced for the crowds and begged their approval. I sold myself for fame. LaRue did me a favor. Now I take what I want. Now I do not debase myself but fight. I will not run.*

She loaded a map into her SmartSphere. There they were. A cluster of red dots. The Rangers. Moving closer across the plains. They were almost here. A hundred Rangers, maybe more. A big force for them.

Rattlesnake stared at the map, his black eyes narrowed to slits. His leathery hand twitched over his enormous dinosaur gun. That rifle could take down a sauropod. Amissa wondered what it would do to a human.

"Very well." Rattlesnake lit a shabu stick. "I fight with you."

Amissa wrinkled her nose, waving aside smoke. "Those things will kill you, you know."

Rattlesnake took a long puff. The little crystals inside the metal cylinder glowed blue. "They say the same about fighting wars, yet here we are."

Clouds moved in from the north, hiding Thanatos, one of Mintari's two moons. Only Hypnos now shone in the southern sky, silvering the distant conifers. Rain began to fall. The drops pattered onto Amissa's helmet. She stood, silent, staring south. The red dots on her map came closer. Closer. The enemy was moving fast. They had jippis, big ones, armored and modified for war.

For a moment, claws of fear grabbed Amissa's heart. She could not breathe.

We should run. Rattlesnake was right. This is madness.

She forced the terror down.

Be strong. You are a huntress. You are a warrior. You are Amissa Triplehorn. You will face the enemy and win!

And if she must die tonight, she would go down fighting.

She looked across the fortifications. Wooden palisades rose in a defensive wall, the logs sharpened to spikes on top. An electric fence provided a second layer of security. Guard towers, some built of metal and others of wood, peered over the walls, full of poachers. Jippis waited inside the camp, armored and mounted with guns. The Rangers weren't the only ones driving those armored behemoths. And Amissa had a few surprises too . . . little treats for the Rangers she still kept hidden.

Originally, this was meant to be a temporary camp. It had become a fortress. Amissa named it Fort Devana after an ancient goddess of hunting. Her fans used to call Amissa the "Goddess of the Hunt," and—

There!

Amissa inhaled sharply.

Lights in the distance! Fog lights piercing the night!

Then she heard it. The rumbling of engines. Jippis were approaching. The Rangers were here.

Amissa flexed her fingers around her rifle, and her lips peeled back in a terrified smile.

The jippis rolled closer, carving paths through the brush. In the dark, their headlights shone like wrathful eyes, and their engines grumbled. They were like great dinosaurs of metal charging forth. Amissa imagined them as a herd of mechanical triceratops hell-bent on destruction.

Then, as they drew closer, Amissa saw it. Real dinosaurs! Real dinosaurs were rumbling among the jippis! One Ranger was riding an ankylosaurus. Another rode a centrosaurus, its central horn thrusting forward like a pike. Several pachycephalosaurs ran alongside the pack, collars around their necks. Their domed heads reflected the moonlight.

Above the jippis and dinosaurs flew a new terror. Three pteranodons flew above, leather wings churning the clouds. The flying reptiles were the size of small airplanes, and Rangers rode in their saddles. Amissa stared upward in silent horror.

"So the Rangers brought an air force," Rattlesnake muttered. He spat a brown glob off the guard tower.

Across the walls of Fort Devana, Hell's Hunters shifted uncomfortably. Mumbles rose among the troops.

"We have to run," somebody said to his friend.

"They're too many!"

"This is madness. We're hunters, not soldiers!"

"We came here to hunt, not to die!"

Amissa took a deep breath. "Hell's Hunters!" she cried. "Do not fear! Together we're strong. Together we will win! I am Amissa Triplehorn. I am with you. We will face the enemy and beat them back!"

One hunter, a bearded man who stood in a nearby guard tower, spat and climbed down the ladder.

"I'm outta here," he said. "I came to this planet to make money, not fight this crazy woman's war. Who's with me? I'm heading back to—"

A gunshot rang out.

The bearded hunter collapsed, a bullet in his head.

Amissa blew smoke off her muzzle. She stared across the battlements. "Anyone else feel like deserting?"

Nobody did.

"Like it or not—this is no longer a hunt!" Amissa shouted. "This is war! I have no use for deserters. Are you soldiers?"

They raised their guns high. "Hell yeah!"

"Who are we?" Amissa cried.

"Hell's Hunters! Hell's Hunters!"

"For the hunt!" Amissa shouted at the top of her lungs, raising her rifle overhead.

"For the hunt! For the hunt!"

The enemy stormed closer. Amissa stared at them, eyes wide, a grin trembling on her face. The jippis and dinosaurs rumbled forth, and the pteranodons cawed above. The Rangers raised their rifles. Amissa saw death charging her way, and it was glorious.

"For the hunt!" she cried, aimed her rifle, and fired.

CHAPTER TWENTY-ONE
This Savage World

"Daddy, no. Please." Tears streamed down the little girl's cheeks. "Don't make me kill him."

Tobias loomed above her, his hands tucked into the folds of his robe. Like many wealthy Cloventians, he emulated the fashion of the silk emperors who ruled from their floating palaces. His crimson robes shone with golden embroidery and gleaming rubies. The silk was soft. His skin was powdered. But his eyes were savage. In his eyes, one could glimpse the Mintarian blood he tried so hard to hide. They were the eyes of a predator.

"Now now, my little Ami," he said. "It's not a *him*. It's an *it*. Just an animal. Kill it."

The little girl sobbed. "Daddy, no!" She gazed at the mouse in the trap. "He's cute. Please don't make me kill him."

"Cute?" Tobias's faced flushed. "It is vermin! A diseased rodent that invaded our home! Are you so weak that you pity a pest?"

Amissa cowered. She had learned to fear his anger. Her body still bore the bruises from yesterday. She had upset him, had left crumbs under her bed. She hid there to read, to play with her dolls, to eat a few pilfered cookies. She made a mess, and she paid the price.

"I'm sorry," she whispered. "I'll take the mouse outside. I'll release him—*it*—in the forest."

"The forest?" Tobias guffawed. "Where do think we live? You've been watching too many Mintarian movies. This is planet

Cloventia. There are no forests. We cut them down long ago. But a few pests survived. You lured one here with your crumbs and your messes. Kill it."

Sniffing, Amissa looked at the trap. Her father had placed it under her bed. A little cage. The mouse was terrified. Trembling. A fluffy little critter. It was the first time Amissa had seen a live animal.

"I . . . I can release it onto the street, I—"

Tobias pulled his hands out from his robes. His rings gleamed. Amissa knew the sting of those crystals.

She sobbed and nodded. That day she put the cage in the freezer, and the next morning, when she pulled the cage out, the little corpse was stuck to the bars and covered with frost. Tobias made her pluck it off with her bare hands and throw it away. It was the first time she had killed.

Another day, Tobias brought her a snake. Just a little thing. Barely longer than her forearm. "Kill it," he told her. "With this knife."

A third day, he brought her a bird. "Crush it. With this rock."

He called her weak. Said she must learn that animals were things. That humans were dominant.

"Mintarian blood still runs hot in our veins," he said. "Cloventia conquered nature. Cloventia cut down its forests and killed its animals. This is how we become true Cloventians."

Every night after a kill, Amissa lay in her bed, weeping, thinking of her mother. Her mother had fled this floating skyscraper above the neon sea. She had taken Joe, returned to Mintari, and now lived in the wild, a place of forests and mice. She abandoned Amissa here. In her dreams, Amissa sneaked into a starship, flew to Mintari, and found her mother. When she was fifteen, she made it as far as the spaceport before Tobias's men dragged her back. And that day he made her butcher a cow he brought in from planet Dagon.

It was that day, as the cow's blood flowed over her arms, that something broke inside her. Her soul burned that day. She rose from the ashes, reborn. A huntress. A killer. No more mercy inside her. She was anointed with blood.

Tobias had completed breaking her and rebuilding her. No more was she little Ami, trembling and meek. She was Amissa Triplehorn, goddess of the hunt. She went from killing cows to killing mammoths. From killing mammoths to killing dinosaurs. And from killing dinosaurs to killing men.

Twenty-five years had gone by since drowning that mouse. Tonight she stood on Mintari. But she had not come here as an animal lover. Not like her mother and brother. Amissa had come as a huntress.

Her gunshot rang out, piercing the night.

Her bullet slammed into one Ranger, knocking the man off his centrosaurus. The rest of the horde kept charging toward Fort Devana, dinosaurs rumblings, jippis roaring. First blood had spilled. The battle began.

The enemy charged closer. Closer still. Their jippi wheels and dinosaur feet shook the earth and raised clouds of dust. The force was larger than Amissa had expected. Twenty jippis. Three screeching pteranodons with demonic wings. Dozens of dinosaurs. Centrosaurs with thick frills and elaborate horns. Domeheaded dinosaurs that could shatter walls. Ankylosaurs like tanks, their clubbed tails whipping from side to side. Largest of all rumbled a diplodocus, its long neck covered with interlocking metal plates. The bastards had actually forged armor for sauropods. Rangers rode the dinosaurs and pterosaurs, carrying guns. The dinosaurs were all herbivores, but they were just as deadly as the toughest carnivores.

We should have run, Amissa thought. *We're all going to die.*

She clenched her jaw. No fear! She was no longer that little girl. She would kill every one of her enemies. Like she had killed that mouse. Like she had killed her own soul.

Amissa scanned the horde for her brother, but she did not see him here. Was the famous Jurassic Joe too cowardly to join this battle? Ha!

At the Rangers' lead ran a massive ankylosaurus, a beast as large as the jippis, a living tank covered in armor and spikes. His tail ended with a club of solid bone. On his back rode a barbarian with a massive head, broad shoulders, and death in his eyes. He looked like Genghis Khan returned from the dead, charging toward the Great Wall of China. Amissa recognized him. Arban Clubber. The chief of the Rangers himself.

Good. She would take him out tonight. They were related through Mina Clubber, but it was a distant relation. Family or not, Amissa would show the man no pity tonight. By killing Chief Clubber, she would end this war with one fell swoop.

"Fire!" Amissa shouted.

For a moment, the entire chaos of battle vanished. The rampaging dinosaurs, the shrieking pterosaurs, the roaring machines—they all faded. And all Amissa saw was the chief before her.

She aimed at Clubber and pulled her trigger.

At that exact same moment, the beefy chief raised his arm. He tapped a button on his wrist, and an energy shield materialized before him, crackling with golden static. Amissa's gun boomed. Her bullet slammed into a shimmering hemisphere, shattering inches away from Clubber's face.

Amissa spat.

"So the Rangers brought some new toys," she muttered.

More poachers opened fire. A storm of bullets flew toward the Rangers. But they were all raising energy shields. Bullets shattered. Amissa snarled and aimed instead at Clubber's dinosaur. Her bullets pounded the ankylosaurus. The dinosaur had no shield, but his natural armor was too thick. The gunfire only enraged the beast. The ankylosaurus roared and rumbled closer.

His name is Bumpy, Amissa remembered. Something her spies had told her. What a ridiculous name. Apparently the Rangers called their dinosaurs rangersaurs. Ha! The Rangers were a bunch of toddlers. Amissa would smack some sense into them.

On the armored dinosaur's back, Clubber raised his fist high. "Fire!" the burly chief howled.

A barrage of bullets flew toward Fort Devana.

Amissa knelt. Bullets pinged against the guard towers. One bullet hit a poacher, a wiry man named Wilhelm. With a warbling scream, he tumbled off the wall. A hailstorm of bullets hit the wooden palisade. More bullets plowed into the electric fence, denting its bars.

"Fire!" Amissa shouted, rising from cover. "Hold them back!"

She slung her rifle over the railing.

The enemy was closer. Only moments away now. This time she aimed at one of the jippis. She fired on automatic.

Her bullets pierced a jippi's wheel. The huge tire ripped open. The jippi slewed and slammed into a pachycephalosaurus, knocking the domehead down, only for another jippi to run over the poor dinosaur.

Amissa's poachers fired with her. Slugs slammed into jippis, chipping windshields. Bullets peppered ceratopsian frills. Gunfire pounded the diplodocus, denting the towering dinosaur's armor. The sauropod bugled in fury and rumbled onward, his feet shattering the earth. Several Rangers rode on his back. They aimed guns around the sauropod's armored neck, firing at the fort. Bullets whizzed around Amissa and pinged against her guard tower. She crouched behind the railing.

They're not stopping, Amissa realized. Her heart pounded. Her hands trembled.

The enemy kept charging closer. Closer. They were almost here. And they all had one purpose. To kill her.

Shrieks tore through her terror.

Amissa looked up, and she saw them above. The pteranodons were diving toward the barricades, bloodlust in their eyes.

With deafening screeches, the pteranodons swooped.

By the silk emperors' underpants, they're huge, Amissa thought.

All three were males, judging by their crimson crests. Their beaks were longer than Amissa was tall. Their wings hid the moons, and their eyes blazed like red stars. The Rangers on their backs were mere shadows. Across the battlements, hunters panicked. A few ran. Amissa wanted to run too. These could not be mere animals. They seemed like dragons of old.

But she stood her ground. As the pteranodons swooped, she raised her rifle and fired.

Her gun rattled on automatic. Pteranodon bodies and beaks were slender, but their wings were like sails. Huge targets. Amissa hit one wing with ease, drawing a line of bullet holes. The perforated piscivore wailed and careened, vanishing into darkness.

At once, Amissa wheeled her gun toward another pteranodon and—

He was too close!

He was reaching out to grab her!

Talons uncurled, each claw the length of a sword. Amissa fired blindly, but the talons knocked her gun away, then grabbed her.

She screamed as the reptile beat his wings, raising her off the battlements.

Panic swelled in her. He was carrying her off!

She crushed the fear. Her rifle hung uselessly on a strap, dangling behind her back. With the talons gripping her, she could not reach the rifle. Instead, she drew a hunting knife. She drove the steel blade into the pteranodon's leg.

The reptile screeched.

The talons opened.

Amissa tumbled down. She thudded onto her guard tower, landing hard on her side. Thankfully, the pteranodon had only lifted her a few feet into the air. Landing still hurt. She nearly rolled over the tower's edge, but Rattlesnake grabbed her. The rawboned hunter pulled her to her feet.

"Get a grip!" he growled.

Amissa glanced at the battle below the tower. The Rangers were storming the barricades, trying to break into the camp. Hell's Hunters were firing on them, holding them back. For now. Amissa could not help her fellow hunters. She had her hands full with the aerial assault.

"Rattlesnake, oversee the ground defenses, I'll—"

She had no time to complete her sentence.

The pteranodon swooped toward her. The same one from before. Her knife was still embedded into his leg.

Persistent bastard, she thought.

A Ranger rode in the saddle. Amissa fired her rifle at him, but the man raised an electric shield, shattering her bullets. The pteranodon dived faster. This time the reptile kept his talons pulled back. Instead he opened his beak wide, prepared to swallow her.

With a savage grin, Amissa drew two more knives. She held one in each hand, hilts pointing inward, blades pointing outward. She did not flee. Even as Rattlesnake cursed and leaped aside, Amissa stood still, letting the gargantuan beak descend toward her.

The open beak slammed down, trapping Amissa like a cage. The beak tips hit the guard tower floor. The gullet quivered above, dripping saliva. The beak formed a huge upside-down V, and Amissa stood in the middle.

The beak began to close around her like a plier.

Amissa thrust out her daggers.

The beak snapped shut around her.

Her blades pierced it—one on each side.

The pteranodon's shriek blew back her hair. The beak opened, releasing her. The pteranodon raised his head, warbling in agony, the knives still stuck in his beak. His talons bent the guard tower railing. The rider on his back swayed in the saddle.

Amissa stood on the guard tower, drenched in saliva. She drew her handguns. She fired one gun at the Ranger in the saddle. The other at the pteranodon's head.

She hit both targets.

The Ranger was too disoriented to raise his shield. Her bullet plowed through his neck. The mighty flying reptile tilted backward and crashed down, impaling himself on the stockade of sharpened logs.

Briefly Amissa glanced below at the battle. The Rangers were still assaulting the walls. Hell's Hunters were firing from the battlements, still holding them off. Three pteranodons had flown here. One lay impaled on the spikes. Another lay on the battlefield, wing full of holes. He wouldn't be flying anytime soon.

But the third pteranodon still flew, and he was the biggest one. His leathery skin was the color of a midnight storm, and his eyes were burning coals. The Ranger on his back was firing a rifle, taking out hunters on the battlements.

As Amissa watched, the winged terror swooped toward a nearby guard tower, one with three hunters upon it. Amissa knew those men well. The Lazarus Brothers, two grizzled old poachers, and young Butterfly (famous for his love of butterfly knives). The hunters opened fire, but their bullets did not deter the huge black pteranodon. The beast kept flying closer, closer, and with a mighty blow from his talons, the titanic reptile knocked the tower down.

The Lazarus Brothers screamed, tumbling toward the ground. The old poachers landed with sickening *thumps*, probably breaking every bone in their bodies. Butterfly was about to join them, but the pterosaur caught the younger hunter. The talons flicked Butterfly into the air. The hunter screamed, spinning above like a rag doll tossed by a petulant child. As Butterfly came falling back down, the pteranodon opened his beak. Butterfly fell right in. Like a worm into the mouth of a baby bird. The pteranodon gulped him down.

"Bloody hell," Rattlesnake muttered, standing beside Amissa on their own guard tower.

Amissa bared her teeth like an angry dinosaur. She grabbed her rifle, loaded a fresh magazine, and opened fire.

Her bullets pounded the monstrous black pteranodon. The reptile cawed and turned toward her. Bullets hit his beak, his leg, and pierced a wing. But still the pteranodon flew, diving across the battlements toward her guard tower.

Rattlesnake opened fire too, filling the black wings with holes, but the pteranodon would not stop flying. The Ranger in the saddle saw Amissa, aimed his rifle, and—

She hit him! The Ranger's head tore open, spraying red mist.

Amissa loaded a fresh magazine just as the pteranodon reached her.

The beak opened wide, prepared to swallow her. She held her trigger down, emptying an entire magazine into the hellish gullet.

The dark reptile crashed into her guard tower, ripping through the railing. He was still alive! Somehow the bastard was still alive! The beak engulfed Amissa and snapped shut. Even in his death throes, the pteranodon managed to gulp.

Muscles gripped Amissa, pulling her down the beak and into the throat.

He's swallowing me. Panic flared in her. *God, he's swallowing me!*

In the shadows, she glimpsed Butterfly. His head was stuck here inside the pteranodon's esophagus. His body was already inside the animal's stomach, being digested. Then the dying pteranodon gulped, and Butterfly's head too vanished into the belly of the beast. Amissa had no intention of joining the poor hunter there.

She still had one knife left. She drew it. With a howl, she carved the reptile open, tearing the esophagus, ripping the skin of the neck, and she burst out the monster into the night.

She dripped blood and saliva. Tears stung her eyes. She was alive. Against all odds, she was alive. She placed a boot atop the dead of the pteranodon, raised her arms in the air, tossed back her head, and howled in triumph.

Across the camp, hunters stared in awe. A few rubbed their eyes. One hunter knelt and whispered prayers.

Rattlesnake stood nearby. He raised his fist. "Amissa, goddess of the hunt! Amissa, Amissa!"

The cry rose across the camp. "Amissa, Amissa!"

She basked in the glory. But only for a moment. She had slain three pteranodons, wiping out the Rangers' air force. But the battle still raged. The enemy still had ground troops. The Rangers, their dinosaurs, and their jippis spread across the dark landscape like a demonic host, ready to break down the walls and storm Amissa's home.

"Grenades!" Amissa shouted from the tower.

She tried to pull a grenade off her belt. Her hands were shaking. Her head was spinning. A bullet whistled above. Another bullet pinged against the railing before her. She grabbed the grenade but dropped it.

I can't breathe. I can't—

In her mind—her father.

You are strong, Amissa. I made you strong. You are a Triplehorn. Fight!

Amissa tightened her lips, grabbed the grenade, pulled off the pin, and hurled it from the guard tower.

The grenade landed among the enemy horde.

In the virtual reality games Amissa used to play, grenades always exploded with fire and light. Reality was different. No fire. No light. The grenade simply gave a deafening *pop*, scattering shrapnel and rippling the air with a shock wave. A kentrosaurus yowled and fell. Several of its dorsal spikes ripped off. Shrapnel flew into the cargo hold of a jippi, and Rangers screamed and tumbled into the night.

Amissa stared, eyes wide. The blood. So much blood. People torn apart.

The other hunters threw more grenades. At Amissa's side, Rattlesnake was snarling in a drug-induced fervor, hurling grenade after grenade. A stegosaurus collapsed, dorsal plates flying off. Rangers tumbled into clouds of dust. A jippi overturned and crushed the Rangers inside.

Stop! Amissa wanted to cry. *Stop firing! Stop this war! Stop everything!*

Her eyes burned with tears.

The enemy charged closer. Closer. Bullets whistled everywhere. A machine gun roared, tearing through the electric fence. Wooden chunks flew from the palisades. Bullets slammed into the guard tower around Amissa, and the entire structure wobbled, and—

Pain!

White agonizing pain!

Amissa fell to her knees, gasping. She couldn't breathe. She was dying! She was having a heart attack! She couldn't *breathe.*

She looked down at her chest. A bullet had hit her, lodging itself into her armored vest.

With great force, she took a raspy breath, shoving the air down. Pain crippled her. She tried to rise, winced, and dropped to one knee. The bullet had not penetrated her vest. But by the gods, it hurt. Her ribs might be broken. Or at least bruised like old bananas.

Rattlesnake grabbed her. "Get up and fight!"

She stood again. The enemy was seconds away now. Right there below.

From her guard tower, Amissa made eye contact with Chief Clubber. His face was hard as a rock. His eyes blazed with fire.

He has my father's eyes, Amissa thought. The two men looked nothing alike. Tobias had round blue eyes. Clubber had dark narrow eyes. Yet those eyes were still somehow the same. They shone with the same malice.

With clouds of dust, a storm of bullets, and howls of fury, the Rangers reached Fort Devana, and the night exploded with light and blood and fire.

While preparing for this battle, Amissa had drawn inspiration from Dinovia, the city she had invaded last spring. Three lines of defense surrounded Dinovia. An electric fence. A moat. And a tall stone wall. Amissa had replicated those three-layered defenses, though admittedly on a smaller scale.

First in line was the electric fence. Amissa knew it would not hold back a determined invader. But she hoped it would at least give the Rangers pause. Well, some of them paused. The dinosaurs did. So did several smaller jippis. But five jippis—big ones with hefty cowcatchers—kept rumbling forward.

"What the hell are they doing?" Rattlesnake muttered, glaring over the guard tower railing. "They'll shock themselves to death."

Amissa stared at the roaring jippis. And she understood.

They were empty. No Rangers sat in those jippis. They were remote controlled.

"Hold on!" she said, gripping the railing.

The five jippis plowed into the electric fence.

Electricity blazed skyward like thunderbolts. Metal twisted, snapped, tore. Electric cables flailed like serpents. Fire blazed across the night and swept over the brush.

The guard tower swayed. Amissa clung on for dear life. Bullets flew both ways, slicing the air. A bullet grazed her shoulder, ripping her shirt, slicing her skin. She yowled.

The power thudded off. Not just the electric fence but power across the entire camp. The spotlights died. The generators shut down with echoing *thunks*. But the fire and moons still lit the night. And the remote-controlled jippis kept rumbling forward. Mangled bits of fence clung to their cowcatchers. Their cabins had shattered. Their frames were bent and cracked. They were burning up. But they kept driving until they reached the trench Hell's Hunters had dug around the camp. The jippis plunged down into the shadows. Their wheels spun madly below, ripping through dirt and roots and rocks. The fire consumed them. They were not getting out of that trench anytime soon.

"Charge!" rose Clubber's cry.

They came racing through the smoke. A horde of dinosaurs and jippis. They looked like an army of demons risen from hell.

Don't make me kill him, Father.

Amissa's legs trembled. Her chest hurt so much.

Please, Father, I don't want to kill the dog. Please.

Her wounded chest ached, an old pain she remembered so well. The pain of jeweled fists.

What am I doing here?

The Rangers reached the trench. Dinosaurs halted and reared and bugled in the dark. Jippis rolled to a halt.

Amissa fired her gun. All her poachers fired. She tossed a grenade, and a stegosaurus mewled and crashed down dead. Another Ranger fell, riddled with bullets. The survivors stood with raised shields, blocking the barrage. The hemispheres of energy sparked as bullets pummeled them.

They can't get over the trench, Amissa realized. *We're holding them back!*

Her heart swelled. She loaded another magazine and fired again, aiming at the chief. Her bullets glanced off his shield and shattered against Bumpy's armor. The Rangers never stopped firing their own weapons. One Ranger fired a grenade, and an explosion rocked a nearby guard tower. Hunters crashed down dead.

"They brought grenade launchers," Rattlesnake muttered. "Perfect." His black eyes widened, bugging out. "Incoming!"

Another grenade came flying—this one right at Amissa. She caught it, threw it back, and ducked.

It exploded in midair. The blast rocked the guard tower. Shrapnel flew overhead. Rattlesnake roared. Blood spurted from his cheek. He fired his rifle, pounding the enemy.

Amissa rose and glanced down. More jippis were roaring forward. Rangers hopped out the moving vehicles, hit the ground, and rolled.

Empty of Rangers, the jippis plunged into the pit, joining the mangled vehicles already there. Jippis piled up inside the trench—big smoldering mounds of metal. And Amissa understood.

They were filling the trench on purpose. They were making a crossing.

With battle cries, the Rangers and their dinosaurs ran over the crashed jippis, crossed the trench, and slammed against the last line of defense. The wooden palisade.

And now it was the dinosaurs' time to shine.

The stockade was built of thick conifer trunks. Individually, each trunk was so wide two men could not hug it. Together they formed a massively thick wall of wood. But the dinosaurs were undeterred. Centrosaurs plowed into the palisade with their armored heads and powerful horns. The diplodocus kicked with his mighty feet, cracking wooden beams. Pachycephalosaurs plowed into the trunks, shattering them. The domeheads stood shorter than the diplodocus's knees, but with their thick craniums, they did just as much damage.

The hunters kept firing. A domehead collapsed, riddled with bullets. The diplodocus reared, his metal armor dented and falling apart. A dead Ranger fell off the dinosaur's back and tumbled into the moat.

The palisade still stood.

Despite all the damage—the wooden wall stood!

Amissa's heart swelled. "Kill them!" she cried. "Kill them all."

More bullets and grenades rained on the Rangers.

Then through the smoke, he rumbled forth. A living tank. Bumpy the ankylosaurus.

Thick plates of armor covered his entire body—his head, his back, his tail. Even his eyelids were armored. Bullets pinged off him. Clubber rode on his back, bent behind his electric shield, gritting his teeth as bullets streaked around him.

Bumpy trudged over the fallen jippis, lumbered through the hailstorm of bullets, and reached the wooden wall. He swung his armored tail.

An ankylosaurus tail was among the most dangerous weapons on Mintari, rivaling T-rex jaws and triceratops horns. The bony club plowed into the stockade like a wrecking ball.

Wooden beams shattered. Splinters filled the air. And the wall came crashing down.

The Rangers cheered. The dinosaurs rumbled. Amissa watched in horror as the enemy streamed into Fort Devana.

In her dreams, Fig was still riding Firewing, but they were not riding in the wilderness. She was a jockey, dressed in a dazzling outfit of red and gold, riding Firewing in the Dino Derby. The crowd cheered. Amissa watched from the balcony, beaming with pride as Fig moved into third place, second place, and the finish line was just ahead. Fig grinned in triumph, racing faster and faster, moving past Strutter and toward the ribbon when—

Boom.

A gunshot!

Firewing went down!

Fig spilled off the saddle, so close to the finish line. She crawled, her leg broken.

Boom.

More gunshots. A bullet hit her leg.

Fire was spreading through the arena. Smoke filled her lungs. She coughed, still crawling toward the finish line, but Strutter had already won. Frankie Lightfoot followed him, winning silver, and Speedy Bandito raced right over Fig, taking the bronze. More and more dinosaurs trampled her as she crawled toward the finish line. She was burning and broken. Even Gallimimus Gil looked upon her in pity as he ran by her, finishing second to last for the first time in his career. A new record.

Boom!

Fig's eyes snapped open.

A dream. Just a dream.

For a moment, she was confused. Was it time for school? Why was her bedroom so cold? And why in God's name was her bed made of feathers?

Then it came back to her. She was in the wild, and she was curled up with an achillobator under overhanging roots. His red and golden feathers tickled her skin. She shivered and burrowed into his feathery coat for warmth.

Another *boom* sounded in the night. The sound seemed distant like the echo of a dream. But Firewing seemed to hear it too. The achillobator snorted, wriggled around the burrow, and sank back into deep slumber. He hadn't even bothered opening his eyes. After a long day of carrying Fig on his back, racing through the fields, and training for the derby, the poor dinosaur was tuckered out.

Was a storm rolling in? Fig had seen no lightning. She sniffed. And there was that distant smell of fire again. Her nose was weak, but even she could smell that.

She nudged Firewing. "Hey, buddy. Wake up."

The dinosaur moaned, curled up tighter, and snored. Lazy bastard!

Reluctantly Fig crept out from his coat of feathers. The cold washed over her, and she shivered. It was November and the night was frigid. She wore her own feathers woven through her dress, but it was hardly enough. Her teeth chattered and her breath frosted in the moonlight. She crept out from the burrow and stood in the open darkness.

Ginkgo trees rustled in the night, their last leaves falling. One of the twin moons hid behind clouds, but the other shone brightly overhead. The sounds of crickets, rustling grass, and a few snoring dinosaurs filled the shadows with the music of Mintari's night.

Then again—a boom.

That was no thunder. That was a gunshot. Maybe even a bomb.

Fig stepped onto a boulder, thrust out her little nose, and sniffed. Fire. But not a forest fire.

A battle.

Fig shuddered again, and this time not from the cold. She had fought a battle before. On the back of an achillobator, she had ridden through the destruction of Dinovia. That most terrible of nights still haunted her. Another battle was being fought tonight, but the city was far from here. Too far to hear.

No, this battle was closer. Fig sniffed again. She tilted her head, cocked her ears, and heard a few distant *pops*. Gunfire.

It was coming from the north. From . . .

"From Amissa's camp," Fig whispered to herself.

Images flashed before her mind. Amissa saving her from Denise outside of school. Amissa buying her pizza. Amissa welcoming her into the Dino Derby arena and changing Fig's life forever. Amissa hugging her. Saying she loved her.

If Amissa was in danger now—Fig must help.

She crawled into the burrow under the overhanging roots. Firewing was still snoring. Fig poked the horse-sized dinosaur.

"Hao hao!" she barked. *Wake up!*

The achillobator stirred, snorted, and buried his head deeper into his feathers. Curled up like this, he looked like a pile of feathery coats. Hardly a dreaded predator.

"C'mon, Firewing," she said. "Haooo haoooo!"

He draped his tail over his ears (bators had holes for ears, often hidden under their feathers), blocking out her voice. He gave a loud, cranky snort, ruffling his feathers, then resumed snoring.

Another distant boom sounded. That one was definitely a grenade. Firewing didn't even stir this time. The sound was dim, the battle distant, but Fig could almost smell the blood, almost hear her aunt's screams.

Fig took a deep breath, lifted a stick from the ground, and poked Firewing in the ribs. Hard.

"Haooo!" she cried.

Firewing bolted up and lunged toward her. His mouth opened in a furious shriek, blasting back Fig's hair. His curved teeth gleamed in the moonlight. His jaws were longer than Fig's arms, his fangs longer than her fingers. He could easily bite her in half. His saliva splattered her, and his yellow eyes blazed with fury.

Terror filled Fig. She was going to die. Right here in this burrow. And nobody would ever find her body.

Instead of running in a panic, she slapped Firewing. Hard across the snout.

"Kraa!" She snarled. "Kraa!"

Down! Down!

He snapped his jaws shut and blinked. The dinosaur had not expected this tiny little mammal to smack him. He was several times her size. He could easily rip her apart. Yet she was snarling at him, showing dominance. Even *slapping* him. What was going on?

He opened his jaws again, letting out an even louder shriek.

Fig slapped him again. Harder this time.

"Kraa!" she demanded. "Kraaa hassshh!" *Down and obey.*

He growled—a deep and terrifying growl that rolled through his throat and ruffled his feathers. His sickle claws rose.

Fig's heart pounded against her ribs. But she stood her ground. She had her own sickle claw. A claw she had taken from a dead bator. It hung around her neck on a leather thong. In a single, fluid movement, she pulled it off her neck, sliced the air, and placed the tip against Firewing's windpipe.

At the exact same moment, he raised his own sickle claw, placing it against her belly.

Fig just had to apply a little pressure and slice his windpipe. He just had to press his claw an inch forward and disembowel her. They remained locked in place, neither daring make the kill.

Fig's instinct was to purr, to make amends, to smooth things over. To be his friend again. That would not work. She could perhaps soothe him tonight and save her life, but he would never obey her again. And if she became a burden, he would not hesitate to end her life. She must not be his friend. She must be his mistress.

So even with the cold claw pressed against her belly, she stood her ground, glowering at him, her own claw steady in her hand.

"Haooo!" she repeated.

Down.

He growled.

"Haoo!" she said.

He bared his fangs.

With her right hand, Fig kept her sickle claw against his throat. With her left hand, she still held the stick she had poked him with.

"Haoo!" she cried, and he opened his jaws to shriek at her.

She drove her stick into his mouth, plunging it deep, scratching the back of his throat.

He yowled, stumbled back, and shattered the stick within his powerful chompers. In his shock, he pulled his claw away from Fig's belly. It was the chance she needed. At once, she scampered deeper into the burrow, leaped onto his back, and reached around his neck, pressing her sickle claw against his throat. He jumped wildly, slamming Fig against the overhanging roots. Her back blazed with pain. But she clung onto the wild dinosaur.

"Haoo! Kass! Aooo ahooo!"

Down! Obey! You will obey me!

He bucked madly, slamming her against the burrow walls, but she refused to let go, wrestling him, ripping out his feathers, keeping the claw against his throat.

"Haoo. Haoo . . . Haoo . . ."

More soothing now. She was in a position of power. She was asserting her dominance—but also offering mercy.

He fought her. He bucked and jumped and lashed his tail and fluttered his wings. But she would not release him. He was a wild beast. He had been alone for so long. He had fought many battles, faced many foes, overcome disease and hunger and cold, survived horns and spikes and bites. His body was scarred, but his soul was scarred far worse.

"Haooo . . . haoo . . ." She purred, soothing him.

I know, friend. I know you suffered. I'm here for you. I love you. I will protect you. But you must serve me.

Slowly his resistance weakened. His furious screeches softened to whimpers. She heard the pain in them. The pain of loneliness and despair and fear.

"Aooooo aoooo . . ."

I know, friend. You've been alone for so long. I'm here. Serve me.

Gently, risking her life, Fig pulled her sickle claw away from his throat. She loosened her grip on his feathers.

He could have seized the chance, slain her there and then. Instead he cooed and flopped down. When Fig climbed off him, he rolled onto his back, exposing his underbelly. During the night, new bugs had bitten him there. Fig pulled them off, cooing as she groomed him.

Gunfire still rattled in the distance. Fig led Firewing out the burrow into the open night. Rain began to fall, and mud sluiced around their feet. Fig climbed onto her dinosaur's back, tightened her thighs around him, and tossed back her head.

"Ayeeee!" she cried. "Yip yip!"

Firewing burst into a run.

He raced through the rain, claws tearing up soil and roots, and by the moons of Mintari, he was fast. Faster than Red Scar. Faster than any achillobator Fig had ever seen. His powerful, scaly legs moved like lightning. His eyes narrowed to yellow slits like crescent moons, and his heartbeat pounded against her thighs.

Fig had tamed him to ride in the Dino Derby, but riding him now, she forgot about the races, forgot about human society. Here in the rain and night, she was a wild child again. Her soul flowed with the energy of this savage world.

I will save you, Amissa, like you saved me.

As Fig rode over the hills, more images of Amissa filled her mind. These ones were older, smudged, dark. Amissa invading Dinovia City with a pack of T-rexes, drugged up with pheromones into madness. Amissa shooting Red Scar, Fig's beloved protector. Tears flowed down Fig's eyes, but the cold wind whisked them away.

She shot Red Scar by accident, she told herself. *She changed. She's good now. She loves me.*

She shoved those ghosts down, slammed the door shut on them, and ignored their clamors. Not now. Not tonight. She narrowed her eyes, clenched her jaw, and leaned forward as Firewing ran toward the sounds of battle.

Tonight was a night of blood.

CHAPTER TWENTY-TWO
We Have Cookies

The Rangers charged over the shattered stockade, roaring into Fort Devana.

Amissa stood on the guard tower, gazing down in terror as enemies swarmed below. They surrounded the guard tower. Dozens of Rangers ran across the mud, howling for war. But most rode dinosaurs. An army of herbivores stampeded all around, shaking the tower. Ceratopsians with deadly horns and massive bony frills. Stegosaurs with deadly spikes. Ankylosaurs with swinging tails. Pachycephalosaurs with battering ram heads. And above them all loomed the mighty diplodocus, rumbling in rage. They were a sea of scales, horns, spikes, and fury.

Amissa had fought saber-toothed tigers with nothing but a knife. She had wrestled a bear. She had shot down a mammoth with a spear. But she had never seen anything so terrifying. These were not like herbivores on other planets. These were not meek prey animals.

My father is right, Amissa thought. *Dinosaurs are monsters.*

She and Rattlesnake stood side by side, gripping the railings. Dinosaurs bumped into the tower, bending its metal base. The tower swayed like a buoy in a storming sea, and below flowed the currents of scales and horns and spikes, a river of Mesozoic fury. The two hunters fired their guns downward, but their bullets scattered off armor. A nodosaur ran by, its spikes like scythes, ripping at the tower foundation. A metal beam shattered. The tower swayed. Amissa gripped the railing and screamed. A stegosaurus hit the tower's other side. The tower tilted the other way, and Amissa nearly plunged into the storm of dinosaurs.

A bugle rose above the battle. A titanoceratops came charging forth, feet shaking the earth and raising clouds of dust. The species was related to the triceratops but even grumpier, and that was saying something. The titan's beak opened with a furious cry. His horns thrust forward like pikes, while his spiked frill rose like the shield of an ancient god. The dinosaur was larger than a woolly mammoth. As he ran by, his monstrous head bulldozed into the guard tower.

And the tower went crashing down.

Amissa screamed.

Her instincts cried out: *Cling to the rail! Hold on!*

She crushed that instinct, kicked off the collapsing tower, and tumbled through the air.

She slammed onto the scaly back of a chasmosaurus. She howled in agony. The fall would have normally killed her, but her body armor absorbed most of the impact. She rolled off the dinosaur, tumbled down, and slammed onto the ground.

Her body blazed with pain. Her breath rattled. Her ribs creaked and throbbed. Ignoring the agony, she rolled, dodging the stamping feet of a charging sinoceratops with a crown of horns. The armored beast plowed onward, probably not even noticing her. An edmontosaurus ran her way, braying. The duckbill dinosaur was colossal, and three Rangers rode on its back. Amissa scampered aside, hitting a stegosaurus. The dinosaur grunted and swung its spiked tail. Amissa ducked and the thagomizer whooshed over her head. She ran at a crouch, leaping left, right, dodging stamping feet everywhere. A kentrosaurus rumbled by, a multitude of spikes thrusting out across its body. One spike slashed Amissa's arm, ripping off armor, cutting her skin. She yowled.

Another dinosaur knocked into her. She fell, rolled, and leaped aside, dodging stamping feet. She coughed. Dust filled her lungs. She was caught in the stampede, and she was going to die.

No.

No!

She gritted her teeth.

She would not die here!

A dinosaur came racing toward her. He was a big bull, snarling and furious. A centrosaurus, Amissa thought, judging by the dinosaur's terrible central horn. That horn was as long as Amissa was tall. The dinosaur charged at Amissa, horn thrusting forward like a lance. A Ranger rode on his back. The pair were like a medieval knight and horse in a joust.

Amissa refused to flee. She cocked her rifle and fired.

The Ranger slumped in the saddle, a bullet in his chest.

The centrosaurus kept charging, carrying his dead master. He lowered his huge armored head, prepared to plow into Amissa and gore her.

Still she stood her ground.

"Amissa, get out of there!" Rattlesnake shouted somewhere in the distance. She ignored him.

The centrosaurus rumbled. The dinosaur almost seemed to smile, eager for the kill. He ran closer, closer, horn at the ready, and—

A second before the dinosaur hit her, Amissa stepped aside. The horn thrust into empty air. She grabbed the horn, pulled herself onto the dinosaur's head, and leaped over his spiky frill.

She landed on the dinosaur's scaly back. The Ranger still sat there, gurgling on blood. Ha. Still alive. A second shot from Amissa's gun took care of that.

She stood on the centrosaur's back, swaying, as the dinosaur charged through the camp. From up here, she surveyed the battle.

The Rangers had made it deep into the camp. Hell's Hunters were firing from rooftops, from jippis, from trenches. Traps sprang open, and dinosaurs plunged into pits full of spikes. One hunter stood atop a caravan, laughing maniacally as he fired a flamethrower, burning dinosaurs and their riders.

So many hunters lay dead already.

We're losing this battle, Amissa thought.

But not for long. It was time. Time to use their doomsday weapon.

Riding the centrosaurus, Amissa coned her hand around her mouth and cried out: "Hunters! Let loose the carnivores!"

Amissa had hoped it would not come to this. She had warned everyone to use this doomsday weapon as a last resort. To unleash this terror only on her order. An order she would give only at the hour of utmost need.

Though if she were honest with herself—Amissa had been looking forward to this.

Across the camp, armored trailers opened their doors. Huge jippis lowered their tailgates. Trap doors opened on the ground, revealing huge pits.

For a moment, nothing happened.

Then Amissa heard it. They all heard it.

Growls. Grumbles. Rolling waves of bass. These were not the sounds of herbivores. These were hunting sounds.

Amissa hopped off the centrosaurus she rode. The herbivorous dinosaur was a target now. She landed on the ground, climbed onto a boulder, and watched.

They burst out from the trailers, the jippis, the pits. Salivating and hungry. Amissa had been starving then, tormenting them, driving them mad, and now they charged to battle. Her army of carnivores.

Raptors leaped through the night, cawing for meat. An allosaurus rumbled and opened his jaws wide, and saliva dangled between his teeth like harp strings. Several dimetrodons scuttled on their reptilian legs, their sails tipped with spikes, their toothy mouths snapping. Largest of all loomed Amissa's personal pet. Asterius, her beloved carnotaurus. He was free from his labyrinth tonight. He had killed many humans, had developed a taste for them, and tonight he would feast.

Amissa gave a loud whistle. Asterius spun toward her, a low rumble rippling his throat. By the gods, he was massive. Saliva dripped from his thick, powerful jaws. His muscles bulged under his scaly skin. Those scales were brown, his two horns red. His orange eyes were mad with hunger. But Amissa had drilled obedience into the carnotaurus. A shock collar beeped around his neck. He had learned who controlled it, who could hurt him. Amissa whistled again, and the gargantuan predator thundered toward her, his talons shaking the earth, and crouched. She grabbed one of his spikes, pulled herself up, and settled in the saddle. He rose, lifting her high above the camp.

"Now charge!" she cried, pointing at the enemy.

The opposing dinosaur forces ran across the camp. The rain steamed on their backs. The firelight danced in their eyes. To one side—herbivores armed with spikes and horns and heavy armor. On the other side—carnivores with claws and fangs. Rangers rode the herbivores. Hunters rode the carnivores. The two armies charged through the mud and slammed together.

The sky shook. The ground trembled. The very foundations of the world cracked. The dinosaurs were like stars colliding, and the force of their impact rocked Mintari.

Horns drove through scales. Clubbed tails shattered legs. Claws ripped off plates of armor. Powerful jaws closed around bony frills. Spikes pierced muscle. Beaks shattered bone. Fangs tore muscle. Blood filled the night as a hundred dinosaurs clashed, reptilian soldiers in the armies of their masters.

Amissa rode her carnotaurus through the battle, firing her gun from atop the towering carnivore. With his fangs and claws, Asterius tore down herbivores (only the claws on his feet, though; his pathetic arms were barely larger than bowling pins). With her bullets and grenades, Amissa slew Rangers. Carnotaurus and huntress. They were a match made in hell, two who fought as one. All around them, the battle raged.

A screech pierced the night.

An enormous dinosaur came thundering forward.

Amissa froze.

Dear Lord.

It was a herbivore. A big, feathery, ugly male. The brute towered over the other dinosaurs. He rose even taller than the mighty Asterius. The fluffy dinosaur opened a beak and cawed. He raised his arms, brandishing claws the size of claymores. Bit larger than bowling pins, those.

Amissa's eyes widened. She had heard of such dinosaurs, but she had never seen one.

"A therizinosaurus," she whispered.

The bipedal herbivore was the size of a T-rex. Shaggy gray feathers covered the dinosaur's back, and a Ranger rode there, holding a bridle. The dinosaur's claws gleamed in the moonlight. A therizinosaurus had the longest claws of any dinosaur on Mintari. Of any animal that ever lived.

With a furious screech, the therizin charged toward Amissa and her carnotaurus.

Asterius opened his jaws, rumbled, and ran to meet his feathered foe.

A therizin wielded deadly claws. A carnotaurus boasted brutal jaws and deadly horns. The two dinosaurs ran across the mud, stepping on corpses, and slammed together.

The therizin swung his claws. Those claws would make a knight's longsword look like a letter opener. They sliced the air, reaching toward Asterius. The scaly carnotaurus leaned back, dodging the assault, then lunged forward, jaws snapping, trying to reach his foe's flesh.

Meanwhile, Amissa aimed her gun. She fired at the Ranger who rode the therizin. Her enemy raised an electric shield, blocking her bullet, and fired his own rifle.

A bullet slammed into Amissa. She screamed.

This bullet too hit her armored vest. Just inches away from the last one. The vest saved her life, but stars above, it hurt. It hurt so much. Tears sprang into her eyes. The Ranger fired again and again. Bullets flew around her. One pinged off her helmet, ringing her head like a bell. She was blind. She was deaf. She was dying. Yet somehow she managed to aim and pull the trigger.

Red mist flew.

The Ranger slumped in his saddle, a bullet in his head.

Amissa took deep breaths, regaining her senses. She was alive. But maybe not for long. The Ranger was dead. And Amissa was stunned. But their dinosaurs were not done fighting.

Asterius had never faced such a foe. He was used to devouring humans. What was this monstrous beast that attacked him? This "therizinosaurus," as his mistress had called him?

Whatever he was, he was big and vicious. The therizin slashed his claws again and again, snapped his beak, and shrieked in rage. Asterius kept trying to bite the behemoth, but he couldn't get close. The claws kept swinging, holding Asterius back. Even with his master dead, the therizin kept fighting, determined to bring down the scaly carnivore. After all, Asterius was smaller than him. Why should the humongous herbivore fear this minute meat eater?

Asterius knew he faced a dangerous foe. He knew he was smaller. He weighed nearly three tons, but standing before his feathery foe, he felt like a dwarf. His enemy was twice his size. And those claws were no joke. The therizin's arms were long and muscular, his claws like triceratops horns. Meanwhile, Asterius barely had arms at all. Even a T-rex had longer arms than a poor carnotaurus. Asterius's arms were vestigial. Just floppy little digits, no longer than a toddler's arms, flapping uselessly from a brawny, scaly body. He wouldn't be clawing his enemies anytime soon.

The therizin pressed the attack. Those darned claws were swinging again. Again. Asterius kept having to pull back, never able to close his jaws around the impudent herbivore. Amissa wasn't helping either. She still rode him, but she wasn't firing her gun. The huntress wanted him to fight his own battles. All he needed was one good bite.

His jaws were his finest weapon. His foe only had a beak. A beak! What kind of dangerous dinosaur had a *beak*? Asterius would show this overgrown bird. He lunged again. The claws swung. This time Asterius ducked under the slashing blades, darted forward, and bit his foe's flank.

Success!

Asterius bit deep, then yanked his head back and . . . began to cough. He spat out feathers. A big fluffy mouthful of feathers. He had bitten so deep, but he hadn't even reached the flesh.

As he stood there, confused, the therizin pressed the attack. Those scythe-like claws swung. Asterius stepped back fast enough to save his life . . . but not his left arm. One of the therizin's claws sliced the arm right off Asterius's body. The vestigial little limb flew through the air.

Asterius howled in fury.

That did it!

Perhaps those arms were useless in battle. But they were still critical for mating dances. When impressing a female, a carnotaurus male stuck out his tail, raised his head, pirouetted, and windmilled his tiny little arms. The females loved it. Asterius had seen lovely females reject perfectly acceptable males simply because their dance had missed a beat. In fact, it had happened to him personally. And it still stung. He had been slowly improving his dancing skills. But without both arms, Asterius could never dance again. Never mate. Never raise hatchlings.

With the loss of that one arm, all his instincts shattered. The primary purpose of every dinosaur on Mintari, even more powerful than eating, was to mate. To raise the next generation. To contribute to this ongoing story of evolution—a story Asterius did not understand in his mind but felt deep in his bones. And he knew his story had been severed like his arm. He was perhaps still alive. But his chapter in the grand story of Mintari had ended.

With a rage like exploding stars, he lunged forward. He suffered claw slashes to his chest, but he didn't care. Bleeding, enraged, he grabbed the therizin's scrawny neck. With a good *chomp*, Asterius ripped off his enemy's head.

He spat it out and kicked it aside. A beak! Ha. Pathetic.

He looked up at his mistress, who still rode on his back. Amissa nodded in approval and patted his flank. She was a dangerous little parasite. So small. He could gobble her easily. Yet she controlled the thorn in his neck, that flashing little thing of metal. Whenever she pleased, she could make it ache. So he traveled the maze for her. And he fought enemies for her. He might never have a mate, but he had his mammalian parasite, and in a strange way, he almost liked her.

A rumble sounded ahead.

His mistress cursed.

Asterius turned his head, saw what was coming, and his heart nearly stopped.

A living tank was rumbling toward him. The dinosaur charged forth on all fours, staying close to the ground. He was bulky and covered in armor. He was shorter than Asterius but probably twice as heavy. Spikes, knobs, and horns sprouted across his body. His tail ended with a bony club.

An ankylosaurus. Great.

The last thing Asterius saw was that club swinging toward him.

The wrecking ball *thunked* into his head, white light flooded him, teeth clattered onto the ground, and Asterius was falling and falling and didn't even feel himself hitting the ground.

But Amissa felt it.

As her carnotaurus collapsed, she leaped from her saddle, hit the ground, and cried out in pain.

Around her, the battle raged, dozens of dinosaurs clashing together. But she only saw the ankylosaurus who stood before her, blood on his tail. Bumpy was in a foul mood tonight. And look who else was here! He was riding the armored dinosaur. Arban Clubber himself. Chief of the Rangers.

As she lay on the ground, Amissa's lips twitched in a smile.

I win this war tonight.

She aimed her rifle at the chief.

The ankylosaurus spun around, swinging his tail toward her.

Amissa leaped aside. The massive club slammed into the ground inches away. That club was the size of a pumpkin. A large pumpkin. A massive monster pumpkin made of solid bone. It came lashing down again. Amissa jumped aside. The club pounded the ground, cracking stones.

She aimed her gun again, but the club swung too fast. She jumped back, and Bumpy's tail knocked the rifle from her hands. It flew into the distance.

The dinosaur stomped closer. He was heavier than a jippi, covered with more armor than a triceratops, and ready to crush her. He snorted, and his steamy breath blew the hat off Amissa's head. He raised his tail, prepared for the killing blow.

Amissa growled. That does it. Nobody blew off her hat!

With a roar, she leaped up and landed on Bumpy's head. She jumped higher, lunging toward Clubber, who rode the dinosaur's back. In midair, she drew her handgun and fired.

But the chief raised his electric shield. Her bullets pounded the force field.

Clubber stood up in his stirrups, leaned forward, and slammed that shimmering shield against Amissa.

Electricity crackled across her. With a scream, she fell back, convulsing, and hit the ground. She groaned in pain, twitching, her clothes smoking.

"Bastard!" she screamed. Coppery blood stung her tongue.

Buzzing, she hopped back onto her feet. She drew a knife in each hand, grinned, and prepared to leap onto the ankylosaurus again.

But Bumpy was faster. He spun and swung his tail.

The gargantuan bony club pounded into Amissa.

For a moment, she blacked out.

She didn't know time and space. When she came to with a gasping, shuddering breath, she was on the ground. Her armored vest had shattered, scattering pieces across the ground. She grimaced, tried to rise, could not. Something was broken inside her.

She lay there, unable to move, barely able to breathe, as Bumpy stomped closer. On the dinosaur's back, Clubber leaned forward and aimed his rifle at Amissa.

"Goodbye, scum," the chief said.

Amissa closed her eyes, ready to die.

A cry pierced the night.

"Ayeeee!"

The cry of a girl.

"Yip yip!"

Amissa opened her eyes, and tears flowed down her cheeks. Through the smoke and fire came racing an achillobator, and Figaro Triplehorn rode on his feathery back.

She leaped through fire.

Her cry pierced the night.

"Ayeee!"

At the Battle of Dinovia last spring, Fig had fought against Amissa and her terrible poachers. Now she fought to save an aunt she loved.

Deep inside her, a part of her screamed. *Stop this! This is madness! This is wrong! What are you doing?*

But another part of Fig still tasted that pizza. Still marveled at the splendor of the Dino Derby. Still felt safe in Amissa's embrace. That part of her could not let her aunt die.

And so riding her dinosaur, Fig raced toward the ankylosaurus, and she raised her sickle claw high.

Ankylosaurs were big dinosaurs. Definitely bigger than achillobators. As if their girth and armor weren't enough, spikes thrust out from them, keeping enemies at bay. And this was a particularly powerful ankylosaurus. Fig recognized him. She had seen him hanging out with Dozer back in the city.

"Bumpy!" she blurted out.

She would not harm this dinosaur. She couldn't even if she tried. Right now she had no beef with Bumpy. Only with the Ranger riding him. She recognized the burly man.

Chief Clubber. Her uncle.

Why was Uncle Clubber here? Why was he attacking her aunt? Why must Clan Clubber hate Clan Triplehorn?

Rage flared in Fig. Sudden loathing for her uncle filled her. Uncle? She barely knew him! He had visited her once! That was all. Just once for ten minutes. She had been back for months, and he barely acknowledged her! He took her father away! And now he rode here, prepared to kill her aunt. An aunt who actually showed Fig affection, who loved her.

So what if he was her uncle? Right now he was her enemy.

Fig let out a wordless, hoarse cry of rage.

Clubber turned in the saddle, and his eyes widened.

"Ayeeee! Yip yip!" Fig cried. *Get him, Firewing!*

The achillobator ran to battle. He was the size of a lion. The ankylosaurus was the size of a mammoth. But Firewing ran to battle nonetheless, screeching for blood. He knew what to do. He did not attack the armored dinosaur. Even in his bloodlust,

Firewing realized this foe was beyond him. Against an angry ankylosaurus, an achillobator stood no chance.

Firewing ran, vaulted off a boulder, and soared into the air. His wings were too short for flight. But he flapped them for all they were worth, gliding forth, his jaws open in a deafening screech.

Spikes thrust out from Bumpy's flanks, as long and as deadly as swords, but Firewing glided above them. The achillobator flew right toward Clubber.

The chief aimed his rifle at Fig, but then his eyes widened. "Figaro?" he whispered.

She could not hear him over the battle. But she could read his lips. Recognition and shock filled his eyes.

All of Fig's anger dissipated.

He doesn't hate me. He's not my enemy.

A second later, Firewing leaped onto the chief.

Clubber managed to fire a shot. But his hesitation cost him dearly. His shot went wide. The bullet whistled above Fig's head, missing her by several inches. Her ears rang.

Firewing shrieked. The sound of gunfire magnified his fury. He closed his powerful jaws around Clubber's arm.

"Wait!" Fig cried. "Firewing, wait, stop! Hai hai!" *Stop!*

But the achillobator ignored her.

The chief had a big, beefy arm. It looked nearly as wide as Figaro's torso. But when Firewing chomped down, his jaws ripped clean through that arm, severing it above the elbow.

Clubber's rifle fell. The weapon bounced off Bumpy's armored flank, released another bullet into the distance, then thumped onto the ground. So did the severed arm.

"No," Fig whispered. "Oh God no."

Firewing planted his feet firmly onto Bumpy's back. He leaned toward the mutilated Ranger, growling, blood on his teeth.

Clubber still sat upright in the saddle, clutching his stump. The blood drained from his body, leaving his skin gray. He stared in horror at the achillobator that was about to end his life.

Then he looked up from the bloodied jaws. He made eye contact with Fig.

"Why, Figaro?" he whispered.

Firewing leaned in, blood on his teeth, prepared to end the man's life.

"No!" Fig cried, horror blazing through her. She grabbed fistfuls of Firewing's feathers and pulled him back. "Don't!"

Firewing paused inches away from Clubber. The achillobator looked over his shoulder at Fig. Bloodlust filled his yellow eyes. Bloody saliva dripped from his mouth. He was frenzied with hunger. He let out a low growl.

I must feed!

"Kraa! Kraaa!" she cried. *Turn back! Back down!*

He growled at her, and for a second, Fig thought he'd devour her first. But then Firewing lowered his eyes, jumped off Bumpy, and raced into the shadows.

Fig leaped off his back, hit the ground running, and hurried toward her aunt.

Amissa lay on the ground, arms wrapped around her chest. Bruises, scrapes, and splotches of blood covered her. But she was still breathing.

"Auntie!" Fig cried.

She didn't have to worry about Bumpy. The dinosaur knew her. Even now, after what she had done, Bumpy would not harm her. And besides, the ankylosaurus had bigger concerns. His master was dying. Bugling mournfully, Bumpy trudged toward a distant group of Rangers, carrying Clubber on his back. Fig could almost understand the dinosaur's moans.

Help my master! Help him, he's hurt!

All around, the battle still raged. Gunshots rattled. Dinosaurs rumbled. Scattered fires burned and ash fell from the sky. In the midst of this chaos, Fig knelt beside her aunt.

"Amissa?" she whispered. Her tears fell, splashing Amissa's cheeks, clearing off the grime and blood. "Auntie Amissa, I'm here. Don't die. I'm here."

Lying on the ground, Amissa gave her a weak, crooked smile, and a sparkle filled her eyes. She was strong enough to clasp Fig's hand. "You were glorious. I'm proud of you."

Deep cries sounded from behind.

"Fall back! Fall back! The chief is hurt. Fall back!"

Fig turned to see the Rangers retreating. They scrambled onto their dinosaurs, formed a protective ring around Clubber, and hurried toward the toppled stockade. A few Rangers were already leaping over the moat, heading back into the wilderness. Across the camp, poachers cheered and fired their guns. Carnivores ran and chomped at the fleeing herbivores.

Amissa tried to rise to her feet, but her legs buckled.

"Help me, Fig."

Her aunt was taller and heavier, but Fig helped the woman up. Amissa stood, leaning against her.

"Let them go!" Amissa hoarsely cried. "Hunters, let them go!"

Fig tilted her head. "You're not going to chase them, Auntie Amissa? To finish them off?"

Her aunt smiled thinly. "Spoken like a true huntress. But no. In the open field, they have an advantage. They'd slaughter us out there. We won this battle. Let's keep it that way."

The hunters took a few parting shots. The carnivores bit a few haunches and tails. But reluctantly the hungry dinosaurs obeyed their mistress. The Rangers and their herbivores fled into the countryside, carrying their wounded, leaving many of their dead behind.

The battle was over. The battle was won.

Holding her wounded aunt, Fig looked around her. Huts burned and jippis smoldered. Dead humans lay everywhere. Fig could not tell if they were Rangers or poachers. In death, they were indistinguishable. Dead dinosaurs smoldered among them. A centrosaurus lay with his ribs exposed. A domehead dinosaur was burning. The mighty diplodocus himself had fallen, his neck curled up, his tail like a mountain range. Amissa's great carnotaurus lay among the dead. Raptors were already ripping into him. Other surviving carnivores were feeding on the carrion. Leaving his new mistress, Firewing ran to join the feeding frenzy, tucking into the diplodocus. It was a feast fit for a king.

Fig looked upon this death and destruction, at all this fire and blood and suffering.

"What have I done?" she whispered.

Amissa pulled Fig's face toward her. The tall poacher stared into Fig's eyes.

"You've joined Hell's Hunters. I took a man's hand, but you took an arm. You will be deadlier than I ever was." She kissed Fig on the forehead. "I love you."

Fig trembled so violently she almost fell, and now it was Amissa who had to hold her up. The fire and blood spun around her, and in her mind, Fig still saw the shock in Uncle Clubber's eyes, still hear his voice.

Why?

But in the vision, Clubber's broad face became her father's weathered, bearded face, and it was Joe who gazed at her with betrayed eyes, and it was his voice that filled her mind, echoing over and over.

Why, Figaro? Why?

She buried her face against Amissa's chest and wept. Her aunt held her, stroking her hair and whispering soothing nothings as ash fell like snow.

CHAPTER TWENTY-THREE
Pun for the Road

As the rain fell, Amissa stood in her trailer, looking at the sleeping girl in her bed. She was a beautiful child. In her sleep, she seemed like a doll, innocent and pure. No one would guess that here lay a huntress.

Amissa stood at the bedside, her torso wrapped in bandages. She had suffered two cracked ribs, lacerations, and bruises that covered her body like poppies. But she was alive. Against all odds, she was still breathing. Because of this innocent little doll.

"You saved my life, Figaro," she whispered.

The girl mumbled in her sleep, hugged her pillow, and sank deeper into slumber. A lamp glowed on a shelf, filling the room with warm firelight. Outside the window, the first hints of dawn gilded the eastern sky. Amissa looked back at her niece.

Fig looked more like a Clubber, her maternal side. The Clubbers traced their ancestry back to Mongolia on Earth (or so they claimed), a realm of fierce riders and warriors. Like other Clubbers, Figaro had olive-toned skin, almond-shaped eyes, and black hair. But her heart was the heart of a Triplehorn. Her heart was woven of flame.

"You'll be everything I'm not," Amissa whispered, eyes damp. "You'll be stronger than me. You won't hurt like I hurt. I love you, Figaro."

Fig's breathing was still deep, her eyes still closed, but even in her deepest sleep, she smiled.

I've never loved anyone more, Amissa thought, gazing at her sleeping niece. *My father hurts me. My mother abandoned me. My brother betrayed me. I have no lover. No friends, unless you count the scum who fight in my army. I'm thirty-three years old, and I've never felt love. Until now. I love you, Figaro. You're pure. I love you more than you'll ever know.*

Lights flared outside, interrupting her thoughts.

Engines rumbled.

Amissa spun toward the window, and horror gripped her heart. She inhaled sharply, clenched her fists, and struggled for breath.

Stars above, no.

Her tears burned dry. Lips tight, Amissa left the trailer.

An astrolite was descending from the sky. It was large for an astrolite. Twice the size of a jippi. Yet it was surprisingly quiet, running on the latest graviton engines. This was no hunting vessel. The hull was adorned with black marble, and a triceratops hood ornament shone on the prow. This ship was made for luxurious comfort. Descending toward a smoldering battlefield, it seemed ridiculously out of place.

The ship thumped down in the center of Fort Devana. A hatch opened, and a ramp extended to the charred ground.

Amissa limped toward the astrolite. She had not washed or changed her clothes since the battle. She still wore bloodstained camouflage and chunks of cracked armor. Dry blood clustered in her hair like little raisins. Pteranodon saliva still gucked up her pants.

A tall, slender silhouette appeared in the ship's hatch, limned in light. The man stepped down the ramp, his hands tucked into the folds of his robes. His robes were black like his ship, embroidered with golden thread along the hems. He smelled like talcum. When he reached Amissa, he gave her a small smile.

"Hello, daughter," said Tobias Triplehorn.

"Nice of you to finally drop by. *After* the battle ended."

He chuckled. "Ah, sweet daughter. I have many talents. Fighting is not one of them. You seemed to have done a good job of it. I see lots of dead Rangers. Very good. Is your brother . . .?"

"Joe didn't come," she said, and the words tasted sour on her lips. "Nor did LaRue."

"Ah. Pity. You could have ended it here. Oh well, this is still an impressive victory. And is the girl . . .?"

The bandages seemed to constrict Amissa's chest. Her ribs creaked. Suddenly she couldn't breathe.

"Amissa! You're pale." Tobias frowned. "Are you hurt?"

Her head spun. She gritted her teeth. "The girl is mine."

Tobias raised an eyebrow. "Oh my my, do I see some motherly instinct? Where is she? Where is Figaro?"

"Keep away from her," Amissa hissed.

Tobias glanced toward the trailer. "She's in there, isn't she? I would quite like to see my granddaughter. Guards?"

Two hulking brutes stepped out from the astrolite and flanked Tobias. They wore black armor from head to toe, visors hid their faces, and cables and tubes snaked across them. Amissa had seen such creatures before. Cyborgs created on Cloventia, trained since birth to defend dignitaries. Only the wealthiest could afford them.

"Seriously, Dad?" Amissa said. "You've got extermaborgs now?"

"One can never be too careful," Tobias said. "They're lovely specimens, aren't they? Seven feet tall. More machine than men. They're costly, yes, but they're worth every clover, believe me. Come now, guards! To the trailer."

"Dad, it's literally twenty steps away. I think you can handle the journey without cyborg protection."

He pretended not to hear her. Holding up the hems of his robes, he walked over the scorched soil. Amissa stared at the rings on his fingers. She touched her cheek. Many times those gemstones had cut her. She still had a scar on her cheek.

The extermaborgs walked alongside their master, their armored feet thumping. The towering cyborgs took position around the trailer door. Tobias stepped inside, robes rustling.

Amissa joined him. They stood inside, looking at the girl sleeping in bed. Poor Fig was so exhausted even the landing starship and thumping cyborgs had not woken her. Tobias stood for long moments, looking down at her.

"Is this her?" he whispered. "My granddaughter?"

Amissa nodded.

"She looks like a Clubber."

"Her heart is the heart of a Triplehorn," Amissa said softly.

Tobias stared at her for a moment in silence. Amissa studied the old man's face, expecting to see disapproval. But she saw . . . what was it? Love? No, not love. But something soft. Something warm that cracked through his icy exterior.

With a ringed hand, he stroked the sleeping girl's hair.

Amissa trembled. Pain flared in her memory. Blood rushed into her head.

She grabbed her father's arm. Gently but firmly, she guided him out of the trailer. He gasped at her rough grip but went willingly.

Outside, the extermaborgs saw her gripping him. They stepped closer, gears whirring, and reached for their guns. But Tobias waved them down.

"Daughter!" he said. "What's wrong?"

Amissa bared her teeth at him. "If you hurt her, Dad, I swear—"

"Hurt her? My own granddaughter?"

"You will not touch her!" Rage stung her eyes. "Do you understand? If you harm a hair on her head, I will kill you, and all the cyborgs in the galaxy would not protect you."

Amazingly, fear flickered in his eyes. Or was it merely shock? She had never seen fear in him. Then again, she had never spoken to him that way.

"I would never harm her," he said softly. "Or you. I love you, Amissa. I'm proud of you."

Dammit. Now her eyes were watering again. He could always dismantle her like this. Manipulate her. Tear her down. And deep inside her, Amissa loathed herself, because she knew she was doing the same to Figaro.

Tobias held her hand. "Amissa, you've done well. You drove the parasaurs to extinction, I'm told. And you won this great battle. I will now fund your labyrinth. Your dream. It will become the premier destination on Mintari, eclipsing even the Dino Derby."

Amissa nodded, feeling empty. She had begged him for this, but it all seemed so trivial now.

"But there is one more thing you must do for me," Tobias said. "I've discovered a way to defeat the Rangers once and for all. To wipe them all out. Listen, Amissa. Listen to your father . . ."

Holding her hand, he whispered into her ear. And with every word he spoke, Amissa's horror grew, and she felt herself falling, falling into a dark pit like the deepest ocean, and the rising dawn could not banish the darkness.

After a long cold night underwater, dawn lit the ocean. The surface shimmered above like a canopy of gold. Beads of light cascaded through the water like autumn leaves, twirling, dancing, then melting among forests of kelp. The morning mottled the seabed, illuminating sandy valleys and rocky peaks.

The ocean life awoke. Eels peered from holes in coral reefs. Fish scuttled to and fro. A nautilus swam by, its shell iridescent, while jellyfish floated near the surface like flowing clouds. The shadows of migrating turtles swept across the sandy seabed, and bottom-feeders peered up, blinking at the passing swarm. Mintari's ocean was lush with life, a world of its own, hidden from those mysterious and alien creatures who lived on land and in the sky.

Through this waking, watery world swam two reptiles. They were long, slender reptiles. Their necks would put giraffes to shame. Their flippers and tails propelled them through the water. Sharp teeth lined their jaws. One of them was male, his body covered with green scales. The other was female, her scales blue, and red spikes grew across her head. At a glance, they looked like two ordinary elasmosaurs. But if one looked closer, they saw one striking irregularity. Flashing electronic bulbs were embedded into their heads.

These two bulbs contained the souls of two humans. Physically, Joe and Simone were back on the coast, floating inside sensory-deprivation tanks. But the illusion was complete. They saw through the elasmosaur eyes, heard through their ears, felt the water flow around them. They had become aquatic reptiles, and they swam through the morning, relieved as the light dappled them.

"I can honestly say that was the longest night of my life," Simone said.

Joe nodded. "Yes, floating underwater in pitch darkness is an odd experience. I didn't get much sleep either."

"Oh, I slept like baby," Simone said. "But never this *long*." She whipped her neck from side to side, grinning. "Get it? Long? Because of my neck?"

Joe groaned. "Great. More jokes."

"Hey Joe, how many tickles does it take to make an octopus laugh?" Simone asked.

"I don't care."

"Ten tickles." She laughed, her head bobbing atop her enormously long neck. "Get it? Ten tickles?"

"I hate you."

She stuck her tongue between her sharp teeth. "Nonsense. You love me. You love me long time." She whipped her head around. "Get it? Because my neck is long?"

"Simone, please shut up."

"Maybe you'll like my neck joke."

"I'm warning you."

"Don't be so neckative."

"Simone, please!"

They swam onward in silence for a while, passing through a school of fish, over a clump of coral, and around a cluster of kelp. The water brightened with the sunlight, and rays swam overhead like aquatic dactyls. Joe soaked it all in. Even with the lurking danger, with the stress of the war, he marveled at the ocean's beauty. He had been fighting for Mintari for decades, but here was a whole world he never much considered, and one he found just as precious.

"We'll find the shipwreck," he said. "We'll find *Darwin's Cradle*. We'll bring home the embryos and save Mintari's dinosaurs."

Simone nodded. "That ship's gotta be somewhere around this neck of the woods."

"Simone, for pity's sake, please stop!"

They kept swimming, following the signal in their heads, and something caught Joe's eyes on the seabed. He looked down to see a shipwreck. But this was not the *Darwin's Cradle*, not a starship from five hundred years ago. It was a cruise ship. The *Maid of Mintari* lay below him on the sand, torn apart.

The two elasmosaurs lowered their heads. Simone told no more jokes. Solemn and silent, they swam over the *Maid of Mintari*. A ship of dreams. A ship of fools. A ship of lost souls.

Ryujin had done this. Ryujin had killed seven hundred men, women, and children. And the mosasaur was still out there. Yes, this underwater kingdom was beautiful, but danger filled it too. And Joe knew he would face horrors before the end.

They left the *Maid* behind. Joe turned his head and looked at the elasmosaur beside him. Simone was humming a tune as she swam along, wiggling her tail to the beat. She looked at him, gave him a goofy smile, and waved a flipper. Oddly, even as a giant aquatic reptile, she was one hundred percent Simone LaRue.

So long as she's with me, things aren't so bad, Joe thought. *I have Simone in my life. I have Fig. I have a home that I love. I have people whom I love even more. With them, I can face any darkness.*

Side by side, the elasmosaurs rode a warm current, leaving one shipwreck behind, seeking another shipwreck ahead. The clement shallows gave way to the cold, cobalt expanse of the deep northern ocean. The seabed dropped below, and the watery vastness loomed ahead. They swam deeper into this ocean of life and death, of wonders and terrors, of light and darkness, seeking in the water hope for a burning world.

The story continues in …

Mintari III

March of the Dinosaurs

NOVELS BY DANIEL ARENSON

Mintari:
A World of Dinosaurs
Where Dinosauars Roam
March of the Dinosaurs

Starship Freedom:
Starship Freedom
The Cost of Freedom
We Fight for Freedom
For Death or Freedom
Let Freedom Ring
In Pursuit of Freedom
The Guns of Freedom
A Time for Freedom

Alien Hunters:
Alien Hunters
Alien Sky
Alien Shadows

Earthrise:

Earth Alone

Earth Lost

Earth Rising

Earth Fire

Earth Shadows

Earth Valor

Earth Reborn

Earth Honor

Earth Eternal

Earth Machines

Earth Aflame

Earth Unleashed

Earth Remembers

Earth in Darkness

Earth, Our Home

Soldiers of Earthrise:

The Earthling

Earthlings

Earthling's War

I, Earthling

The Earthling's Daughter

We Are Earthlings

Children of Earthrise:

The Heirs of Earth

A Memory of Earth

An Echo of Earth

The War for Earth

The Song of Earth

The Legacy of Earth

Kingdoms of Sand:

Kings of Ruin

Crowns of Rust

Thrones of Ash

Temples of Dust

Halls of Shadow

Echoes of Light

The Moth Saga:

Moth

Empires of Moth

Secrets of Moth

Daughter of Moth

Shadows of Moth

Legacy of Moth

Dawn of Dragons:

Requiem's Song

Requiem's Hope

Requiem's Prayer

Song of Dragons:

Blood of Requiem

Tears of Requiem

Light of Requiem

Dragonlore:
A Dawn of Dragonfire
A Day of Dragon Blood
A Night of Dragon Wings

The Dragon War:
A Legacy of Light
A Birthright of Blood
A Memory of Fire

Requiem for Dragons:
Dragons Lost
Dragons Reborn
Dragons Rising

Flame of Requiem:
Forged in Dragonfire
Crown of Dragonfire
Pillars of Dragonfire

Dragonfire Rain:
Blood of Dragons
Rage of Dragons
Flight of Dragons

Misfit Heroes:
Eye of the Wizard
Wand of the Witch

Standalones:

Firefly Island
The Gods of Dream
Flaming Dove
Utopia 58
Star Stuff

KEEP IN TOUCH

www.DanielArenson.com
Daniel@DanielArenson.com
Facebook.com/DanielArenson
Twitter.com/DanielArenson